ROSYLAND

A Novel
in
III Acts

Doug Ingold

Wolfenden

ROSYLAND

Copyright ©: 2016 by Douglas A. Ingold

ISBN-13: 978-0-9786951-9-4
ISBN-10: 0-9786951-9-4

Library of Congress Control Number 2015918414

Published by

WOLFENDEN
780-A Redwood Drive
Garberville, CA 95542
wolfendenpublishing.com
Phone: 707-923-2455

Cover Design:
Robert Stedman Pte Ltd
Book design and layout by
Robert Stedman Pte Ltd, Singapore

Printed in the USA

Also by **Doug Ingold**

SQUARE

The Henderson Memories

In the Big City

To
A. & J.
&
G. & S.
For the good times.

With thanks to
Jan, **Lindsey**, **Frank** and **Nina**,
close readers all.

"It's like a dream, see.
We are leading you into a dream...."

E. Gilbert

Some characters who appear in *ROSYLAND*:

In Oregon:
Elisa Gilbert, nee Bolcar, a.k.a. Binks. Elisa is a costume designer with the New Oregon Repertory Theatre.
Rafe Gilbert, Elisa's husband, an actor with the company.
Tiff Bointon, an actress with the company.
Neal Bointon, Tiff's husband, a renowned set designer.
Tom MacElhenney, the director of the theatre company.
Tim Ferguson and Ollie Rand, two bachelor actors.

In San Francisco:
Lawrence "Pug" Bolcar, an attorney and Elisa's father.
Ruth Bolcar, Elisa's mother and Pug's former wife.

Harold Manx, the head of a law enforcement agency.
Lydia Manx, Harold's wife.
Janet Manx, their daughter.
Noony, Harold's mother.

Employees at the law enforcement agency:
Robin Durham, divorced from Liese, father of Denise and Julie.
David Gordon—his wife is Roseanne Harden, a television personality.
Randall Chin.
George Fernald.
Gordon Tessler, from the prosecutor's office.

Vince Lackner, a pilot and the owner of Pacific Rim Transport.
Carlos, a Colombian rancher.

Tripper McLain, a long-time friend of the Bolcar family, owns a professional basketball team.
Ramona Livingston, one of Pug's clients.

Dot Hilliard, Ruth Bolcar's friend and the widow of Ed Hilliard, Pug's former law partner.
Tyler Conden, Ruth's brother, a politician and Pug's former client.

Becky, Pug's office manager.
Pete Miller, Pug's assistant.
Tom Behel, Pug's accountant, married to Niedra.
Rayford Huddleston, Pug's attorney.
Patricia Pendar, a gossip columnist.
Norm Freuhoff and Rendleman, Pug's partners in Angelica Estates.
A cat.

ROSYLAND

I

TAHOE

IF asked she'd say Buddhist. Like that time in Corvallis when Rafe had a chance to play Puck in a summer stock production. They were still in school then, living together but not yet married. The director, one of Rafe's profs, had gotten him the part and a stipend, enough to cover their room and board if the room was small and the board slim. She'd done stitching that summer gratis. So they were in the office of a property management company looking for a place to rent and the guy they were talking to had that fresh-scrubbed, newly-converted, evangelical look. He was going on about the different parts of town and where they wanted to be and to figure it out had asked what church they belonged to.

So she had said, "Well, I'm Buddhist." Meaning not so much that she was Buddhist but that this guy was a jerk to ask such a personal question, thinking later she should have said, "Islamist, creep, and where do you live?"

Then later after they were married and working with the company in Oregonia, Jehovah's Witnesses started coming to their door unannounced. She, thinking she'd get them to stop, explained that she was Buddhist. Big mistake. The very next day they were back. The same two, only the two of them standing back now, sending a young Hispanic girl to tap on her door and hand her a tract on sorcery and cults, as if Buddhism was one of the two or both. Every couple of days a new recruit with a shy smile handing her a pamphlet about devil worship, or some such. Rafe said she'd become their blocking dummy. Count on Rafe to come up with a sports metaphor.

So, she was a Buddhist. Not a saffron-robes, begging-bowl Buddhist. Buddhist, meaning she believed…well, what's there to believe, really? There was a word she heard her grandmother use once in reference to a glass of sherry, that it was her "restorative." Buddhism was Elisa's restorative. She lived her life along the axis of justice. Actions were right or wrong, fair or unfair. Not just her actions but everyone's. They made life better or they made it worse. Newscasts were dramas for Elisa; the world was in constant flux ever in danger of sliding off the dark edge. So she sat zazen three mornings a week with a small group at the house of a woman friend to give herself some perspective, some stillness at the center. And that made her, if she could be said to be anything, Buddhist. And being Buddhist made her vegan, though she might have an egg now and then, and resisting a piece of cheese was always a challenge. But vegan, mostly. Where was the integrity, she thought, in sitting zazen and chewing on a cow?

Which meant cooking two meals most nights, one for her and one for Rafe, who loved steak and all its derivatives and accoutrements.

"Mindfulness." That was a Buddhist principle she could be said to believe in. Being in the moment and mindful of where she was and what she was doing. Which didn't keep her from locking her keys in the car shortly before noon on the Thursday after Christmas in downtown Oregonia a block from the theatre company where she and Rafe worked. It was ridiculous. Walking around the car checking the hatch and doors, all the windows up tight, she could see them dangling there, inches away and completely out of reach. She couldn't even remember what she had been thinking about the moment she jumped out of the car. Whatever it was, it had been engrossing enough to make her forget the keys and ignore the little bell that tinkled whenever you left the keys in the ignition and opened the driver's door. Go figure.

Beating herself up for being so stupid and thinking she would have to find a hammer somewhere or locate a phone and call a lock guy, she remembered that Rafe had to be somewhere in the theatre complex. He had come down an hour or so before to look at the set design for "Henry the Fifth," something to do with a fight scene he was going to be in. She had been on the phone with her brother Michael when he left and hadn't paid much attention.

The New Oregon Repertory Theatre was dark over the holidays, always was between November and February. Lights off, everything locked, she going from door to door, her keys useless in the car. Finally, at the Period Theatre, the outdoor one, she found an unlocked entrance in the surrounding wall. Access through it to the stage and then backstage a doorway and stairs descending to the underground corridor connecting the three venues. Quiet down there, a bit spooky, too, walking along with only the emergency lights on, the place deserted. Where the hell was Rafe? Then she heard a sound, a moan actually, and some kind of movement coming from the prop room. Elisa reached the doorway, paused, and then peered around the corner.

Before that moment whenever Elisa had thought about Tiff Bointon—and before that moment she seldom thought about Tiff at all, and then only in passing—she pictured the dainty little floral-patterned tea set and the matching platter of small concentrically arranged cookies that Tiff would deliver to her husband Neal's study. This back three years now, the second season Elisa and Rafe had been with the company. It would be about eleven and Tiff's arrival would signal the end of Neal's and Elisa's work session. Neal Bointon was designing the set and Elisa the costumes for the company's upcoming production of "The Three Sisters" and to find some uninterrupted time together they had scheduled those evening sessions.

Collaborating with Neal Bointon had been very important for Elisa. She had begun work with the company as a stitcher the summer following her junior year, the year after the Corvallis gig. Then after graduation they had taken her on as a designer. Her first assignments were contemporary plays, two or three characters, exciting, challenging work, but nothing compared to costuming "The Three Sisters" for Neal Bointon. Bointon, the acknowledged master, having designed sets for everything from Sophocles to Mamet including most all of Shakespeare. So she was never ready to quit, and seeing Tiff enter the study after a polite knock, a coy smile emerging above the carefully balanced rosewood tray, always sent a wave of annoyance through Elisa.

They never seemed to annoy Neal Bointon, those late night arrivals by his wife. Regardless of how intently they had been working he would always and literally take the bait. A refined tweedy man he seemed to have a voracious affection for Tiff's herbal tea and little store-bought cookies, dunking them up to his finger tips and muttering happy nonsense worlds removed from Czarist Russia. Tiff in her pale sweaters with their cowl collars and tiny knitted flowers above the heart never dunked her cookies. It seemed inconceivable that she would. An actress, perhaps fifteen years younger than her husband, Tiff had a face as pale and cultured as her china. And while her Lady Macbeth was still talked about and her Cleopatra, which she had performed the year before Elisa and Rafe had arrived, was legendary, her offstage demeanor was that of a precious doll, a model of propriety, a woman the company sent to woo dollars from its older, richer patrons.

Elisa and Neal Bointon worked together on several major productions in the three years following "The Three Sisters" but Elisa's perception of Tiff didn't change until that Thursday when she looked into the prop room and found her and Rafe hastily disarrayed and displayed in a sexual tangle on the same bed where the season before as Desdemona, Tiff had met her cruel fate in sixty-four successful performances.

The full moon showed itself rising up behind Mount Shasta, the mountain's snowy flanks still blushing faintly from their time in the sun. But roaring south on I-5 Elisa neither acknowledged nor noticed this striking tableau. She and the mountain were two volcanic cauldrons passing in close proximity, the heat of one contained, the other's in full eruption.

Amazed now that she had been speechless back there, a condition rarely encountered in her twenty-six years on the planet.

"This is not what you think!" Tiff had shouted. The actress exiting stage left pulling on her pants, boots and vest in hand, blouse unbuttoned, exclaiming as she passed out the door, "Oh, my God!" as if Elisa had committed a faux pas by walking in on them. Rafe, meanwhile, was insisting that the whole thing was meaningless. He in the dim light, even now stunningly handsome, his curly dark hair, those brows, those achingly familiar shoulders, sitting bare-chested on the edge of the bed waving his arms, that trained and resonate voice turned on her: "An act of shared impulse, El, a moment of passing clumsiness. Regrettable, naturally, embarrassing, certainly, but El, it was meaningless!"

She remembered removing the key ring from Rafe's abandoned jeans, driving to the apartment, packing what she could and setting forth in a roar for her mother's San Francisco condo. Thank God it was not snowing when she crossed the summit. Had she been forced to wrestle in the gathering dark with a pair of tire chains she might have done damage to herself or someone else.

She drove too fast into the night and as she drove she shouted sermons at her failed husband: "Some things are basic! Loyalty is basic. Honesty is basic. Keep your promises. Do what you say you're going to do. Don't do what you promise you're not going to do. It has to do with trust, and trust is precious and fragile and once it has fallen from your hands...."

December 27, 1979, a Thursday. Elisa Gilbert, a costume designer from the small town of Oregonia, had begun her journey toward Rosyland, and the taillights ahead swam in her tears.

"Hello?"

"Oh, my God! Oh, my God!"

"Tiff..."

"Where is she?"

"Wha...?"

"Where *is* she?"

"I don't know. Gone, she's...she's gone...."

"Oh, my God! She is going to squeal. She will, I know it. "

"No, it's…"

"She will too! What a fucking disaster! She will, I know she will."

"No, I…"

"Oh, my God! Oh! My! God!"

It was nearly midnight when Elisa reached San Francisco. She found her mother waiting up, wrapped in a purple housecoat, half drunk listening to the talk shows. Ruth's impulse to comfort soon turned into a rant. First Rafe, naturally, but soon on to husbands in general and then to her favorite subject: Lawrence "Pug" Bolcar, her former husband and Elisa's father.

The next morning Elisa telephoned her father, the devil himself, and he invited her up to Lake Tahoe where he was vacationing. She took an eleven o'clock flight and by early afternoon was skiing recklessly over moguls too dangerous for her level of skill and practice. It was cleansing work, exhausting, exhilarating, a high road on the edge of injury, and she kept at it until a wind came up and the light was nearly gone. But then on the shuttle back to the hotel a man seated behind her said to his companion, "Where I come from the land's so flat you see a snow-covered hill, you know a car must be buried under it."

That silly remark sounded so like something Rafe might have said that Elisa had to gasp.

"How could you?" she blubbered aloud as if her accused husband were standing before her, she stomping the floor with her boot, stinging tears again filling her eyes.

"Hello?"
"What was that bitch doing down there? Tell me that."
" I..."
"You said something. You had to have said something."
"No, I..."
"So why was she down there? Tell me that."
"No, I..."
"Oh, my God! I am so miserable! I am so fucking miserable!"

— 2 —

Back when he was eighteen, nineteen, maybe even twenty, Robin Durham used to give the finger to anyone he saw driving a Cadillac. He did this as a matter of principle he liked to believe, though it may have had more to do with resentment than principle. It wasn't just that the owners were conspicuously rich and their cars big and ugly, though to his eyes both were true, but that they behaved as though entitled, rolling through stop signs, exceeding speed limits, changing lanes without troubling to inform anyone with signal lights. "Take that, asshole," he would mutter, thrusting his finger from the battered Chevy pickup he owned at the time. That was back before he left Missouri, before the Army, before Liese and the girls and all that followed.

He remembered the practice now, fifteen years later, sitting in a casino hotel room on the south side of Lake Tahoe. Sitting with Harold Manx, the Chief, as he was known in the department, a man who himself drove a late model black Caddy and dressed like, well, as Robin's co-worker, David Gordon, had been known to say, like he was about to have an audience with the Queen. The shirt was always white, the suit dark and custom tailored, the tie wide and full-Windsor-knotted. The stickpin, fashioned of gold and diamond, matched the cufflinks one could glimpse glinting at his wrists. On the lapel a flag, always. Shoes spotless and black; and topping the bald head now and then, reportedly, a homburg. Robin, being new to the department, had yet to witness the homburg. One never knew about the homburg, Gordon had told him. It might not appear for weeks and then it might show up for a few days in a row. The staff, ever mindful of the Chief's moods, sought to find meaning in the comings and goings of the homburg, but, according to Gordon, no theory had as yet earned consensus.

But none of the usual garb was visible on this Friday afternoon at Lake Tahoe. They were in the field, as it were, and the Chief was attired in what Robin took to be his idea of casual dress. And what he noticed now as he watched the Chief drop down on the bed, lean back against the headboard and stretch his legs out on the gaudy gold spread was that casual included a pair of argyle socks. Navy-blue argyle socks with yellow and red diamonds. Who would have guessed?

The Chief was apparently embarrassed by the socks. "A Christmas present," he said, pointing at them.

"Your daughter?"

Harold Manx frowned. "The wife," he said. "I don't have a daughter."

"Ah." Robin removed the headphones that had been draped around his neck and glanced again at the notes on the table. Harold Manx was staring at him intently so he added, "I'm glad it's over."

"What's that?"

"Christmas. I'm always glad it's over. Presents. I don't like buying them. The kids aren't so bad. It's my ex-wife, my parents, my sister."

"You buy a Christmas present for your ex-wife?"

"Not much. A token, the kids expect it."

Harold Manx seemed to be enjoying this. He leaned forward, his heavy shoulders curling. "So what's a token for an ex-wife?"

"Earrings, that's what I got her," Robin said. "She got me a watchband." He held up his arm displaying the watch and band. "Nothing much."

"I see. Did you need a new watchband?"

"Not really. She said the paint was chipping off the old one."

"Was it?"

"Somewhat," he admitted, looking away.

"In my generation when people divorced they

hated each other. Now I see they exchange presents." Manx leaned back against the pillows. He smiled slightly, though not particularly at Robin. "Chin's divorced," he said, "as you may know. He says he and his ex-wife are good friends, they just can't live together. Perhaps you can understand that better than I. She's Caucasian. Some kind of writer, I believe. I had the pleasure of meeting her on a couple of occasions. Are you and your ex-wife good friends?"

"I wouldn't say so."

"Is she Caucasian?"

"My ex-wife? Yes, Chief. "

Manx leaned forward again, his eyebrows arching slightly. In contrast with his nearly bare scalp and otherwise fastidious appearance the eyebrows were tangled and unkempt. "I have now learned from this brief conversation that you have a Caucasian ex-wife for whom you buy a present at Christmas, a sister. Older?"

"We're twins."

"Interesting phenomenon, twins. And you mentioned children, I believe. That was plural, wasn't it?"

"Yes, two girls."

"Also twins?"

"No."

"I see. The mother has custody?"

"Joint. But she has them most of the time."

"Of course. You have your work, don't you."

Robin nodded but did not speak, letting stand the false impression that he, rather than Liese, had been the major earner. This small misfeasance brought to mind a blurred image of his super-busy, super-organized former spouse, firm of lip and clear of eye and ever ready to offer direction to her less adept, less ambitious and now former husband.

"And you come to us from the military," the Chief was going on. "Office of the AG wasn't it?"

"Yes, sir. Investigatory arm."

"Then a try at private dick?"

"That's true."

"Cost you your marriage I suppose. Usually does. So, in from the cold to us. Regular checks, retirement pension to look forward to, health insurance for you and the girls. Something to cover those monthly child support payments. College ahead for the little ones. Any alimony?"

"No, sir. She's employed professionally." This confession, though partial and glancing, perhaps atoned for his recent error and in his mind's eye he recognized the smug expression Liese wore when a point she had made had at least in part been conceded. My life with a superior being, he thought, how familiar it still was.

"You're doing better than most, Durham." Harold Manx rose from the bed. He stretched his back and flexed his knees slightly. He was a large man in his early sixties. Six-two or three, Robin calculated. Two hundred, maybe two-twenty. His wide feet stretched the argyles exposing dots of the pale skin underneath. He wore dark slacks, a woolen sweater he must have had since his college days. The Chief had mastered dressing up, it seemed to Robin, but at dressing down he was less adroit. That dark green sweater with a large brown football-shaped patch sewn across the front was, well, dated.

"So, what do you think of the conversation we just monitored?" Harold Manx asked now, stretching his back.

"Lackner…?"

"Yes, and his friend Carlos."

Robin Durham picked up the headphones and seemed to weigh them with his palm. His hesitation was understandable. Vince Lackner was Harold Manx's man. The Chief had his thumb on him and was using him to every advantage.

"I was disappointed, if you want the truth."

"I always want the truth." Manx grunted as he sat down at the table, facing the younger man. "So, 'disappointed,' you say."

"I expected better work from Lackner. Some rambling talk about birds, but Lackner'd already told us Carlos ships a few illegal birds now and then. The Colombians aren't going to be impressed by that information. The conversation was abstract, nothing pinned down. Carlos showed more interest in the poker game they're having tonight than dealing cocaine. And Lackner didn't even bring it up." Manx did not react and after a moment Robin felt compelled to add, "Why, did I miss something?"

Harold Manx slipped a mint into his mouth and puckered his lips momentarily. "That depends on what you expected to hear."

"I expect a deal. This Carlos agrees to sell ten kilos

of coke to Lackner and Lackner gets him to say it on tape. That's what he agreed to do, isn't it?"

Manx nodded but did not respond.

"We tip the Colombian authorities. They nab Carlos and keep half the haul for evidence. Lackner is let loose to fly home. He peddles what's left to that bad apple in customs, Webster, is it?"

"Yes, Webster."

"…and we nail Webster, leaving Lackner free to go his merry way. But first he's got to cut the deal with Carlos. Isn't that why we're here?"

The two men stared at each other for a moment before Robin looked away.

"Lackner will make his deal," Manx said finally, sucking on the mint. "But you can't expect it to happen the moment we plug in the microphone. It might not happen in Lackner's room. We might not hear it at all. I told you, this is a routine training operation, nothing more."

Robin frowned. "Surely Lackner has the sense to get Carlos' compliance in front of the bug. That should be elemental, with the deal we're cutting him."

"It would be elemental," Manx said, subtly rolling the word the way Robin had, "if Lackner knew."

Robin's eyes widened. "Are you saying Vince Lackner doesn't know about the bug? What's the…?"

"A routine checkup, as I told you."

"On Lackner?"

Harold Manx did not bother to respond.

Robin was astonished, and without thinking blurted out: "A fishing expedition? Can you get a warrant for such a thing?"

In the silence that followed the implication of his remark hung in the room like an electrical charge. Manx turned now and faced him full on, thick necked, his wide hands resting on the table.

"Young man, I secure my own warrants, and what I do is always authorized. Remember that."

"Of course."

He was about to turn in his chair so he could face the Chief directly. If the boss insisted on playing grade school "stare-me-down" they might as well do it right. But Harold Manx had finished playing. His slight smile was almost friendly. "I don't mean to be unpleasant, Durham. This is a training mission and my job is to teach."

Robin felt spanked. And he had to belch. Manx was giving his stomach fits. He needed some antacid but he was damned if he was going to take any in the old man's presence.

But then to his relief the Chief pushed himself away from the table and began putting on his shoes. "Lackner is meeting his friend Carlos again this evening and we'll want to listen in on that. If something comes up in the meantime call my room. Otherwise I'll be back before their appointment." He crossed to the door. "Order yourself some food, Durham. But have everything out of sight before room service arrives."

"I know the procedure."

"Good, follow it."

***

Harold Manx stepped from the elevator and began to ease his way through the crowded lobby. An orchestrated rendition of "Frosty the Snowman" flooded his ears as if management were determined to ring a few final dollars out of Christmas, now nearly a week past. As he approached the outside door he saw a young woman trying to enter with her arms full of ski equipment. One of the poles caught against the door and fell with a clatter to the floor.

"Shit," the woman said.

He picked up the ski pole and held it out to her. It was then he saw her face for the first time. She appeared to be crying. The two of them stared at one another.

"Mr. Manx?"

"I…" Harold Manx started to turn away.

His profile made her certain. "Mr. Manx, I'm Elisa Gilbert, Elisa Bolcar. Don't you remember? A friend of Janet's growing up?"

"Yes, I remember."

Then Elisa, too, remembered. She blushed.

"Do you hear from her, Mr. Manx?"

"No, never," he said. "She's dead to us."

"I'm sorry."

But Harold Manx had averted his face and he turned now to go. Elisa ran after him, wiping her eyes, ski equipment clutched against her body, reaching for his arm.

"Mr. Manx. Wait, please."

He stopped, not looking at her, this imposing man poised like some sculpture in the hotel lobby wearing a ridiculous green sweater with the image of a football sewn on the front, leather patches on the elbows.

"Lydia, Mr. Manx, is she…?"

He turned and looked down on her, eyes cold. "Alive? Yes, my wife's alive. Her life has been ruined, thanks to your father. But she endures, Binks, if that's what you're asking."

There was a pause. Him glaring, Elisa feeling anger, deciding not to go there. Deciding to keep it bubbly.

"I would love to see her. I so remember that kitchen. The smell of coffee, rolls baking. Things like that, when you're a kid…"

"It's the same kitchen, but…"

"And Noony! Noony talking about growing up in Colorado. Those stories!"

"My mother's in a home," Harold Manx said. "Her mind's gone. She's waiting to die."

"Oh, I'm sorry…"

"You'll excuse me, then."

"Yes, yes of course."

Elisa watched as he passed through the door. He was much older than she remembered, but his posture was still straight. He moved with careful precision. He did not look back.

— 3 —

In Elisa's room the message light was blinking.

"I don't understand why you couldn't have just stayed here," Ruth Bolcar began. "It's not like there's nothing to do in San Francisco. And after what you've been through."

"I know, but it felt right. And since Dad offered to pay...."

Ruth Bolcar snorted. "How is dear Pug anyhow?"

Not a favorite place to be, talking to one parent about the other. "I don't know. He seemed fine. I just saw him for a few minutes. We're going to have dinner." Elisa decided to change the subject. "Mom, you'll never guess who I just ran into. In the lobby a couple of minutes ago, Janet's dad. Remember? From back in Oakland."

Ruth sighed. "That would be Harold Manx. It's been years. Still straight as a pencil, I'll bet. Held his figure?"

"Yes. Older, of course, but fit seemingly."

"I'm not surprised. The man was a gentleman from head to toe."

"I always found him frightening," Elisa admitted. She and Janet both had. Did they talk about it? She didn't remember. But their childhood cunning had made them wary, that she did recall. How they would close themselves in Janet's room when he came home. Janet had a collection of Indian dolls that Elisa had loved. The image of them lined up on the white shelving flashed through her mind now, the thick black hair, the leather, the bright beadwork. And his voice as he entered the house, how it filled the place, not loud or angry but deep and forceful. Or were they outside when his car pulled in they might sneak next door to Elisa's where the backyard was smaller but there was a sandbox and a fence that hid them away. They were small children. The Bolcars had moved from Oakland to the City when Elisa was twelve, shortly before Janet turned thirteen and the trouble with her parents began.

"You were children, Binks. Of course he seemed that way to you."

Elisa wasn't sure. "He's still a large intimidating man, Mom. I felt it right away, seeing him again."

"He gives off a sense of command, no doubt about that." The tone of Ruth's voice suggested admiration. "He is in law enforcement, after all. But he was always considerate, never a harsh word. And such a dresser! Your father knows how to dress, of course. I'll give him that. He was selling suits when I met him, you know, and he learned a lot about style from old Feldman, the owner of the place. Nothing in Pug's growing up would have taught him anything, so it had to have come from Feldman. Feldman took Pug off the street and gave him a polishing, that's what my dad used to say." Ruth laughed and the laugh caught Elisa by surprise. Her mother had a husky, smoker's voice, but her laugh just then was spontaneous and joyous as if it retained some remnant of an earlier happier time. Hearing it now gave Elisa pleasure.

"'Took Pug in and gave him a polishing,'" Ruth repeated, still chuckling. "Daddy could turn a phrase all right. Pug sold a suit to my father, that's how I met him. Did you know that?"

Elisa had heard the story multiple times. She was still standing in her skiing outfit, feeling sweaty and sore, her gear tossed on the bed. She shifted her weight from one foot to the other as Ruth went on.

"But Pug has never dressed like Harold Manx. That man looked impeccable. Always, even sweeping his driveway on a Saturday morning. And he did sweep his driveway every Saturday morning. Then he washed the car."

"He said that Janet has never come back. 'She's dead to us.' Those were his exact words: 'She's dead to us.'"

"That's a shame, though I can't say I'm totally surprised. I know you loved her, Binks, but Janet was a strange child, plain as a slice of unbuttered toast. Those heavy glasses, head always in a book. That child had the dullest, most lifeless hair I've ever seen on a girl. Well, such is life. You love what is yours even if it's plain as a post. That's just the way it is. Still, it had to have broken her mother's heart."

"I did love her. And Mrs. Manx, and Noony. Noony's in a home now."

"Of course you did. One moment, dear."

Elisa could hear ice tinkling, gin being poured.

"Well, tonight's the poker game probably," Ruth speculated when she returned to the phone. "You'll have the dubious pleasure of Tripper and Helen McLain at dinner. God, those horrible jokes. And maybe the new one, the one who took Tony Licari's place. What's his name…Lochness or something. No, that's the monster, isn't it. He's a pilot or some such. I met him two years ago. The man has eyes like a wolf, I swear." Ruth paused for a sip. "That was the last time I was invited on Pug's annual trek to the mountains."

"Well...."

"It's all right, Binks. No comment required. I'm lucky to be rid of the bastard."

"I hope you're happy, Mom. I know he treated you badly."

A snorting, not-at-all-merry, laugh. "My dear, you have an astonishing gift for understatement. Anyway, I almost forgot the news, and here we were talking about bastards all along. Rafe called. Imagine the gall, as my mother used to say. You're gone twenty-four hours and he's on the horn claiming there's an emergency. I hung up on him, of course, but not before informing him in what I hope was clear and concise English just what I think of him and his kind."

"What did he want, Mom?"

"What he wants is to have his cake and eat it too. Don't call him, Binks, that's the important thing. Have nothing to do with the man. Let the lawyers do the talking. That's what I should have done the minute your father started running around."

"He said there was an emergency?"

"There's no emergency. He's a whipped puppy wanting back in the house. Forgive him once and believe me, there'll be no end to it." After a hesitation and the sound of ice sloshing in gin Ruth added: "Forgive him once for this kind of thing, and you'll be forgiving him all your life."

***

Rafe Gilbert was not home the first time Elisa called. But after she had showered and dressed for dinner she tried again. This time he answered.

"You're all right?" he asked. "I'm worried about you."

"You told mom there was an emergency."

"Yeah, I got a list of them actually. You are all right, aren't you? You sound funny. Like one of those women who give out welfare checks or something. You know, and act like it's their money."

Elisa did not respond. She was afraid to, afraid that saying most anything would lance the boil of pain swelling inside her.

"Okay, sorry, that was lame. Look, El, I am so sorry. What can I say? It was terrible for you, I know…"

"What's the emergency, Rafe?

"El…. All right. My goddamned keys, that's the first one. What'd you do with my keys? I can't get in my car and the theatre key is on that ring. I'm worried sick about that. And if I hadn't remembered the spare we stashed under the mat I'd never have gotten in here." He paused but Elisa again did not respond. "This is the pits, El. Please come home. We need to talk. We need to sit across from each other and talk…. And where are you, anyway? Your mom said you were unavailable…. El?"

"I threw them."

"What?"

"The keys. I used them to get into my car. My keys were inside so I threw yours… in some bushes.

I was parked in front of the library, I think."

"You threw them? Jesus Christ, El. In front of the library?" Rafe seemed to be describing an event of astonishing violence.

"Well, Jesus Christ, yourself!" Elisa yelled, and hung up.

"Hello?"

"Can you talk?"

"Never call here! Are you fucking crazy?"

"It was an accident."

"What…?"

"She didn't know. She locked her keys in her car."

"Oh, my God!"

"Keys, she came looking for me to get my keys!"

"Oh, my God! You are both idiots! Do you think it matters *why* she was down there?"

"Well, you…"

"What matters is that she *was* down there! That's what matters!"

"Well, I…"

"Oh, my God! I cannot believe this!"

— 4 —

Lawrence "Pug" Bolcar leaned out over the curb and looked down the street. It was an act of some grace considering the breadth of his chest and stomach, proportions accentuated by the gray turtleneck he wore beneath an unbuttoned blue blazer. Elisa, her arm through his, thought he might tumble them both into the street, but he poised there, his thick wavy hair graying from brown, his squat flattened nose, his thick lower lip protruding like the edge of a bagel, and for all his ugliness he conveyed a presence, a dynamic that Elisa had never in her lifetime felt she could quite touch or get enough of.

Night had fallen and the temperature had dropped back below freezing. The road was thick with traffic that churned the slush and fogged the air.

Elisa stomped her heels against the pavement to warm her feet. "Why don't we just go to the corner?"

"Too easy," her father said. "Anyone can cross a street at the corner."

"It's better than freezing to death. This traffic is endless."

"You won't freeze. You've got your father's warmth." He leaned still further out, staring down the line of traffic like some aging bullfighter.

"You mean fat."

"You're not fat."

"I feel fat. To the extent I can feel anything."

"Your generation has been bamboozled by Madison Avenue, Binks. Look at the women on TV. All collarbones and concentration-camp arms. How's it look in that direction?"

"It's possible."

"Go!"

They plunged into the street, reached the center-line, stopped abruptly for two cars and then raced to the far curb. Laughing they entered the warmth of another casino and worked their way to the third floor where the maitre d' led them to their seats.

A man sat alone at the table. He rose, took Elisa's hand and then embraced her. He was tall and thin with graying blond hair and a gentle, refined face that opened when he saw her into a smile that was impossible not to trust. To anyone who regularly read the Bay Area papers Tripper McLain would have seemed at least vaguely familiar. He'd made a fortune with that smile, converting orange groves around San Jose into subdivisions, and now he owned a distant professional basketball team that always ended up in the middle of its division. Back in the early forties, he and Pug had shared a paper route. He had known Elisa since her birth.

"It must be three or four years," Tripper said as they settled into their seats. "Your wedding, probably. Have I seen you since then? I don't believe I have."

"That was four years ago last August," Elisa said.

"You were a lovely bride."

"Thank you, Tripper. Unfortunately, it didn't take. We're separated."

"Your father told me. I'm sorry."

Elisa acknowledged his understanding with a soft smile, hoping her eyes weren't about to tear up again. "So, how's Helen?"

"Helen's fine. She flew home this afternoon. She's chairing a fundraising drive for the symphony and there's a meeting tonight. She was here for two days with her little paper cup full of dimes and quarters."

"And the boys?"

"Kevin's in Central America, something to do

with aerial mapping. He doesn't say much about it, which leads me to suspect our government's up to something it shouldn't be. And Terrence has finally moved into his own place. It was our Christmas present."

Had the McLains bought their younger son a house? Elisa could not believe it. As a Christmas present?

Tripper's disarming smile spread grace across the table. "No, my dear. I mean when he asked Helen what we wanted for Christmas she said we wanted him to move out. Mothers can be so tough."

Tough mothers. The observation returned Elisa to her present, uncertain, circumstances. Terrance was moving out while she was moving back in. "I'll be staying with mom, I guess, at least for now."

"Move in with me," Pug suggested. "You can have your own condo."

"Your choice of several from what I understand," Tripper said. "Your father got into real estate at the wrong time, I'm afraid. If these interest rates don't level out soon we'll all be in trouble."

"They'll turn around," Pug Bolcar growled. Then to the arriving waitress, "A martini for me, up, dry with a single olive. Binks?"

"Chardonnay, please. With an ice cube." Elisa was starving. She began to scour the menu for something substantial that was close, something even on the same continent with vegan.

"Perrier," Tripper said.

"I'm dining with a couple of lushes as you can

see," Pug explained to the waitress.

A few minutes later Elisa's father rose from his chair and waived to someone across the room. The woman approaching the table was tall and elegantly thin in a red dress with dark hair and eyes. Her age, Elisa quickly estimated, was roughly the same as her own. Ramona Livingston. Pug introduced her somewhat uncomfortably as a client.

"Pug's going to make me rich," the woman said, sitting down.

"Justly compensated, I hope. Hardly rich."

"But I want to be rich," Ramona said, pouting. "I want to be fabulously rich."

"Then you'll have to do more than fall down and break your leg."

"Even with the scar?" she asked flirtatiously.

"Even with the scar." Elisa saw her father redden slightly. Then he turned to Tripper, "Get that waitress over here, I'm starved."

Well he is divorced, Elisa kept reminding herself during the meal. He's entitled to his own life and I have no right to pass judgment on him. These admonitions, though sincere and often repeated, did little to improve her mood.

The bill arrived with their coffees. Pug Bolcar pulled out a credit card and slid it into the folder.

"We should be going, Pug," Tripper said. "It's set for nine."

"The poker game," Pug explained to the women. He glanced at his watch and pulled out a cigar.

"Vince can wait a few minutes. This is a vacation."

"They have this game every year," Elisa said to Ramona, the first words she had addressed to her. She was disturbed at herself for being irritated at her father and at this woman. It was because of Rafe, she decided. It was really Rafe she was angry with. "So, who's playing these days, Dad? I remember when it was you two, Ed Hilliard and Tony Licari."

"After Tony retired and moved to the Islands we brought in Vince Lackner," Tripper explained. "He's a few years younger than us. A pilot, has a transport business. But since Ed's death we haven't picked a fourth. Each year one of us brings the fourth player. This year Vince is the banker so he brings the guest."

"Who's he got, Tripper?" Pug asked.

"Some South American fat cat according to Vince. A Carlos something."

Bolcar shrugged. "The banker has to stand behind his guest so we're covered. The stakes are a little higher than they were twenty years ago, but the game's the same."

"Speaking of old times, Dad, you'll never guess who I ran into this afternoon. Harold Manx, Janet's dad."

"Manx," Tripper said. "Didn't they live next door when you had that…?"

"Oakland, yeah." Pug Bolcar rubbed the ash off his cigar. "That sorry bastard."

"They've never heard from her apparently. He still blames you for that, Dad."

"The man's got nobody to blame but himself. I didn't put her in the damn cult. She was eighteen. She had the right to do what she wanted. Believe me I got no pleasure from it. But they came to me. What could I do?"

"So, tell us. What did the good attorney do?" On Ramona Livingston's left forearm were a half dozen thin metal bracelets that tinkled seductively as she nudged Pug's arm. Elisa found herself making mental notes about Ramona, her hair, her makeup, her dress, her accessories. It was a professional habit. If she ever had an opportunity to costume a certain kind of role this woman would make a good starting point. And what would that role be? It wasn't real elegance, she was seeing. There was something *overt* about it. The false lashes, the deep eye shadow, the dress a size too clingy, the décolletage too low…. She felt herself blushing. She knew absolutely nothing about this woman. But it was true. Ramona's every move seemed calculating and coy. And her father, though obviously annoyed by her blatant sexuality, couldn't keep his eyes off her. Collar bones and concentration-camp arms, Elisa thought. Pale sweaters with neat little knitted flowers.

"I didn't do anything," her father was saying, his voice almost angry. "Manx had kidnapped her."

"His daughter?"

"That's right, his own daughter. They were holed up in a little travel trailer out by Concord. 'Deprogramming' her was the way he put it. Holding her against her will and trying to brainwash her or unbrainwash her until she agreed to not return to the cult. The church came to me, just a bunch of hippies is what they were. She had given them my name if something like that came up. I was probably the only lawyer she'd ever met. She knew her father, all right. Knew what he was capable of. And she was an adult by that time. She hadn't committed a crime. The court had to issue the order and I had to serve it. That's all, no big deal."

"And the girl?" Ramona asked. "Did she go back to the cult?"

"Of course. What would you do if your old man had dragged you into a car while you stood in a parking lot with a bag of groceries. Then locked you in a travel trailer and harangued you for hours on end." Pug exhaled a cloud of smoke as if ridding himself of the memory. "How about the two of you gals having a night out? Juliet Prowse is in town. My gift from the twenty-one tables."

Elisa's eyes met Ramona's. Obviously neither of them liked the idea.

"Thank you," Ramona said, standing. "It would be great fun but I've had a long day following a longer night. A bath and an early bed is what I'm looking forward to. You understand, I hope."

"Of course," Elisa said. They were all standing now. Ramona, Elisa noticed, was an inch taller than her father.

The woman leaned forward and kissed Pug on the cheek. "Win big," she said.

Tripper McLain whistled softly as they watched

her walk away. "That is one lovely young lady."

"She's just a kid, Tripper," Pug Bolcar said. "A kid I'm trying to help out." He signed the authorization and returned the credit card to his wallet. When he finally looked at Elisa she saw in his eyes a range of her father's moods and powers: embarrassment, a glint of anger, an abundance of pride. "So, Binks, the offer's still open. Want a century note to blow?"

She was tempted. It would be a kind of revenge. "Thanks, Dad. I'm not up for much either."

"Have it your way." He slapped McLain on the shoulder. "Okay, Tripper. Let's go take a look at this Don Carlos and his money."

"Hello?"

"Listen to me. I've got to be quick. If that bitch tells Neal…."

"No…"

"Listen! Listen to me! If that bitch tells Neal. If she so much as hints to anybody in this company…"

"No…"

"…you will be lucky…listen to me…you will be lucky to find work anywhere on this planet, you understand?"

"I…"

"You'll be lucky if…"

"I…"

"… end up playing an aging clown in some tiny Bulgarian circus!"

"I…."

"If you're lucky! You hear me? Some cold and

gray communist shantytown. A clown! If you're lucky!"

— 5 —

Seeing that girl again had disturbed Harold Manx and he knew it. It had ruined his intended nap, tainted the over-cooked steak he had eaten alone in his room and now as he started back to Durham's room it continued to sour his disposition. It's a myth that time heals, he thought. The most you can say about time as a healer is that it scabs over a wound. But seeing that girl again, seeing how she had grown into the full flowering of adulthood while his own daughter…that had torn the scab away, and what lay beneath was as fresh and raw as ever. Maybe time itself is the myth. Maybe everything is always happening right now.

Well, so what? he said to himself as he stepped from the elevator into the empty corridor. There had been other wounds, many of them. He was covered in scabs. This is what life is about. You live or you cower. The scabs make you tougher, thicker. You just have to be ready, that's all. You have to be alert. You have to act, not react. That thing back in the lobby had taken him by complete surprise, that was the problem. So, forget about it. See your duty and do it.

Robin Durham was in his headphones when Harold entered the room. He pointed at them and motioned excitedly. Harold sat down and slipped into his set. Vince Lackner was speaking with his habitual whine, an annoying trait that Harold immediately identified.

"With all due respect, Carlos—and I believe the two of us are capable of treating each other with great respect. I personally have great respect for you, Carlos."

"Oh, and I for you, Bincent." The voice was soft and distant. Harold thought he must be standing near the door. But the accent was unmistakable, the Colombian no doubt.

Word of Carlos had come to the department from a disgruntled card player who was in the states illegally and trying to avoid deportation. Carlos was not much of a catch given the volume coming out of Colombia these days. A small-time independent working cautiously outside the forming cartels. A cattle rancher with a taste for cards and two sons accustomed to jet-setting the globe, he needed the extra cash. But when Harold approached the Colombian Ministry of Justice they were eager for dirt on Carlos. Some unsavory political connection apparently. So for Harold, Carlos was a puzzle piece that slid nicely into place: a small gift for the Colombians, one they could safely handle, and a neat fit with Lackner whose business took him all over the Pacific Rim, including Bogota and Medellin. It had been easy to arrange some business for Lackner in the river valley where Carlos had his ranch. And of course, Lackner, too, had a fondness for gambling as well as an obligation to the department.

As he sat forward, straightening his back, Harold felt his attention harden. It was a pleasant sensation.

In a certain sense he never experienced himself as quite alive anymore unless he was in the field. And there had been less of that in recent years. The weight of personnel decisions, intra- and inter-agency turf disputes, budgets and the never ending scramble for funds, the currying of needy grand-standing politicians—these were the minutiae that clogged Harold Manx's daily calendar and dulled his appetite for work.

But now the game was on and he was in the midst of it. Forget that other thing and get yourself fully into it.

The American was going on about the great respect he had for Carlos. "I have been a guest in your wonderful home," he was saying. "I have met your family. Enjoyed your hospitality...."

"It is my honor to have you, Bincent. I am only telling that your needs mean complications for me. I am made at risk for this idea you have."

Lackner's voice rose in pitch, taking on an edge of hurt. "It is not my desire to place you at risk, Carlos. That's the last thing I want to do. But look who's taking the real risk here. I'm the one flying the cargo. I wouldn't trust this to anyone else. And my risk is the same if it's ten kilos or twenty." A sudden loud rasp came through the headphones causing the two men to momentarily lift the sets away from their ears. "Would you like to try it?" Lackner asked after the sound had stopped.

The Colombian said something they could not understand.

"It's all good for you," Vince Lackner added. "Banana, soy milk, wheat germ, an egg, a little carob powder."

"Much thanks," the Colombian said, "but no." After a pause he continued. "Twenty is a big problem for me. Suppliers, you understand. I must be very careful. The others, you know."

"I know, I know that," Lackner said impatiently. His voice reminded Harold of a little boy whose baseball bat had been taken by the neighborhood bully. "But I've got to tell you something, Carlos. I'm in big trouble here. These guys don't mess around. I was sure from the way you talked there'd be no problem with twenty, so I've committed for twenty. I've staked my business on this operation. My airplanes, the whole thing. This is not something I do every day. You know that. The only reason I got involved in this scheme in the first place was because you were my friend. But I can't back out now, Carlos. I am counting on you. Do you understand how serious this is for me?"

"I understand, Bincent. But…"

"It was your idea! That's why I'm so upset about this. I would never have put myself in this situation if it hadn't been for you."

"I don't remember it my idea, Bincent." The Colombian's voice had lowered. He was becoming annoyed with Vince Lackner, Harold thought. An easy thing to do.

"Of course it was. That night at the ranch you started talking …"

"In a general way, I may…"

"You brought it up! You think I go around making deals like this with anyone? I fly out of Colombia all the time. Bolivia too now and then. I never touch the stuff. The subject never comes up. I'm a legitimate businessman. Now, I've gone and risked it all and you're telling me you can't get me a lousy twenty kilos. I put myself in this situation because of you, Carlos. Because you were my friend and…."

"We never talked twenty kilos, Bincent."

"You talked like you had suppliers. Like you could put together a shipment. You know I can't risk everything for a few ounces."

"Twenty kilos is not…."

Vince Lackner's voice slowed down. "Let's not argue, Carlos. We are friends. We shouldn't argue. Let's not forget our friendship. Here try one of these bars. They're sweetened without sugar, Carlos. Fruit juice only. Unrefined. Do you know about sugar? The processing is very bad. And brown sugar is not brown sugar. It's processed sugar with caramel added. Try one, Carlos."

"Much thanks, Bincent."

"I also have carrots here. Apples. I get these near Sebastopol. No sprays whatsoever." Harold Manx could hear the rattling of paper bags.

"No, Bincent. But thank you. This cookie is good."

"It's a bar. But no sugar, that's the thing. So, Carlos, it is absolutely necessary that I get twenty kilos. We must find a way to make that possible."

"Twenty is big problem for me."

"You want more money per kilo, don't you?" Lackner said now. His voice was also more distant. Manx instinctively leaned forward but Carlos's answer was muddled by the distance and the munching of food.

"As I said, Carlos, I respect you. This is not your line of work either, I know that. The cattle, that's your pride, isn't it? I saw that when I was there. Those wonderful cattle, and your sons. They're here with you, your sons?"

"Yes, Bincent. Skiing."

"Of course. Of course."

"The risk…"

"Of course," Vince Lackner said again. "The risk is real for both of us. I am only a pilot. You are only a rancher. So, this is difficult. I understand, but I must have twenty. If you get me twenty I'll give you ten percent more per kilo than we discussed. That will flatten my cut. My risk will be the same, my cut less. But if it makes the deal, Carlos, I'll do it. If not, I'll have to look elsewhere. There is no backing out for me. I must have the stuff."

"That is kind with you, Bincent."

"I try to be kind, Carlos. If that is acceptable we have nothing further to discuss."

"Acceptable. Yes, that is acceptable. Now we play poker?"

"Of course. Mr. Bolcar and Mr. McLain will be here in about an hour. You spoke of taking a shower. We will wait if you have not returned."

"That is kind with you, Bincent."

"I try to be kind, Carlos."

Harold Manx and Robin Durham heard a door close. They removed their headsets and looked at each other.

"Did he say Bolcar? One of the players coming was a man named Bolcar?"

"Something like that." Robin's face gleamed with excitement. "Did you hear what he's up to? The bastard's playing both ends against the middle. We've authorized him to buy ten kilos, five for the Colombians and five to bring home for delivery to that rogue guy in customs…"

"Webster."

"Yeah, Webster. But he's just cut a deal for twenty. He's flying in under our protection so his entry is absolutely safe. He works the deal with Webster in exchange for which we drop that thing in October, and he's left with ten to peddle himself."

"Or five," Harold pointed out. "The Colombian authorities might take half of whatever they find. That's the understanding, though Lackner will be clever enough to stow the second ten separately."

"Okay, worse case five. He's still miles ahead." Admiration flashed across Robin Durham's face. "You were a genius to plant this bug, Chief. I mean that."

Harold Manx smiled. He was very pleased by the information they had just received. His private thoughts about Robin Durham were less enthusiastic, though his critique was more generational than personal. Durham looked all right, clean cut, seemingly bright enough. And he had a good physique. A large man himself, Harold Manx gave points for size. When push came to shove you wanted someone beside you who had the will and the physical strength to move the line forward. In his career Harold had been there for others and others had been there for him. And he was alive today because of it. Durham appeared to have the strength. Whether he had the will was another thing. This new crop of agents, men like Durham, struck him as extraordinarily uncommitted. Kids, really, in a certain sense, though this one was hardly a kid. Thirty-two according to his file, a military vet, married and divorced, father of two. But devoted, it seemed to Harold, not to the department, not to the society it served, but to himself, to his own career. The kind of recruit who in the introductory interview asks about retirement and disability benefits. That's the way it was now. Office memos descending from above advised personnel to stress such benefits when interviewing applicants. And the result? Men in their forties running off to doctors with an eye on disability and early retirement. There were now doctors, apparently, who specialized in that kind of thing. Harold remembered the agent in his office last year, forty-seven years old this guy was. His hip had gotten slammed by a car door while on a bust, and as a result the man now believed he was entitled to spend the rest of his life lounging on a beach somewhere, compliments of the taxpayer.

"You've done a fine job yourself, Durham," he said now. "But the excitement is over and I'm giving you the night off. Take in a show or try your hand at the tables. Your own funds, of course. Remember, I personally review all expense accounts."

A few minutes later as he combed his hair in the bathroom the now jovial Robin Durham called out in a joking manner, "You going to listen in on the poker game, Chief?"

"Of course not. Whatever Lackner's up to he's entitled to his private poker game. No, I'm going to listen through this last conversation and turn in." He was rubbing his knee when Durham re-entered the room. "I do a have slight problem, however, and I'd appreciate a favor if you don't mind."

"Whatever, Chief."

"I seem to have thrown my knee out coming back from dinner. An old rodeo injury, and I know its course. A couple of aspirins and it'll be fine by morning. But if you would switch rooms with me I can avoid walking on it."

"No problem." Robin delivered the aspirins and a glass of water and began packing his bag. "Want me to run your things over?"

"That won't be necessary," Harold said, tossing him a key. "Old cowboys can sleep wherever they find themselves. Just ignore my mess and make yourself at home. I'll call you in the morning." He turned back to the table and began to rewind the tape, not speaking again until Robin was ready to leave. "For now, Durham, we need to hold the information on this tape in the strictest confidence. No reports, no discussion in the office, not a word to anyone. Understand?"

"If that's what you want, Chief."

"It's not what I want, Durham. It's what I require." He put on the headphones and did not respond when Robin Durham said goodbye.

— 6 —

When Pug Bolcar and Tripper McLain arrived at Vince Lackner's hotel room they found a round table covered with green felt and stacked with multi-colored chips. The table was situated in front of a wide floor-to-ceiling window with a view of the lights of South Lake Tahoe, the dark lake, the shadowy mountains. To the left stood a bar with glasses and cups, bottles, ice, a pot of coffee.

"Nice view, Vince," Pug said, his hands on the back of a chair, "but a ridiculous place to set a poker table. Pull the drapes."

Vince Lackner, already annoyed that McLain and Bolcar had showed up a half-hour late, looked contemptuously at his accuser. "You may not have noticed, Pug, but I have carefully placed each chair so no player's cards will be reflected in the glass. And since your chair, in particular, faces the window more or less, I don't see what you have to complain about."

"I came to play poker, Vince. Had I wanted to go sightseeing I wouldn't be here. Close the goddamned drapes and let's get started."

"Carlos? Your chair and mine are in theory the most vulnerable. What are your feelings about this?"

"It is no matter." The Colombian shrugged.

"Tripper?"

"Vince," Pug growled, "we don't need a show of hands here. This is a poker game, not an annual stockholders' meeting. Poker is played in private. I want the drapes closed."

Tripper McLain smiled benignly. "Close the drapes, Vince. The view is lovely but it could interfere with our concentration."

The drapes pulled, Vince Lackner brought out two bowls of sunflower seeds. One, he pointed out, was salted, the other not. He was an angular, thin-faced man with close-set yellowish-brown eyes, a long hooked nose, a pronounced Adam's apple, short carefully styled hair. He wore a gray running suit trimmed with maroon and had before him a half-empty glass containing a substance that to Pug vaguely resembled orange juice but left a powdery residue on the sides of the glass. Best not to ask. The last time he made that mistake he'd had to suffer through five minute lecture from Vince on the merits of seaweed.

"Have you explained the rules, Vince?" he asked when Lackner broke the seal on the deck of cards.

"Carlos knows the rules, Pug."

The Colombian nodded. "Draw poker according to my friend Bincent. Only draw poker. No wild cards, of course." He was small, thin. He wore tinted glasses, a half-opened gray metallic-colored shirt.

A silver cat-shaped pendant hung from his neck. "Gentlemen, I am appreciating this opportunity. In my small community it is difficult finding a good poker game. I have electric poker. Computer. But its game is…lifeless." He smiled as though pleased to have pulled the correct word from his memory.

Bolcar accepted the cards from Lackner. He examined them briefly before passing them along to McLain. "And no empty chatter," he said. "Ed Hilliard had a rule. Every unnecessary sentence costs you ten bucks into the pot. And in those days, ten bucks meant something."

The Colombian nodded. He accepted the cards from McLain and brushed their edges with his delicate manicured fingers.

Ed Hilliard, Pug thought. A Monday morning on the Bay Bridge three years ago last spring. A massive heart attack. Ed had been Pug's law partner the previous twelve years, and he was dead before his Mercedes crunched against the guard rail. A true friend, a decent, square-shooting man. With Ed's death, Pug now realized, his luck had soured. Their partnership agreement obligated him to purchase Hilliard's interest from Ed's widow at a value based on the firm's gross for the previous two years. Those two years happened to have been the best two in the firm's history. So for the past three years and for the next three, approximately thirty cents of every dollar the firm earned flowed into Dot Hilliard's plump bank account.

There had been other reversals. His last three

major trials had not gone well. Two he lost outright, the third settled at mid-point when his client got nervous—and she had been right to get nervous. The young surgeon made an excellent witness while his client sounded evasive and unsure. Not a liar so much as a person who had always had problems and always would, the kind of victim juries love to despise. Not his fault, but then fault wasn't the issue. You won or you lost. You settled well, or you settled badly.

Then there was Ruth. Their divorce became final a year after Ed's death and the alimony payments were staggering. The old "put him through school" argument, an argument he had used often enough himself to respect. That plus the judge, bending over backwards to not appear as if she were favoring a fellow lawyer, accepted a ridiculously high valuation on the condo units and then assigned them to Pug. Dot Hilliard and Ruth Bolcar were good friends. They could be seen nearly every weekday lunching together at one or another dining spot, feeding on poached salmon, enjoying crisp chardonnay and good company, all complements of Lawrence Pug Bolcar.

But he felt solid now. He sensed a turning of the wheel. At the twenty-one tables the cards had fallen like green rain all afternoon. Dinner with Tripper and Binks had reminded him of how he started out, working his way through night law school selling suits and ties. He and Tripper hawking papers on Fishermen's Wharf as kids. He had scraped for every penny and had made his own damn breaks, and there was not an attorney in San Francisco who could relax knowing Pug Bolcar was on the other side. Then there was Ramona. That she accepted his casual invitation to join him in Tahoe seemed to suggest that the thing that happened a couple of weeks before meant more to her than a quick roll. And now poker; few things in life gave Pug Bolcar as much pleasure as a good poker game.

Vince Lackner passed the cards along without a glance and counted out ten thousand dollars worth of chips to everyone in denominations of twenties, fifties, hundred and five hundreds. With Carlos, arrangements had apparently been made in advance. From Pug and Tripper Lackner accepted personal checks. It had been that way for years and no one had ever defaulted.

The four men tossed twenties onto the felt and Pug dealt the first hand. McLain opened with twenty. Jacks or better. Carlos went along. Lackner folded. Bolcar doubled the bet. Three ladies. A pleasant way to begin the evening.

An hour later he was thirteen hundred dollars ahead. McLain and Lackner were close to even. The profit had crossed the table from the Colombian. Getting up to pour himself some coffee, Pug's reserve softened. He asked Carlos whether his computer dealt cards in a truly random order.

"On my ranch is old man," Carlos said. "Very old black man. Nothing is random, he says. No such thing as chance. They saying he never loses at dice, though I personally have not played with him. Some say he is healer. Others afraid of him. How you say...a caster of evil spells."

"And what is your opinion of this man?" Tripper McLain asked.

Carlos shrugged. "An old man who insists on working though I no longer require it of him. He lives in small cabin and grows garden. His people believe in him."

Pug sat down heavily. "A charlatan, of course. They always are. I knew Jones, remember. Some know they are charlatans. Others fool even themselves, and of the two the self-deluded are the most dangerous. At first Jones knew what he was about. But by the end he believed all the bullshit he was dishing out, and he slurped it up along with the Kool-Aid."

Carlos shuffled the cards slowly. He seemed to ponder Pug's words for a long time. When he began to deal he said, "The world may be more mysterious than you suppose, Mr. Pug."

— 7 —

The world did seem mysterious to Ramona Livingston at that moment. She lay in a tub of very hot water, submerged but for her knees, head and neck in sea of white slowly dying bubbles. She preferred her bath as hot as she could stand it, so periodically she reached out with her left foot, curled her long toes around the handle and admitted more hot water. Gently, so as to not disturb the bubbles she stirred the new water into the old until pleasure merged with pain and her foot reemerged to turn it off. Be very still. To move at all was to send pain running along the shoreline of her skin.

In a beauty parlor that afternoon, as she had waited for her shampoo and manicure, she had looked up from her magazine to see a woman walk in. Normally, Ramona would have dismissed this woman after a quick summing up: the mink coat worn over a garish-pink outfit, the gold at the neck and ears, the black dye that gave her hair its false sheen. But for some reason Ramona had been unable to look away, and the woman's eyes heavy with makeup had turned toward her while a plume of smoke unfurled from lips curled down in perpetual disgust. One look from this once beautiful, still prosperous, but obviously miserable woman had produced in Ramona a sudden and uncontrollable command to retch. She had fled the parlor, rushed across the corridor and into a restroom where she had fallen onto her knees before the toilet like a supplicant.

Lying now in the bath she felt again the cold tiles against her knees, smelled the overwhelming reek of toilet cleaner, the taste of partially digested prawns and Parmesan cheese, the rasp of stomach acid against her throat. At the time, the whole bizarre episode had seemed unconnected to the food she had had for lunch, the lack of sleep, the small amount of alcohol she had consumed. Inexplicable, it had called forth demons: stomach cancer, some form of epilepsy—it was as if she were being assaulted by a force outside of her. The thought of a curse had crossed her mind, or worse, that she had slid through a crack in time and the woman was a vision of her future self. Best to lie very still, she told herself. Let it pass. Let it all slowly pass.

Robin Durham stood among a crowd of people looking at a large glass structure approximately the size and shape of a telephone booth. The bottom two feet of the booth—and the reason Durham and other others were drawn to it—was filled with paper currency. The money lay rumpled and loose as if it had been tossed in by the bushel-basket full.

A man stood beside the booth holding a microphone and turning a drum filled with slips of paper. He stopped the drum, pulled out a piece of paper and read a name and address. This information reverberated through the casino but no one came forward. Around went the drum and out came another name. An Anita Wallace was summoned. Ms. Wallace, a forty-five-year- old high school teacher from Durango, Colorado, made her way forward as the crowd cheered. Moments later she was wading into the money. The door closed behind her and the crowd tittered with sly greed.

"All right, Anita Wallace," the man said. "Do you see that slot in the side of the booth there?"

"Yes, I see it."

"Good. Now, in just a second that money is going to begin flying around in there and your job is to grab all you can and stuff it through the slot. You have one minute and all the money you get through the slot is yours. You understand that, Anita Wallace?"

"Just through the slot there?" A full-figured woman, Anita Wallace stood awkwardly in the money. She looked uncertain and embarrassed, as if she had just stepped into a mud puddle and was unsure how to extract herself.

"That's right," the man said. "Grab the money and push it through the slot. Are you ready?"

"I guess so, it seems very silly."

"Really! Ridiculous is more like it." This sudden interjection came from the woman standing to Robin's immediate right. He chose to ignore it.

"Silly?" The man with the microphone was saying. "Silly? Would you consider changing places at this moment with any of these nice folks out here?"

"No," Anita Wallace said, "I guess not."

The man chortled. "No," he repeated, "I guess not. All right, Anita Wallace. Now, before we start the money flying and your Minute of Riches begins, I want you to take a moment to just look down at that money. What do you see when you look down at all that money, Anita Wallace?"

"What do you think she sees, you fool, Swiss cheese?" That same voice again, and Robin glanced toward the woman beside him and then looked away. She was not speaking loudly enough to be a heckler, and her comments did not seem directed at anyone in particular. She appeared to be simply expressing an uncontainable exasperation.

"Well, bills," Anita Wallace responded. "Bills of various denominations."

"That's right!" the man exclaimed. "Various denominations! Those aren't all singles, are they?" He leaned forward and peered at the money. "There's a twenty. There's a ten. There's another twenty. There are fifties in there, Anita Wallace, there are hundred-dollar bills, tens, fives. Money, Anita Wallace. You are knee deep in money, and all you can grab in the next minute belongs to you. Go for it!"

A fan started in the bottom of the booth and the money began to fly around. Anita Wallace stood in a blizzard of bills while frantic music pulsed loudly and the crowd yelled encouragement.

"Don't worry about your skirt, Anita Wallace," the man shouted. "Grab the money! That's it. Grab the money and stuff it through the slot there."

A frenzied energy seemed to overtake Anita Wallace. She was beating at her skirt and slapping at the flying bills and trying to stuff them through the slot, which it now became apparent was very narrow.

"Whoops!" the man shouted. "Look at those legs! Hey, there goes a fifty over your shoulder! Here comes a twenty! Go for it, Anita Wallace!"

"This is disgusting!" That voice again. The woman turned slightly toward Robin now as if offended by the very sight of Anita Wallace and her Minute of Riches. "Here is a dignified, seemingly intelligent woman, who is being reduced to a grasping, lunging idiot."

"She knows what she's doing," Robin Durham said, adding after a pause: "She *is* a big girl."

"You're disgusting. That woman is being used."

The music stopped, the fan stilled and the money slowly settled around the ankles of Anita Wallace as the crowd roared its approval.

"They made a fool of her," Elisa Gilbert continued, "just to teach us all a lesson."

"A lesson? So, what's the lesson?" Robin Durham asked, his smile condescending.

"That money is everywhere, obviously. That it flows like water. That you can throw it away because there's always more and if you're lucky you may win a fortune."

"So, that's the lesson?"

"That's right. That's the lesson."

Anita Wallace, disheveled and seemingly stunned, stepped from the booth and was handed a hundred and forty-seven dollars.

"A lousy hundred forty-seven bucks," Elisa said.

"I'd take it," Robin said. "Put me in there. They can laugh all they want. I'll even wear a skirt."

"You probably would."

"And I wouldn't waste one hand trying to hold it down. Hey, what's the problem? She's a big…pardon me. She's an adult. What'd she say when the guy asked if she wanted to trade places?"

They were walking away slowly now with the dispersing crowd. On one side of the aisle dollar slots rang, on the other was a row of silent twenty-one players, Keno numbers bellowed through the sound system.

"The problem," Elisa said, waving her arms, "is

this, all of this. I feel like I'm in an elaborate cage." She pointed up toward the ceiling. "Look, see those little glass panels? Windows, I bet. We're being watched at this very minute, probably listened to as well." She shook her fist at the ceiling.

"They're watching for cheaters," Robin explained. "Their dealers mostly, their own people. Money's the game here. Lots of money, and everyone keeps his eye on everyone else."

"No, it's a cage and we're the hamsters. On the inside, here where we are, it's all glitter and razzle dazzle and hyped up excitement. But on the other side of the walls, I hear large gears grinding. I hear the law of averages relentlessly turning. I imagine that beneath these tables and machines there are chutes. Money enters those chutes and it flows down into vaults where greedy men sit counting and laughing."

Robin stopped and looked at her, bemused. "May I ask you a simple question?"

"What?" Surprised, she looked seriously at him for the first time.

"What the hell are you doing here?"

"Me? Well, skiing."

"No, I mean here. In this casino. Lots of people come to Tahoe to ski who never enter a casino. You obviously hate the place. What are you doing here?"

"Well..." Elisa looked perplexed. "I just had dinner upstairs and I was....." She stopped and glared at him. "So, what business is that of yours? You a cop or something?"

"A cop?" Now it was Robin's turn to look flustered.

"Yeah, you know, one of those people you were talking about. The ones who go about looking for cheaters. A security guard or something? Are you going to bounce me out of here because I'm not falling for the company line?"

Robin Durham grinned and slowly shook his head. "Actually, I was just going to ask if you wanted a drink."

A young man walked into Tomasino's, a popular hangout in Oregonia. He took a stool at the bar and ordered a beer.

"All right," said Marthe, the bartender. "We have several to choose from."

"Whatever you have on tap will be fine."

"This one's local."

"Yes, fine, that'll be fine."

"Well, Ferguson, look who we have here," said one of the two other men seated at the bar.

"I see, Ollie. It's our young leading man. Out on the town are you, Iago?"

"Hey, guys."

"My guess, Ferguson, is that our star here has ventured out on this cold and wintry night for the sole purpose of sharing a glass with we walk-ons."

"Come on, guys..."

"He might even deem to purchase the first round."

"Or it could be a spat with the wifey, Ollie. That has been known to happen in the best of circles.

And such things do drive men out into cold and wintry nights."

"No, no spat," said the younger man.

"So, no spat, Ferguson. The gentleman has spoken."

"Spoken and well stated. Then I am honored as I am sure you are, Ollie, that this gentleman has 'deemed,' as you so finely stated, to join us. It reminds me a bit of Good King Wenceslas now that I think of it."

"Good…?"

"I delight in your reference, Ferguson. The image is most apropos, given the season. A dark and wintery night…"

"Royalty stepping out among commoners…"

"Come on, guys!"

"The snow deep…

"…and crisp…"

"And even, I believe." The young man sighed.

"Yes, very good, lad. Very good."

"Okay. Bartender, pour these guys a drink. One round. And one round only before I head home."

— 8 —

By the midnight break it seemed to Pug Bolcar that he and Carlos were locked in a strange unvoiced struggle for dominance. Lackner and McLain had become foils, cardboard images stood up to balance the table and square the game. Their stacks of chips stood approximately the same as when the game started while his and the Colombian's moved back and forth in increasingly dramatic shifts as the magnitude of their bets grew. By now each of them had twenty thousand in play, each having needed an extra ten at one point to pull himself from a hole.

Carlos departed for the bathroom while Lackner began doing stretching exercises near the door. As he poured Tripper and himself some gin, Pug asked his old friend what he knew about real estate prices in Humboldt County. He had some land there, he explained, a piece he'd secreted through the divorce. If the price was right, he might dispose of it.

"What I own is a corporation," he explained. "Rosyland Timber Company. I got the shares as a fee several years ago. I own all the outstanding shares but the only asset in the corporation is a hundred sixty acres of timber."

"What kind of timber?"

"What do I know about timber? I drove up there once. There's a small cabin on the place. Evergreens, firs I suppose."

"Any redwood?"

"Maybe some, Tripper. I don't know. I remember old stumps. It had been logged in the fifties, they told me. I didn't walk the whole parcel, of course. The client told me it was good timberland."

"Is it rural?"

"Rural as hell, as I remember it."

"I'm wondering if it could be subdivided," McLain said. "That's a lot of acreage if you could break it up. I've got some contacts up there. Shoot me the assessor's parcel numbers and I'll check it out."

When he and Carlos returned to the table Lackner pulled back the drapes for a moment.

"A full moon," he said.

"Last night was full," Tripper said. "Helen keeps track of those things."

As they sat down, Carlos glanced at his watch. "It's three hours later at home. With moon like this, drums are beating."

"Drums?" McLain asked.

"Santeria," Carlos said, looking to Lackner for assistance.

"What we would call voodoo," Lackner explained. "An Afro-Christian religious practice. It comes from the Caribbean but forms are found in many parts of Latin America."

"Your old man, I suppose," Pug said with a suggestion of contempt.

"Yes, he is part of it." Carlos took up the cards and began to shuffle them. "You say Christian, Bincent, but the rituals you would not recognize as Christian. During full moon there are many."

"Sacrificing a virgin most likely," Tripper McLain suggested. "Did I ever tell you about the Aztec god who…"

"Tripper," Pug growled. "If I'd wanted comedy I'd have gone to Reno to see Rickles."

But then moments later as they were pondering their hands, Carlos spoke again.

"It is strange," he said. "I can feel his presence tonight."

"The old man?" Lackner asked, honestly interested.

The Colombian nodded and the fingers of his right hand rose to absently caress the cat-like pendant at this throat. The move was so casual and yet so obvious that Pug nearly laughed out loud. He thought he had witnessed every hustle known to man but this was a new one. All this dribble about a mysterious old man had obviously been designed to put him on edge.

"I suppose your old man is standing behind me. Sending you signals about my cards." Pug held his cards back over his shoulder as if to give the spirit presence a better look.

Carlos, he saw with satisfaction, looked embarrassed. "I only need to see my own, Mr. Pug."

"I thought we were finished talking," Lackner said, throwing in forty to open the pot.

Over the years the rules had grown specific and time honored. The host-banker announced the time hourly. After midnight the dealer would call for bets as each round of the original five cards was dealt, a procedure that reduced the number of hands played but increased the size of the individual pots. A loser could retire at any time but a winner must be willing to continue until four o'clock if anyone remained to challenge him.

The passing hours, far from tiring Pug Bolcar, seemed to have filled him with heightened expectancy. McLain began to lose consistently now and was nearly five thousand down, most of which was stacked in front of Pug Bolcar. Lackner was short a thousand or so, and the Colombian held this. Carlos was a calculating, usually conservative but occasionally very daring player. Once, shortly after the one o'clock call, Pug drew a third jack and bet a thousand against what he calculated were lackluster hands. Carlos met his thousand and doubled it. Pug's call found the Colombian holding only a pair of aces.

Pug continued to feel very good about his game. The cards were falling well. When he lost it was with respectable hands. Twice in a row he successfully drew to fill an outside straight, though one of them cost him five grand to see a full house held by Carlos. The Colombian, too, became freer with his money. There was no more talk about old men beating on drums, though at crucial moments his hand sought the pendant. Once Pug caught him glancing up to see if he had noticed. Pug countered this by blowing the Columbian a kiss. Frowning, Carlos held Pug's stare for a long time before looking away.

It was after two now, and dealing the next hand Carlos called for bets after each round, a thousand a round. McLain and Pug dropped out and Lackner snared the pot with two pair, jacks over eights. With his deal Lackner continued the high stakes and this time Pug accepted the challenge. His first card was the king of clubs and being the first to bet he set down a thousand. Both Carlos and Lackner went along. His second card was the king of spades. The two black kings felt as heavy as weapons in his hand. He threw in five thousand and watched as the manicured fingers reached for the pendant. After a moment Carlos went along, glancing at Lackner who folded.

Sweet Jesus! His third card was also a king, the king of hearts. This, he realized, was the moment he had been waiting for. He looked at Carlos. Slumped in his chair the Colombian fanned his three cards, drew them together and fanned them again. For well over a minute neither of them moved. Finally, fingering a stack of chips but not looking up, Carlos asked Pug if he was going to bet. The move was Pug's but he did not respond. No movement, no word. He sat quietly watching the face of the Colombian. Lackner and McLain, sensing the drama, held themselves very still. At last Carlos looked toward his opponent. Pug smiled and blew him another kiss.

"It'll cost you ten to see another, amigo," he said, counting out the chips.

The Colombian's eyes returned to his cards but Pug could see the anger pulsing in the veins of his neck. Carlos counted out the chips and slid them to the center of the table.

Pug's fourth card was the ace of diamonds. "Another ten, Carlos," he said, his voice dismissive, a tone he used with opposing counsel at that point of negotiations when they were coming to realize the superiority of his position. Whatever its effect, Carlos went along. But it seemed to Pug that the charade had ended for the Colombian. The pendant rested forgotten at the base of his neck as he counted out the chips. Like Pug less than a hundred dollars remained in front of Carlos when he had met the terms.

He turned toward Lackner. "Deal the last one, Bincent."

The card Pug Bolcar received was more than a card and for a second he thought his eyes had tricked him. He glanced quickly at the five of them and more carefully studied them again. Yes, all four were there, the single ace resting among them. Slowly, almost casually, he brought the cards together. He set them face down on the table and placed his heavy, folded hands on their blue backs. For the moment he was content to revel in the pure pleasure of his good fortune, a pleasure he would have felt as intently had these cards fallen to him back in high school when he and Tripper had played penny-ante in the boiler room and the pot rarely exceeded a quarter.

But then a whole new line of thought entered his mind. In that pot were twenty-seven thousand dollars that were not his own, and of the twenty-six he had invested, six he had won that night. Thirty-three thousand was not a sum to be trifled with. He turned to Lackner.

"How much," Vince asked, anticipating his request.

"Ten."

Lackner nodded. "Write the check and place it in the pot. I'll guarantee it, Carlos. And you're covered if you want to go along."

"I do, thank you, Bincent."

Lackner counted out the chips for the Colombian and slid them to the center.

"Cards?"

The marvelous thing about four-of-a-kind is

that you do not need to take any cards, and the assumption your opponent makes is that you hold a straight, a flush or a full house when in fact four-of-a-kind defeats any of them.

"No cards," he said.

"No cards," Carlos said. He had slumped even lower in his chair, staring at his hand.

"Bets?" Lackner asked, quietly.

Carlos had paid thirty-six thousand dollars to purchase those cards. Surely, Pug thought, he could squeeze some more out of him. The question was how much. Ten he would go for, twenty he might not, and then Pug would have lost the additional ten. And he must persuade Lackner.

"I want to bet fifteen, Vince."

Vince Lackner blew out a mouthful of air. "Pug, I'm holding your two checks for ten each and I've just guaranteed a third for that amount. This would make a total of forty-five."

"You'll get it, Vince."

Lackner frowned. "You're right. I will."

Pug withdrew his checkbook. He wrote the check and tossed it onto the pile. The moment it landed, Carlos looked up.

"I think you're bluffing, Mr. Pug. I go your fifteen and I raise you another ten."

Lackner counted out the chips. The little Colombian must be worth some coffee beans, Pug thought. He should have started with twenty. Then he told himself to stop and think. No hurry here. The pace was his to set.

Why is Carlos betting like this? Of all the hands in poker only three could defeat his, and two of those were impossible. He could not have a royal flush because Pug had all four kings. And he could not have four aces because Pug had one. Only a straight flush: five sequential cards of the same suit could defeat his four kings. The odds against drawing a straight flush in five cards had to be something like fifty-thousand to one. He might be bluffing. The Scotch, his anger at Pug's antics had made him reckless. Or he might have four-of-a-kind as well, though the cards would have to be lower than his. Possible, but most likely was a full house, aces over. His second, third and fourth cards had been aces, and the last had matched the first. That would explain his betting. And he may think Pug was bluffing; he was known to. All the better. Too bad he couldn't raise him again; the rules prevented that. He looked at Lackner.

"We're talking fifty-five thousand, Pug."

"I know what we're talking. Will you guarantee it or not?"

Lackner thought it over. "I'll guarantee it."

Pug was tempted to look at his cards again. No, that was not necessary. He withdrew his checkbook and wrote out another ten thousand dollar check payable to Vince Lackner. He tore it from the book and set it on his stack of cards.

"It's going to have to be good, Carlos."

"Are you calling me?"

"I am." Pug reached out and dropped the check

on the pile of chips and paper.

They were red. Hearts. They began with four and ended with eight. He studied them carefully: four, five, six, seven and eight. All red, all hearts, a neat row of them. He took the deck from in front of Vince Lackner and shuffled in the four kings without showing them to anyone.

"It's yours," Pug Bolcar said. He sat back and sighed.

— 9 —

"Let me guess," Robin Durham said. "A Pink Lady."

Elisa Gilbert looked at the waitress and rolled her eyes. "A Black Russian, please."

"One of the reasons I don't gamble."

"Reason enough, I should think."

They sat at a small precarious table in a gloomy bar just off the casino. A slot machine had surrendered nearby causing a bell to ring urgently as if in alarm.

"And you, sir?" The waitress bit the end of her pencil.

"Scotch and milk."

"Scotch and…"

"Milk." Robin nodded. "I'll take it on the rocks."

"Chocolate?" The waitress was having a long night.

"Very clever," Robin said. "White, and low fat if you got it."

"Hmmm," Elisa said when the waitress had left.

"My stomach's bothering me."

"Have you considered scotch and Maalox? It has

a certain ring, scotch and Maalox on the rocks."

"Next round, perhaps."

Elisa's mind kept wanting to rewrite the script. Why was Tiff Bointon anywhere around between Christmas and New Years? No one worked between Christmas and New Years. She and Rafe had just returned from visiting his parents in Santa Fe. She felt angry suddenly at Neal Bointon for not taking Tiff away for the holidays. They had money. If not family, they could have gone to New York or London to see the new shows. Insane. Her thoughts were insane. Neal Bointon had nothing to do with it. None of that stuff had anything to do with it.

"So," she said now, "you're not a bouncer and not a cop. And your nose isn't sun burnt. What are you doing here?"

"Business," Robin said.

"Business."

"Yeah, we're checking the snow. Depths, temperatures. We're working on a computer program that will help predict avalanches." Robin Durham rubbed his nose. "I'm inside most of the time, assembling the data."

"That's interesting. You're with a university?"

"Government. Your tax dollars at work."

"Are they being well spent?"

"We're making progress. Had a small breakthrough today. Picked up some information on a pattern snow uses to enter the area."

"It didn't snow today," Elisa pointed out as their drinks arrived.

"Immaterial. I work from models. Actually I create models."

"Is that the cause of your stomach problems? The breakthrough?"

Robin Durham shook his head. "The boss is in from the home office."

"You've got a problem with your boss?"

Robin could not resist looking around before he responded. At the next table a woman lit a cigarette. He watched her and then looked back at Elisa.

"I don't want to talk about the boss."

In the embarrassed silence that followed, Elisa remembered that Rafe had gone to the theatre because of a battle scene in "Henry the Fifth." That's what he said. That he wanted to do some blocking. He would be playing Fluellen, a fool. He had taken up the script when they returned from Santa Fe. Going to the studio to have a look at the physical setting. The image of him at the door, she on the phone talking to Michael, her brother. Then she remembered Iago. Last season Rafe had played Iago to Tiff's Desdemona. Sixty-four performances. It could have started months ago. It almost certainly did start months ago. She was the one playing the fool.

Elisa began to wave at the smoke coming from the next table. "I hate cigarette smoke."

"You have to expect some smoke in a place like this," Robin said, trying to soothe her.

"That doesn't mean I have to like it. Smoking is a

disgusting, very rude habit." She said this loudly and addressed it directly to the couple at the next table.

"Well, pardon me." The woman's response was more confrontational than apologetic.

"Could you blow it somewhere else?" Elisa asked, adding a tiny lie: "I'm allergic." Part of her problem may be the woman herself, she realized, that flamingo-pink pant suit, hair dyed the color of charcoal.

"Then you should move, lady." This from the smoker's companion, a dark-haired, pasty- skinned man who gripped his beer bottle by the throat as if it were an unruly dog. "This is a bar. People smoke in bars."

"Yes, and most of them have the courtesy to not blow it in the face of another customer."

"I wasn't blowing it in her face," the woman explained to her companion. "I didn't even know she was there."

"That's not true! You blew it out of the corner of your mouth right in my direction. Why do you think I said something? See that man over there? He's smoking. I'm not complaining about him. It's you. You blew it right at me and now you're lying about it."

The beer bottle was suddenly hovering within inches of Elisa's face. "Listen, bitch. This is a public bar. People smoke in public bars. It's the law. You don't like it, get the fuck out of here."

Then this man she was sitting with, this man who had bought her a drink and whose name she didn't even know, was half standing, his hands reaching past her. One grabbed the man's arm, the other pulled the bottle free. The man's wrist hit hard against the table almost knocking it over. It was beyond embarrassing. Had there been an escape route she would have been running.

"Wait," she stammered.

"Apologize to the woman." A slightly southern accent in his voice, at least to her ears.

"She's the one should apologize," the man said, wincing. "She started it."

"Oh shit." Elisa hands covered her nose, watching as the man's arm was torqued.

"Apologize. You called her a bitch."

"All right. All right. Jesus, you're both of you crazy. Oooh, all right. I shouldn't a said bitch."

"Say the words!"

"I'm sorry, Jesus."

Robin released his grip. The man pulled his arm back and began to rub his wrist. "Let's get out of here." The woman was standing now adjusting the waistline of her pink slacks. She slipped on her mink coat, and bending forward blew a dense cloud of smoke in Elisa's face.

"Break out in hives, creep."

Elisa, her eyes on the table, did not respond. Ever since she walked around that last innocent corner she had felt herself clinging to a dragon's tail. Even now, in the midst of all this, her mind was fumbling with distant probabilities. Maybe they were just joking around, doing a little scene. Nothing meant by it. No, that's ridiculous. They were…..they had been for months. They were laughing at her.

"God, I'm sorry." Tears now forming in her eyes. Blurting out, "I…I left my husband yesterday."

"Yesterday." Robin Durham studied her a moment. "He smoked, I take it."

Elisa shook her head. "No, but I used to. And I really wish I had one now." She stood up, smoothing her skirt. "And you, you're what? A computer nerd does Errol Flynn or something?"

Now he was embarrassed. "It was stupid. Really. Had it gone another way, somebody might be dead now. Literally over a puff of smoke."

"There was more to it than that."

"No," Robin insisted, "that's the point. That's all there was to it."

Her humiliation complete, Elisa listened as an amplified voice blared out winning Keno numbers.

"Would you like to take a walk?" she asked. "A real walk, outside in the air. I promise I won't start another fight."

"That's a real commitment," Robin said.

Later, thinking back over the evening, Robin Durham would try to remember when his perception of this woman began to change. Certainly not in the casino. He would wonder why he had bothered to speak with her, let alone buy her a drink. Muttering like that in a crowd of strangers, her abrupt unjustified anger. He valued self composure in himself and others. Liese, his former wife, was the same. Had they been together and seen a woman behaving like that they would have entertained themselves speculating about the odd duck. There's a future bag lady, Liese might have said. Scolding her favorite garbage can oblivious to the passing crowd.

So, why had he gone along with the walk? Because he had loved Liese and now felt only sadness and loss and failure when he thought of her? Because his daughters had asked him six times over Christmas if he was coming home? And that would not happen. Would simply not happen. Because Harold Manx had been dead right? He had come to the department a failed private investigator, unable to scratch out a living prowling flea markets in search of a client's stolen goods, or interviewing reluctant witnesses, or being in the employ of the kind of men, who if you wanted a fee out of them, you damn well better get it up front.

Because he was alone. Because he was alone and she was alone. Because he felt his aloneness and her aloneness to the core of his being.

They walked a mile or more into California, past motels promising hot tubs for bone-weary skiers, her heels skittering in the thin refrozen slush. She talked without pause: her work with the theatre, her mother's drinking, her father's weakness for skirts. Perhaps she was trying to justify her behavior in the bar: look what I'm going through. Though not another word about the husband.

Before starting back to the neon excitement at the Nevada line they stopped for hot chocolate at a small place with too Swiss a décor where after a quick perusal he was pleased to see that none of the customers was smoking.

Perhaps an hour later they reached the lobby of her hotel. She had a way of standing, cocked on one hip, the other leg forward, her hands sunk in the pockets of her sweater, her face flushed from the outside air.

"Thanks, Robin." Her right hand emerged and was extended toward him. "The walk was just what I needed. I'll sleep like a baby."

They stood a few feet in front of the elevator. It was almost midnight but the dolls were still twirling in the Christmas display and "Rudolph" bounced out of the intercom as though it were mid-afternoon the day before Christmas.

Too pat, he thought.

"Let's go up to your room." That's all, just that. What was he thinking as he said those words? The old game? Was there even a glimmer of the other thing?

Elisa Gilbert blushed—she appeared quite rosy, all in all—but said nothing. The elevator bell rang and the door opened. She turned and walked toward it. Was this goodbye? He didn't know. Anything was possible, given the history. He stood a moment, perplexed, then followed her.

The two other couples in the elevator knew each other. One man said to the other: "Pornographic films? We don't even have a pornograph." The women were talking about cilantro. One loved it, the other said it tasted like soap. Elisa watched her shoes, hands in her pockets. They could be a couple in the middle of an argument, he thought, holding their tongues while changing venues.

Still silent she opened the door of her room and reached for the light. Durham caught her hand and held it. He bent down to kiss her.

"You have this habit of grabbing other people's arms," she said, turning her face toward his.

— 10 —

When she woke him, it was still the middle of the night. She was nudging his shoulder with the heel of her palm, just the heel as if that large toughened muscle could endure the contact without risk of contamination.

"You're going to have to leave," she said. She stood at a cautious distance from the bed, wrapped in a robe. They had pulled open the drapes at one point, and the light from the moon falling now on the table near the window had a harsh mineral quality about it.

"Well…" He rubbed his eyes. "What time is it?"

"I don't know. It doesn't matter." Going about the room now gathering up his clothes. The plaid flannel shirt, the gray cords, good quality both of them. She had complimented him on his apparel over the hot chocolate. "My wife dresses me," he had said. "I mean my ex-wife. She bought all my clothes." What to make of that? Well, it didn't matter now. A turquoise down vest, the image of it clear in her mind, seeing Tiff exit the room again. 'This is not what you think!'

The double arrogance of that, Elisa thought: that she knew what I was thinking and that I was wrong to think it. Tiff Bointon stumbling around without a script, having to make it up herself. 'Oh, my God!' The arrogance underlying that.

He found his watch on the nightstand. "It's three-thirty."

"Here." She held his clothing, arms extended, and when he did not take them, she dropped them onto the bed.

"Now?"

"I don't even know your last name."

"I can tell you my last name if that's the problem."

"I don't want to know your name. I just want you to leave."

Mumbling he rose on the far side of the bed and began to dress himself while she went to the window and stood looking out. When he had dressed he began gathering up her clothing.

"You don't..." she began, turning.

He ignored her. Working methodically he hung each item across his left forearm and walked to the window and presented them to her. She reached to take them and he leaned forward to kiss her. It was a foolish need-filled gesture, he realized later, poorly timed and certain to frustrate his wishes. But seeing her standing at the window, wrapped tightly in her robe, she seemed to him all the loveliness of spent desire, the tenderness of confused impulses.

Elisa averted her face and pushed at him with the bundled garments. "Please, just go!"

He found himself in the eye of a gathering incongruity. "Listen, I think something special might have happened here."

"Special? It's common as dirt." To hide the tears filling her eyes she turned back toward the window. "Just go," she said quietly. "It's not you, okay? It's me. I just want you to go."

"Okay, I'll go. But give me your last name. Tell me where you live. Maybe we could meet in the morning, have some breakfast." How he would work that out with the Chief he had no idea.

Her head shook. "It's a bad dream. I want it over." The dark mountains shaping the skyline swam in her tears. They were like guardians watching her. She focused on them, wanting to draw them closer.

"A phone number? At least that, Elisa."

"Just go! Please!"

It took a long time for the elevator to make its way to the fifth floor. When it opened a man in baggy slacks and a sport jacket stepped out. He pulled out his empty pockets, showed them to Robin Durham and laughed.

"I know the feeling, pal," Robin said.

In a small apartment in East Palo Alto a woman woke from a dream. She lay on her back looking up at the darkened ceiling. Beside her, puppy-like, a small child was sleeping. The child's posture expressed several of the meanings we hope to convey when we use the word "grace." The woman was thinking about magic, and about the dream, and about the telephone on the counter in the kitchen. How the receiver had felt that afternoon when she held it in her hand, its smooth weight, its curious balance, the sense it gave of being alive and possessed of mysterious powers. In the dream she had been gigantic, capable of stepping over freeways, able to leap across cities, and to run and run without becoming tired. Yes, she had. She had picked up the receiver that afternoon, and had held it at a distance as if it were a dangerous thing. Dangerous, but also potent and capable of magic. She had forced herself to listen for a few seconds to the urgent, demanding dial tone before she returned it to its cradle. And now she had had the dream.

"A serious man," said Ollie Rand, "sits at the bar. A serious man does not sit at a table. And most certainly he does not sit in a booth."

"A serious *drinking* man," said Rafe, who saw his reflection in the mirror behind the bar and did not like what he saw. "You are talking about a serious *drinking* man."

"Redundancy!" claimed Ferguson from his other side. "Redundancy, you are slipping into redundancy."

"What?"

"He's right, lad," said Ollie Rand, "an obvious redundancy. Explain, Ferguson."

"Many men drink, lad, and many who do are not serious about drinking or anything else. But a serious man always drinks. Ergo, to say 'a serious drinking man' is to commit a redundancy."

"And a redundancy," explained Ollie Rand, "reflects

badly on the speaker, suggesting as it does a word-waster...."

"Word-waster, I like that Ollie."

"Thank you, Ferguson. Moreover a man of confused thought, of muddled phrasing, perhaps a man whose mouth has wondered free of his mind."

"In short," summarized Ferguson, "a not serious man."

"All I know," said Rafe, "is that I am a man who is very tired and very drunk who dreads going home to an empty apartment. It's empty, Ollie. It's very empty. And I thought, maybe a booth. In a booth I could slump and maybe have one more drink and every time I looked up I wouldn't have to see that guy over there staring at me."

"Ah," said Ferguson, "now there's the confusion."

"Yes," agreed Ollie Rand, "we're making progress. Bartender, one more round if you will."

"Is he...?" asked the bartender, coming over.

"I'm not sure I..." began Rafe.

"He's in our charge, Marthe," said Ollie Rand. "We take full responsibility for his wellbeing and his eventual journey home."

"As serious men," added Ferguson.

Marthe poured the drinks and returned to the far end of the bar where she picked up the remote and began yet another fruitless tour through the channels. Tomasino's was empty. It was sometime after midnight in the dead of winter with the theatres closed, the visitors gone, the company dispersed, the precipitation vacillating between snow, sleet and rain. About the time that stacks of many-colored chips had begun to lunge dangerously back and forth across Vince Lackner's carefully-appointed table. About the time two strangers coupled in a flurry of confusion, passion, anger and despair. About the time Ramona Livingston climbed from her bath and, wrapping herself in a towel, walked to the window saying to herself, though not quite believing it: I am Lady Bounce, the one who survives. The one who comes away unscathed.

In East Palo Alto a car passed down a street. Its headlights raced up the wall and across the ceiling. The woman wanted to catch and hold that light, but it was gone.

"Raise your glass, lad," instructed Ollie Rand.

The three men raised their glasses and touched them together.

"Now look clearly at that gentleman you see before you," said Ferguson.

"To him," said Ollie Rand. "We drink to him."

"To a serious man," said Ferguson.

And they drank.

II

SAN FRANCISCO

A phone rang. It rang a second time. It rang a third time.

"Uhn?"

"Have you talked to her?"

"Unuh."

"You coward! You have to talk with her!"

"Uhn."

"And she's lying about the keys."

"Wha…?"

"This has kept me up all night. She has to be lying about the keys. The entire complex was locked! She couldn't have gotten down there without her keys. The bitch is lying! Or you are! What did you say to her?"

"No, I…"

"And poor Neal. Oh, my God! This will break his heart. That man worships the ground I walk on."

"Uhn."

"Oh, baby, I am so miserable. I am so fucking miserable!"

"Uhn."

January 3, 1980, the first workday of the new year,

that day of days when reality stops by with its list of reminders: all those obligations that we in our haste to enjoy the holidays had put aside.

By 8:30 that morning Pug Bolcar was at his desk hovering over four sheets of yellow paper. The desk was walnut, heavy and huge. On its massive surface, he had been told, a client's ancestors had played with railroads, gold mines and oil wells. The client was a grandson of a former president of the Southern Pacific Railroad. A young Pug Bolcar had taken the desk as his fee. The heir had come to him charged with driving under the influence, his third in fifteen months.

On one sheet of paper, he had listed the cases set for trial in the next four months, their probable settlement figures, and the amount of each settlement the firm would receive. Scanning down the list he knew that seventy percent of them would be put over to a later date because courtrooms would not be available, and defense lawyers, the bastards, never settle until they reach the courtroom door. At the bottom of the page he had set down all of his liquid assets, including money owed him.

On the second sheet, Becky, his secretary and office manager, had enumerated the expenses the firm would have over the next four months: rent, library costs, office supplies, the monthly payment to Dot Hilliard, the salaries of three attorneys, three secretaries, malpractice and other insurance premiums, an estimate of costs the firm would front for clients, utility bills, etc. Becky had neatly aligned and totaled the numbers. To her total he added fifty-five thousand dollars representing the four checks he had written to Vince Lackner. Checks that at the end of the night Lackner had endorsed and handed to the Colombian. The liabilities on the second page exceeded the estimated income on the first page by forty-seven thousand dollars.

On a third sheet of paper he now set out columns comparing his personal income with his personal expenses over the next four months: alimony to Ruth, payments on the Audi, on the condominium (he had moved into one of the units and was paying for it), his share of the condominium joint venture's overall obligations, meals (he took all his meals out since the divorce), more insurance, laundry, dry cleaning, alcohol....

He stopped writing. This was ridiculous. He was too old and too comfortable to be fretting over the cost of booze and clean shirts. On the fourth sheet he began to write the names of possible contacts: his accountant, his banker.... Who else? Tripper? He could not bring himself to do that, though he would send Tripper the information on the Rosyland property. Maybe that could be sold off quickly. From several people on his list he could get ten grand, no questions asked. Unless one of them found out about the others, then there would be questions aplenty. Gossip rolled over Pug's San Francisco like early morning fog. He picked up the phone.

"Becky, have you got hold of Behel?"

"Yes. He just walked in. Ah...Pug?"

"What?"

"Have you read the morning paper?"

"Christ, no. Why?"

"Well, there have been several calls."

"I told you, hold all calls. And send Behel in."

"Right." Becky smiled at Thomas Behel. "Mr. Bolcar will see you now." To Pete Miller, the senior associate standing at the door of his office, she shook her head.

As soon as Thomas Behel had entered Pug's office and closed the door, Pete Miller placed his hands in prayer position, the tips of his fingers touching the end of his nose, and bowing toward Becky, pleaded: "Please tell me he could not have done that."

Becky shrugged her shoulders. She had stopped years ago trying to predict or explain Pug Bolcar's behavior.

Like Pug, Thomas Behel had not read the morning paper. News made him angry and so he avoided it. He was a large, careful man. Joining the Marines near the end of World War II, his one rash act, had satiated for life whatever urge he possessed for adventure. He had a lovely, sophisticated wife who patronized the arts, two grown children, a granddaughter, a new Oldsmobile every year and a house in Marin with a backyard full of roses that he cultivated with loving care. An accountant by profession, he had overseen both the firm's and Pug's personal financial matters for years.

Notwithstanding this long association, Tom Behel

felt somewhat uncomfortable stepping into Pug's office. His wife, Niedra, whose wisdom he never doubted, had witnessed a drunken food fight several years before in the Venetian room of the Fairmont between Pug and Erwin Bloom, an equally notorious attorney. And if that hadn't been enough, Niedra would remind him of how Pug had treated Ruth, his flagrant unfaithfulness toward a woman they both knew and felt sympathy for.

And yet Tom Behel enjoyed handling Pug's business. Every April when the tax returns had been prepared, he and Pug went out to lunch. He enjoyed Pug's stories. He liked the wine Pug chose, the way his client always picked up the tab, and how every year he had to remind Pug to keep the receipt.

Pug had his coat off and his sleeves rolled up to his elbows. His desk was cluttered with stacks of files and sheets of yellow paper. Across the arms of one chair laid an artificial leg with a court reporter's tag attached. Seeing it, Thomas Behel winced slightly. He chose another chair, plucking on the creases of his slacks as he sat down.

"How are things, Tom?"

Behel started to answer then noticed that Bolcar was writing on one of the papers and not listening. After a moment Pug looked up.

"So, how are things, Tom?"

"They're fine, Pug, and you?"

"Fine. I need some money though, short term thing."

"I see."

"I need fifty-five thousand, and I need it by next Thursday."

"Next Thursday." Tom Behel rubbed a finger back and forth along a cheekbone barely discernible in his fleshy features. The skin of his face had a shine to it, as if his after-shave contained wax. Now it was his thumb, up and down on his cheek. "Fifty-five thousand, you say?"

"That's right."

Behel sighed. Sometimes Tom Behel reminded Pug of a banana slug, the shiny skin, the seemingly lack of internal structure, the agonizing deliberateness of the man.

"Do you intend to borrow that amount?"

"I'll have to borrow a chunk of it, won't I?"

"I see." Behel leaned forward and gently rested his briefcase on some files at the edge of the desk. He clicked open first one latch and then the other. He removed a file, closed the briefcase and set it on the floor. He opened the file and removed a sheet of lined and ruled green paper.

"Becky gave me the latest figures when she called."

"Well?" Fumbling in a desk drawer, Pug pulled out a cigar.

"The last quarter looks like it was slow. We don't have all the figures."

"Yes, I know." Pug pulled the cigar free from its wrapper. "How do you propose I raise what I need? Two or three months. I'll have made it back. Just a short term loan, Tom. I can pay top dollar."

Behel stared at the green financial statement. "Your situation was altered significantly by the divorce."

"I know, Tom."

"Then there's the monthly disbursement to Hilliard," Behel added, eyes on the paper. "That removes a large amount off the top."

Pug placed his elbows on the desk and leaned forward. "I need fifty-five grand, Tom. And I need it by Thursday."

Tom Behel's hand returned to his cheekbone. "You have an investment in mind, I take it."

"You could say that," Pug said, lighting the cigar. "But nothing I can borrow against."

"I see. Well, there's the certificate of deposit."

"I've thought of that. I could borrow against it but that's twenty at most."

"At last maturity $21,735.46. We reinvested the interest along with the principal apparently."

"Probably."

"You've always held the certificate against slow periods in the firm. You need that cushion, I should think."

"Then what about the condo venture? I've sunk a wad into that. Could we paint it up so a bank would loan against it?"

Behel set the paper down. He opened the file and shuffled through several sheets. "Your contribution stands at $130,342.17 as of the end of the year. Your obligation on the outstanding note is well over that. Do you have a recent appraisal?"

"I could call Freuhoff. He might have something."

"I see." Behel studied the file and stroked his cheek.

"A bank would require its own appraisal, wouldn't it?" Pug realized, souring.

"I should think so."

"Christ. That could take a month."

"Ten days to two weeks, if they rush it." Behel glanced curiously at the man sitting across from him. Must be a hell of an investment, he thought. What he said was: "Prime rate was running at twenty-one percent a couple of weeks ago, higher, of course, on short-term loans. Plus incidental charges."

"I can write the damn interest off," Pug said, blowing out a cloud of smoke, "but I need the money now."

Behel nodded but said nothing. It was just not there. Not fifty-five thousand, and certainly not in a week.

Pug Bolcar coughed slightly. "You know my daughter, Tom. You were at the wedding, I believe. Well, she's got a problem on her hands and I want to help her out if I can. She and her husband separated over the holidays."

"I'm sorry to hear that."

"Yeah, it's a shame. I hope they can salvage the damn thing but in the meantime they got a balloon payment to make on a house they bought up there. A fixer-upper they were hoping to sell before the due date, and that hasn't happened. Fifty-five grand and it's well over due."

Thomas Behel had set down the file and was

examining his coat sleeve for lint. Pug leaned the cigar against the ashtray and rubbed a finger across his lips. God, he hated this.

"Here's the problem, Tom. They got a buyer who's interested but unless they can stave off the lender, they'll have nothing to sell. All their equity gone, not to mention the work they've put into the place. I think it's the damn money problem that's wrecking their marriage."

"I see." With a thumb and index finger Tom Behel lifted the crease of a pant leg and crossed one leg over the other.

"Twenty-five I can come up with, but that leaves me thirty shy of what the kids need." Pug took a deep breath. "Tom, if you could loan me the thirty, I'll make it very worth your while. Ninety-day note, you name the interest. Becky can type it up and you can tie it to whatever you want, future earnings of the firm, the condos, whatever makes you comfortable."

"Well, I...." Tom Behel rubbed his cheek and looked out the window at the gray, featureless fog. "Security wouldn't be a problem, Pug. But Niedra insists we go to Bayreuth this season, and Courtney's back living at home...."

Pug Bolcar just looked at him. No relief. Let him squirm through it. This account is not Behel's biggest, but it's not insignificant either.

"I can't do it, Pug."

It's his goddamned wife, Pug thought. He holds up a finger every time he needs to tinkle and she would never forgive him. He felt betrayed. Twenty years, he'd been giving Tom Behel his work, sent other clients his way. He pushed his palms against the desk and stood abruptly.

"If you can't do it, Tom, you can't do it." He watched as Behel pulled up the briefcase, opened it, deposited the file inside and closed it again. Deliberate as all hell. One fast move and the man might start running and not stop until he hit a wall or leaped from a precipice.

"I wish I could help, Pug."

Walking toward the door Pug did not bother to turn around. "No problem, Tom. You put this time on the account."

"No, that's all…."

"No, I insist on it," he said, hand on the door knob. "Business *is* business, after all. By the way, how much did the firm's account come to last year? Something over three, wasn't it?"

"Yes…I don't have the exact figures…"

"And the joint venture? I got you all that work as well, I believe. That must have been over five, start-up costs and all."

"I appreciate the business, Pug, you know that. It's just…."

Pug Bolcar opened the door, and slapping Tom Behel's shoulder directed him out. "Becky, if Mr. Behel doesn't send us a bill for this visit, you call his girl over there and insist on it."

"Yes," Becky said, looking out past the crowd of employees who were clustered around her desk, studying an open newspaper.

"And Becky, bring me in a cup of coffee."

The employees watched silently as their boss stepped back into his office and closed the door. They stood watching as Thomas Behel pulled on his all-weather coat and carefully straightened the lapels.

When he had left, Fran said, "Take it in with the coffee, Becky. You have to."

Becky entered Pug's office, coffee in one hand, the folded newspaper held in front of her like a shield. She always entered the room tilted back, her chin tucked in, her face slightly averted. It sometimes amazed Pug that she didn't fall over backwards.

She placed the coffee and the paper in front of him, pointed to Patricia Pendar's column and stepped back. The pertinent item had been circled in red:

> Less than six months after kickback charges against him were dismissed, former supervisor Tyler Conden is ready to try again; this time for state senate; look for an announcement in two weeks. Meanwhile his attorney (and former brother-in-law) Lawrence "Pug" Bolcar has been taking a few risks himself. He reportedly received an unpleasant verdict from a straight flush in a private poker game at Lake Tahoe over the weekend; damages were a punishing $61,000.00.

— 12 —

"Lunch is my meal, darling," Ruth Bolcar said that

morning while Elisa ground the coffee. She was so happy to have her daughter's company she had agreed to some cereal, though in the end she ate only a few bites.

"Breakfast is for children and pets—you know cats and those furry little dogs that yap you insane if you don't feed them. Dinner can have its charm, especially dinner in the form of a party, but it's a charm that ends in the hips. Ugly hips are one of the few human failings I've escaped in life, Binks, and I've done it by avoiding dinner in the main. But lunch, now that's an occasion. A girl's entitled to an occasion every day and lunch is mine."

Elisa was only half listening. She caught herself spinning the grinder so fast that coffee beans began flying out and bouncing off the butcher block table. There were moments, now, when she had begun to doubt her actual sanity. That thing with that man. One black Russian? She wished she had guzzled a parade of black Russians. At least she would have an excuse, however lame.

Ruth was still expounding in high style when Dot Hilliard called. Pendar's column poured out of the phone, Dot's voice shrill and loud as if she were reporting a fire. Elisa, on her hands and knees picking up coffee beans, could hear every word from across the kitchen. Then at her mother's direction she had run down to the foyer for a copy of their own which they spread on the table, the two of them leaning in to stare at the words as if they had to be closely examined before they could be trusted as real.

The plan had been for the two of them to go downtown this morning. Ruth would reintroduce Elisa to a few family acquaintances, people she had known one way or another since childhood. The idea was to get a start on a new life. Find some temporary work until she could make better arrangements. "Surely, darling, someone will have something. A nice, comfortable position while you get your bearings."

But now, Ruth decided, Elisa could not possibly go out looking for work on this of all mornings. Everywhere she went they would be asking her about the newspaper column. And poor Dot was beside herself. Each of them had been damaged by the antics of this man and it was essential that the three of them show themselves together for lunch. They could not let Pug's behavior shame them into being housebound. She knew Elisa would help calm Dot, and Dot, for her part, might have suggestions where Elisa could find work. "It would help take her mind off it, Binks."

So, Elisa did not go job hunting, though more than anything she wanted to sustain her momentum away from Rafe. And the way to do that, it seemed to her, was to establish a life for herself in San Francisco. If she became stalled she would hear Oregon calling. She still felt bruised inside, as if she had survived a car accident, and her thoughts, whenever she wasn't using them to beat herself up about what happened in Tahoe, strayed to her husband. She found herself raging at him, or blaming herself, insisting she must have caused it all by failing him in some way, or in more innocent moments she heard herself telling him things as though nothing had happened between them.

One thing about Rafe was you could talk to him. It wasn't like he saw himself as a star or particularly handsome, or something special. He would listen to you. He was patient in that way. And that hadn't changed since they were in school together. Other people commented to her on how regular a guy he was. He comes off stage after a packed house has been on its feet applauding him and he's just a regular guy. Not show-offy, not snooty, not hyper intellectual. Even kind of jocky—don't get him started on tennis. A craftsman, they say. An artist who knows his craft but is not going to get obsessive or theoretical about it.

Her father was someone she wanted to talk to Rafe about. The money he reportedly lost dazzled Elisa. She found herself going back over their dinner sifting for evidence of other bizarre behaviors. The Ramona thing, what did that mean? A woman his daughter's age? She would have talked with Rafe about that. Women and gambling were not news when it came to her father. But the extremes—had he lost the fine control he always had? If the paper was correct, he had squandered a small fortune on a single hand of cards.

Elisa had always thought of her father as the consummately capable man. He solved problems, he made things better. He took responsibility for situations people could not handle themselves, and he found solutions, made it right, got them justice. He was the kind of man who might win thousands of dollars in a card game, but it stunned her to think he had lost.

At other moments it was not Rafe so much as work. She had fled, she was beginning to realize, not only her husband, but also her job. And doing so had placed her career at risk. There were not that many companies producing great theatre who could afford to employ costume designers, and those that did were not desperate to hire new ones. The opposite was true. The process that led to her hiring had been as rigorous as the auditions Rafe had gone through. Should she allow Rafe's behavior to cost her her position? She was free to return to Oregonia, find a new place to live and resume her work. But Elisa knew she could not return. The community was small, the company a large family. She would be in constant contact not only with Rafe but the Bointons as well. It would be impossible. She was too much her father's daughter to go meekly about her business. She would end up back with Rafe, or she would encounter tension and ugliness wherever she went.

Following their breakfast, and as her mother was indulging in her customary forty-five minutes in the bathroom, Elisa braced herself and picked up the phone. She dialed the theatre's administrative office and asked for Tom MacElhenney, the company's executive director. She was going to tell Tom she was leaving. No sordid details, but she and Rafe had broken up and it would be best for both of them if she started a new life. Kathy Hill answered at the other end. Tom was traveling in Greece, she explained, and not expected back for a week. Neal Bointon was available. He was handling things in the interim. Did Elisa want to talk to Neal? No, she did not want to talk to Neal Bointon, not at this moment. Kathy would have Tom call when he returned. "I'm sorry to hear about your mother," she added. "I hope it's not serious."

So Rafe had already spread a cover story, including no doubt a line about the poor husband forced to fend for himself while his wife was away playing nurse. Easy bit for an actor and it might get him a meal or two. He's a fraud, Elisa wanted to shout, and now he's lying for both of us. Instead, she told Kathy that, yes, that would be fine. Have Tom call when he returned.

As she set down the phone Elisa felt herself sliding into a form of paralysis. She had been prepared to explain to Tom MacElhenney, if not everything, enough to let him know that she was not coming back and why. And following that she would march off to a new life. Instead, she had let Rafe's lie stand uncontested.

So she spent the morning at home with to her mother, who, since she could not talk directly to Pug, talked about him to Elisa.

Lunching with Dot Hilliard and Ruth Bolcar meant dining in the presence of pronounced shoulder pads, with hair color chemically preserved, with eyebrows plucked and drawn. Dot wore the perpetual expression of a person waking from a nightmare, ceding to Ruth the role of the older, more-worldly friend, though she was in fact the younger by a year.

Elisa felt docile, bored. It was all so familiar. Dot, her voice high and nasal, competing with her mother to see who could paint the worst picture of the evils that had befallen them. Pug, of course, was the principal subject, but they were careful to throw in Rafe from time to time lest Elisa felt left out.

And Elisa did feel left out—she was the little girl again playing on the floor among the chair legs—but she had no desire to talk about her husband, however angry she was with him at the moment. It was all too easy a song to sing, this a-cappella diatribe against absent wrongdoers. She found herself tempted to defend the guilty if only to balance the conversation. It made her sad and exhausted. She wanted to use her anger, not wallow in it. But in the course of the conversation, somewhere between the mixed greens and the grilled snapper (Yes, her mother had insisted that Elisa order the snapper—"After what you've been through, dear, you must have protein and lots of it.") Dot Hilliard said something that Elisa took to heart:

"Don't underestimate what's happening to you, Binks. You have just met death. It's no different from what happened to me. It was as sudden and just as real. One moment you're married and secure, and the next you're lost and alone. My husband died, for you trust died. But it's all the same in the end. We're both in mourning, one way or another. And that's how you should think of it."

— 13 —

"Jesus Christ!"

The concussion from Pug Bolcar's fist hitting the desk spilled the coffee and seemed to hurl Becky halfway across the room.

"Becky, get me…Oh, Christ, I'll do it myself." He reached for the phone. "Clean this up."

As Becky hurried through the outer office for paper towels she nodded her head to the other employees. The article, the nod said, was true.

Pete Miller slapped his forehead. "Man the fucking lifeboats! And certify the paychecks."

Pug Bolcar was told by a soft and pleasant female voice that Tripper McLain was not available.

"Where it he, goddamn it?"

"He's on his way to Chicago, an owners' meeting."

That McLain should be off trading one seven-foot giant for another struck Pug at this moment as particularly irritating.

"Where's he staying?"

"The Palmer House, Mr. Bolcar, but…"

"You get the Palmer House and you tell them to have McLain call me the minute he arrives. Is that clear?" Without waiting for an answer he broke the connection and punched seven more numbers.

"Pacific Rim Transport."

"This is Pug Bolcar. Give me Lackner." He waited, thumping the desk with the end of his stubby index finger.

"Good morning, Pug." Vince Lackner's purposeful, whiny voice was more than irritating. It reminded Pug of who had invited that damn Colombian into the game.

"Vince, if you or that runt are responsible for this, you'll both freeze in hell before you see a penny from me."

"What's the problem, Pug?" Lackner sounded like he had more important things on his mind.

"The goddamned paper."

"What paper?"

"The *Courier* for Christ's sake. Pendar's column. Have you read it?"

"I don't read the *Courier*."

"Then let me fill you in," Bolcar said sarcastically and then read the item.

Vince Lackner looked up from his desk and out the window. On a clear day he could see a strip of runway and beyond it, the bay. This morning the bay was hidden by fog.

"Does it say who else was involved?"

"It says what I read, damnit!" Pug's fist came down again, this time within inches of where Becky's hand was wiping with a towel. "This thing nails me to the fucking wall, Vince, and I intend to find out who did it."

Lackner picked up a pencil and began tapping

the eraser on a legal pad. "That's exactly right, isn't it? Sixty-one thousand."

"To the dollar. And when I left your suite only four people in the world knew it. Now everybody in town does."

The rush of nerves sparking in the back of Vince Lackner's neck caused him to take a slow breath. "So, what are you saying, Pug?"

"One of you let this out, that's what I'm saying. And when I found out who there is going to be hell to pay." He tore a towel from Becky's hand and began to furiously wipe at his desk. "Goddamnit there was no reason for this! No reason at all."

Lackner moved the receiver away from his ear. He turned the pencil around and slowly, wrote two fives, a comma and three zeros. In front of the first five he drew a dollar sign. When Bolcar had wound down he said in the same flat voice, "Have you talked with McLain?"

"McLain's on his way to Chicago."

"Well, Pug, this is the first I've heard of it." He drew three parallel lines beneath the numbers.

"Who've you told?" Pug demanded.

"No one."

"You sure of that?"

"Absolutely," Vince Lackner said, Pug's breath loud and raspy in his ear.

"Where can I get hold of the Colombian?"

"I have no idea. He'll be here next Thursday to present the checks. You said they'd be covered by then."

"Not if he leaked this they won't. Those checks will bounce all the way to Colombia. There…"

Lackner again put distance between his ear and the receiver. With the pencil he retraced the numbers making them darker, more bold.

"Carlos didn't do it, Pug," he said when Bolcar paused to suck in more air. "Carlos is a gambler and a very discreet businessman. He has no more interest in Bay Area gossip than I do. But that's all beside the point. I guaranteed those checks. I endorsed them. If you don't pay, I'll have to and it was you who lost the money, not me."

After a long silence Pug Bolcar said in a soft voice, "Well, Vince, you did bring the little bastard into the game."

"Yes, and he took you fair and square. And he took you because I was willing to back your paper." Lackner paused. He drew a box around the numbers. "Of all people, Pug, you are the last person I'd suspect of reneging on a promise. I didn't hesitate to stand behind you because I knew I could trust you. I'm amazed you would even suggest backing out."

"Somebody betrayed me!" Pug Bolcar shouted, his voice filled as much with anguish as rage. "For no reason, no reason in the world. There are rules, Vince. You don't go around talking about who won and who lost. That breaks every rule. It's cheap and it's low and if I find out who did it he'll regret it to his dying day."

Vince Lackner took a long deep breath. "I didn't do it, Pug. I had nothing to do with it. But you're talking like you want me to pay the price. I resent that. I trusted you and now you're threatening to renege."

A growl-like sound rose from Pug Bolcar's throat. "I'll talk to McLain. Somebody had to do it. Somebody let this out and if it was Carlos he's not getting my money, Vince. I can't do that."

Lackner studied the numbers in the box. "Talk to McLain. There has to be a rational explanation."

"That's true," Pug said thoughtfully. "There has to be a rational explanation."

He had been back from lunch for half an hour when Tripper McLain finally returned his call.

"What's so important, Pug? You scared my secretary half to death."

"Listen to this." He read the item.

"Christ, how'd she get hold of that?"

"I was hoping you could tell me."

"I love a joke, but I wouldn't do that, Pug, and you know it."

"Has to be the Colombian then. Him or Lackner."

"Could have been an accident," Tripper suggested. "A loose tongue. Somebody overheard it and passed it on to Pendar. People do that kind of thing. Feeders they call them."

"I didn't tell a soul, and Vince claims he told no one."

"I mentioned it to Helen," Tripper admitted after a pause. "No details, just that you were the big loser. She probably thinks you lost four or five hundred dollars."

"Anyone else?"

"No."

"Then it has to be the Colombian," Pug said again.

"Sounds like it. He must have let it slip out somehow."

"Well fuck him. This is going to cost me no end of problems. I made a fool of myself in front of Tom Behel this morning. I was a laughing stock at the club during lunch. Every lawyer in town is going to think I'm desperate to settle and I'll have to tough out every penny. Well, fuck Carlos. He can tack those checks on the wall because I'm stopping payment the minute I hang up here."

"That's coming down awfully hard on Vince. He can't shoulder this."

"Then he can tell the Colombian to get fucked. These are gambling debts. A California court might not look kindly on him coming in to collect them."

"That might not be possible, Pug. Carlos could be an important business contact for Vince. He might have to pay him off regardless. What a mess. I think Harry Morgan might know Pendar. Maybe he can learn something."

"Put him on it. Meanwhile I'm holding onto my money."

"You should have thought of that sooner."

"Very funny."

McLain chuckled. "Is Conden really thinking about running for senate?"

"How would I know? Conden hates me about as

much as Ruth does, and the feeling is mutual. He's probably fool enough though."

"Well," McLain said, "he was found innocent."

"Correction. I got the case dismissed on a technicality. There's a world of difference."

He felt better. He could put it somewhere, on the Colombian where he most wanted to put it. At the bank he wrote out the stop-payment orders. Back at the office he called Lackner and told him what he had done. Vince said nothing. He was too smart to argue and too angry to not argue if he opened his trap.

Then, cigar in hand, Pug Bolcar returned all but one of the calls that had stacked up during the day. Attorneys arranging depositions, asking for extra time to answer, communicating offers from insurance companies. To those who knew him well enough to raise the issue he responded with humor. Yes, he felt them thinking, the same old Pug, not showing his cards unless you paid to see them. To Freuhoff, one of the partners in the condo venture, he was relatively more forthright. Freuhoff needed to be comforted. He was ten years Pug's junior, stretched so thin by the condo deal he could no longer blink, and in general given to panic.

"Norm," he began, "I suppose you read the line in the paper."

"On the way in this morning, Pug. Is it true?"

"No, Norm, it isn't true but like most things there's some truth to it."

"It's not just the payments…sixty-one thousand is a lot of dollars, Pug."

"A lot of dollars and I'm glad I didn't lose them." He allowed a bit of gravel to enter his voice, "Norm, have I ever failed to make my contribution when it was asked?"

"Of course not, Pug. I'm not saying…,"

"Have I ever asked for a few extra days to get it together?"

"That's not my point. I simply…."

"The point, Norm," Pug said, "is that you read in the morning paper where a business partner lost sixty-one thousand bucks in a poker game and that made you nervous. Well, it would make me nervous too, Norm. And you can be certain if I ever read that about you, I'll be on the horn before I put down the paper. I understand that and I don't resent you calling to discuss my personal finances. You have the right to know these things. So, I'm going to be frank, Norm. I did lose, nothing like what was reported, but enough to hurt. I may end up making a few personal adjustments as a result, but you can rest assured Norm—and you can pass this along to Rendleman when you talk with him— if and when the partnership calls on me I'll be there. I still believe in the project and I remain behind it one hundred percent."

He heard a long sigh at the other end.

"That's what I wanted to hear, Pug."

"Good," Pug Bolcar said, and hung up.

After fifteen minutes in the library, he called Becky

into his office and dictated a formal demand that the *Courier* issue a retraction. It was after five and the office quiet when he returned the one remaining call.

"Hello, Ruth," he said, when his ex-wife answered.

Her delivery allowed no pause, her voice brooked no hesitation. He imagined a school of words lunging against the backs of her incisors all day. Soon as she opened her mouth they rushed for him, eager as piranhas.

"Well, it's the great poker player! Years ago I thought I was beyond being dismayed by you. I thought I had seen everything, that nothing you could ever do would hurt or embarrass me again. But now you take our daughter to Lake Tahoe for the weekend and you end up losing sixty-one thousand dollars and getting it announced to half the world. And you were the one who told me time and time again that I didn't know how to handle money! Ha! Well, you have hurt and embarrassed me again and that must make you feel better, but that's all right because I'm accustomed to it, and my real friends know all about you anyway. But you've also embarrassed Tyler and severely hurt his chances for election to the senate—being connected to you is like being tied to an anchor, as I realized after years of being dragged down by you—but Tyler's a gentleman and after all the slander he's been put through and all the embarrassment and pain you've caused him— taking his case for your own glory, pandering to the press and now this—dear Ty will go on and make the best of it." Ruth paused to gasp in more air. "So I can live with that too, Pug, but you've also mortified Binks, and for that I'll never forgive you. She was in tears this morning, tears! Did you think her friends are illiterate? The poor girl is struggling to make a new life after that dismal marriage and now you've made a fool of yourself, and indirectly her, in front of the whole community. I will never forgive you for that, Pug, and what is more neither will Binks. It has taken her a long time to see you for what you are but the poor child is beginning to understand. You're losing her, Pug. All the love she feels for you is flowing away, just as my love did. A person can stand to be hurt, embarrassed, made a fool of only so much, Pug. Love is a tender thing and under abuse it withers and dies. You abused me for years and now you're abusing her too. Well, you've made your bed and you can lie in it, but I want you to understand one thing and I want it understood very clearly: what you do with your money is your business, and what you do with your daughter's affection is your business—though God knows I'm the one who has to comfort her as best I can—and you can wreck your life any way you choose, but I'm telling you this, Lawrence Bolcar, I am entitled to twenty-two hundred dollars a month from you every month until the day I die or remarry, and I'm going to get every penny coming to me. I called Cleary today and he told me no judge in the country would let you off the hook after this. So, go blow whatever money you want, but don't come looking to me for comfort and don't be a day late sending me what's rightfully mine or Cleary'll have you in court so fast your head'll spin. And that goes for Dot Hilliard as well. She called me this morning distraught. Distraught! 'Does this mean I'll be left without my money?' Terrified. The poor woman is terrified! First she loses Ed and then that cancer scare and now she has to depend on the likes of you for her livelihood. And you throwing away thousands in a card game! Well, I told her very carefully: 'Dot, don't give him any rope. Insist on those payments every month to the penny and on the date due.' And I told her if she had any problem with you to go see Cleary. Cleary's as big a bastard as you are and the smartest thing I ever did was hire him to fix your ass."

Pug Bolcar released a long, slow breath. Then, in a quiet voice he asked, "So, how are things with you, Ruth?"

The answer was a dial tone.

— 14 —

When Ruth Bolcar got off the phone after railing at her former husband she looked defeated and badly in need of more alcohol.

"My God," she said, walking to the bar, "I have come to loathe that man. He's become a millstone around my neck. I swear he has. I loathe him and I can't get him out of my life, I just can't. I divorce him and he's still there. If I killed him, he'd still be there, a millstone." She poured herself more gin and waived the bottle in Elisa's direction. "And that's the only reason I don't, believe me. He would still be there. Another small one?"

"No, Mother, I don't.. ."

"Oh come on, Binks. At least share a drink with me. I know I shouldn't but after the day I've had. The day we've both had. Have a drink with your mother."

Elisa went to the bar and offered her empty glass. "I wish you could forget him. Move on with your life."

"That's easy for you to say. You weren't married to him for thirty-four years. You aren't depending on him for food to eat and a roof over your head."

"Okay, but maybe you can learn to not concern yourself about him so much. Daddy has always done whatever he wants and your suffering has never changed that."

"God, isn't that the truth! Not a millimeter. All my shoving and pulling. All the pain I've gone through. Say when, dear."

"Stop!" Elisa jerked her hand away causing a splash of gin to land on the carpet. Neither of them noticed. Not Ruth, who was refreshing her own drink, not Elisa, who stared with horror at her half-filled tumbler. Back home, she thought, she regularly went a week or two without a drop of alcohol, and now this. She stepped toward the bar seeking tonic and ice. Maybe if she diluted it and sipped slowly.

"He just hangs there around my neck," Ruth went on in a despairing voice.

But as Elisa poured the tonic water she was reflecting on her own thoughts, not her mother's words. 'Back home?' she had thought. What did she mean by 'home?' What an empty-calorie, junk word that was. The apartment in Oregonia was not her home. She had no home. She was a twenty-six year-old married woman trained to design costumes for theatre productions and she had no home, no husband and no job.

"I tell myself, get occupied. Get into things. I started volunteering at the de Young. Did I tell you that?"

Elisa became aware again of her mother's voice and she did a brave and generous thing. She forced herself from the wallow of her own misery, squared herself at the bar and directed her full attention back to Ruth.

"You did, Mom. You told me that on the phone. How did it go? I never found out."

"Museums are nice places to meet people. You know, the right kind of people."

"Of course. An excellent idea. Are you still doing it?"

"They give you name tags. ID cards you pin to your blouse or jacket. It's for the guards, and also the public, of course. So they think they're talking to a person."

"I understand," Elisa said. "So, what did you do?"

Ruth took a swallow of gin. "Bolcar is not that common a name. It's not Smith or Jones or something. Even Gilbert, Binks. That's a blessing for you. Everyone's not going to say, 'Oh, are you Rafe's wife?'"

"They did though." Elisa brought the glass to

her lips. "It's a small community up there. And Rafe being an actor with the company."

"How smart you were to leave. I am so proud of you. That's what I should have done years ago. Should do now. I should leave San Francisco and start over somewhere new. Am I too old for that, Binks? Am I just talking fanciful again?"

"No, I…"

"You have to be honest with me, Binks. I need someone to be honest with me." Ruth took a large swallow of gin and then placed the glass against her forehead. "Oh, Christ. That man has made my life so miserable. He took my name and sapped my strength and left me empty. Empty of everything but despair. That's the truth, Binks. That's the goddamned truth." Ruth Bolcar had begun to cry.

"Mom…" Elisa set down her glass and was about to put her arms around her mother when the phone rang. "I'll get it."

"No!" Ruth grabbed Elisa's arm and held her. "It might be Rafe," she said, starting for the phone. "I am going to protect you from that man if it's the last thing I do. You were so brave to leave him, so right. I will not allow him to pressure you into coming back. There will be no end to it, Binks. I swear to you. No end."

"Mom, I can…"

"Hello." Ruth wiped her eyes and thrust her jaw forward. "No, she's not here."

"Mother!"

"And even if she were she wouldn't talk with you.

She's made that very clear. You are not to call this number or bother her in any way."

"Mom…"

"Her father is a lawyer, you know. You have treated our daughter shamefully and she will have nothing more to do with you. Goodbye."

"Mother!"

Turning from the phone, Ruth Bolcar looked splendid. "What did I tell you, we just have to be firm and he will give up after a while. Just like any other whining puppy. One of those machines! That's what we'll do. I'll answer when I'm here and the machine can take the calls if you're home alone. Don't let him think there's a chance, Binks. That's the secret."

"Mother, I know you are only trying to help, but there are things I need to discuss with Rafe."

Ruth shook her head. "Make a list, Binks. The next time he calls I'll read it off to him. You are not going to talk to that man. You did the right thing, the courageous thing. And there is no reason for you to suffer more than necessary. Your mother will handle this. It's the one thing I can do for you." She swallowed what remained of her gin and straightened her shoulders. "First thing tomorrow we'll get one of those machines. Might be fun, don't you think? We'll put on funny messages. We'll be like a couple of college girls here." Ruth Bolcar looked positively happy.

Elisa had been in bed for an hour before she finally stopped crying and fell asleep. Then at three she woke again, her head thick from the tears and the gin. A street lamp in the alley lit the sand-tan drapes. She pulled them aside, opened the sliding glass door and stepped out onto the little balcony. Moisture dripped from trees, the air surrounding her was damp and cool. As she drew her hand along the metal railing a curl of water rose up and rolled off, slapping on the pavement below. In those frantic moments as she was packing to leave Oregonia, her mother's condominium had promised a safe refuge. Now she wanted to melt into the night air, be dispersed like vapor. It had all become too real. At center stage large and immobile stood Rafe's betrayal while she, a black-gowned mime working in a spot of light, might dance around it, might kneel down and hug it, might spread a blanket over it and have a lonely picnic. But none of these, nothing she might devise to do, would make it go away.

From below came a scratching noise, some small creature scrambling in the dark, and then the eucalyptus branch beside the balcony began to stir. "Go back," she whispered. A gray and white kitten looking impossibly ambitious came inching now along the branch making its way toward the balcony. On it came, ignoring her pleas to stop, and the branch sagged ever more heavily beneath its weight until, two feet away, unable to retreat and meowing incessantly, it paused. Such was the course her life had taken, Elisa thought: she could not so much as step out onto her balcony in the middle of the night without provoking a crisis in someone's life.

The meowing became desperate and Elisa stretched out her arms. Continuing to complain, the kitten leaped, though the effort resembled a fall more than a leap. The front paws cleared the railing, one extended claw raking across Elisa's inner wrist, but the back ones hung up momentarily scratching furiously against the glass panel, until twisting and tumbling the cat finally landed in an awkward muddle on the cement floor. Watching this graceless arrival Elisa remembered that time in rehearsal when Rafe had slipped on his way over the wall to the Capulet's garden. Prone on the boards, cast and crew standing hushed between laughter and concern, he had recited, "He jests at scars that never felt a wound."

Jesus, she had loved that man. And now her new Romeo rose too without complaint and began to rub against her ankles with a purr.

— 15 —

As the kitten was landing gray and white and devoid of grace on Elisa's balcony floor, Lydia Manx lay awake, unmoving, her husband snoring beside her. The snoring was irregular in cadence, a kind of stumbling march through the night, but not loud enough she had to nudge him. Lydia woke frequently in the night. Sometimes it was his snore that woke her. Whatever the cause, she was reluctant to disturb Harold in any way. His responsibilities were heavy enough. No need to compound them by interrupting his sleep.

Over the years a pattern had developed with regard to her husband's profession. When an arrest made the papers, he would point it out explaining how accurate or inaccurate the reporting had been. About the personalities of his staff he commented frequently. Lydia knew, for example, that David Gordon had taken to wearing strong-smelling cologne, that Harold's secretary, Nancy, was less patient during football season, that George Fernald's wife felt he worked too many hours and spent too little time with the children. That the man he called Chin was sly and ambitious, perhaps even devious. But on the subject of pending investigations, about the day-to-day problems he had to face and resolve, he said nothing.

On one occasion, many years before, a man had arrived at their home in the middle of the night bleeding from a gunshot wound in his leg. This man, Lydia speculated, might have been an undercover agent of some sort though Harold never explained who the man was or how he knew where they lived or why he had come to them rather than to an emergency room. At Harold's direction she had held a towel pressed tightly against the man's bare thigh while Harold used the telephone to arrange for medical assistance. That was as close as she ever came to the vivid immediacy of Harold's work and closer than she wished to be again. She saw his rigid code of confidentiality as a gift he gave her. His willingness to bear the burden alone saved her from endless worry. She accepted without question that his work was difficult, that it was dangerous and invaluable, and that he did it very well. Her role was supportive, which meant among other things not asking questions, not complaining about his hours, not worrying overtly about his sudden and unexplained absences, not disturbing his sleep.

Lydia did not find it unpleasant to lie awake in the night. The darkened room, the lack of traffic on the street, Harold's heavy presence (his weight on the mattress never failed to astonish her—they turned it regularly to keep the two of them in relative balance), yes even that heavy presence, maybe that more than anything, brought her comfort. Soon her thoughts would quiet, and if she relaxed her body and concentrated on the fleeting images her mind presented: a pattern on a fragment of cloth, a small black object screwed to a piece of red wood, a glimpsed view through a cabin doorway, a building seen from an impossible angle—images fleeting and unrecognized from her own experience—hold them dear, she had learned, and they carried her into dreams.

But on this night, the roaring thoughts were far too vibrant to be ignored. She even tried reciting a Bible verse, her lips moving silently in the dark, but the moment she began to relax the voice came back. Her daughter's voice. Janet speaking on the phone that afternoon. A voice Lydia had not heard in seven years.

"Mom?" How sad and afraid and shy that voice had sounded. Or was it just that her daughter, being older now, her voice would sound more mature? Nothing about where she was, or how she could be reached. No word about how or where she lived or who she was with. No mention of coming home or meeting or even calling again. She had called to say she was alive, to apologize for the many years she had left her mother in doubt. The two of them sniffling on the phone.

"Is this a good time to call?"

"Of course," Lydia had blubbered, "anytime."

"I mean, does he still work during the day?"

"Yes," Lydia had said, understanding now. "Yes, he still works. And yes, yes, during the day he is gone."

Then came the urgent demand: "You have to promise, Mom, that you won't tell him about this call."

She would have promised the world.

The tears flowing now terrified her. If he woke and sensed her crying, if he felt moisture on the pillow, what would she say? She was hopeless at lying. Absolutely incapable. Then she remembered the strangest thing. Those silly argyle socks she had bought him for Christmas. And how the other morning when he was leaving on that trip. She had been making the bed when he came out from the shower. He had taken the socks and had sat down in the old rocker that had belonged to Noony before she went into the nursing home and pulled them on.

"Are you going to be embarrassed?" she had asked.

"Of course not," he had answered. "It's what they'll all be wearing." Then he had raised his feet and wiggled his toes at her, as if they were puppets in a children's show.

Her Harold making a joke like that, like old times, so light and teasing. And that is what she would say. That she had thought of that and it had made her cry to see him happy for a moment. And it was true, she had thought of that. And the thought of him being happy did bring tears to her eyes.

"Hello."

"Well, have you?"

"Have I?"

"Talked to her! You have to talk to her."

"I can't talk to her. I've tried but I can't. Her mother won't let me."

"Her mother?"

"Yes, her mother. I call and I ask but she won't let me talk to her."

"Her mother? I cannot believe this. Her mother?"

"Her mother controls the phone. I hear her in the background but I can't talk to her."

"Oh, my God! I have been cast into a pit of vipers!"

Harold Manx always arranged to meet Vince Lackner at a place he knew Lackner would despise. Harold knew the city, knew its nooks and crannies. This time it was a bar frequented by house painters, mechanics and other heavy smokers. It was afternoon just before the rush and Vince sat alone at a table drinking bottled water. Manx ordered a beer and some chips.

He slipped into the chair across from Vince and set his bottle on the table.

"So?"

"I made the deal."

"All right."

"It's going to cost a little more than we discussed."

"That's your problem." Harold Manx used his teeth to tear open the package of chips. He poured the contents out on the table between them. He enjoyed being a little crude in front of Lackner.

"What do you mean, my problem? You're paying for the stuff. My job is to make the deal, carry it out. You refuse to understand the risk I'm taking here."

Harold fed himself several chips and took a long swallow of beer. He had loosened his tie before entering the bar. Now he motioned toward the chips with the back of his hand. Lackner shook his head.

"I know the market," Manx said. "If you offered too much, that's your problem."

"I had to pay that price to get the deal," Vince whined. "What difference does it make? You're getting two busts out of it."

"How much more?" Manx asked, his mouth full.

"Twenty-five percent more than you quoted." Lackner waited while Manx had a coughing spell. "Maybe the market's changing. He was firm on it. It was that price or nothing."

"Impossible." Harold cleared his throat. "Maybe I can get you five. Not a penny more. This is how many kilos again?"

"Ten, of course. What we said. I'm just a pilot. I

don't know the ins and outs about this stuff. Maybe your prices are based on a larger volume. All I'm trying to do is help."

"Come on, Vince, you wouldn't help your own mother cross a street unless there was something in it for you."

Vince looked hurt. He squeezed more lemon into his water. "Well, I can't pay an extra twenty-five percent and risk my life in the process. I'm getting a bad rap. I'm better off fighting it."

"That's your prerogative. Want to talk to the prosecutor?"

"Get me fifteen?"

"Five, like I said."

"This is unfair, Harold."

"Life's like that, Vince. I thought your mother would have told you."

Vince Lackner glanced around the bar. It was beginning to fill now. The volume up, the smoke thicker. "I got another problem."

Harold waited. As a boy back in Colorado he had been sent to the chicken coop one morning to fetch the eggs. He was what, eight, nine? Overnight a weasel had gotten in. Across the table from him now sat a weasel. If Vince Lackner had his way, the world would look like the inside of that chicken coop and Vince would be convinced he'd only gotten what he deserved.

"Carlos plays poker. He's crazy about it. I promised him a game, like I told you. That was part of the set up, a private poker game."

"How much did he lose?"

"He didn't. He won. Won big."

"So, how much did you lose?"

Lackner shook his head. "It's more complicated than that. Most of his winnings came from a lawyer, a guy named Bolcar. The problem is, I guaranteed Bolcar's checks for fifty-five grand and now Bolcar's refusing to honor them."

Harold Manx picked up a potato chip and carefully examined it before placing it in his mouth. "So?"

"So, if Bolcar doesn't pay, I'll have to. Otherwise, Carlos backs out of the deal."

Harold Manx was being very deliberate. He swallowed some beer and set the bottle carefully back on the table before nodding his bald head. "You're right, Vince. You got a problem."

"I'm a pilot and a businessman. I got a payroll to meet, payments on the fleet, fuel costs, on and on. I don't have that kind of money."

"I hope you're not asking the department to pay your gambling debts."

"Their not my debts! The debts belong to Bolcar."

"Don't even think about it."

"You want Carlos, don't you?" Lackner's whine threatened to rise above the ever-increasing din in the bar. "I can't handle this."

Harold Manx was three inches taller than Vince Lackner, twenty or more pounds heavier. He placed his elbows on the table and leaned forward.

"Let me tell you what I got. What I've got, Vince, is you." His thick blunt finger jabbed Lackner's left shoulder. Poked it hard, hard enough it felt for a second like the sting of a wasp. "Your life, as you understand it, is in my hands. And what you promised to do for me, Vince, is to deliver Carlos to the Colombian authorities and the balance of the shipment to the bad guy at this end. Do that, Vince, and I give you back your life. But what you need to do to accomplish the task, that's your problem."

He sat back, brushing off the elbows of his suit coat.

"There was an item in the paper," Vince said. "A gossip column thing. Told about Bolcar losing the money. He thinks Carlos leaked it. That's why he's not paying."

"What difference does that make? If the man owes the money..." Manx looked away for a moment. "Make the asshole pay," he continued, his voice angry. "If the guy owes the money make him pay. Don't come to me, asking the department to pay it."

"Could you at least find out who leaked it? If it wasn't Carlos, and I can prove that, then Bolcar'll have to pay."

"You're a real card, Vince. So now you want the department to act as your personal private eye? Initiate an investigation on your behalf? Get serious." He stood up and straightened his jacket. "This lawyer, if I were you, I'd lean on him. Tell him a little bit about Colombia's national pastime."

Lackner looked irritated. "What's that?"

"Think about it, Vince. By the way, when's the buy?"

"Three weeks."

"So, you've got some time," Harold Manx said, turning toward the door. "I'll be checking in."

— 16 —

Robin Durham and David Gordon were about to leave the office when Harold Manx returned from his meeting with Vince Lackner.

Manx said, "Durham, a moment, please." When Gordon had stepped away Manx explained where he had just come from. "I thought you might like to know. According to Lackner, the price is up twenty-five percent."

"We pay, right?"

"Of course." The Chief was grinning, eyebrows quivering.

"That was chummy," David said when Robin came up. "You join the Chief's church?"

"No," Robin said, starting down the stairs, "I got him tickets for a Grateful Dead concert."

"You wha…?"

They preferred ethnic and hated pretense, by which they meant high prices, small portions and waiters who talked about wine in terms that would make Bacchus blush. "Wild strawberry?" Gordon would mutter after the sommelier had left. "Hints of cherry with vanilla? How about a wine that tastes like grapes?"

No one cooked for either of them. Not Durham

since the divorce from Liese, not Gordon since he married Roseanne Harden, everyone's sweetheart on Channel 3 Golden Gate News. Watching her newscasts, Robin would have assumed she could put together a Thanksgiving dinner for twelve while minding three kids and playing a game of Scrabble. But according to Gordon she detested kitchens and rarely ate. A candy bar on the run or a restaurant three-star or better, that was her diet according to David. A Vietnamese maid came in three days a week and a caterer whenever they entertained. "Have the neighbors over for cheese and crackers and a bottle of grape after a movie and it's catered," he explained.

Robin understood when David Gordon went on like this that he did not intend to convey a precise truth. Gordon was a punch-line kind of guy. What mattered was the cleverness of the remark, not its factual accuracy. But to Robin, stark in his aloneness, Gordon's company and entertainment were gifts. That the Gordons' marriage seemed bizarre and inexplicable did not surprise him. To Robin lots of things seemed bizarre and inexplicable.

They went to a place off Fillmore that Gordon had heard was cheap and served something called blackened redfish. His stomach better, Robin ventured a beer and the gumbo. Gordon was younger than Durham but longer with the department by three years. He wanted to know about the Tahoe trip.

Robin explained that he met a woman.

"Whoa. Could it be we're nearing the end of the post-Liese blues? Who's the lucky girl?"

"I don't know."

"You mean you're not telling. A married woman, I take it. Do I know her or something?"

"No, I mean I don't know, as in I don't know. I don't know her last name or where she lives or what she does for a living."

Detective Gordon pondered that for a moment. "So, what do you know?"

"She hates smokers."

"Okay, you don't smoke. Anything else?"

"She'd just broken up with her husband. Like the day before."

"Well, that's encouraging. For you that is, not for the husband. Anything else?"

"Not really. I was in her room but she kicked me out. End of story."

David Gordon was a handsome man, long lashes, wavy hair, a strong jaw. When his eyes squinted, as they were now, you could assume calculations were in process.

"That sounds more like the beginning of a story," he said. "What happened?"

"I don't know what happened. It might have been me. It might have been her or her husband. His ghost or something. Middle of the night. She ordered me out and I left."

"You had a fight."

"Not really. I was asleep. She woke me up, told me to leave."

"Middle of the night."

"Right."

The squinting eyes again. "Okay. Take me there. Give me the picture. It's the middle of the night. You're standing in the hallway outside her room. You been kicked out in your skivvies."

"She let me dress, but yes, otherwise that's correct."

"At that moment, did you want to see her again?"

Durham sniffed the bowl of gumbo that had just been set in front of him, pink prawns floating in brown sauce amid the pale okra.

"Yes," he said to Gordon, "yes, I did."

David thought about that. "Okay. So, you knew the hotel she was staying in, right?"

"Right." He started with a spoonful of broth, hot, tasty.

"I mean you're standing in the fucking hallway of the hotel in question. And the room number is on the door, right?"

"That's true."

"And the door is right in front of you."

"Yep." Not just temperature hot, spicy hot. He took a swallow of beer. Better start with the bread. Dip some bread in. Get the digestive track acclimated.

"And you're telling me you didn't go straight to the front desk, flash your badge and get her name? Her home address, the fucking license plate number of her car?"

Robin Durham looked up from his bowl. "There had been no crime, David. That information would've required a warrant."

Gordon looked disgusted. He set down his knife and fork and grabbed his wine glass. "You are hapless.

You're state of ineptitude is unparalleled."

"Hmm."

"Who's gonna be at the desk at that hour? A teenage girl doing her nails. Some acne-rich young man who takes a toke on a joint out back every thirty minutes. They see a badge what they going to do? It's called a goddamn perk, Robin. A benefit of the profession. Tell me something. Say you're driving a car and a cop pulls you over. Lights flashing, maybe a burp from the siren. You pull over, right? Of course you pull over. Cop comes up to the window. You roll the window down. He says you were speeding, asks to see your driver's license. What do you give him?'

Robin was chewing bread soaked in gumbo. He stopped, mouth half full. "My license of course."

"Your badge, idiot. You show him your badge *and* your license. You don't have to lie. You don't have to say the reason you're going a hundred and ten in a fifty-five is you were chasing public enemy number one. Just show him your badge."

"But?"

"No but. Put yourself in the cop's shoes. Say he's off duty driving home from a bar and a black and white pulls him over. It can happen. Does happen. What's he do? He shows the officer his badge. You got a badge, another cop expects to see it. He may give you a ticket, he may not. Nothing wrong here. Nothing inappropriate. You're not offering a bribe. It's a courtesy. You show your badge, he decides."

"I'll remember that."

"Please do. Now, as to the illusive lady, all is not

lost. Give me the name of the hotel. Give me the room number, the night it happened and I'll come back bearing gifts. Full name, home address, make and model of car. The lady's driving record. Maybe the name of her employer, all for you. A new life."

"Your fish is getting cold," Robin said.

"Ineptitude," Gordon said, returning to his food. But then after a few bites, "So, tell me what happened up there with Manx?"

"The Chief wore argyles. Socks, I mean. Argyle socks. He seemed embarrassed about them."

"Splendid piece of information. Come on, whose tail were you sniffing? That is, beside the young lady's. The operation, what was it about?"

"Didn't you tell me once the Chief had a daughter? I blundered into saying something about that and he turned cold as ice."

"Before my time, but I think it was a daughter ran off with a band of goat farmers or something. Manx got heavy handed and had his knuckles rapped by the politicos. Chin told me about it."

"Word to the wise. Don't mention daughter to the Chief unless you're talking about your own. By the way, Chin might be on the Chief's shit list. He wanted me to critique his performance on the Waggoner bust. Pushed me on that. Seemed disappointed I couldn't come up with anything."

"No surprise, there. Fernald's senior but Chin's the up-and-comer. Manx sees him positioning himself as successor to the throne. Doesn't go over well with the Chief, since he knows he's immortal, not to mention irreplaceable. So tell me about it."

"Routine backup operation's the way he described it. A little listening in. A training mission. Me being the trainee."

"Listening in on who? Or is it whom?"

"'Whom,' my mother would tell you. But back to warrants and being hypothetical here. How they handled in the department? What's the protocol?"

"All applications go through the Chief. He reviews the request. If he approves he takes it to the judge. Assuming the judge issues the warrant you find the papers in your inbox."

"And his?"

"His?"

"The Chief's."

David Gordon smiled, and a mischievous smile it was. "I see. You're asking me, 'Did Harold Manx have a warrant for the little training session in Tahoe? The little...how did you describe it? The little 'listening in?'"

"No, David. I'm asking about office protocol. What I'm asking has nothing to do with Tahoe."

"And if he did," Gordon continued, "how would we know? And if he didn't, how would we know that?"

"No, David."

"Well, I'm going to answer your questions, my boy. The ones you are so carefully not asking. We wouldn't. We don't. So, tell me."

"How's your fish?"

"You're not going to tell me."

"You got a good mind, David. You'll go far."

Afterward he and Gordon took in a movie. Then he walked for forty-five minutes. When he reached his apartment above the tobacconist, Camew was on the landing waiting to be fed, his front paws curled beneath his chest.

The apartment was not much, a kitchen, a bath, a ten-by-twelve room for all the rest. It was temporary, he told himself. The light switch inside the door twisted rather than toggled and there was a tension in the turning that disturbed him. He woke from dreams of fire.

The sink was rounded and old and separate from the small counter. The stove small but clean, the refrigerator an ancient guzzler of electricity, and most troubling, always empty, or nearly so: cheese, a corner hard and yellowing, some bread moving toward mold, condiments, a quart of milk, a few carrots going soft on him. At home—that is, at his former home with Liese and the girls—the refrigerator was huge and always stuffed. Liese did all the shopping and threw nothing out. Little plastic containers jammed in around the bags of vegetables and fruit. Milk by the gallon, cheese by the block, margarine boxes stacked up. Sour cream, pork steaks, hamburger, bacon in precise rows beneath the plastic window, artichokes, grapes, apples, eggs, bottles of juice. Coming home late, he would happen upon lengths of salami, a slice of lemon meringue pie.

The empty quarters, the lack of stored food,

had less to do with finances than his hatred of shopping. Necessities he purchased on the run from small convenience stores, paying the higher price to avoid facing the interior of a large supermarket. His vehicle, a gray Rabbit with a single decal proclaiming membership in the Cousteau Society affixed by a previous owner, he had purchased when his bug threw a rod near Los Gatos. The Rabbit was the first vehicle the salesman at the dealership showed him, though he had felt obligated to drive two others before deciding. He never did it right. "Nobody buys the first car they look at," Liese complained. She was a CPA, she had a head for these things. Durham had been proud to get the guy down four hundred bucks. "But that was the trade in for the bug," Liese told him, "That was his starting price."

Robin turned on the radio and poured some food out for the cat. He had chosen the apartment because of its age and smell, the floorboards steeped in the aroma of pipe tobacco, the ancient tobacconist and the cat who came with it rent-free. It just needed some cheering up, he told himself. Some of the girls' drawings on the refrigerator, some food within.

— 17 —

A winter storm came in during the night and in the morning it was still raining. Gusts of it slammed against Pug Bolcar's Audi at eight o'clock as he emerged from the empty parking garage beneath the lonely condominiums. The radio announced flooding in San Rafael and they were worried about the slide again north of the tunnels. A string of brake lights flashed in front of him. He geared down as the radio informed him of delays northbound on 101 south of the city, something painfully obvious from his perspective. There had been an accident on the Nimitz southbound; the Richmond Bridge was one lane westbound because of stalls. Thousands of people sat in cars listening to descriptions of their own miseries and the idle flapping of windshield wipers.

Pug pulled out the morning's first cigar. He had two trials set for Monday, one in San Francisco, the other in Contra Costa. For the case in Contra Costa he had received an offer he thought his client would accept. The problem was the other one. As he considered the options, traffic sped up and he passed the airport and the exit to Pacific Rim Transport. Tomorrow the checks were to be presented. Nothing had changed his mind about Carlos. Thoughts of the trial only stirred his irritation. Normally he would have called the defense attorney by now and hashed out settlement options. But that was normal, and normal, he estimated, would not return for six months. In the meantime it was back to the old days: assume all cases are going to trial. He would make no settlement offers until the other side opened the door, and he would have to try a few cases, cases that should have settled, and try them well enough that he won. Which meant between now and Friday, unless Weinstein called, he would put in hours preparing for a trial that would almost certainly settle at the door and never happen.

Last night, Tripper had phoned. Lackner had called him and Tripper was feeling sorry for Vince. "I am paying," Pug explained. "And I'll still be paying three months from now." He asked if Harry Morgan had gotten anything from the columnist. Turned out it wasn't Pendar Harry Morgan knew, but the other one, the one with the Oakland paper. "Vince needs this guy for his business, Pug. And Vince says he doesn't have the money to cover the checks."

He had no reason to hurt Vince. But he was not paying out fifty-five grand for the privilege of being made a fool of. "Can't do it, Tripper. Not going to do it. This has cost me a world of hurt."

When he reached the office Vince Lackner was on the phone. According to Becky he'd been calling every five minutes since before eight.

"I spoke with Carlos, Pug. He didn't do it. He did not discuss the game with anyone. Not even his sons know the names of the other players. He denies everything."

"Of course he does," Pug growled. "Why should he admit it? I don't care if he leaked it on purpose or got to babbling in a bar. You saw how he drank. So he denies it. Everybody denies it but somebody did it. Somebody did do it, Vince, and that somebody is lying. I'd rather think it was him than you or Tripper."

"Carlos is very upset."

"Good, so am I. This has made my life miserable. If it causes him some grief, so much the better."

"He's coming tomorrow to present the checks. No way can I cover them."

"I was hoping you wouldn't."

There was a pause. Then Vince said, "I'm not sure you understand these people, Pug. There's a sense of honor, the principle of the thing."

"The principle of the thing?" Pug shouted into the phone. "Well, the first principle is 'Thou shalt not fink!' That's what he did. He finked. You can tell your friend, the fink, that he will never see a penny from me. That's it. It's over and done with. I have work to do."

Elisa, out job hunting, stopped by the office. Pug found her chatting with Becky and invited her to lunch. He was happy to see her. He wanted to talk to her about the thing in the paper and to reach her by phone, he would have had to go through Ruth.

At the club he ordered wine for each of them. "I've given up gin," he explained, "for lunch, that is. Those were the days. Ed thought martinis were mandatory for lunch."

Elisa was seeing someone at the opera at two. She wasn't sure she should have wine on her breath.

"Binks, this is San Francisco."

She was fragrant, dressed to the nines, and he was proud to be lunching with her. But he was aware of her watching him with a new caution. Even his daughter saw him differently now. The cost of this disaster continued to mount. And she had grown up. They grow up and move away. They get married, they separate, they evolve into new selves. She had become someone he could speak candidly with, the subject of her mother aside.

"I learned something during all this," he told her. "Something you apparently know about. Your mother too, I suppose." This was not easy. She waited, watching him. "I felt betrayed when I saw that piece in the paper. Profoundly betrayed."

She let settle what she took as an apology to her mother and herself.

"Do you know who did it?"

"Can't prove it yet, but I think so. There were only four people in the game and Tripper was one of them. That leaves the other two. I'm coming out all right and the burden's on the right donkeys. But that doesn't alter the way I felt."

The wine came, a half carafe of chardonnay, and Pug filled their glasses. It was true that she was watching him closely, this familiar mystery that was her father. This man alone in the world, charting his own course.

"Salute," he said when he'd set down the carafe and lifted his glass.

Their glasses sang as they touched, good crystal at the club, and after she had sipped the wine Elisa asked, "Do you exercise, Dad?"

"What?" He looked startled for a moment.

"Well, you've given up martinis for lunch, I was just wondering."

"You think I'm getting fat? Is that it?"

"No, it's just that a lot of people are into it these days."

"Let me tell you. Those guys go to the gym every day? Walk the treadmills, lift the weights. Ninety percent of them I could put flat on their backs in thirty seconds. Your uncle Rollie, my older brother, he fought Golden Gloves, did you know that? Rollie was a contender for the city championship. I used to hang out with him and his gang down at the gym. I learned the ropes inside the ropes, understand? The trainer down there, Rollie's trainer, the guy ran the place, they called him Doc Smoltz. This guy had a schnoz you wouldn't believe. You seen the famous drawing from the war: Kilroy Was Here? Doc Smoltz, had that kind of nose. Anyway, he wanted me to get into it. He thought I had the instincts, the toughness. And he was right. I do."

He did have good instincts, Elisa thought. She had been thinking he had gained weight.

"They say it can extend your days, though," she suggested, ordering the squash soup and the salad with the roasted pecans. "Regular exercise, that is."

"Interminably probably." Pug chose the steak sandwich with a side of onion rings. "What's the point?" he added when the waiter had left. "To be a hundred and ten? To be alone, broke, bored silly and too damn healthy to die?"

Elisa found herself laughing. "Rafe has a theory, Dad. This exercise craze is the doctrine of original sin returned. The body in its natural state is seen as evil, see, slothful. For salvation you must do penance. You know, no pain no gain. Or as he puts it, 'You have to grunt and groan and make yourself smell bad.' Of course he says all that and then he runs four days a week."

"Hmmm," Pug Bolcar said. "I don't know him well, Binks, this husband of yours. The holidays, that time we came up to see the plays. You've been better about coming around than Michael, of course. Michael ran east and never came back. But we understood all that, your mother and me. We wanted nothing to do with our parents either, starting out. But Rafe always struck me as all right, a regular sort of guy."

"He has good qualities," Elisa responded pensively. "It's just that he can't resist sharing them."

Her father did not respond to that. He was looking down, spreading the white cloth napkin across his lap. The light striking the top of his head at that moment made Elisa look more closely at his hair. Something about the color was not right. My God, she realized, her father had tinted his hair. A garish golden sheen rose out of the darker graying brown. Yes, she was sure of it. The contrast astonished her, not the colors so much as the realization that her father would do such a thing.

He looked up, eyes alert questioning her. Those instincts again.

"I may end up going back to him," Elisa said to cover her embarrassment.

"Ah."

"You think I should?"

Pug Bolcar's hand paused half way to his glass of wine. He thought for a moment, then came the mischievous grin. "Daughter, you're asking a member of the pack."

Late in the afternoon Vince called again. It was essential, he said, that they talk.

"So, talk," Pug said, his voice booming.

"Not over the phone. Will you be coming past on your way home?"

"Not until much later. I have a trial to prepare for."

"I can wait."

Pug looked at the booklets stacked in front of him. An assistant had marked and tabbed the important parts in all the depositions, but he never felt he could trust their decisions. He needed to read each word, draft each question, anticipate every objection. That was the way he won.

"Midnight," he said finally.

"I'll be here."

It was twelve-thirty when he pulled into a parking slot at Pacific Rim Transport. But for Lackner's red Alfa, the lot was empty. The rain had stopped momentarily but the wind, still arriving in warm sweeps from the ocean, brought assurance of more. He tried the door and finding it unlocked, stepped inside. From the rear of the office he heard a strange screaming noise. He made his way through the darkened reception area to the lighted doorway. Lackner sat on a floor cushion facing a large sheet of paper covered with Asian characters; he was playing a bamboo flute.

Pug listened for a moment then shouted, "Let me know when you've killed it."

Vince finished the passage. He set the flute deliberately across his legs and turned.

"You're late."

"You're lucky I'm here at all. Got any gin?"

Vince motioned toward a cabinet. "There's ice in the refrigerator through the door," he said, swabbing out the flute. When Pug returned he pointed to a second black cushion. "After hours I prefer these to a desk and chairs."

Bolcar ignored the invitation, swirling the ice. "Out with it, Vince. I've had a long day."

"All right. I have too, most of it on the phone with contacts in Colombia. I've known Carlos for a while. He's a respected rancher. The land has been in his family for generations. But I needed to know more before I told him of your decision. Colombia is not the most important country to my company, but it's not insignificant either. It's on the flight line, you see, for points further south. I get a run to Santiago, say, and whatever I can drop off in Bogota, is gravy. Same way coming back."

"So," Pug said, sipping gin.

"So, if I'm going to leave Carlos hanging out because of you, I need to know what that means for the rest of my business. What his influence is. I need hanger space from time to time. I may need to rent a warehouse. People have other choices, they don't have to ship with me. I hold my customers because I'm a reasonable guy to work with. I get the job done on time and for a reasonable price. I pay my bills. Unlike some people I never go back on my word." He paused, looking at Pug. "I've been in and out of Colombia for six years. I'm building a future there."

"You're getting to the point, I hope."

"You son of a bitch. I should let you find this out in your own time."

"I think you want to tell me, Vince."

"You're right, I do. What I've learned is disturbing and I don't want to be disturbed alone. If I'm not going to sleep, neither are you."

"Try me, Vince."

"Do you follow Colombian politics?"

"I don't follow San Francisco politics. Conden was closer than I wanted to get."

"San Francisco is a nursery school compared to Colombia. Here they buy influence. In Colombia they drive by with AK-47s. We're talking a few hundred bodies just to clarify the issues. They got political parties, they got cartels, they got guerilla movements, they got armed militias. It's not just politics, it's a way of life. It's been going on for over a hundred years and it's not stopping anytime soon."

"If you don't come out with it pretty soon, Vince, it'll cost you more gin."

Vince Lackner picked up the flute and turned it slowly in his hands. "What I'm saying, Pug, is this decision could cost you your life. Mine too, maybe, but I don't think so. I'll work something out with

Carlos over time. It will cost me dearly, but I'll work it out. I didn't throw him kisses across the table. I didn't insult that old man he talked about, the one lives on his ranch. I didn't write fifty-five grand worth of checks and then refuse to cough it up." He stood then and walked to his desk where he slipped the flute into a leather pouch.

"That's your speech?" Pug said.

"That's the gist of it. I know it's late."

"The bastard betrayed me!" His voice was a hiss.

Vince Lackner shrugged. "If that's the way you see it."

— 18 —

On Channel 3 News Roseanne Harden's weather guy was calling it the Pineapple Express, the warm Pacific storm coming at them all the way from Hawaii. But moving east the front turned to snow above the Sierras depositing ten inches of fresh powder on the runs where Carlos and his two sons were enjoying their holiday. By daybreak it was breaking up over San Francisco but in the mountains the radio reported that roads leaving Lake Tahoe would be closed at least until mid-afternoon. Carlos and his sons breakfasted at the lodge, taking seats near a window where they could watch the snow blowing across the side of the mountain.

Later Carlos called Vince Lackner and explained the situation. He would not get there until the following day, probably in the afternoon. Lackner said the delay would not be a problem. Carlos and the boys should drive to his office before going to the bank. They could turn their rental in at the airport and then use one of his cars for the bank run.

"That is very kind with you, Bincent."

"I try to be kind, Carlos," Vince said. He put the phone down and rubbed his temples. That guy has to be kept happy. He wasn't going to make the same blunder Bolcar had made, underestimating the Colombian. Which is why he hadn't mentioned the problem on the phone. Hearing it for the first time, face to face, Carlos would have to react in front of him. If he had been responsible for the leak, even accidently....

Vince closed his eyes and did a slow neck roll, first clockwise and then in the other direction. This mess had no redeeming features. He was supposed to have been on his way to Singapore for a data processing fair with a half dozen executives and a new line of products. It was costing him business as well as sleep.

He was still massaging his neck when Harold Manx called, demanding a meeting, naming the time and place before abruptly hanging up. Vince went to the stationary bike and began to peddle furiously. Maybe if he could draw the tension down into his legs his head would stop throbbing.

Ruth Bolcar was in the bathroom that afternoon when the phone rang. Nature's call momentarily diverting her diligence allowed Elisa to answer. The fatherly voice was familiar.

"Elisa, this is Neal Bointon. I found your message here and thought I'd check in with you."

"Hello, Neal."

"Tiff is here with me, Rafe too. We're all thinking about you. How's your mother doing?"

This would be Tom MacElhenney's office. The one with the shield and crossed swords on one wall, the map of Elizabethan England and Wales framed in pale myrtle wood on another, the Bard himself in the form of a granite bust near the west-facing windows. Tiff and Rafe probably side by side on the leather couch, separated the one from the other by a respectable distance, concerned expressions on their lying faces.

"May I speak with Rafe, Neal?"

"Well, yes, of course." She heard shuffling.

"You son of a bitch," she said when Rafe came on.

"El...hi... Sure glad it was you. I...I told Neal your mother might..."

"You son of a bitch."

"Yeah...well, just, you know, trying to keep the door open here. We're all hoping you're able to hurry back. We miss you, we need you. All of us."

"You son of a bitch," Elisa Gilbert said a third time, hanging up.

"Good for you! Good for you!" Ruth Bolcar stood in the doorway shaking her clenched, tendon-streaked fists, a crone of a warrior. "That son of a bitch!"

Sobbing, Elisa ran to her room, closed and locked

the door. She was a child again, cowering in the face of her mother's emotions and her own.

"Binks?"

"Leave me alone, Mom."

"Binks, what's the matter? You were magnificent. That's just what he needed to hear."

Elisa abandoned her room and took refuge on the balcony, a box of tissues pressed against her chest. It was brisk out there, cooler air following the storm, wind in the trees. She looked over the railing to the narrow sidewalk below. How could she get down if she really had to? Hang from the base of the railing and drop? And then where would she go?

From the trunk of the eucalyptus she heard the cat's claws seeking purchase. Yesterday afternoon on her way back to the condo she had bought a can of food in case it came back. To get to it she would have to face her mother but that might not be a bad thing. She wasn't going to have a life here until she did. And something occurred to her at that moment, something that she had not realized before: other than her mother, there were no women in her life now. The women friends in Oregonia, those with the company, those in the Zen group and elsewhere in the community, all were far away. Their absence counted as yet another price she had paid by leaving.

And however tense the relationship between them, however imprisoned she felt on the tiny deck as she watched the intrepid kitten make its noisy journey up the tree, she and her mother really did share something beyond the obvious: each had been betrayed by a man.

The fast food restaurant where Harold Manx told Vince Lackner to meet him was hosting a birthday party that evening for a five-year old and his nine enthusiastic friends. While the jukebox roared, the guests ran around the tables wearing paper hats and screaming the names of fictitious characters popular on Saturday morning TV. As usual Manx was late. Vince sat alone at an empty table as far from the celebration as possible. He studied the menu posted behind the counter but could not find a single item he would allow past his lips.

Harold Manx had become his personal devil. Vince could taste the glee with which the man tormented him. It was in the air, palpable. His attorney, though, had encouraged him to play along. That or be prepared to find other work. They can confiscate assets now, the lawyer explained: planes, office equipment, bank accounts, even before the trial. There was no fairness to it. The big guys were untouchable and men like Manx needed something to show for their time and salaries.

All day he had waited for a phone call from Pug Bolcar. The Colombian history lesson delivered the night before had put Bolcar on edge, that had been apparent to Vince. But he had not called. Apparently he was willing to risk the consequences rather than honor the checks. An intensely private man himself, Vince felt a grudging admiration for

Bolcar's stubborn resistance, an honest sympathy for the man's predicament.

Among the oversized coats and sneakers, the stocking caps, the skateboards tucked under arms, the chunky Hispanic girls, Vince saw now the bald head of Harold Manx as he waited in line to order. The tallest man in the room, and the only one wearing a suit. Vince had been watching the doors but had not seen him enter. Like a bad dream Harold Manx appeared out of nowhere.

"Fries?" Manx offered, setting the box in the center of the table. Beneath the strong lights, his head glistened. Vince declined, smelling the grease. "You should eat, Vince. Keep your strength up." The scraggly eyebrows twitched merrily.

Vince ignored this. Manx's mockery infuriated him. "If you want Carlos, you're going to have to help me."

"Your man hasn't paid up."

"No."

"You couldn't persuade him?"

"He didn't budge."

Manx lifted a long fry and held it between them. "My old man broke horses. Back in Colorado, eastern Colorado where I grew up. A very large man, my father, a ranch hand, a cruel man in many ways. Men, animals, a cruel man. But he knew horses, the old man did. He could pick them, he could train them, he could get the best out of them. I'm thinking this, Vince, because it occurs to me sitting here that you have a way of betting on the wrong horse. How many times have you flown into the country clean?"

"Every time but once."

"Right." Manx chewed the fry. "Now this poker game. Fifty grand was it?"

"Fifty-five."

A look of feigned awe and the accompanying sound coming from Harold Manx's mouth sounded like that of a chicken clucking. "A lot of money, Vince. I'm surprised you backed it."

"I had to guarantee his checks to keep the deal."

"So, you did it for me? Vince, you're breaking my heart."

"I had to back Carlos to keep the deal and if I was backing Carlos I had to back Bolcar. I was trapped. Besides, I've known Bolcar for several years. I thought I could trust him. And I could have if it hadn't been for that damn newspaper…"

"My, my." Harold Manx stuffed three fries into his mouth and chewed them thoughtfully. The slowly pulsing cheeks reminded Vince of a sleeping rodent, its belly rising and falling. "I'm even more surprised you haven't figured that one out."

"Carlos has to have his money. Bolcar won't pay it. I can't pay it. You figure it out."

"Not that. The leak to the paper."

Vince Lackner had kept his windbreaker zipped up to his throat as if to protect himself from the salt and grease and empty calories flying around the room, but now he unzipped.

"The leak? You know something?"

"I have a theory."

A pain shot through Vince's right temple. A theory. Well, anyone can have a theory. "So, what's your theory?"

"So, you tell me." A sense of malicious mockery hovered about Harold Manx like an aura, his head lowered, his eyes peering intently through the brows. The man must have been a classic schoolyard bully, Vince thought. Still was.

"McLain told his wife and she spread it to the wrong person. They travel in those circles."

"Possible. What does this McLain fellow say?"

"Absolutely denies it. I talked to him."

"So do you," Manx said.

"So does everybody. It's not something Carlos would do, though I hope to hell he did."

Manx chuckled. "You're desperate, Vince."

"He had reason to. Bolcar treated him like shit."

"What does a Colombian cattle rancher know or care about gossip in San Francisco? The idea is preposterous."

"You're right. Has to be McLain."

"Vince, you astonish me. You keep ignoring the one person who stands to profit from all of this."

A parade of screaming children ran past the table just then, their balloons bouncing off the other customers. There arose in Vince Lackner's throat something akin to vomit.

"That's impossible. He was furious. I've never seen him so upset."

Harold Manx shrugged. "He comes out the winner. Besides, I've been looking into the fellow. His business is wringing grief out of juries. Histrionics is his stock in trade. And then there's this." He pulled an envelope from a coat pocket and handed it to Lackner. As Vince was fingering through Bolcar's divorce papers, Manx added, "As you will see, the poor man is being bled."

Vince Lackner looked through the documents, though later he would not be able to remember a thing about them. It was so obvious when you thought about it.

"The bastard," he said.

The man across from him nodded. "Seems we have a file on the fellow. Old stuff we knew but couldn't prove. There are men in the department would like to get him. So, you're in luck, Vince. You got a problem, we got a problem. The question is what can we do to make it all better." Harold Manx sat back. He waved an arm expansively, looking around the room. "Cute bunch of kids, don't you think?"

— 19 —

It was after eleven and Pug Bolcar pulled off 101 and down Palos Verdes Avenue to the condominiums named Angelica Estates, Angelica being the name of Norm Freuhoff's eldest daughter. Lights on here and there among the apartments gave the semblance of life but in reality only two of the seventeen units were occupied. He had one and Terry and Carol Fruera the other. The Frueras managed the place. They hustled the curious, guarded against vandalism, turned a few lights on each night in an empty room or two.

He pushed the button on his sun visor and descended the ramp to the garage. The door went up and lights went on. People want a lot of lighting in their parking areas, they had been told. Thirty years of television crime shows. Even the best-lit garages are filled now with eerie echoes and ominous shadows. Two parking spaces allotted to each unit. Wire storage cages against the wall. No mud on the floor, no rubber streaks, no smears of grease, the white lines freshly painted, and the whole place empty but for the Frueras' Camry and a Boston Pop's rendition of the "Dance of the Flowers" from the Nutcracker Suite. It would go off in five minutes along with the lights. January. Fruera needed to change the tape.

He rode the elevator to the second floor, walked down the empty corridor through a green door marked POOL and into the presence of humidity, chlorine and the soft hum of motors. After passing through another door he poured himself some gin, undressed and showered. With the tumbler of gin in his fist he lowered himself into the spa and sat staring at his square yellowish feet with their twisted lumpy toes and gnarled protrusions. In Tahoe Ramona had described his feet as sexy. He had laughed then, and even now the thought made him smile. His foundation, she had said, the base from which he rose to confront the world. People had told him, though he was never conscious of it himself, that when he argued to a jury he rocked or swayed in the air, his feet planted in one spot. He was, they said, like some thick building swaying in an earthquake, a motion both mesmerizing and graceful. Regardless of how you justified them, though, the feet remained ugly as sin. And the gin did not taste right so he set it aside.

The few times in his life when he had been unable to drink he had been either sick or afraid. He knew which this was, the knot in his gut had not gone away all day. This thing had felt wrong from the beginning and nothing since had made it better. A call had come in that afternoon from an editor at the *Courier*. No retraction. They were sticking by the story, which meant they had some support for it, though the editor refused to say what. Bolcar knew the way to find out. He called a colleague and asked him to prepare a complaint for libel. Ray Huddleston tried to talk him out of it. "In this town everything's forgotten in twenty-four hours, Pug. You're just going to bring it up again." But Pug had to know. So he lied to a man he respected, acted wronged and aggrieved. If Huddleston knew how frivolous the suit was, he might not be willing to represent him. So he was proceeding with the suit and holding firm with Lackner, but everywhere the ice felt thin.

When he reached his apartment the phone was ringing.

"How'd you get this number?" he asked Vince Lackner.

Vince claimed he had a friend with the phone company. "I met with Carlos this evening. He did not leak the information. Something has to be worked out."

"Send him over. I want to hear that from him face to face."

"It's too late. He flew back tonight."

"Good."

"Not really. He's got people here."

Pug paused. "Not a penny, Vince. Not until I find out who did it."

"How you going to do that?"

"I'm working on it."

"There's no time. Carlos wants his money. He's entitled to it, but barring that he's made a proposal. I think it's a very generous proposal but he's not playing around. This is it. You take it or face the consequences. And he wants your answer in twenty-four hours."

"I'm always willing to listen."

Vince said he would be jogging in Golden Gate Park in the morning. He wanted Pug to meet him in front of the Tea Garden at eight.

"Impossible. I'm in a settlement conference in Redwood City at eight-thirty. Tell me the goddamn proposal and I'll give you my reaction."

Lackner refused to reveal details over the phone. Maybe seven at the Tea Garden, he suggested. It was just another negotiation now. Familiar turf. "I'm going the other way, Vince. I'm tied up all day. Your man's in a hurry, what's the problem with the phone?"

"I'll run in the evening. Say six-thirty at the Tea Garden?"

"I'm working late."

"Come on, Pug. Would seven be better?"

"I won't sit around."

"You won't have to," Lackner said.

The bastard did do it, Pug Bolcar thought when he hung up the phone. No other reason to offer a deal.

Tiff Bointon took her exercise on a bicycle. Most mornings Neal went with her. They would start at the house, follow the trail up through the park and then along the paved road that led past the water plant. It wasn't ideal. The first part being uphill meant the return was down. Nobody liked it that way but if you live in a valley it's that or you stay in the bottom where you get no climbing, where the traffic is angry and exhaust fouls the air.

Rafe was a runner. He followed the same course, though he did not go so far up. He knew a dirt foot trail that began near the water plant and then followed the heights south along the west side of town. The trail surface was irregular, broken by stones and roots but he could run twenty more minutes that way before he had to descend. It was not that he loved Tiff Bointon. He wasn't even sure he liked her all that much. But the attraction their bodies had for one another had been undeniable. He and Tiff were like two herdsmen, it seemed to him. They brought their animals into proximity and the rest was automatic.

Sometimes they met in the mornings. If Tiff

was alone and passed him in the park she would wait near the water plant, pedaling in circles till he appeared. They had never made love on these occasions. The course was too popular but even if privacy had been assured, Tiff's idea of an affair did not include rolling around in leaf mold. So they talked absently while their bodies hummed, invigorated by the exercise and each other. The hum was what they were after. They had surprisingly little to talk about.

Then came the disaster in the underground followed a few days later by that terrible half- hour when Tiff and Neal ran into Rafe in Tomasino's. Neal remembered the note he had seen in Tom's office, the one requesting that Tom call Elisa as soon as he got back. Concerned, he started asking Rafe questions and then decided they should all go to Tom's office and give her a call, only to be perplexed by Elisa's abrupt and unfriendly response and Rafe's tattered and rather theatrical explanations. Neal thought he had done something wrong and was troubled by it all evening. Did Tiff know if they were having marital troubles? Tiff chalked it up to immaturity. A couple of kids, she said to Neal. Remember the mood swings?

The next morning at the water plant, immaturity was still on her mind. But watching Rafe's bulging thighs as he steamed up the grade she had to look away. He wanted to continue running so she rode alongside him. "Part of this is very simple," she said. "Get your story straight."

"My story?"

"Of course. 'We' have no story. Except with Elisa, 'we' don't exist. The problem is your story. Why did she leave so suddenly? Why was she so unfriendly with poor Neal last night? And with you? It was painfully obvious to everyone, my boy, that you were talking into a dead phone at the end there."

"Her mother took sick," Rafe said. They had passed his turn off and the road steepened here. His breath was heavy, his voice rough.

"So, why the hostility?" Tiff asked rhetorically. "No, that line was flawed from the beginning because it requires her cooperation, and given the circumstances she's not feeling cooperative. And that thing you said to Neal about pre-menstrual syndrome. Really, Rafe!"

"I was desperate."

"Obviously." She rode ahead a few feet, circled and then came up beside him again. "There's nothing wrong with a lovers' quarrel, you know. You had a fight and she ran off to San Francisco. You can say you told the first story to justify her actions."

"I did. Really, I did." He glanced at Tiff. "So, what did we fight about?" She wore a pink sweatband and her hair was being tousled by the breeze. Her jersey hung low on her shoulders revealing the base of her neck and the upper part of her back.

"That's nobody's business. They're not going to ask you that."

"Okay." The steep slope was making him pant. "Unless she tells."

"Oh, my God! I know, I know. That bitch has the power to destroy all of us! A fucking costume designer. It's infuriating!"

"It's not her fault."

"All of us, baby. You, me, poor Neal. Neal's heart will break. Oh, that poor man. Even her! It will destroy her! Yes, that's what you have to tell her. That it will destroy even her! And it will, goddammit, if I have anything to say about it."

"You don't understand," Rafe began, and it took him several seconds to complete this little speech because his breath was rasping. "She has this thing… about fairness…about justice…about truth. She might tell. She might just out with it."

They were quiet awhile and then Tiff laughed thinly. "Well, in that case I guess we'll do what thespians have always done. We'll drop the curtain and run for the nearest exit."

Rafe Gilbert did not laugh. He circled in the road and started back down the hill. It occurred to him for the first time just how different their circumstances were. Her marriage was untouched, his leveled. Tiff made a broad slanting sweep on the bicycle, glided close and then away again. He was the first man she had ever known whose sweat turned her on.

"I know this," Rafe said now, "I want you at this minute more than ever."

"Oh, my God," Tiff responded. "Did you have to bring that up?"

***

Four days had passed since Lydia Manx picked up the phone and heard her daughter's voice at the other end. Not a word in seven years, then that call, and not another for four long days. For Lydia the enduring silence seemed to stretch like an expanding rubber band that grew ever more tense. Was it something she had said, or failed to say? Had she been too enthusiastic? Too distant? That she could not talk to Harold about it compounded her apprehension. In more than thirty years of marriage there were few things she had been unable to discuss with her husband. Most, if not all of them, thinking back on it, had to do with Janet. Her teenage years had roiled with turmoil, from failure to do chores and homework, to B's and C's that should have been A's, to curfew violations, skirmishes over clothing, dating, eating habits, a patch of anorexia, even shoplifting. Finally, their child, their precious only child, ran away. Then captured and freed again by the court she ran a second time, like some wild animal desperate to be away from them. Through it all Lydia had stood between Harold and Janet, a feeble mediator, fumbling apologist, a nervous confidant, a porous barrier, an inadequate protector.

It wasn't simply that Lydia wanted to tell Harold about the call. She felt she should. Though he refused to mention Janet's name, claiming she was dead so far as he was concerned, she knew better. Harold worried the same as she did. Was Janet safe? Had she made a new life, or was she wandering some city street homeless, mentally disturbed perhaps, or addicted to one of the terrible drugs Harold worked so hard to keep off the streets. Then that thing happened in Florida, the serial killer that started talking, and they began digging up bodies of young women all over the United States. Almost every night new footage appeared on the news, the two of them watching, silent, sharing but not expressing the same dread.

When the article appeared in the paper about their former neighbor Lawrence Bolcar losing all that money in a poker game Harold read it to her at the breakfast table. He was gloating. According to Harold that man was getting only a fraction of what he deserved.

Lydia made the mistake of doubting the article's authenticity. A man that smart, she suggested, that educated, wouldn't squander a fortune in a poker game. When she said that, Harold's anger flared fresh and raw, as if it had never left. The man cheated on his wife, he told her. He milked insurance companies, shaved his taxes, freed the guilty by whatever device he could find. He had built a career filing spurious lawsuits just to get what he wanted. All of that Harold said, and more, but Lydia understood that what really angered her husband about Lawrence Bolcar was the court order that had freed their daughter to run away again.

And she knew Janet was alive and poor Harold did not. The predicament terrorized Lydia. She could not tell him but she was incapable of telling a lie. Should Harold suddenly ask if she had heard from

Janet, or reaffirm that she was obviously dead, her features would betray her. They would, she knew it. Or what if she talked in her sleep? Harold was a light sleeper. Or just the fact that Janet was so alive in her mind, wouldn't her thoughts somehow impinge on his awareness even if she never uttered a word? But Lydia felt she had failed her daughter many times in the past and could not, must not, fail her again. It was in this state of dread that Lydia shared time with her husband and answered calls from magazine salesmen, charity drives and wrong numbers. Then, around two that afternoon the phone rang.

"Hello."

There followed a long silence before a soft voice said, "I was so afraid he was going to answer."

"It's all right, my dear. He's not here."

"I've picked up the phone a dozen times these last days…. I don't want to hear his voice. I know I could just hang up, but…"

"No, he…"

"And I have to wait until Noah is sleeping."

"Noah?" Lydia blurted out without thinking. She pictured the large dangerous man snoring in the next room, the cult leader, the one who dominated her every move.

"Oh, Mom," her daughter gushed, "I have a little boy!"

— 20 —

That same sunny afternoon, Ruth Bolcar was working the phone on behalf of her brother, Tyler Conden.

He was making his announcement at the Regency on Thursday and had asked her to invite a few people. Ruth had given a lot of hours to Tyler's two supervisorial campaigns and she was comfortable calling friends and old family acquaintances. There were a lot of them. The Conden family had established itself in San Francisco before the 1906 quake and it was well known that much of Pug Bolcar's early success had come from clients he had picked up through Ruth's connections.

She was feeling rather well this afternoon. The night before, she and Elisa had enjoyed a long talk, like old times, and Ruth felt they understood each other better now. She would no longer try to prevent Elisa from speaking to Rafe, if that was what Elisa wanted to do. And Elisa assured her mother that while she did not know what would ultimately happen, she would not go running back to Rafe because of a phone call.

As Ruth chatted away she was pleased to learn just how many people were aware of Elisa's work in Oregon. The New Oregon Repertory Theatre was popular with Bay Area residents. Its season was reviewed in local papers and many of Ruth's acquaintances traveled to Oregon for a weekend of plays. They remembered Elisa and Rafe from their huge wedding and continued to follow their careers.

Harriet Landau, who had supported Tyler through thick and thin and who would be a major contributor to the upcoming campaign, told Ruth that she always chose the plays that Elisa had costumed or

Rafe appeared in.

"Oh, my dear," she said when Ruth explained that Elisa was no longer with the company. "And Rafe? He made the most gorgeous Romeo I have ever seen."

"Born to the name, if not the part," Ruth said, dryly, going on to explain the circumstances of the breakup. "But Binks is home now, and soon you may not have to travel so far to see her work. The opera is interested. Also a company in Berkeley."

A few minutes later Harriet asked about the object of Rafe's desire. Had it been a woman in the company? It was, Ruth acknowledged, though Binks had not named the woman, only that she had found them under "delicate circumstances."

"In the act?" Harriet exclaimed, and Ruth would swear later to Dot Hilliard that she heard Harriet smack her lips.

"Presumably."

"You poor dear," Harriet replied, her voice confidential. "And after what you've been through."

This from Harriet Landau, who many years before as Harriet Nicoletti at a harvest party given by the Hilliards at their place outside Napa, had been seen emerging from between rows of vines, her white shorts stained with grape and with Pug Bolcar looking sheepish, following only moments behind.

In Golden Gate Park, Pug Bolcar paced up and down in front of the Tea Garden. If Carlos had returned to Colombia, maybe Lackner had paid him, maybe not. It made no difference. If the threats had been serious, he would be having kneecap surgery by now. Something had happened and it was time to make a deal. He lit a cigar. He was always ready to talk deals.

"Let's walk, Pug," Lackner said when he arrived, running down from the museum. "I need to cool down." He wore a black scarf beneath the maroon jacket of his running clothes, and black leather driving gloves, his sharp white knuckles exposed. Vince Lackner, it occurred to Pug, dressed as though an *Esquire* photographer might at any minute jump out from the bushes. As they walked he took deep breaths and rhythmically waived his arms.

"Carlos is very upset."

"Is that right?"

"He thinks you did it."

They continued on a few paces before Pug asked, "You going to tell me what he thinks I did, Vince? Or is this Twenty Questions?"

"You informed the paper."

Pug Bolcar stopped. "About the game?"

"Precisely." A smug expression.

"That's preposterous! You have any idea what I been through these last few days?"

Vince Lackner spread his legs and began to stretch his ham strings. "Carlos sees you saving, or I should say, trying to save fifty-five thousand. That's worth some inconvenience."

"That son of a bitch. Did you tell him?"

"What can I tell him? I don't know who did it."

Lackner was stretched low near the ground and Pug resisted the temptation to lower him the rest of the way with a punch across the back of his skinny neck.

"Well, you know damn well I didn't do it. I'm suing the damn newspaper to get proof. That's how much I did it."

Vince Lackner straightened slowly. He arched his back and then did a couple of neck rolls.

"Anybody can sue anybody, Pug. You know that even better than I do."

It was enough to make Pug Bolcar walk away a few steps.

"You can forget any deal. I'm not dealing with that S.O.B."

Lackner shrugged his shoulders. A woman approached, three children strung before her in bright coats. They stopped talking until she had passed.

"He's been looking you up, Pug. Or having it done. He knows about your family, your son, your daughter. The apartment buildings. Angelica, wasn't it? He showed me a copy of your divorce papers. He's on your case."

It was dark and a wind had come up. Pug felt cold. All of that he could have gotten from the divorce papers, public documents. Still.

"My car's just down the street," Vince Lackner said. "This wind's not good for my warm muscles." When they reached the car, he added, "I have to ask that you leave the cigar behind. Outside I can't complain. A private poker game in a motel room, that I tolerated. But not in my car."

Bolcar stubbed out the cigar and settled into the

passenger seat. The interior smelled of the cologne Lackner always wore.

"I should be in Malaysia by now," Lackner complained when he got in. "This thing is costing me. I had to call up a competitor and offer him a very lucrative contract."

"If you're expecting tears, Vince, you're going to be disappointed."

Vince Lackner drank slowly from a bottle of water. "I offered to pay him part of the money. What I could. The rest he could take in transport. Carlos refused. Wouldn't accept a dime from me. He wants it from you. It was you who lost the money."

Pug felt crowded in Lackner's small car. "Vince, I'm a busy man. I've had a long day and I've got another tomorrow. You mentioned a deal. I'm always willing to listen, but let's get on with it."

"All right. Carlos says you own a corporation and…."

"A what?"

"A corporation."

"He's crazy. I don't own a corporation. That's ridiculous."

"Rosyland Timber, something like that."

"Oh shit, where'd he get that? That wasn't in…." Pug felt his chest tighten suddenly, a cramping sensation. There, and in the center of his back as well.

"The man is on your case, I told you. Anyway, according to him, this corporation owns some land north of here, timber land."

"So?" He was trying to roll down the window but

there wasn't a handle and the button wouldn't work. Lackner watched him but made no move to activate the electrical system. "So, what's he want?"

"He wants you to grow marijuana on the property. He'll take the crop as payment."

"That's preposterous. Christ! Open the damn window. I'm suffocating in here." Lackner turned the key in the ignition and Bolcar lowered the window. "The man's crazy. I could lose my license having anything to do with that. If that's his deal, you can forget it."

"He's not going to forget it, Pug."

"I don't give a shit. I'll call the goddamn cops. I'll hire a body guard. I'm not going to let this bastard intimidate me."

"He'll kill you," Vince Lackner said quietly. "You or a member of your family. And when it happens he'll be miles away engaged in some other quite legitimate business. Now sit there a minute and listen to me. I knew you'd have a problem with this so I've been thinking. I know a guy who's done some of this in Hawaii. He grew a field of the stuff and got away with it. What if I could get him to take the job? He grows enough to pay off Carlos and keeps the rest for his share. You have to put up the land and the financing but then you have nothing more to do with it. Carlos takes his share, my guy gets the rest and everyone walks away a winner."

"And if he gets busted?"

"Carlos says that's your problem. We try again next year."

Bolcar snorted. "Except it's my land and my financing. I get investigated, perhaps indicted. I've gained nothing and my license is out the door. The idea's absurd. What are we talking, startup costs?"

"I'll talk to the guy. Five grand maybe, I don't know."

"At five grand, I might consider it. If all I have to do is give the money. Nothing more. But it has to be a one shot deal. Your man gets busted, everybody's even."

"I don't see him going for that, Pug. You owe him fifty-five thousand dollars. That obligation is not going away until it's paid."

Bolcar opened the door. "That's all he's going to get. My land, my five grand, your guy, one time only. If he accepts those terms we got a deal. If not, I call the F.B.I." He climbed out of the car cussing under his breath, the damn thing was slung so low getting in or out was like doing calisthenics. He closed the door and leaned in the window. "Next year, Vince, let me pick the fourth player, all right?"

— 21 —

"Listen, El. I'm sorry about the other day. That was an impossible situation for me. Neal sitting there, Tiff. It was impossible."

The whole thing seemed impossible to her. Sitting on this bed in her mother's condo in San Francisco. This familiar voice coming from the throat of a stranger. This voice she wanted to cuddle beside, where she could sleep again the sleep of the innocent.

"Yes," she muttered into the phone, meaning that she understood what Dot Hilliard had said about mourning. That even "innocent" victims lose their innocence.

But the single word from her caused Rafe's voice to brighten. "So, you do understand that it wasn't my idea to call? Of course you understand. You've always understood me. We understand each other. That's what we have together." There followed a silence they both clung to, the breath of each just audible to the other. Then Rafe spoke again, "Oh, God, El, I am so sorry, and I miss you so much. This is making me miserable. Come back. Please do come back. I want to sit across from you. Just to talk if nothing else. I want to look into your face and talk to you."

"Oh, miserable are you? And just whose fucking fault is that?"

Elisa hung up the phone and threw herself against the pillow. And when Rafe called back, which he did three times in the next five minutes, the phone ring until the machine took it. The new machine and Ruth's laughing, somewhat drunken voice announcing that the caller had reached the "abode" of Ruth and Elisa and they would be delighted to receive the caller's message.

With one hand Pug Bolcar held a phone to his ear, in the other he held a pencil. As Rayford Huddleston talked he drew a stark cityscape, thick with vertical lines, angles jutting sharply, lots of heavy shading.

The paperwork was finished but Huddleston didn't feel good about it. "You'd be smart to drop the whole thing."

Pug pushed the paper away. "That's not your decision, Ray. That's my decision. Yours is to handle it or not handle it."

"You know I'll handle it. I'm your colleague. But I want you to know what I think."

"You told me. I appreciate it, I do. But I have to go through with it. I'll run somebody over to pick it up. I want to file it this afternoon."

Pug explained that his firm would see to serving the papers and that he had already prepared a press release.

"I'll probably be hearing from Clenton and Leonard," Huddleston said. "They're house counsel for the paper."

"Fine. You can tell them I'm serious about this. And I do appreciate it, Ray."

They had dinner at a small Italian place on Columbus Avenue which was jammed between a pawn shop and a night club featuring male dancers. When she learned that Paulo, the owner, was his client and that Pug had helped him modify his lease so he could make structural changes to the building, Ramona began quizzing him about real estate as an investment. What were the problems, how much of a down payment would be required? He explained about insurance, building codes, maintenance, dishonest and underfunded tenants. Soon she moved on to realtors. Could you trust them? Was it cheaper to go around them? She had taken some business classes at SFSU but that was all theory, she said. He was the real thing. He knew the real stuff, the nitty gritty. Her questions came in rapid order through the chard-filled ravioli and on to the pudding with apricot sauce and finally an espresso. Pug enjoyed his role as a reservoir of practical information. When he teased her about it, she said:

"I've been far down, dear Pug, and I don't intend to ever go back."

On route to the Regency Hotel she asked, "So, where we going? You're being very secretive."

Pug chuckled. "To the world of politics, young lady, where the sun never shines."

Ramona had read about Tyler Conden's scrape with the law. She wanted to know more.

"My former brother-in-law and former client? Just what you might expect: tall, blue in the shirt, red in the tie, an attractive wife, the proper number of children, vague positions on all the right issues. He's already squandered most of the family's fortune. Conden's idea of work is being briefed by subordinates over lunch."

"Why did you represent him if you find him so disgusting?"

Pug looked at her mock surprise. "What makes you think I find him disgusting?"

The lobby of the hotel was crowded. He placed a hand on her elbow and led her to the bank of elevators.

"Was it for the money?" Ramona persisted.

"I hope not," Pug said. "He still owes half my fee. No, the DA thought he had Conden, the papers thought the DA had him and Conden thought he had been had. Who could resist?"

"He must be very grateful."

"Are you kidding? Conden hates me as much as Ruth does. No, that's not true. Hating may be Conden's best emotion, but he's wimpy even at that. Ruth is far the better hater in that family, though it is true that my getting him off made him hate me even more."

In the elevator and again in the ballroom Pug was busy shaking hands and acknowledging acquaintances, Ramona at his side. During spare moments, he provided her with capsule descriptions of the people they had met or were about to: "Low life in the mayor's office." "If that one starts talking about sailing, run with the first tide." "Sleeps with the world and doesn't care who knows it." "Sleeps with the world and cares very much who knows it." "Very rich." "Very dishonest, and in this crowd that's saying something." "A closet gay, and in San Francisco, if you can believe it." "One of the few people who has jumped off the Golden Gate Bridge and survived, to the regret of all who know him." "A decent man interested in little more than chess." "Follows his wife and carries the money, her money." "Lives for racquetball, a game I understand is even less enjoyable than tennis." Then, "You know Elisa, I believe," followed by, "And this, this is Ruth, my former wife."

They made their way to a clearing near some windows where they stood sipping champagne. Pug held his glass against his belt. His lower lip jutted forward as he whispered. "They're ogling you, my dear. It gives me pleasure."

"Is that why we're here?"

"Not at all but it is a fine thing to observe." A waiter approached. Pug emptied his glass and took another. "Drink," he instructed her. "Let's spend as much of the bastard's money as we can."

A few moments later Tyler Conden entered the room. Shaking hands and followed by his smiling family he made his way toward the podium.

"Time to get to work." Pug took her arm and led her on a course that caused them to intersect with Conden a few feet from the podium.

"Oh, Pug. So glad you could make it."

"Tyler, this is Ms. Livingston."

"A pleasure, Ms. Livingston." She felt a smooth hand slide into hers and out again. No time for a squeeze.

Conden started to turn away but Pug placed a hand on his shoulder.

"I haven't received a check yet, Ty."

Conden's eyes squinted with anger, but then he smiled. "Really? Must be some mistake, Pug. I'll check with my accountant."

Again he turned away, and again Pug placed a hand on his shoulder. This time with more force. "In the meantime you can do me a favor."

"Anything, Pug." Decidedly unfriendly.

"Before you make your announcement I want you to introduce me. I have few words to say."

Conden looked flustered. "This is an important announcement…I…"

"Your choice is simple, Ty. You introduce me and I make a short statement that has nothing to do with you, or I walk up there right now and make a statement that might prove less kind."

One of Conden's aides stepped forward. "What's your statement about?"

"You'll hear it when I give it," Pug said leaning toward the podium.

"Okay, you bastard," Conden said, "but this will not get the check to you any faster. And from what I read you can use it."

"Nothing will get me the check any faster. Just introduce me." He handed Ramona a sheaf of papers. "See the large woman in the front row, the one wearing the blue suit? When I get to the microphone, ask her if she is Patricia Gale Pendar. When she says yes, hand her these."

Tyler Conden gave a warm introduction to his former brother-in-law and trusted counselor. Then Pug stepped to the microphone. She walks like a model, he thought, as he and many others watched Ramona cross the open space between the podium and the first row of chairs. That's what she had testified to at her deposition. That she worked as a model and her injury had cost her work and why the scar on her leg threatened her career. Then this evening at Paulo's place she had finally brought him some evidence, a few receipts from a modeling agency. Not a lot, a thousand, maybe fifteen hundred bucks, he had put them in his briefcase after a glance. But what she wanted, she had told him, her eyes bright with determination, what she really wanted was to be an employer of money. To earn money and then set that money to working for her. That comment and the one preceding it, the one about having been a long way down and not intending to ever go back, had fomented the barrage of questions about real estate. Could she figure ten percent? she had asked. If she had a million, say, could she count on a hundred grand before taxes? It had made him smile in spite of himself, that youth, that enthusiasm. But he was impressed now, watching her cross the room. She had come a long way from the rail-thin nineteen-year-old he first met in a hospital room almost four years ago and then didn't see again for three or more.

Pendar had a surprised smile when Ramona leaned forward and spoke to her. She nodded and Ramona handed her the papers.

"This afternoon," Pug Bolcar announced, "the law firm of Huddleston and Munro filed a civil action on my behalf against Patricia Gale Pendar and the *San Francisco Courier*. The complaint alleges that on January 3rd the defendants, through a column allegedly written by Ms. Pendar, stated that I had lost over sixty thousand dollars in a poker game at Lake Tahoe. This article, the complaint alleges, was false, and that at the time it was published, the defendants knew it was false. The complaint seeks damages in the aggregate of five million dollars. Ms. Livingston will be distributing a press release which provides more detail." He removed the papers from his briefcase and handed them to her. For a moment he and Patricia Pendar stared at one another, and then to her credit, Ms. Pendar placed the unexamined papers in her purse and began a conversation with the person sitting beside her.

Members of the press began shouting questions, but Pug waved them to silence. "Ladies and gentlemen, your answers are all in the press release. I have taken enough of the Supervisor's time. If you wish to speak with me I can be reached through my office."

He jumped lightly from the stage and taking Ramona's arm, led her toward the exit.

"When you came back to the room that night, I thought sure you had lost," Ramona said, as they descended in the elevator.

"It's complicated, my dear. It's complicated."

— 22 —

Robin Durham and David Gordon were playing eight ball in a bar not far from their office. Just after five and Durham's gut was bothering him again. He had seen Liese and the girls over the weekend and was beginning to recognize a pattern. His stomach troubles following along faithfully behind visits to the girls and the ex.

Of the two players, Robin was the better. He occasionally ran the table, Gordon was lucky to string three. Early on Gordon bet him but now they played for drinks. Beer for Gordon, apple juice for Durham.

"The old man called me in today," Robin said as David studied the table. "He gave me a book. Wanted to know if I'd done any acting."

"You?"

"Did some," Robin said. "In high school. You know 'The Crucible?' Arthur Miller?"

"Can't say I do."

"I was the guy Danforth. Anyway, the Chief says, 'Read this like you're learning a part.'"

"The book."

"Right. A how-to book for marijuana growers. I didn't know you could get such a thing."

Gordon lined up a complicated bank shot. He had given up beating Durham. Now he went for the glory.

"You thinking about a career change?'

"I don't know, haven't read it yet."

Gordon made the shot but then scratched. Or would have had he not caught the ball at the pocket and tried to nudge it back onto the table.

"I think we're ready for dinner," Robin said.

Outside they found a stunning mid-winter evening. Temperature hovered in the low sixties, the breeze gentle. They decided to ride the ferry to Sausalito and were soon standing among the commuters on the deck looking back on the receding city, its pastel colors still glowing from the recently-set sun.

Gordon pointed out a young woman at the back rail. She could not have been more than twenty, slim, wearing a sky-blue sweater over a white turtleneck and slacks. Reaching toward the sky, a potato chip held in the tips of her fingers, the woman's body seemed to elongate through her arm, her spine, her legs. Robin noticed the delicate bones of her extended wrist, her feet arching free of her sandals, her bottom taut in the evening air. A gull, flicking its wings with careless ease dropped down. It picked off the chip and then veered away, its wings spreading out to catch a rush of air and falling back until it dropped to the water, a white speck on the dark blue bay.

"I think I'm in love," Gordon said, still watching.

"Julie, my youngest, has that kind of grace. That's be her in twenty years."

"The Liese blues have returned. You should have let me check out that Tahoe dame."

"She was clear about what she wanted," Robin said. He turned toward the coming shore which lay in shadow now against the Marin hills. He wanted to feel the wind in his face.

"I did something for the old man last week," Gordon said as they were finishing hamburgers and fries. "On the way back from Del Norte where I hand delivered Fulton."

"Was Manx responsible for Fulton?"

"Don't think so, Fernald's boys. But Manx learned I was going up there. He had me stop on the way back and run a title search on a piece of property. Ever done that?"

"Tried to find some liens for a guy once. He had

this idea his wife was piling up debts against their property. She wasn't, at least not so far as I could tell."

"Then you know about the big books."

"Recorder's office?"

"Right. Huge books. Every document comes in gets listed in these indexes. You can follow the history of a piece of land from the present back to the time it got stolen from the Indians, I suppose. Anyway, Manx had the name of a company. He wanted to know what land was owned by that company. If I found any I was supposed to get a map and a description."

"Of the property?"

"Right. And all I got's the name, right? So I begin at the present and I start going back. I go back to 1953 before I find any mention of this company, Rosyland Timber. I find they picked up a piece in 1953, two in '52 and another in '51. I go back ten more years and find nothing. This is the index listing the names of everyone receiving property, right? Then I go to a second index, those getting rid of property."

"Okay." Durham wiped his fingers, then decided to finish the remaining fries.

"And I start back in 1951 and go from there forward. By 1956 all but one of the properties has been sold off. I continue on all the way up to the day I was there, and one parcel is still in the company's name. That's the Chief, all right. He said there'd be at least one and he was right. So, a helpful chap makes me a copy of the deed and sends me along to the assessor's office where another public servant prints me a copy of a map. Happy Chief, happy me."

"Do you eat popcorn?"

"Sometimes with my wife. She likes it with Parmesan cheese. At least she did the last time I saw her. Why, you want some popcorn?"

"No, I was thinking about my girls. They got this idea all we ever did as a family was eat popcorn. Every time they see me they want to have popcorn. It's a fixation."

Gordon was looking at him strangely, waiting for a connection. "So, you had popcorn with your kids?"

"Right," Durham said. "You know what popcorn husks are?"

"Well, yeah…"

"Knives," Durham said. "Little knives in the gut."

It was almost ten by the time they got back to the city and Robin had reclaimed his car and found a parking place a block from his apartment. In a convenience store, garish with neon glare, he bought a box of Graham crackers and a bottle of antacid. Back on the sidewalk he saw someone crouched in the shadows near a cyclone fence at the edge of a small park. The neighborhood was home to a small flock of street people—a couple of them regularly slept in the foyer at the foot of his apartment stairs. But this was a woman wearing a plaid skirt, a suede coat, a large leather bag hanging from her shoulder. The cat she was talking to was Camew, his cat. One of its ears was bleeding.

"What's the problem?"

"He's been in a fight, obviously," the woman said, not looking up. "Come on, Romeo, let mama take a look."

"Romeo? His name's Camew."

"Not at my house." The woman reached for the cat but Robin stepped in and picked it up. The ear was gashed all right and he had scratches on his nose as well. "Oh, you poor fellow," the woman said, touching his ear, "you been in a tussle, haven't you?"

"Elisa?" He was astonished.

"Do I…?" She looked up.

"Right?" His face, he realized, was in deep shadow. "It's Robin Durham. I met you at Lake Tahoe." Moving now so she could see him better.

"The avalanche guy." Elisa turned her attention back to the cat.

So that's what she remembers, he thought, the avalanche guy. He stroked Camew's back. "I can take him home and clean him up," he said. "I'm just up the street."

"No," she said reaching for the cat. "I'll take care of him. He's sort of my cat, I guess."

"Actually, he's mine. I mean he comes with the place, sort of like the refrigerator. I feed him every day."

"That's not likely, as much as he eats at my place."

"I'm definitely not mistaken," Robin said. "I've known this cat for a couple of months. I pour food into him." He named the brand.

"I give him canned," Elisa said, in a voice that sounded to him smug. "I have a friend back home who has three of them. Cats, I mean. She told me this. Dry food is not good for cats, especially males."

"Well, mine's not dry really," he said defensively. "It's moist." My God, he thought, I'm sounding like a commercial. "Besides, he loves it."

"That's not the point. That kind of stuff contains ash and magnesium. In male cats that can cause urinary tract blockages. And those can be fatal."

Robin stepped back. "Look, would you just stop grabbing for him. I'm not hurting him. I'm trying to help him. You can talk all you want about your urinary whatever but at the moment his ear is the problem. If you want to help, grab this package. I live just down the block."

At the top of the stairs he put the cat in her arms so he could unlock the door. Inside she looked around.

"How does he get in and out?"

"Through the door," Robin said, heading for the bathroom. "Just like everyone else."

"At my place he climbs a tree up to the balcony. "It must be twenty feet above the alley."

"Wonderful," he said without enthusiasm. "Bring him in here." He turned the water on at the lavatory. "Stick his ear under here."

"Poor Romeo. It's not too hot?" She checked the water with her finger then lowered the cat's head until its ears were beneath the spray. The cat began to struggle and she pulled away.

"Just hold him," Robin said. "I'll wash it with my fingers."

She stepped back. "Wash your hands first."

He dutifully washed his hands, then cleaned the wound and squirted it and the other cuts with antiseptic. The cat kept reaching up with his paw, trying to brush him away.

"Do you think we should get it stitched?" she asked, sitting down on the stool, the cat still in her arms. There were splashes of water and blood on her suede coat. She held the cat out until its face was directly in front of hers. "Should we stitch you up, Romeo?"

Robin wiped his hands and sat down wearily on the side of the bath. "It won't heal right like this. We could tape it, I suppose. Where'd you put the package?"

"He'd pull the tape off in no time. You saw what he was doing." She motioned with the cat. "On the table."

Robin went into the other room, pulled the antacid out of the bag and took a couple of swallows. He put a flame under the water kettle and went back to the bathroom.

"Would you like some tea?"

She had set the cat down and was dabbing at her coat with a piece of wet toilet paper.

"Do you have some?" She sounded surprised.

"It's not swank, I realize." Then borrowing Liese's phrase he added, "I'm in transition."

"I'm sorry." Now she looked embarrassed. "Yes, that would be nice. Herbal if you got it."

The water boiled and he made the tea while she

searched the yellow pages for a late-night veterinarian. Robin poured the tea and then sat watching her until she looked up from the directory. It was the first time she had allowed her eyes to meet his since they recognized each other in the park.

"You live around here?"

"My mother does, up the hill." When he did not respond, she added. "I'm staying with her, for now."

"I see." She had just left her husband, he remembered. He noticed now she no longer wore a ring. He wanted to inquire further but held back, suddenly conscious of how often he had thought of her.

"I'm sorry for what happened that night," she said, as though reading his thoughts.

"Sorry?"

She blushed. "The way I sort of kicked you out."

"Middle of the dark night," he agreed. "Cold too."

"Poor boy," she said returning to the directory. "Anyway, I think I've found a place that's open." She took the phone and called the number. When the party answered she described the wound, in his opinion exaggerating it slightly for dramatic effect. "Rabies?" She looked at Robin, who shook his head. "So far as we know he hasn't had any shots. And I think he has worms." When she looked back at Robin, her face seemed so familiar to him. "Do you have a car?"

Durham glanced at his watch. It was after eleven. "Yes, I have a car."

"I'll pay."

"We'll split it," he said.

Descending the stairs they came upon a man in khaki slacks and a trench coat who was spreading his sleeping bag on the landing. The man smelled of alcohol and sweat. Seeing the cat, he paused.

"Hey, Rolfe," the man said to the cat. Then to Elisa, "That your cat, lady? He's always hungry."

At the clinic there was some confusion about what name to give the cat and which human to list as the owner. Together they held the animal on the table while the veterinarian stitched the wound and bandaged the ear. More antiseptic on the cuts, a series of shots. The bill came to $153.49.

"You mind if I keep him?" she asked when they were back in the car.

"If you promise to let him out again. I have an investment."

"Soon as he's better," she agreed.

He got directions and drove her home.

"I'd like to see you again," he said when she was getting out of the car.

She paused thinking about it, the cat in her arms, its bandaged right ear gleaming in the dim light.

"Well," she said turning now and smiling at him for the first time, "you do have an investment."

— 23 —

"Thing is, Pug, what if I get asked about it?" Tripper McLain was uncomfortable, uncomfortable enough to have broken two appointments to have lunch with his old friend. "I dislike depositions under the best of circumstances. Especially when I have to testify against you."

"You won't have to," Pug said.

"I was there. I'm a witness."

"They don't know that."

"How do you know what they know? They know about the game. They know you lost and how much. I think you should have dropped it, Pug, I really do. It was just an item in a gossip column. Every day Pendar has to fill a column. Who can remember a single thing she wrote last week? I can't. Nobody really reads the stuff. We skim through it, get a laugh or two and forget about it."

"I can't forget about it." Pug's head had been aching for two days and he couldn't shake it. He took a long swallow of wine.

"And the way you upstaged Tyler Conden. The Shiros were there. Must have been close to midnight when Lilly called Helen. She couldn't wait until morning to report the news. And the mysterious woman in red? Our lovely dinner companion, I suppose." Pug Bolcar nodded his aching head. "And Elisa was there. Ruth, too, of course. I'm beginning to think you need a vacation, Pug."

"I just got back from vacation. My vacation was the cause of all this. No, what I need is to find out who did it. Who did it and why."

"Has to have been Carlos, don't you think?"

"The bastard claims I did it."

"You?"

"To keep from paying the S.O.B." Pug emptied

his glass and poured a second.

"Sounds plausible," Tripper said, "the way you been acting lately."

"I want to shove the proof of it in his face, Lackner's too."

"Of course, if he did do it," McLain reasoned, "and now wants to hide it, he might blame you."

"Damn right. The runt is not your average coffee bean picker, I've learned that. According to Lackner he's got ties to the other Colombian export."

"No shit?" McLain seemed pleased by this additional intrigue. "You haven't paid him I suppose."

"Lackner says he'll off me."

"Jesus, if you don't?" Pug nodded and the two men were silent for a moment. Then Tripper said, "Well, you've got to then, don't you? I mean, what's it worth really?"

"We're talking, through Lackner. Remember that property I told you about? The timber land up in Humboldt?"

Tripper nodded. "Sorry, I haven't had a chance to look into it."

"He knows about it. Knows the name of the corporation I hold it under. He showed Lackner a copy of Ruth's and my divorce papers."

"Christ, where'd he get those?"

"The courthouse, presumably. They're public. But the thing is, Tripper, the Rosyland property wasn't part of the divorce. The papers don't mention it."

"Jesus."

"So where were we when we talked about it? You

remember?"

"By ourselves, I think." McLain thought for a moment. "He and Vince had left the table…"

"And we were by the bar…"

"Right, and then they came back…. We could have still been talking about it."

"It's possible," Pug said, "though I can't imagine we said anything in front of them. Another possibility is someone in my office or yours. I would hate to think that."

"I opened your letter myself. It's in the to-do box on my desk along with a dozen other things."

"Your secretary?"

"Jennie? She's been with me for years. You know that. She could have gone through those papers and found it. But why?"

He didn't know. It made no sense to him. Even a private investigator would have a time tracking that property down starting from scratch. He felt Tripper looking at him.

"You know, Pug, if there's any problem with the money…I can get it for you in a minute. You don't want to mess around with something like this."

He considered that for a moment before thanking his friend. "The money's not the problem. Hold off on the property for now, it's one of the things we're talking about."

Back at the office Becky handed him a phone message. Lackner needed to see him. "Six o'clock," the message said. "The usual place." What the hell did that mean, the usual place? If Lackner wanted to see him he could come to the office.

"I got any space on my calendar?"

"Four-thirty, the last half hour."

"Give him that. If he asks, I'm in conference."

Since that night of Tyler's announcement, Ruth Bolcar had felt herself beneath a shadow. Seeing Pug with that young woman had stunned her in a way she hadn't thought possible. Her first impulse had been to make a scene. She was tipsy at the time, though far from drunk, and the fact that Binks was with her and the moment being so important for Tyler, she had restrained herself. But then at the end, after Pug had made his statement and he and this woman were leaving, she found herself standing along with some other people beside their exit route. It was like— she would say this to herself later—it was like those columns of adoring cheerleaders that football teams run through on their way onto the field. Yes, like that, and she had stood there as if in frozen honor, she the defeated saluting her conqueror. During that brief moment, before she became badly drunk and had to be assisted by Elisa to the elevator and down to the car, she had realized something she would have thought impossible. All the fights, all her terrible rages had in some sense been crudely calculated to bring him home. Hurt him deeply enough, the reasoning seemed to be, and he might waken to the knowledge that he cared for her, that they were meant to end their days together. And seeing him with that young woman made her realize it was not to be. It was a realization made recognizable by its impossibility.

She was mostly drunk now. In the mornings, a time she used to stay straight—after an eye-opener, which didn't count, being but a readjustment from the night before—she now found herself drinking steadily. It was the only way to still what she called the itch. Not that it was really an itch in the physical sense, though the sensation was certainly physical. It began as an almost pleasant anticipation, not for the drink itself, but for something unnamed and unknown. But if she did not drink the anticipation quickly became an anxiety followed by raw pain.

So, she drank. And most days now she was not up for lunch with Dot Hilliard, though she promised every day that the next day she would be. She listened to talk radio and puttered about the house running a hand sweeper, straightening the kitchen—she always made her bed. So it was that at ten-thirty on this morning she took a message for Elisa that a man named Tom MacElhenney had called, writing it down carefully with her fine hand, and then at eleven-thirty as she went about straightening things, she threw the paper with the message into the wastebasket.

Elisa had just started working for a firm downtown that distributed educational films to schools and businesses. Not a career choice. Mostly she answered the phone and chatted with pleasant people in different parts of the country taking their orders. But it was all right. Everyone understood it was temporary, even her employer, an old friend of her Uncle Tyler's. She had feelers out. The opera company was interested. Apparently there was a committee, but she had been led to expect good things and she had sent portfolios to other regional theatre companies. Meanwhile she had two one-acts in Berkeley to play with, though there was no money to be earned there.

She had not spoken to her husband in a week, or to her father since the night of her uncle's announcement. Rafe had tried to call twice but both times Ruth had hung up upon hearing his voice. Any improvement on that score had disappeared with the new bout of drinking. Elisa heard what happened but had no enthusiasm for calling him back. And she had not talked to her father because his conduct had so angered her that she was afraid she might act toward him in the same ridiculous way her mother did. But this afternoon, after getting off work, she realized she had to talk with someone about her mother.

She arrived at her father's office just as Becky was leaving. Becky was in her final countdown, she said. Eleven more days and the Super Bowl would be history and the spell her husband was under would presumably break. Her father, she explained, had someone with him, but that was his last appointment for the day.

Sitting alone in the outer office Elisa realized just how tenuous her mother's position really was. Pug was under an order to give her money every month, but beyond that he had no legal or ethical duty toward his former wife. She considered Uncle

Tyler but he was in the middle of a campaign, and besides he had already helped her find the job. And Dot Hilliard was hysterical at the best of times. She had called her brother Michael that afternoon from work. He was as always a patient listener, but his empathy was for Elisa not their mother. A gentle family man, he taught early childhood education and directed a preschool lab for his university. It was not a coincidence that he lived almost three thousand miles from his parents. "Well, she needs to be dried out, Binks," Michael had said. "Put away somewhere. But how you're going to do that, I have no idea."

She could hear her father talking through the closed door, not the words themselves, just the rhythms of language, the rise and fall of emphasis. The other voice, she thought, might be that of a woman or a boy, but when the door opened she saw it was a man. A man in running clothes with short, carefully styled hair.

"Not here, Pug," the man said back into the room. "I'll let you know where."

She could see her father standing in shirtsleeves behind his desk fiddling with pink telephone slips.

"I'll want a receipt," Pug said. "And that ten comes off the obligation regardless."

"Making it forty-five."

"Making it forty-five. And if your man gets busted that balance is halved. The forty-five, not the fifty-five."

"He'll accept that," the man said.

"Good." Looking up Pug spotted his daughter.

"Well, it's Binks, the working girl."

The man in the running suit jerked around to face her. Lean, intense in the eyes, he looked astonished for a moment, paralyzed. Then he nodded, a brisk formal nod, crossed the waiting room and left.

"Handsome," Elisa said. "Gay?"

"Neither," her father responded. "Unadulterated narcissist."

Pug looked tired. To Michael she had described their dad as looking older. "Would you believe he's dying his hair?" She had to tell somebody about that. The revelation had been bustling around inside her head and had to get out somehow. It was the kind of thing she would have told Rafe and couldn't now.

That Michael wasn't surprised at this, she found astounding. "A grandstander," is the way he put it, adding, "Maybe you're finally starting to see through him."

Though her brother would never admit it, Elisa believed that Michael shared at least one quality with their father, a quality she described to herself as "nuance deficient." Both of them tended to view the world through a black and white lens. They labeled people and things and then moved on. A family joke, long repeated, happened on a trip to the Grand Canyon when she was eight and Michael twelve. Their father walked to the edge, took a quick look and announced, "Yeah, it's big." Then he turned and was ready to leave.

"Drink, Binks?"

"No, thank you."

"Well, I am." He was already standing at the liquor cabinet. "I've got things to celebrate. Freuhoff called today. Looks like we've sold a condo unit. Yuppie couple. Junk bond peddlers. They got so much money they're having trouble spending it." He chuckled, pouring gin over ice. "I suggested to Norm maybe they'll want to buy another for the mother-in-law. And Lackner, the guy that just left. I think I've worked something out with him as well."

Elisa sat down on the couch. It felt familiar. She had worked in the office a couple of summers as a teenager. Weeding out old files, mostly, organizing them in banker's boxes and hauling them to a warehouse to be stored. Sometimes Pug took her and Becky to lunch. He knew everyone and people were always stopping him in restaurants to talk. She came to enjoy the intermittent crises as trials approached, the celebrations when they won or settled well. For a while she considered going into law. He wanted her to, especially when it became clear that Michael was moving in another direction. Elisa remembered all of this as she watched her father doing his ritual with the drink. The stuff never seemed to hover over him the way it did her mother.

"Dad, I've got to talk to you about mom."

"Ah, your mother." He moved a chair to get closer. "She's been unhappy with me, hasn't she? That gambling thing in the paper, I understand was done to torment her. The action against the *Courier* was filed, no doubt, for the sole purpose of inflicting pain on Ruth." He sat down heavily, his knees nearly touching hers. "I hope I haven't ruined her taste for scaloppini. Dot Hilliard would never forgive me."

"She's drunk, Dad. All day, every day."

"I see," he said quietly.

"She doesn't want to eat. I'm very worried about her and I don't know what to do."

"Your mother is a bitter woman. A very angry bitter woman."

"Michael says she has to be detoxed."

"Michael does. Michael knows? What does Michael know?" Pug pushed himself out of the chair, grunting. He crossed the room as if passing before a jury and then turned to face her.

"Look, Binks. I know my role in this. I'm the villain, I know that. The turd in the sauce. You've gotten your mother's version over and over, I'm sure. Poor Ruth Conden, beaten down, abused, betrayed, humiliated, pummeled…whatever the descriptive phrase is these days. Future wrecked. Gave the best years of her life to that no good Lawrence Bolcar and now he's tossed her aside. No wonder the poor woman drinks. The man might as well have poured it straight down her throat. Well, read the literature, Binks. You think I haven't read it? You think I haven't carried her out of parties? Or cleaned her puke out of my cars and off my suit coats? You think I didn't prop her up for your wedding? Or Michael's graduation? Or a thousand other times and places? It's a sickness, I know that. A chemical dependency they're calling it now. But that doesn't change the facts. And the fact is, so long as she's blaming me for all her problems she's not going to recognize what she has to do. I'm not going to tell you I'm a hero, or even a decent husband, I wasn't. And I didn't do the noble thing; I didn't leave her because I wanted to force her to face reality, though if it helps in the end I'll be happy for her. I left because I wasn't doing any good and I was tired."

Pug's posture changed then. He softened, as if realizing it was his daughter, not a judge or jury he was talking to. He came back to his chair and sat down. Elisa noticed a heaviness in his breathing.

"When you get to be my age, Binks, you start seeing things in a different way. As you read the paper or watch TV or practice your profession you start to notice how many of the people shaping the world are younger than you. They didn't have the same experiences you had. My entire youth was spent before TV, for example. I remember something of the depression. I collected tin foil for the war effort. World War II I'm talking about. These new attorneys, many of the people I'm seeing on juries now, and increasingly the judges I stand before have not had those experiences. And to the extent we shared them, the fifties, say, the sixties, now the seventies, they were experienced differently by people your age than by me. And it gradually begins to dawn on you: the world is being handed down to new generations. And soon, too soon, no matter what you do you're going to grow old and die. I can eat nothing but tofu, raw carrots and brown rice. I can run twenty miles a day—like that

Vince Lackner you just saw probably does—and I'm still going to die.

"I'm growing older, Binks, and I'm going to die. Ed Hilliard left San Francisco that morning for a court date in Alameda Superior Court and he never got there. One of these days I won't get there either. I know that. And that's why I left your mother. Because I wasn't doing any good, and because I have relatively little time left to enjoy myself." He grinned then, his familiar mischievous grin. "And I do like to enjoy myself, Binks, as you know."

Elisa knew but she had nothing to say about it. She wanted a drink herself, but was afraid of the desire and so resisted it. She felt herself lulled by the large, gentle presence of her father that she remembered so fondly from her childhood.

Pug finished his gin. "So, Michael's right that she needs to be dried out. Easy for him to say, of course, being on the other side of the country and staying there. And saying it does precious little to make it happen."

"It helped me accept the fact," Elisa acknowledged. "I'm grateful for that."

"Have you talked with her about it?"

"She says it makes her a better person, funnier, happier. She claims to have it under control. We haven't talked since...since this bad turn."

"Maybe she's closer to the bottom now. She might be ready to listen, but she won't hear it from me, that's a certainty." Pug pushed himself out of his chair. "What you say we eat? Szechuan?"

That was true. He was the last person she would listen to.

"I think I'd better go home. I'm very worried about her." Her father's disappointment was fleeting but obvious. He had had some good turns this afternoon and wanted to celebrate. He was alone now, she realized, and the recognition surprised her. She had always thought of the divorce as liberating him, but that was only half the equation. "Maybe, Ramona?" she suggested.

"She's a hard one to catch in the evenings," Pug said, starting for the liquor cabinet. "I'm a minor player in that game. But I have plenty to do, daughter."

Pug Bolcar, the man Elisa had never felt she could get quite enough of, poured himself some more gin.

— 24 —

Spent, moist, warm, Tiff Bointon lay quietly that snowy afternoon looking at her lover. He was breathing slowly, softly. Asleep. He had fallen asleep after they made love and she had found this behavior somewhat irritating. The first time, that time at his friend's cabin, he had jumped up and down and done a crazy dance around on the wooden floor, chanting nonsense, genitals flopping. He had done this without warning, as if the orgasm had popped free a genie. Now he slept, his forehead damp, the dark curls. This sleeping, she thought, was spawned of familiarity. Granted, he had his worries. He probably wasn't sleeping any better these days than she was.

It was late afternoon, light failing, snow falling, the first time they had been intimate since the disaster in the underground. They were in bed at Rafe's place, up the outside stairs—plants brought in off the railing on the landing by Elisa and crammed together to winter on the sill above the kitchen sink. Modest digs, Tiff thought, a step above student level. Certain of Elisa's design drawings framed and hung on the walls, a photograph or two of Rafe in full Renaissance regalia. Nothing much had changed in Elisa's absence. (Tiff had known the place from before. She and Neal had been invited for lunch a couple of times, gazpacho, greens with tofu, onions, nuts and fruit. Lentils, yes, one time she had actually been served lentils in this place.)

Rafe had a quirky neatness about him that she appreciated: clothes picked up, dishes washed and stowed away. But Elisa's sudden departure had allowed an element of domesticity to seep into their affair. They had a place they could go now, a refrigerator, shower, a sound system—Rafe enjoyed country of all things.

She raised herself to one elbow. The bed was nicely situated near a window with a view out over the roof of the back porch toward a small river—everyone else called it a creek, Puma Creek, but Tiff disliked the word "creek" which for some reason evoked thoughts of sewage for her. In this late light the world seemed shut down and closed in. She felt safe for the first time in days. Enclosed by snow, and Neal away for three days in Los Angeles. Outside, the porch roof was snow-shaped, tree branches hung thick and drooping. The field that lay beyond a laden loose-wire fence was white and lumpy and marked here and there by stalks of dried caramel-colored grass protruding through the mounds. At this elevation snow was precious, doomed to a quick departure. It added a poignancy to Tiff's realization that this, too, had to end.

Oh, my God, she thought now. She did actually feel relaxed. Felt it for the first time since…. She couldn't remember, frankly, having drawn a single calm breath since the disaster. Neal on edge and Tom MacElhenney home from Greece, wandering about thinking out loud, mostly to Neal. Three weeks away and on his return—well, he was saying, it was as if he had brought a Greek tragedy home with him—his prized young designer gone and not returning his calls while her husband stumbled over his own inconsistencies. And Neal confiding all of this to her, wondering if his phone call had aggravated an already tense situation. Seeking her advice and comfort. And all the time that bitch was out there with a fucking bomb in her hand behaving erratically, and who could say really what she was capable of?

This afternoon of sex, this coupling, was not supposed to have happened. The boy was showing a certain neediness, it seemed to Tiff. He wanted more of her than she could safely or willingly give. It wasn't desperate, he didn't push it. It was just there, a need. And she was aware that he, at some unconscious level, might want her to share the destruction their affair had brought to his marriage. What had been a beautiful, deliciously tantalizing, and yes, perfectly harmless little adventure had become a tawdry, fucking farce which might at any moment explode into a full blown tragedy.

Time, in short, to end it. Zip up the pants, kiss the cheek and walk away. But Tiff found herself, even now, lingering. She was thirty-five, would be thirty-six when the plants were placed back on the landing, and Rafe was probably the last and the sweetest in a line of damp-browed boys. Teas with blue-haired ladies, speeches before social clubs, playing continuo for her dear and accomplished husband, roles with the company that demanded crustiness more than coquettishness, and less of them, that was the lay of the coming landscape. You will do them all well, she told herself now. You study your scripts, whether on stage or off. You play your parts with finesse.

Still she paused. She had intended this afternoon to introduce the subject to Rafe. Set the boy down, prepare him for the change of scene. He was of good alloy; the problem was not that he would run off and do something crazy. Just say the damn thing, get it out there.

But the lovely snow started falling to the surprise of everyone. The idea had been to meet and walk the trail and talk. Her idea, her invitation, Neal being away. Meet on the hiking trail that paralleled the little river and take a walk. But he had arrived on Nordic skis, coming down on her in full voice through a tangle of brush, poles and snow flying.

Hiding up there, who knows how long, wearing a red stocking cap and looking for all the world as if Santa had wrapped him up just for her.

Damnit. As she lay now watching him, a sticky thought entered her mind that she had to forcefully dismiss. No, absolutely not. That was intolerable. She would not, absolutely would not, go back to a one-floor walkup with no dishwasher and a car that had outlived its warranty. Not at this point in her life. No matter what he said, no matter how he pleaded. She would not even consider the possibility.

And so it was that she leaned forward in the dim and failing light and softly kissed his temple where the skin was moist and as wrinkle-free as a child's. He woke warm and urgent and slipped himself inside her without so much as an introduction, the muscles of his chest and shoulders broad and firm, and still smelling just faintly of melting snow at the tips of the curls along the base of his neck and around the lobes of his ears.

When they had finished, being slightly worn now and less comfortable, and it being dark but for the reflection of gray evening off the snow, she sat up and started to speak.

But before she could get any words out, Rafe spoke in that simple, declarative way he had: "Tiff, I'm sorry, but we need to end this. I love El. I want to get her back and this is not the way to do it."

"Yes! No! Wait."

"What?"

"That was my line! You trampled...!"

"Your…? So, you agree?"

"Yes! No! Wait!"

Returning home from her father's office, Elisa steadied herself for the coming encounter with her mother. There was the question, first of all, of timing. In the morning, sick and sedate, she might be more willing to listen. But Elisa's experience suggested that in the early morning, Ruth devoted herself to getting back to even, and even, these days, meant drunk. Or, if not drunk, far enough down the road to want to keep going. By nightfall she was bombed, if not bombastic. Traditionally, evening was the time Ruth reserved for phone calls to friends and radio talk shows. She had a remarkable ability to sound reasoned and erudite on the radio while at the same time being incapable of setting her glass safely on the table. Off the radio she would stammer and rail at distant enemies, and then moments later discuss with literate passion the plight of the homeless, the nation's foreign policy in Central America, the inequity of bridge tolls. They all knew her, the talk show hosts. "How's it going this evening, Ruth?" She reported on aches and pains, the misfortune of friends, criminal behavior in her block, the disappearance of good neighborhood markets. And she was always polite, her voice refined. "The gentleman caller," she would begin before laying waste to his position on the drug problem. She had been a singer and knew music. She had a gift for visual memory and could describe outfits she had seen at an art opening in great and colorful detail. Understandably her control faltered when the discourse came to lawyers or local politics, but on other subjects her calls were always welcome. Some nights, driving home alone, Pug would search the radio dial for her voice, a fact he never considered mentioning to anyone.

But in the last few days Ruth's behavior had changed. Now in the evening she was relatively docile. The radio off, she sat before the TV confining her ridicule to sit-coms, a target, it seemed to Elisa, unworthy of her skills. Evening might be best. She and her father had made some calls. She had learned some options, lengths of stay, prices. She would meet resistance, she knew that, but the resistance had to be brought to the surface and dissolved. Coercion was out of the question. Ruth would have to choose.

Braced thus, Elisa entered the front door to find the phone ringing. Invaders from outer space filled the television screen, a pecked-at TV dinner congealed on the coffee table and her passed-out mother slumped on the couch.

It was Rafe. "The daughter's voice," he said. "My lucky day." When Elisa did not respond or hang up he added, "Well, somebody flipped the paperweight up here. It's stopping now, but we've gotten four inches or more of clean, heavy snow. Huge flakes, particularly at the beginning. They looked like tissue papers drifting down. I got out on the boards. Skied the walking trail probably half way up to Leland, you know, where the sports fields are? I turned around there. You should see it, El. You'd love it." Then after a pause, "Can you talk?"

"She's asleep," Elisa said, putting it charitably.

"I was thinking more in terms of did you have the capacity. You're not saying much."

"You're the one who called."

"That's true."

"So?" she asked when he did not say anything.

She heard a sigh at Rafe's end. "So, it's over. Today. A little while ago."

"Tiff."

"Mrs. Bointon, you might say. That's not why I called though…. Well, maybe it is. But I've been trying all along. The other times it was your mother who answered."

"And now you want me back."

"I never wanted you to leave, you know that."

"You show it in strange ways."

"Yeah, well…"

"Yeah, well…" she repeated. They hung on that for a while. "So, all that talk about a one-time thing…" She had known, of course, and hated herself now for asking the question.

"More than once, yeah. But it was never what you'd call serious, El."

"Don't tell me what I'd call serious!" Elisa shouted into the phone. "Maybe *you* don't call it serious."

"El…."

"Are you hearing yourself? You carry on a long term affair with another woman. Married like yourself, and you tell me it's not serious?"

"Not long-term. It wasn't long-term, El. Three

or four times. Okay, serious, yeah, but not…"

"Who are you? Talking like this. That's not serious?"

"El…"

"I thought we…" The pressure flooding into her eyes and sinuses was overwhelming.

"I mean I didn't love her, El. We had sex, okay? All right, three or four times. But I never loved her. It's you I love. Not her. You, I love you."

"And how did you think I would feel? Did you think about that at all? You say you love me and you're busy shacking up with…with Tiff Bointon of all people. With Neal Bointon's wife. You know how I feel about Neal…."

"El…"

"I'm sorry. I don't know who's talking here. I feel like I'm talking to a stranger."

"El…"

"How can you say you love me and then subject me to something like this? Those two things aren't compatible. They don't belong in the same sentence. They don't belong on the same page. Did you give one thought to how I would feel? Did you think maybe I'd say, 'Oh, it's just Tiff, so that's okay?' 'Oh, it's not serious? So, it's okay?' Did you think that? How could you possibly think that?"

"I love you."

She was sobbing now.

"I do. I love you," he said into the sound of her crying. Then after a long time he added, "Listen, El, I wish you'd call Tom MacElhenney at least. The man's…"

"He's back?"

"Of course he's back. He's been trying to call you. You didn't know? "

"Tom…?"

"He came here tonight just after dark. He'd left messages with your mother. Two at least."

"I didn't know."

"Well, call him. Call him tonight. Call him at home. He wants you to." Rafe read off Tom MacElhenney's home number.

She had an image then of their apartment. How it was in the snow. How you could lie on your back at the edge of the bed and look up through the window. It was as if the snow was falling straight toward you, the flakes dancing as they fell. It could make you dizzy, that snow.

"I'll call him."

"And, El," Rafe could not resist adding this, "be careful when you talk to him, okay? Please be careful."

"Right! Be careful you say." And she hung up the phone.

— 25 —

Elisa turned off the television and covered her mother with an afghan. She found some jazz on the radio and put what remained of Ruth's dinner in the refrigerator. She cut a slice of sourdough, poured some oil to dip it in, made a simple salad and opened a can of soup. The woman at whose house in Oregonia where she used to sit zazen said to always think good thoughts when you prepare and eat food. But on this night, eating alone at the kitchen table, Elisa's were dark and confusing.

Tom MacElhenney asked her to hold a second so he could take her call in the library.

"Jesus," he exclaimed, a moment later, "I come back and the whole hive's in an uproar." Not surprisingly, Tom had a flair for the dramatic. He saw the world in terms of monumental struggles and last-minute victories. His fundraising letters read like dispatches from the final refuge of embattled civilization. Had he not found legitimate work, Rafe had once joked, Tom might have ended up in the television ministry. He was also not one to waste time. "Was it, Tiff?" he asked, voice booming.

"Wha…?" Elisa was flabbergasted.

Tom MacElhenney hardly paused. "I received the strangest phone call yesterday. A large contributor from San Francisco. I'm not going to mention a name or even the gender. The strangest things happen in this business. I come back and my young designer is gone without explanation. A thousand other things have piled up. Do you know what our insurance did? Doubled! In one year, liability coverage has doubled. They're making it impossible to operate. And health insurance! If I can't find another company that's more reasonable, the board's going to insist we drop vision or dental coverage, maybe both. When all a person wants to do, all any of us wants to do, is produce memorable theatre. Exciting, stimulating, challenging theatre. And we're going to have to cut back on health insurance for our people! You can imagine when that hits the fan. Sorry, I shouldn't be bothering you with this stuff. Anyway, in the midst of all this, a call comes through from a patron. I don't even want to take it. But here I am, what can you do? Thank you, dear. Marilyn just brought me some decaf. I'm trying to give it up. Caffeine, that is, not Marilyn. Anyway, this caller reports that you have left town because Rafe was 'running around,' the caller's phrase, with another member of the company. No name, you understand, but you caught them in the act. That's what I was told. And to that minute I was understanding it was that your mother was sick. I've meant to call from the day I got back but I haven't had a free minute. So, I called immediately, of course, after hearing from the patron. A woman answers, presumably your mother. She's polite, genteel. She say's you're at work but she'll have you call. Working? I'm thinking, what do you mean working? She's my designer. She works for me. That was yesterday. No return call. Same thing today. I call, your mother answers, she'll have you call. No call. So tonight I stop by to see Rafe. I'm thinking maybe he has another number for you. Perhaps he knows if you're working. We've had a ton of snow up here, by the way. It's beautiful. We've had the outside lights on all evening, just looking out the window at it. Anyway, I slosh through the snow to your place, and guess who I find leaving?" Tom MacElhenney stopped for a moment. "Perhaps I shouldn't even mention this."

"No," Elisa said, "that's all right."

"Tiff Bointon. I meet her at the bottom of the stairs. She has a casserole under her arm. She and Neal had had Rafe over for dinner, she said. He'd taken the leftovers home in the casserole and she'd stopped by to pick it up. Sounded reasonable to me. After all, we're all family, right?"

"Yes," Elisa said after a moment.

"You have to help me, Elisa. I'm way out on a limb here. It's none of my business really. I run a theatre company, that's all. It's just that now we're talking about my set designer and two of my leading actors in addition to you." He stopped and released a long breath of air. Elisa could not bring herself to speak. "Anyway," he finally continued, "that phone call from the contributor is still on my mind, and I know Neal left this morning for L.A., and now I'm walking up the stairs to your apartment, and it suddenly occurs to me that Tiff's tracks coming down are the only tracks on the stairs. Oh, there's some others but they're snowed in, hours old. So unless she's just walked down stepping in the exact same spots she took going up...." He let the possibilities hang there for a moment. Then he said, "Elisa, I feel awful. Just tell me this. Does it surprise you that I should meet Tiff at the foot of the stairs to yours and Rafe's apartment?"

It occurred to Elisa as she pondered his question that the apprehension Tom MacElhenney was suffering from the fault line spreading through his company was tempered by the enthusiasm he felt for his detective work.

"No," she said.

"Shit! Double shit! The bastards. But you two are everyone's idols around here. You know that, don't you? The happy couple with everything: beauty, talent, youth. And he has to go and do this? No wonder you're in San Francisco." Tom released a rush of air. "You are coming back, aren't you?"

"I…I don't think so, Tom."

"Elisa, don't tell me this. I want you back. You owe me something too, you know. You're my young designer, goddamnit! I picked you out of a crowd. I need you. I haven't been unfaithful!"

"I know," she said, laughing through her tears.

"You're working?"

"Yes, part time."

"In theatre?"

"No, not really."

"Good!" Tom MacElhenney exploded. "I know that sounds crass but damnit you're mine. I love your work."

"Thank you."

"I do, really. And you've got to think about that. You've got a gift, you've got a career."

"I know."

"You like working here, don't you?"

"You know I do."

"Then, goddamnit you can't trash your career just because Rafe ran off with his glands, for chrissakes. I don't want to cheapen this, Elisa. I know how painful it must be. But this is a theatre company.

You're a theatre person, like it or not. We're a family of young, intelligent, creative, egotistical—God, are we egotistical—beautiful people, and every one of us has an appetite for melodrama, or we would have become doctors or professors or something sensible like that. What I'm saying, dear, is that this kind of thing is going to happen. You can't go out there every night and stir hormones the way we do and not have it happen. That doesn't make it right. Or painless. Rafe was an absolute idiot getting involved in this. They both were. Poor Neal! Have you talked with him?"

"No."

"Is he aware?"

"Not that I know."

"You're part of our family, Elisa. Kill the bastard if you have to. I'll get you the best lawyer in Oregon. But don't leave me."

Laughing, Elisa remembered the rule Rafe had: allot seventy-five percent of everything Tom MacElhenney said to bullshit. But even using that ratio, enough remained.

"Thank, you, Tom. It helps me to hear this."

"Take some time, Elisa, if that's what you need." He sounded quieter now, fatherly. "Give yourself a chance to heal. Is there any truth about your mother being ill?"

"She's having her difficulties," Elisa admitted, glancing toward the couch.

"Well, stay there as long as you need. You'll be getting a check on the first, just like always."

"Tom..?"

"No, that's only fair. You're my designer and a member of this company. You've got a personal crisis in your life. If you need some time, it's yours."

"Thank you."

"Just don't sign any contracts, you hear me. You're mine. Do not sign any contracts!"

On the coffee table beside Ruth's cigarettes stood a glass half full of gin. Elisa poured it down the drain. As water heated for a cup of coffee she did the same thing with the twelve bottles she found in the bar cabinet, and then the cooking sherry she remembered in the cupboard beside the stove. With the coffee and a Dick Francis novel she settled herself in the stuffed chair at the edge of the couch.

Her vigil ended shortly after midnight when Ruth Bolcar sat up and reached, hand quivering, for her cigarettes.

"What time is it?"

Elisa told her the time.

"The bewitching hour," Ruth said. She managed to remove a cigarette from the pack and light it. She sat back in the corner of the couch, blowing out a cloud of smoke. "Time flies when you're having fun."

"A woman of promise," Elisa thought. The quote came from a newspaper article now nearly forty years old. She had seen it in a scrapbook her grandmother had kept during the years Ruth attended Mills College and was singing at various functions.

"You bear a somber cast, daughter," Ruth said

now. "Immersed in your horsey mystery?"

Elisa closed the novel. "I want to talk to you about your drinking."

"Oh my, a set-me-down-and-have-it-out talk. Isn't that sweet? Aren't we witnessing a confusion of roles here, Binks? When I lay down for my little beauty snooze, I was the mother and you were the daughter. And late coming home, too. I had to go at my foil-wrapped delicacies alone." Ruth rambled through this speech as though distracted, uninterested, her eyes meandering the room, not expecting a response.

"Mother, you're killing yourself."

"Ah, marvelous lead in, Binks," she said, not looking at her daughter. "So subtle." She roused herself to high distain. "Is this a professional opinion you're rendering? 'Costume designer on lam from wandering husband opts for proffering medical advice to those in need.' Take this on the road, Binks, and it might earn you a small but well-earned fortune. Or talk radio, now there's a prospect. Save yourself the travel fare. Always a line of old drunks like myself anxious to call in and get scolded by an arrogant voice on the airwaves." Ruth laughed, pleased with her exposition, but the laughter soon turned to hard coughing, which, when it ended, left her weak and haggard and feeling somewhat nauseous.

Elisa watched her mother and said nothing.

"Well," Ruth continued after a long drag off her cigarette, "I was prepared to trundle off to my cozy nook for a night of pleasant dreams. But if we have before us a discourse on the evils of drink, perhaps I should fortify myself with a sample of the subject at hand." Her eyes scanned the coffee table, then the floor and the couch around her. "Binks, dear, would you find a glass and pour me a tad of gin. I seem to have misplaced my vessel."

"No, Mom, I won't."

"Well, so kind," Ruth said, rising. "Fruit of my loins. Has your father put you up to this? So like him. Torment by saboteur."

"Dad doesn't care," Elisa said as her mother made her unsteady way toward the liquor cabinet. "Not really. He would just let you die."

"So true," Ruth agreed. "Save him a bundle."

The bar was located across the room to the rear of Elisa's chair. Without turning she waited, listening as Ruth fumbled free a glass and opened the cabinet door. There followed an awkward, pregnant pause. Then some intuition caused Elisa to stand and turn. Just in time, too, for with a scream of anguish, Ruth was rushing toward her, the glass tumbler held tightly in her raised fist.

Elisa caught her mother's wrist and held it as they stumbled together onto the couch. She held on until the both of them were exhausted with struggle, weak and crying, and Ruth had begun, fruitlessly, to beg.

— 26 —

"Am I rich yet, my dear Pug?"

Two weeks had passed since the night of Tyler Conden's announcement and in the intervening days his attempts to reach Ramona Livingston had failed: messages left with her answering service, a letter typed by Becky and sent out with his signature. No response. He had never seen her apartment, had no personal home number. The mailing address was a post office box in the city. She had always surrounded herself with a layer of mystery, but her case was nearing trial and they needed to be in contact, professionally if for no other reason.

Mid-afternoon on a Tuesday, she finally called and that was the first thing she said: "Am I rich yet?" She had been on a shoot and was obviously in high spirits. Modeling in the snows around Mammoth. "You should see my tan!"

"I would enjoy that."

"You know Mammoth? They say the earth up there is moving against itself at a rapid pace. Tension is mounting. It's like a nut being twisted too tightly on a bolt. That's how a man described it to me, the guy driving the van for the shoot. He says you can feel it, and it's true. Energy. Like it's rising up out of the earth and flowing into you."

"Hmmm."

"So, am I?"

"Rich? Not at this end, but we do have news."

He had found an expert on asphalt paving, a man who had testified in a number of successful slip and fall cases. Great credentials, and attorneys he had worked for said he made a good appearance on the stand.

"I flew him up from Fresno to look at the edge

of the parking lot. He's prepared to testify that the asphalt, or more particularly the sealant, had been applied without sand, or at least without the proper mixture of sealant and sand."

"So, what's that mean?"

"Well, according to our expert that was contrary to the manufacturer's instructions because the lack of sand makes the surface slicker. Especially during the first few months after it's put down."

"And it was fresh, right? I remember how black it was. Believe me, I had a good view of it, lying there afraid to move, knowing I had broken something. I told you I heard it crack."

"You said as much at your deposition. And that's correct. The lot had been resurfaced just over a month before you fell. Another factor is moisture. The lack of sand makes the surface particularly slick if it's wet."

"It was wet, all right."

The National Weather Service had confirmed her testimony on the subject, he told her. The city had gotten a quarter-inch of rain in the early hours of that morning.

"All right! So what does this mean in terms of dollars?"

Pug Bolcar found himself smiling. The timid, skinny, teenage street kid who had first come his way four years earlier now talked like an investment banker. In the meantime no money had been made on the case and all the money spent had been his own.

Their expert was going to issue a report, he told

her, and when it arrived, he would send it on to the defense. "The important thing is that the paver is the one with insurance. All this costs a bundle, of course, and they'll want to take his deposition. But if his report reads like he talked, I think we've got something that will get their attention."

"Any chance I could get some of my counselor's attention?" Ramona asked, coyly. "Say tonight? You know, before I lose my tan?"

Soon as he set down the phone Becky came in, begging him to call Vince Lackner. The man was driving her nuts, calling over and over for the past half hour.

"Where's the fire, Vince? I have an office to run here. I can't have you tying up our phone lines."

"The ten thousand, Pug. I need the ten grand today so we can get started on this."

"I have it in hand. You know where I am. Come and get it if it's so important."

That was out of the question. Vince was leaving the next morning for South America and juggling a thousand details. He would be meeting Carlos on the last leg of the journey and he must be able to report that the money had changed hands and the project was underway.

"I would think, Pug, considering what I've gone through for you on this that you would show a little cooperation. You'll be coming right past here on your way home anyway. I can stay here until six."

"Six is impossible, I have a dinner engagement. It will be eight at the earliest."

"Eight will be very inconvenient for me, Pug. I've been here since before seven this morning. I have to drive home, pack, get my personal matters in order. I'll be out of the country for five days. I need a good night's rest."

"Between eight and eight-thirty, Vince."

"Eight. No later than eight."

"A little business to take care of this evening," Pug told Ramona over dinner. "Unavoidable."

She was delighted. "Does this mean we're going to another party? Am I becoming your favorite process server?"

"Not tonight. You won't have to get out of the car. It should just take a minute. I have to deliver an albatross to a man. One that's been hanging around my neck for some time."

"Sounds intriguing. Can't I come in?"

"Not on your life, darling. The idea is to end the intrigue, not sustain it, which is what your being there would do."

They sat in a small Thai restaurant in Oakland. Robin Durham's friend David Gordon happened to be sitting two tables away with his wife, Roseanne Harden, everyone's sweetheart on Channel 3 News. Roseanne had run over after the six o'clock edition and would soon be going back to prepare for the broadcast at eleven. Roseanne had an inside tip, which is why they were there. Although the menu was Thai, the owners and staff were Laotian and would, on special request, prepare a

Laotian feast. The one requirement was you had to eat everything with your fingers, an activity Ms. Harden appeared to be enjoying more than her husband. Pug recognized the news lady. Ramona did not, though she did observe the commotion and the finger play at the table. Roseanne noticed her husband noticing Ramona. Pug noticed both of them noticing his date and it made his martini taste even better than usual.

Ramona was still enthused about Mammoth, going on about the beauty and the energy she found there. And it was true about the tan. Her face was robustly colored. There was something of the repressed tomboy in her mood and manner.

"Probably not a wise place to invest though. Do you think? With the earthquakes and all."

Pug was content to let her talk, enjoying the food and her company. "The last time we met, I understood your enthusiasm was for urban properties."

"Right. Well, when I finally got away from home, I thought I'd never again want to see snow or climb a hill or walk through a field. Those couple of days in Tahoe I never went outside." She looked reflective for a moment. "Whatever I associate with my childhood I reject out of hand. You know, the basics: sun, wind, earth." She giggled. "I'll be content to never see another animal. Certainly never smell one. But being up there. Outside on the side of a mountain. Feeling that air, I began to think, maybe I'm an outdoor girl after all. Wouldn't that be funny?"

He remembered that age, when a weekend could

change your view of the world. And maybe that was part of it, to touch that fluidity again. He still knew next to nothing about her. Hints of a miserable home life in some rural place in the west. A street kid, perhaps a runaway, falling in a parking lot. The day she came to his office to prepare for her deposition two years later she wore black tights, a pink sweater and pink leg warmers. He suggested something less tantalizing for the deposition and she appeared in a skirt and blouse, sensible shoes. She could have been a primary teacher at a parent's conference.

And now he noticed that something else had changed as well. She seemed to be wearing no make-up, no blush, no extensions on the lashes, no eye shadow, no lipstick. The photographer on the shoot had spoken to her, she explained, reddening, her eyes on her empty plate. An older man, graying. He had taken her aside. Given her beauty and her age, he had told her, anything that she added to her face only lessened what was already there. Ramona started to look up as she spoke and it seemed to Pug that she back away slightly from the table. "I feel exposed," she admitted. And her eyes, large, dark and, at that moment, vulnerable, rose and met his.

They arrived at Vince Lackner's office shortly after eight-thirty. Pug kept the engine running and the radio on for her. It was a cold clear winter's evening. Temperature felt to be in the low forties. He carried his briefcase with the money inside. Lackner had insisted on cash and that made him uncomfortable.

He had taken the briefcase into the restaurant with them, something Ramona had teased him about.

The front door to the office was unlocked. He stepped inside. Every light in the place was on and Vince was not alone.

"Who'n the hell is this?"

"Pug, this is Jake," Vince said, rising from the desk where he had been working. "The Hawaii fellow I told you about. The one who's going to grow the marijuana for you."

The man stood up, pulled off his watch cap and offered his hand.

"Pleased to meet…"

Early thirties, probably, Pug thought. Around six feet, solid, hair the color of wet river sand. He wore denims, crusty boots, and a plaid wool jacket.

After an initial glance Pug Bolcar turned toward Vince Lackner.

"I got nothing to do with this guy. What the fuck's he doing here? You tell me to deliver the money and this guy's here?"

"I thought you'd want to meet him," Vince sounded hurt. "He's the one doing the job for you."

"Hell no I don't want to meet him."

"He's got questions, Pug."

"Yeah," Jake said. "I got to know about water, got to have water. And access. I'm figuring a hundred'n twenty marijuana plants to get what we need out of this. That means hauling in a lot of pipe, steer manure, storage tanks, plastic sheeting. Going to need a greenhouse for the seedlings. Drying sheds. Can I truck it, or am I going to have to carry all that shit?"

"Sit down," Pug said to the man. "Sit down and shut up." Jake sat down holding his cap. "This is not like you, Vince. That you're an asshole I can accept. But you're not stupid. I'm dealing with you, not Mr. Green Jeans here. You know that."

"This man has questions, Pug. Legitimate questions. He needs answers if he's going to do this job for you. He's never seen the place and neither have I. Did you bring a map?"

"I have a map," Pug said, opening the briefcase. "I have the money, and I have a lease. But it's got nothing to do with him."

"A lease. What do you mean, a lease?" Vince glanced sideways at Jake.

Pug removed the documents and handed a copy to Vince. "Nothing complicated," he said. "It's all very straightforward. The corporation leases the property to you..."

"To me? What?"

"Let me finish. You told me you got a guy does this kind of work. So the corporation leases it to you and you sublease it to him. The term's a year. You pay the corporation ten thousand in rent, but the rent is paid in work, not cash. The work is that he plants ten thousand fir and redwood seedlings on the property during the year. The ten grand is to buy the seedlings. Clear enough, I should think."

"But that's a sham," Jake said from the couch. He looked at Vince. "I'm supposed to grow dope, right?"

"Of course," Vince said. "Pug, there's no reason

for this run around. I've known Jake for years. This subterfuge is silly. Jake is going to grow marijuana on a large-scale basis. You know that. I know that. Enough marijuana for you to pay off Carlos, and enough for Jake to make it worth his time. We don't need anything in writing to confuse the issue."

Pug was leafing through the pages of the lease. "What your man does up there on his own time is his business. But I do want to point out paragraph 14 of the lease, in which the lessee, that is you and indirectly your man there, agrees to not engage in any illegal activity on the leased property. The map is attached to the lease. He should have no trouble finding it. I know nothing about water but there's a road leads right to it. I've already signed both copies on behalf of the corporation."

Vince Lackner and Jake looked at each other, baffled. Then Vince said, "This is your debt, Pug. That's why we're going through all this." He handed back the unsigned lease. "I don't like it. It's like you don't trust me. After all I've put out for you on this."

"Those are my terms," Pug said. He opened the briefcase again and turned it toward Vince. "Here's the ten grand. It's yours when I get the signed lease back. I'll also want a signed receipt from you for ten grand." He pulled that form out of the briefcase and handed it to Vince. "The receipt confirms that the money's for seedlings."

"This man is growing marijuana for you, Pug. That's the deal."

"It's a sham," Jake added.

"Yes," Vince said, "a total sham." He seemed at a loss.

Jake got off the couch. He took a copy of the lease from Pug and looked through it quickly. "Okay, what the shit, I'll sign it. It's just a piece of paper, right?"

"No, not you. You're not here. Vince signs the lease."

"I'm the one going to grow the dope, not Mr. Lackner. I'm going to grow it on your land with your money to pay your debt." Pug had turned away and the words were addressed to his broad back.

"If you want the money, Vince, sign the lease and the receipt."

Vince and Jake looked at each other again. Then Vince sat down at the desk. He signed his name on the lease and the receipt and handed them to Pug.

"You heard what Jake said, Pug. I wish you'd just acknowledge what's going on here."

Pug Bolcar accepted the papers. He counted out the money and set the stacks of bills on the desk. Then he smiled at both of them.

"I know what's going on, Vince. And I have a signed lease to prove it."

"Well, dear Pug, It seems as though you still have it."

They had driven directly to the empty Angelica Estates. Ramona had been there before. It smelled of new carpet and fresh plaster. Pug's unit was essentially unfurnished but for a waterbed, a liquor cabinet, some sound and video equipment, a table and a couple of chairs. They had passed quickly through, grabbing towels and drinks and had gone on to the spa where they stripped unceremoniously and dropped in, the jets pulsing.

"What's that?" he responded after a moment. "Sexy feet?"

Ramona laughed. "Well, that too, of course. But I was thinking of the albatross."

"Ah. I'm sorry. I guess I was still thinking about what happened back there."

He had been thinking of Roseanne Harden actually. Everyone's sweetheart up to her knuckles in sticky rice. But it wasn't the restaurant or Ms. Harden herself that had brought her image into his mind. It was Vince's office. That guy with the black watch cap, Vince's uncharacteristic nervousness. And the feel of the place. On his other visits the lighting had been subdued, indirect. This time the place had been lit up like…like a television studio.

— 27 —

Vince Lackner, Robin Durham and Harold Manx sat through three viewings of the videotape before Harold Manx would say anything beyond, "Run it again." After the third viewing he said nothing at all.

"Well," Vince suggested finally, "He as much as admitted it. When you look at the thing as a whole it's clear he knows what's happening and he did turn over the money."

Robin wanted to agree with Lackner and he was tempted to defend his acting job. They had gotten the money, damnit. And Bolcar had made that crack about what the grower did up there was his business. No question he knew what was going on. He was about to add his comments when he looked at his boss's shiny head, at the eyebrows protruding like brambles, at the absolute concentration on the man's features. He decided to not say anything.

After a sustained silence Harold Manx finally spoke: "That son of a bitch."

Robin Durham decided to confess all to Elisa Gilbert. It was no longer funny that she kept calling him the avalanche guy. They had enjoyed a couple of casual encounters in a coffee house, ostensibly to discuss their multi-named cat. One afternoon, picking her up after work, they hustled over to the Strybing Arboretum in Golden Gate Park for a walk through the climates of the earth.

"I'm a newcomer," he explained. "I still take this town like a tourist."

The days were getting noticeably longer and some light remained as they walked back to his car. At a Chinese restaurant on Clement she learned that he had come west with the military. Born and raised in Missouri, he said, her thinking that might explain the soft inflections that she found so pleasing in his speech. His father worked on the river, a man of cargo, of boats and moving water.

"Which side of the Mississippi River is Missouri

on?" he queried.

She guessed wrong, squeezing the "show me" state in somewhere between Kentucky and Tennessee, thus proving his point that native-born Californians are pathetically ignorant about the geography of their homeland.

"Reno, Las Vegas. East of that it's all a blur for you people. Until you get to New York."

"Why bother," she countered. "California has everything." Adding after a pause, "Plus Oregon."

"I rest my case," he said, pouring more tea.

Elisa ordered a vegan lo mein while he asked the waiter about beef, choosing a beef and broccoli stir-fry, which led her to wonder if she was for some reason naturally drawn to carnivores.

Her brother, she told him, had once locked himself in his room for three straight days. Her mother wanted to knock down the door but her father said he would come out in time and he had. Later he went to college at the University of Iowa. He's only been back to California a couple of times since.

"Iowa is above Missouri," he informed her. "Same side of the river. I know it well. I did a paper on the Amana Colonies and a Mennonite colony further south."

He had majored in anthropology. The impracticality of his choice of major pleased her. "My brother likes it there. There's a river apparently. Early childhood education, that's his thing. And he took up golf."

"Rafe?" Robin asked her later in the meal. "That

his real name?"

She looked somewhat embarrassed. "It's a British thing, comes from Ralph, though in this case Rafe is his given name. Ellen, that's Rafe's mother. She was…is…loves theatre. It's the name of a character in "HMS Pinafore," the Gilbert and Sullivan operetta. Rafe's father claims his wife married him because his last name was Gilbert. He's a surgeon, Rafe's father, that is. It does fit him though, Rafe. He was born to act. One year he went to high school in St. Louis. He was in a school play that year. Found he loved it. He was about sixteen, I think. His father had some kind of teaching gig there that year."

"St. Louis."

"Right. Isn't that somewhere near Missouri?" she asked with feigned innocence.

He studied her for a moment before asking, "Are you going back to him?"

Elisa blushed deeply and suddenly. It was not the answer he had hoped for. Later, alone in his apartment, he could not remember what she had actually said in response to the question. It was the blush that mattered. But by then, by the time he was back in his apartment, stepping over the sleeping man on his way up the stairs, Camew greeting him with his tail in the air, by that time everything had changed anyway.

All evening he had waited for the right moment to confess the lie about his work. The right moment never came so as she was munching on her fortune cookie he just told her.

Elisa seemed untroubled by his deception "Oh, really," she said, brightening. "Then you must know Harold Manx."

Her best friend as a child, it turned out, had been Harold Manx's daughter. Their families used to live in neighboring houses. Robin was about to marvel at all this and make an inquiry about the mysterious daughter when Elisa added as an aside, "He really dislikes my father, I'm afraid. You might not want to mention that you know me."

"Your father?"

"Yeah, Pug Bolcar, he's a lawyer."

"Pug…?"

Elisa laughed at his obvious confusion. "It comes from his nose," she said. "It'll make sense if you ever meet him."

Lydia Manx was in the kitchen washing dishes. Harold stood beside her, one of their long white dish towels in his hands, standing there solemn and large and silent. She washed and rinsed a saucer and handed it to him. He dried it off, moved to the cupboard and put it away, then returned wordlessly to his duty station beside her. Except for the occasional nights when work kept him away, and the years when the drying role had been forced upon their rebellious teenage daughter, they had followed this routine since they first married more than thirty years before. Shortly after Janet ran off the second time he had purchased Lydia a dishwasher, but they never used it. She always washed, he always dried; a ritual of shared domesticity that Lydia found comforting. Drying dishes is what Harold did around the house, that and sweeping the driveway, polishing her shoes, lubricating noisy hinges, peering into the rare malfunctioning toilet or slow-to-empty drain, moving furniture when and where she wanted it moved.

Lydia was talking, Harold was not. She almost always talked more than he did, but on this night the discrepancy was exaggerated. So it had been over dinner and so it continued now as they cleaned up. Her first thought was that she had done something to annoy him and that sent her mind to the calls from Janet. But if he knew about that, if he had any inkling, silence would not be his response. No, it must have something to do with his work. His mind, she told herself, was still at the office. She knew better than to probe him, draw him out. The few times she had tried that had resulted in prompt dismissals. Some subjects, while of vital importance to his work life, were off limits at home. She understood and respected that.

So Lydia rattled on about whatever came into her mind, and on this evening it had mostly to do with the ongoing dilemma at the church. Their minister of thirty-two years had announced that he was retiring in July. Their children and grandchildren had settled in Arizona and he and his wife were called to move there.

"The new pastor might be a few decades younger than us, Harold. That would be an adjustment, wouldn't it? And it could even be a woman! More and more women are coming out of seminary these days, Sybille tells me. She's on the exploratory committee, you know." Lydia giggled as she handed Harold a dripping plate. "Imagine having a pastor's husband in the congregation. Of course, it's no different in principle than a pastor's wife, but still…"

"Has the Bolcar daughter ever gotten in touch with you?" Harold asked in the middle of her monologue.

"The Bol…do you mean Binks?"

"Yes, Binks. She's the only daughter I know about, though with a man like Bolcar who can say. Given his character, or lack of it, there could be daughters scattered all over the state like some random plague of vermin."

"No, I…." Lydia had stopped washing. She stood at the sink, her gloved hands sunk unmoving in the soapy water, her attention focused on the window. "I…I don't understand, Harold. Why? Why would Binks want to contact me after all these years?"

"She said she might. I saw her over the holidays. In Tahoe during that operation we had going there. Just for a moment in the lobby of a hotel. She had asked about you. I thought I'd told you about it."

"No, I…"

"She was crying."

"Binks was?"

"She looked worse for wear, frankly. Could have been on something, now that I think about it. She wanted to know if we were still in the same house. I got the impression she was thinking of stopping by."

"No," Lydia said lifting a plate from the water and rubbing it with her sponge.

"No call? No visit?"

"No," she repeated more strongly. "I would remember something like that."

"Yes."

"The last thing I recall about Binks was in the newspaper. Her wedding announcement. That was several years ago. There was a write-up in the society pages. They made a lovely couple."

Lydia remembered cutting out the article and putting it away in her lingerie drawer, slipping it into the album she kept there with the photos they had of Janet.

"Bolcar would have seen to that," Harold said, taking the plate. "That man plays the press the way he plays everything else. Always to his advantage. That he would milk his daughter's wedding for some publicity, that's just what you might expect."

"I'm sorry to hear…"

"Binks? Yes, she didn't look good," Harold said. "If she calls or stops by, let me know, you understand?"

— 28 —

Elisa's blush back at the restaurant did not reveal, as Robin had erroneously supposed, that she intended to return to her husband. It meant she was happy and surprised. Happy that Rafe wanted her back, happy that Tom MacElhenney wanted her back and surprised that Robin, as his question presupposed, was himself eager to know what her plans might be.

The way he had asked like that: sudden, sincere and out of the blue.

But of all the feelings flowing through her, the most pleasing was the realization that she had no idea how it might turn out. The unknowing was delicious and she was content for now to watch the possibilities dance around her. What she actually had said to him, following the blush, and what Robin would later fail to remember, was just that: "I have no idea." How delightful it had felt uttering those words. She did have no idea. And just then she was open to life, to whatever might come along.

What did she think of this guy anyway? He was pleasing enough to look at. Not gorgeous like Rafe, but pleasing enough. And she loved his voice; its timbre suggested an attentive, quiet spirit. With the sticks he had been clumsy but game, and not offended when she teased him about it: "Just look at that, would you, a Missouri boy with chopsticks." He seemed to enjoy both listening and talking, a rare combination in her experience. He appeared unhurried but not mousy. God, that night in the casino with the smoker! The way he had stood up for her even though she had been abrasive and intolerant. What a state she had been in. Her own mother smokes, a fact he had observed and wryly pointed out the one time he had come to the condo and met Ruth.

He was bright but she hadn't seen as yet much evidence of humor. Could he be "humor deficient?" Another of Rafe's "deficient" categories, employed when he encountered the super-serious. No, it wasn't that, she decided. He was far from super-serious. But there was an element, an undertone of something that troubled her. His apartment that night with the injured cat had put her off. Not its austere modesty. But hominess, yes, it lacked hominess. The place had struck her as drenched in a quality more powerful than tobacco smells—a sense of…not despair exactly… but loneliness, regret. Could he be a wounded bird? One of her college friends had been obsessed with the species, running off to bars in search of them, bringing them home and trying to fix them up. Elisa had no such inclinations.

Later, in the private capsule of his car after they left the restaurant, all of this had passed briefly through her mind. The mood had changed. Not night for day, more a cloud passing before the sun. If not a chill, then a shadow, a fumbling, as if he had suddenly remembered another engagement.

"I may be away for a while," he said as they waited at a light in North Beach, neon colors glinting on the surface of the hood. "Work."

A man was walking in the crosswalk in front of them, his shoelaces untied and flopping about as he passed. A large brindle dog walked beside him. The man had removed his belt and looped it around the dog's neck. He held the end of the belt in one hand, with the other he held up his pants.

They watched him pass in silence and then Robin added, "It's not nine-to-five, my job."

Why this sudden declaration, she wondered. So glum and apologetic. He had to have known his work assignments all evening.

"Galloping off on a white horse are you?" she had joked, hoping to revive the mood they had shared in the restaurant. "Bringing justice to the world? That's what my dad used to announce when he left home for the office: 'I'm off to bring justice to the world.'"

"Yeah? Your dad did?" The light changed and he resumed driving.

She had assumed he would invite her up to his place on some pretext or other and she hadn't made up her mind yet if she was going to accept. The uncertainty tantalized her. She wanted her decision to be a last minute one. Robin flicked on the radio, and then to her surprise drove them straight to her mother's condo.

"I really like you, Elisa," he said with embarrassing sincerity when he had stopped the car.

She realized then that his problem was a momentary failure of nerve. She found it charming, and not surprising given her inexplicable behavior that night in Tahoe. The memory of that night made her blush again in the dark of the car. To ease his fears she leaned over and whispered in his ear, "My mother's home."

And the implication of that remark struck her suddenly as hilarious. Two adults, one divorced, the other separated, conspiring around the unseen presence of a mother. "Is your mother home too?" she stammered through her giggles. He was looking at her strangely. "Maybe we can sneak in, climb the eucalyptus to my room. That's what Romeo does."

She started giggling uncontrollably as the prospect took hold of her. My God, and all she had drunk at dinner had been tea.

"Elisa…"

"No—wait, this is it—I go in, and then I slip out onto the deck and help you up. Tell me, sir, can you climb trees? Quietly? Can you climb trees very quietly?"

"Elisa, listen. I think I'm getting sick."

"You're…what?"

"Yeah, something. The sauce on the beef maybe, something keeps coming back to me. I don't know. Maybe it's the flu." He did look miserably forlorn.

"Oh, no, that's terrible," she said, patting his face. "You want me to drive you?"

"No, I…."

"Then come up for a minute. I can get you something. Antacid or something."

"No…no, thank you. I just need the rack for a few hours."

"You sure?" She was babying him now, lips pursed, touching his face with her fingers. "You poor boy," not wanting him to leave.

But he did leave, and the next morning he called and said he felt better, but it looked as though he would be out of touch for a while. "I like you very much," he said again.

Ruth Bolcar was staying sober but she was not enjoying it. In fact she hated it. Each morning she woke to a featureless, seemingly endless expanse of time. And time had become a desert. She experienced pain, a physical craving, but that was not the worst part. The worst part was time itself, time without the possibility of diversion. Time with just herself and no hope of salvation.

She smoked constantly, drank coffee cup after cup, but these humble vices were simply the raw ingredients necessary to maintain a bearable existence. They gave no real pleasure, offered no true respite. Nothing she said was capable of a graceful turn, no insight contained a barb of truth. The idea that she might conceive and express a thought capable of provoking a laugh seemed preposterous. She no longer telephoned the talk shows. She had nothing to say, and if she had, no wit to say it with.

In the middle of one interminable afternoon, an afternoon spent measuring time by the changing soap operas and hourly refills of coffee while waiting for Binks to return home from work, the day's big event, Ruth saw herself with an almost disembodied clarity. Saw what she truly was: a lumbering, fumbling vehicle for alcohol. All her personal qualities to which she could assign any merit had in fact been the qualities of alcohol. It was alcohol that had loved and hated, booze that cried and laughed. It had been sauce that held the audience and drew the friends. It, not she, that had fought the fights, had turned the phrase and scanned the world with wit and wisdom.

Binks, of course, kind Binks, who settling in after a day of work, slipping into a robe and booties, would spend the evening bringing her mother small engagements about food, about the news, about whatever she could dredge up to challenge her with, dear Binks insisted on turning her mother's argument on its head.

"A clever one, that alcohol," she agreed, acceding the vitality her mother had given an inanimate substance, "but he's trying to trick you. He needs you much more than you need him."

"Should have known it was a he," Ruth said listlessly.

"Obviously. The point though is that he only makes you think you're clever. Actually…"

"I see. I wasn't clever then either. Well, the illusion at least was comforting."

But Binks was not buying. "That's silly. You're always clever and you know it. Too clever for me. The booze has so deadened you that you no longer recognize yourself without it, that's the problem. But you're down there, you old cob," she said, pinching her mother's cheek. "I can hear you rumbling."

She didn't sleep well at night either. Lay awake waiting. Waiting for what? Day or night, the same endless desert of ticking time. Binks blamed it on the coffee and lack of exercise. They would start going out in the evening, she threatened, a short walk in the park. Get some exercise. Exercise! The word brought to Ruth's mind images of those baggy, shapeless, god-awful blue outfits she had been forced to wear in gym class years ago. Yes, and those ponderous, ugly medicine balls you had to toss around. And what were those other things called, those horrific wooden things that could knock you out cold? Indian clubs, that's it. Indian clubs. Terrible things. People would throw them at you. Balls heavy as anvils, and those bizarre clubs like bowling pins.

Binks did not know medicine balls, had never heard of Indian clubs. They would just walk, she told her mother, stretch their legs, look at things. And yoga? Had she ever had an impulse to try yoga?

It sounded ghastly. And it wasn't the coffee keeping her awake, Ruth was sure of that. She had been drinking coffee since she was a teenager and it had never kept her awake before. No, what she needed was a sip of wine before bed. Just a small glass and she would sleep like a baby. Surely, every human being, however harsh their station, however odious their sins, was entitled to a few hours of unconscious bliss every night.

Ruth would climb from her bed after Binks had gone to her room and scour the house. But her daughter had everywhere preceded her: the kitchen, the medicine cabinet, the den where Pug used to hide to do his work.

And finding nothing, it was useless to lie back down. Light a cigarette, watch Cary Grant or Jimmy Stewart in an old black and white feature that the station managed to cut into pieces and send out in slivers between those pathetic late-night commercials. She needed a bit of lilt in her life, damnit. Some sleep at night, some prospect for lilt during the day.

Dot Hilliard had lilt. But Dot was in on it. She refused to dine out with Ruth anymore. She would come over, or have Ruth to her place but she refused to lunch out. Too tempting she claimed. But Ruth knew the converse. Lunch at home was not lunch, it was housework.

She could have gone out at any time, of course, and bought herself a bottle. Her funds had not been frozen, her car keys not impounded. She was not under house arrest like some deposed dictator. The thing that kept her, the only thing that kept her indoors and dry was her daughter. Here was Binks bearing up so well against her husband's pleading calls, finding work, meeting this new man who seemed nice enough, that one time he stopped by. Binks calling a couple of times a day from the office, coming straight home after work, insisting on at least a walk around the block before dark, grousing about her lack of appetite. Her daughter was being tough as a leather bone; her devotion even gave Ruth a certain tolerance for the cat. In the right mood she would allow it to curl up with her on the couch. But it was Bink's face, imagined in pain, her leaving in disgust, returning to a life of misery with Rafe, that was what kept Ruth clean.

Then one morning, it was mid-February now, Ruth's brother Ty called with a scoop. That woman, the one Pug had escorted to the announcement? Yes? Someone had recognized her. Who? Ty had promised he wouldn't say.

"Well?"

"She's a whore," Tyler Conden announced. "A high-class, very expensive hooker."

"No!"

"You know those escort service ads in the classifieds? Call the right one and you get her. And she don't come cheap, sis. He probably put down seven-fifty, maybe a grand for that little performance. Not bad for serving some papers and spreading your legs."

Ruth Bolcar was astounded. The news revealed a weakness in her former husband that she had never imagined. Desperation, that's what it was.

"Bought and paid for," Ty was saying.

"The man has lost control of himself," Dot Hilliard said when Ruth called her soon as she got off the phone with Ty. Dot's voice conveyed a sense of awe as if she were describing an eclipse or the sudden eruption of a volcano. "You think we should have someone appointed to look after his funds? A guardian or something? It's our money he's blowing. Oh, I wish Ed were here to advise us."

Ruth was beginning to feel a heady triumph. The revelation seemed to substantiate every condemnation she had ever made of her former husband.

"The man really is pathological," she said to Dot, amazed herself that it should finally have been proven true. "And in the midst of this epidemic. He will surely get himself infected."

They lunched at a favorite restaurant off Union Square. Grilled mahi-mahi like old times, a single glass of chardonnay for each of them. Ruth knew she could handle it now. The great curse of her life had been lifted from her shoulders. The man was exactly what she had always claimed he was.

Dot had telephoned Cleary, the lawyer who had handled Ruth's divorce. So long as Pug was making the payments there was not much he could do, he said. But keep a watch on him and if the man is at all late let him know.

On the drive home Ruth picked up several bottles of wine. She would limit herself to wine, and then just a glass before bedtime. It would be smart, she realized, to hide the bottles for a few days. And hard as it might be, she would not tell Binks the news about her father, not yet anyway. As to the wine, the only way to convince Binks was to have a track record.

— 29 —

Randall Chin, third in command, called Robin Durham into his office. Robin did not take it as a good sign. Chin was known as Manx's hatchet, the guy doing the dirty work, like a vice principal at a middle school.

But being the first time in Chin's sanctum, he looked around. On the walls, sailing craft. On the desk a photo of Chin's blond, bookish ex-wife (Wasn't she an ex? Hadn't Manx said that?), glasses against her forehead, a pencil in her hand, the tip of the eraser touching her upper lip. She was said to edit a poetry magazine. Chin wore a gaudy gold watch and looked agitated, pacing the room with his coat off, insisting that Robin take a chair by the desk.

On his mind was a field operation Durham had

worked with Manx in late December.

Robin thought for a moment. "That would be Lake Tahoe?"

"Is that right?" Chin said, looking out the window, giving nothing away.

"That's the only one."

"All right. Tell me about it."

"There's nothing I can tell you. You should talk to the Chief if there's something you want to know."

Randall Chin turned. "You wrote a report, I presume."

"No. Chief said he'd handle the report."

"So, no report?"

"Not from me. Like I said, the Chief…"

Chin waved his arm, the watch flashing, loose on his wrist. He was a slight man with a long full jaw, straight black hair refusing to conform to the shape of his head. Holster on his belt.

"I'm authorized to ask these questions, Durham. Departmental policy may have been violated. Your full cooperation is expected."

Caught between the proverbial rock and hard place, Robin thought. And it was not hard to guess just who would get squeezed when they collided.

"All right," he said finally.

"Was there a wiretap?"

"We monitored a conversation or two."

"Monitored. Did you record them?"

"We did, yes."

"Vince Lackner?"

"That's correct."

"Did the conversations include a poker game?"

"No."

"No poker game?"

"There was mention of one but we didn't monitor or record it."

"I see. Any talk of who won or lost the poker game?"

"It hadn't happened, the game hadn't. This guy…"

"Lackner?"

"No, a Colombian. The guy talking to Lackner. He wanted to play but the game hadn't happened."

"At the time of the conversation you recorded."

"Right."

"It hadn't…"

"No."

Randall Chin sat down, put his hands on the desk. More gold, the wedding ring gleaming. (Maybe they weren't divorced? Maybe they got back together.) Another on the pinkie of his right hand. The gold seemed out of place. As if he'd gotten too close to the bad guys they were pursuing and some of it had rubbed off on him.

"Did you and the Chief share a room?" Chin asked after a moment.

"No. We each had our own."

"The operations room, the recording equipment, was it in your room or his?"

"Look, sir. I'm becoming uncomfortable with this. The Chief was clear. I was not to speak with anyone about this operation. You should talk to him."

Randall Chin was back out of his chair and

undeterred. Hands on the desk, gold flashing, he leaned forward. "I have authority, Durham, as I told you. Your cooperation is required. Your room or his?"

"Mine."

Chin paused. "So it was in your possession, the equipment?"

"Yes it was." So that was it, Robin thought, some problem with the equipment, some piece missing probably. Or protocol, some form not filed.

"Did you ever leave it unattended?"

"No, of course not."

"Never out of your control? Never out of your sight?"

"No," Robin repeated, getting annoyed. "Well, yes, but the Chief was there. If I was gone, the Chief was there. We kept it secure at all times. No room service, no visitors, nothing like that. It was a training mission for me. The Chief was real clear about the procedure."

"If you were gone, the Chief was there?"

"Absolutely. We never let it out of our sight."

"When did that happen?" Chin asked, casual now, fingers toying with a pen.

"When did what happen?" Robin took a deep breath. His guts had started to cramp.

"You leave the room, the Chief stays. Did you go out to grab some sandwiches, say, the Chief staying behind?"

"The second night," Robin said. "After we'd finished the job. The Chief's leg was bothering him and we switched rooms."

"You switched? He was in your…"

"All night. And I'm sure he didn't leave. His leg was hurting like I said, that's the reason we switched. So the equipment was never…"

"…with the equipment."

"Look, it was all there the next morning. I helped him pack it up."

"Of course," Chin said. "The next morning. And the tape?"

"It was there. The gear, the tape, all of it together."

"And you brought it back here."

"We came back together in his car. We brought it all in, took it to his office."

"The tape?"

"Everything."

Randall Chin thought for a long time before saying, "One last question, Durham. Did you make a copy?"

"Of the tape? Me, personally? Why…?"

"Did you?"

"No, of course not."

Chin got up from the desk, saying "You're free to go," and began to pace again behind the chair, adding, "This is confidential, what we talked about just now."

Just what the Chief had said after taping Vince Lackner, Robin thought. Almost word for word.

Vince Lackner touched down on the runway at San Francisco International shortly before one-thirty on a Thursday morning.

He was beat, badly in need of a smoothie. Some orange juice, he was thinking, protein powder, a banana. Six days in transit including a seventy-four hour stretch in the Bogota jail. Not the fancy prison, the so-called Hotel Escobar they were building for the drug king. More like what you might expect of such a place: cold, dark and dangerous. But now he had only one more task to perform. Then he would be free of Harold Manx and at long last able to resume his life.

He wasn't worried much about the Webster end of the operation. Webster, the man in customs who was dealing stuff in the south Bay. He had been pestering Lackner for a while, wanting him to deliver product. Vince thought Webster an obnoxious man, sloven, a pest, and wanted nothing to do with him, but when he needed currency to give to Manx, Webster came immediately to mind.

Manx just wanted to know when Webster took possession so he could find out what he did with it. Lackner had been assured by his lawyer and by Manx that he would not have to testify, that his name would not be mentioned. If Webster ratted on him, nothing would come of it. Vince's job was to make the delivery. Innocent, neutral, like a medical technician handing a patient a glass of barium sulfate before his X-rays. The cash coming from Webster would, of course, go to the department.

When he stepped into customs Lackner was directed to a side office where Webster personally inspected his luggage. He found five kilos of cocaine among Vince's carefully folded clothing and replaced it with stacks of bills bound by rubber bands.

"That's it," Webster said. "You're free to go."

"Not until I count them."

"Did I check the stuff, or even weigh it?"

"You don't have to," Vince said. "If I cheat you, you kill me."

The observation seemed to please Webster in a grumpy sort of way. "Well, count them then, damn it, but be quick about it."

A few minutes later he was approaching his office when he saw Harold Manx standing beside the entrance.

"The report I have from Colombia gives you high marks."

"I understood I was to deliver Webster's money in the morning. To my lawyer in his office."

"That's fine, or I can take it off your hands now and give you a receipt. The formal paperwork will take a few days."

"Take it. Then I won't have to worry about it."

They went inside. Lackner handed over the cash and accepted a signed acknowledgment.

"You did good work, Vince. Perhaps you'd prefer working for us rather than against us."

"I'm not going to do either. I'm in the transport business. That's what I'm sticking to." He picked up his suitcase and started toward the door.

Harold Manx did not move from the side of Lackner's desk, his briefcase resting there with the cash inside.

"I need to talk to you a few minutes about Bolcar. I ran the tape for the prosecutor's office and they agreed we don't have enough for a conviction. We need your cooperation to finish the job."

"Why me?" Vince Lackner said, annoyed. "Why not your man Jake?"

"Bolcar suspects my man, that's obvious. No, it has to be you."

Lackner reached the door and turned. He was a good fifteen feet from Harold Manx now, his head glinting beneath the lights. Something was wrong with this picture. This was his office, his turf. He was leaving and Manx was not. His next step would be to switch off the lights. Maybe that would encourage the old bastard to move.

"I've got an airline to run," he said. "That last little movie you produced in here cost my company two days worth of productivity and rattled my staff in the process. I want nothing more to do with it. And right now I'm tired, Harold. I want to go home and hit the sack." He couldn't remember that he had ever called Manx by his first name before, but why not. They were on equal footing now.

"Of course, Vince. It's been a long day, I know that. For both of us, a long day. But give me a moment. Hear me out. I thought you hated Bolcar. Remember the gossip column, the way he planted that leak and then accused you? The way he reneged on the checks. What was it? Fifty some grand? And you had to come begging to me for the money. That couldn't have been fun, Vince. Asking me for money."

"I carry no affection for Pug Bolcar and it's a shame he outfoxed you. But I've done my share. I would think you'd be grateful for all I have done."

"Oh, we are grateful, Vince. The department holds you in the highest esteem." Harold Manx clicked the locks opening his briefcase. He removed some papers and extended them toward Lackner. "The department is always grateful when a public-minded citizen like yourself is willing to sacrifice his time and resources in the service of law enforcement."

The warrant authorized the department to search his airplane. "This is illegal," Vince said, shaking with fury.

"Something is, Vince." Harold Manx directed Lackner out the door and toward the plane where a crew of men stood waiting.

III

ROSYLAND

THERE was more light and it lasted longer. The first week in March Lydia Manx had her garden rototilled by a neighbor who backed his pickup down Harold's immaculate driveway and unloaded his tiller in front of the garage. Afterward he came inside, removing his boots at the door, and enjoyed tea and warm coffee cake baked for the occasion. During the following days Lydia planted radish, carrot and lettuce seeds, marigolds and nasturtiums along the borders. The garlic cloves she had set deep in the earth shortly after the first of the year had green shoots now eight inches high. At the Marin home of Thomas Behel, Pug Bolcar's former accountant, jonquils appeared against the board fence enclosing the backyard. Along the south wall of the house came the long yellowish-green leaves that would later produce the naked ladies that Niedra so enjoyed. Behel spent a pleasant Sunday afternoon removing blankets of leaves and debris from his rose beds.

Death came to the woman who shared Noony Manx's room in the nursing home. Noony appeared to take no notice of her passing, but Harold did.

Other than her wild, seemingly electric silver hair, he remembered very little about the woman. She was small, motionless, a pale mound beneath the bedspread. Every Sunday afternoon her son would come bringing the woman's husband, himself aged and unsteady on his legs. Seated in the outer lobby beside Noony's wheelchair Harold would see them approaching the front door. To steady the old man, and possibly to comfort him, the son would hold his father's hand. A part of Harold Manx, the part that was still a boy, wanted to mock this tenderness the first time he saw it. He stifled the urge, of course, and was left to peer across the vast expanse that separated him from such easy affection. The father and son also brought to mind the realization that there would be no faithful child to assist him and Lydia or to visit them in their last years. Bolcar had seen to that. In his mother's eyes Harold occasionally saw now the last emotion she would express. He mentioned this to Lydia but she said it wasn't so. To Lydia, Noony appeared content. But he could see it. Somewhere in that prison, usually far submerged but now and then rising to near the surface, resided an awareness as alive and restless, as angry as that of any child.

The opera company called Elisa. Politics had won out and a position could not be offered her until next summer with no guarantee of that. The news was depressing, though she was far from certain she would have accepted had it been offered. Two regional theatre companies, having seen her portfolios, wanted to set up interviews. But she already had a position with a regional company and where would she find another Tom MacElhenney? The check had come in February and another in March. With the March check a list of the plays the company would be staging next season. A note said, "Pick the three you want, but I have to know your position by the first of April." She could hear Tom's voice in the scrawled words and it was saying, "That, or get off the pot." Had it not been for her mother she would have telephoned immediately.

Ruth Bolcar was drinking again, though she kept the gin hidden from her daughter and made a show of limiting herself to wine. She was doing better, Elisa told herself. She almost always stayed straight until noon and drank only moderately before dinner. She was eating some, lunching with Dot Hilliard and phoning her favorite talk shows in the evening. They had talks, shopped, went to movies and plays together. Her presence, Elisa thought, was important to her mother, and in that strange way Rafe's lie had become the truth.

Ruth, for her part, took it as a sign of her new stability that she had never spoken to Binks or Pug about his prostitute. And she no longer railed when Rafe called. While she never so much as said hello to the man, she would without complaint hand the phone to Binks and walk away. And sometimes Binks talked to him for half an hour or longer. From Ruth's perspective, she and her daughter had constructed a fragile compromise: she could drink and Binks could talk to Rafe on the phone. It was a transaction Ruth recognized, if Binks did not, of exchanged weaknesses.

The last Monday in March Harold Manx was out early, driving his personal car. He had observations to make, a pattern to discern. He crossed the Bay Bridge and merged with the dark-suited hoard flowing into the financial district. On the northwest corner of Davis and California he stood out of the wind, hands in his pockets, his back to a building, watching the parade of pedestrians as they entered and left the intersection.

Twenty years remained in the century but as he observed the passing crowd that morning Harold sensed the end of things. Tired centuries tend to rub up against decadence and this time was no different. Sexual perversion flowering and the rampant diseases that accompany it. A Pacific Rim city, they were calling it now. As if that were a good thing, a city looking west, its back turned on its own country. Minority populations growing seven times faster than white. Commerce flowing in and out, values, ideas in flux. The color of a man's skin was not itself the problem—hadn't he hired the first Hispanic in the office, the first Asian, the inscrutable Chin? But color did suggest heritage, traditions, values, there was no denying that.

He noticed then a man coming toward him pushing a bicycle. Soiled bags, stuffed to breaking, hung from every available bar of the old contraption making it impossible to ride. The man was tall, gaunt, the indeterminable age of a homeless alcoholic, his hair greasy, his skin dark from weather and grime. Caucasian though, Harold noted. That was clear enough from the man's height, his jutting cheekbones, the cut of his jaw, the hook of his nose. And how appropriate! Here came western civilization itself limping along, crippled by self-indulgence, weighted down with worthless possessions, pushing a useless carriage, its direction aimless, its focus distracted while the new and vibrant multicultural world bustled around and past him.

Brooding thus, Harold watched as the laden bicycle angled toward him. The man lifted a dirty hand from the handle bar and opened the palm in a listless, almost disdainful gesture. Harold gave a slight but abrupt shake of the head and the man passed on.

It was then that he spotted her on the other side of the street, half running along the sidewalk. He watched as she reached the southwest corner, crossed Davis with the light and proceeded west on California to the building where he already knew she worked. She had a bounce, Binks did. He had always felt a certain fondness for her, and seeing her now rushing along with the crowd brought a slight smile to his lips. He glanced at his watch to note the time. Five minutes before eight.

Thursday morning of that week, the day in the church calendar known as Maundy Thursday, Lydia

Manx drove south. Harold had been very busy all week. After services on Palm Sunday and the regular visit with Noony he had gone into the office for the rest of the afternoon. And every morning he left early and returned late. On Wednesday she spoke with Janet on the telephone and Janet had offered to meet her. The weather was growing warmer by the day, though more rain was predicted for late Thursday. The meeting in a park in Palo Alto would be their first. At ten-thirty? her daughter had asked. Ten-thirty would be just fine, Lydia had assured her. Janet was familiar with the grounds and described precisely where Lydia could leave the car and how they would find one another. The detailed directions were just what they both needed. Each was disturbed by the possibility that she might not recognize the other. "We'll be right there in the little playground, Mom, and I'll have a yellow scarf around my neck."

"I'll be there too," Lydia had responded. "And I'll wear the same."

Parking the car was an activity of intense concentration for Lydia. She drove only occasionally and rarely far from the house. Not until she had slid the transmission into park, had set the brake and turned off the ignition, did she look up and see her daughter standing at the curb, the yellow scarf unnecessary at her neck, the little boy tugging on her arm in a futile effort to pull her back to the playground. She was pale, a few pounds heavier than Lydia had remembered. She wore a white blouse beneath a blue cardigan, a full-length skirt that had experienced many washings. She was not a particularly pretty girl, never had been, but coming off her was the same light, clear and innocent, that Lydia had recognized at her daughter's birth and which was as familiar to her now as the movement of her own breath. She was clean, her hair washed and combed, her eyes clear and alert, though perhaps a bit tired. In the next few moments, before and after their embrace, Lydia scanned her daughter's hands, her face, her neck and found no marks or bruises. The things we can learn to be grateful for, she thought, given time and circumstance. And the light. That was the important thing. The light was still there.

"Mom, this is Noah." Janet lifted the child and balanced him on her hip. He was handsome, rambunctious, his hair a mass of dark curls, his skin the color of creamed coffee. "Dad would kill me, wouldn't he?"

"No, I..." In the child's eyes Lydia saw fire, a clean flame intensely burning. Where he able to see objectively, she thought, Harold could love this child.

"He would, I know him," Janet continued. "Or take him away." She was agitated now, her eyes fearful. That too was familiar and hardly bearable.

"He will never know," Lydia said quietly, running her finger first along the child's cheek and then over and down the cheek of her daughter. "Not unless you choose to tell him."

Tiff Bointon had chosen as her new role in the

Tiff and Rafe saga, that of the big sister. Implicit in her lines were a superior wisdom and a restrained judgment, both of which annoyed the hell out him.

She delivered these pronouncements at parties, during rehearsal breaks or after a performance when they would by chance end up seated at the same table at Curoletto's for Irish coffees. Such things as, "My dear, this solemnity will lead to unfortunate wrinkles." Or, "Rafe, we should all be spending more time with you, shouldn't we? Let's have you over for dinner. I'll talk to Neal." All this in a crowd. During rare private encounters she was more frank. "You're moping, silly boy," she would whisper, passing him in a hallway, or "Your new friends are among the dregs, both literally and figuratively." This last comment whispered over his shoulder as she, Neal and another couple were leaving Tomasino's one night while he sat at the bar drinking beer with Tim Ferguson and Ollie Rand. Part of what annoyed him was the accuracy of her observations. Except when a show of anger was required, his work had become labored, heavy. He recognized it, and he assumed everyone else did as well.

While Rafe recognized how the affair had pummeled his life and career, he had not noticed what the breakup had done to Tiff. Had he seen through the character to the actress standing behind it, he might have recognized what she saw when she caught her reflection in a mirror. And seeing herself in a mirror happened to Tiff with what was now disturbing regularity: most anyone entering her and

Neal's home—certainly every woman—noticed how many mirrors hung on the walls. Yes, she had aged. Without doubt, suddenly and significantly. Vertical lines now streamed down her neck as if it were a sack holding a pile of rocks and snugged by a drawstring. And it had spread her face as well, a drawn tense look that thinned her cheeks and pulled at the edges of her mouth. Everyone, she thought with horror, must be seeing what she saw.

For his part, Rafe did not particularly enjoy drinking with Ferguson and Rand anymore. Their cynicism had become crusty and corrosive. He ended up when he drank with them feeling both empty and full, the way one does when he has watched too much football on TV. But stoked following a performance he could still not bring himself to face the empty apartment without ingesting a generous dose of booze.

The other thing he did was call Elisa. He called her every night when he did not perform, sometimes early in the evening when he did, and on Saturday and Sunday mornings before lunch. When she wasn't home, he worried about where she was. When she was home he told her the same thing. Every time. He had made a mistake. He was very sorry he had caused her pain. He wanted her to come back. Everyone did. But that wasn't it. It wasn't because Tom or the company wanted her back. He was calling because he, Rafe, loved her and wanted her back.

He didn't dwell on it. He just made his speech and then related some gossip about the company, or the audiences, or the way the car heater fan had stopped working that morning but when he took it to the mechanic and the mechanic turned the engine on the heater had worked fine. Or how, eating out so much, he was becoming tired of hamburgers for the first time in his life. Or the new running shoes he had bought and the support they provided his arches.

Then finally, early that Thursday evening, the same Thursday that Lydia Manx had driven to Palo Alto, Rafe told Elisa he was coming to see her. He had scheduled a flight after the matinee on Friday. He would be at the San Francisco airport by six-thirty that evening and he had booked a return flight for Saturday afternoon in time for a Saturday night performance. He wanted to spend those twenty or so hours talking to her, non-stop if necessary. If at the end of that time their marriage was over, he would not bother her again.

"That's crazy," Elisa said.

"I can't make you come to the airport. All I can do is put myself there. I will be there, El. If you are certain our marriage is over, don't come. If you think we have a chance than please do come, and page me on the white courtesy phone as soon as you arrive." He gave her the airline, the flight number and time of arrival. "I love you. I feel terrible about what happened and I want you back." He waited, hanging on the line.

"I'll think about it," Elisa said after a long pause.

"Wonderful!" Rafe said, and hung up.

When Elisa got off the phone Ruth was nowhere

in sight. Then a few moments later she stepped into Elisa's bedroom. She had a glass in her hand, newly freshened with gin. From the anger on her face it was obvious she had been listening on the extension. Rafe could bear waiting to learn Elisa's response, or perhaps he wanted to put off knowing, but Ruth had to know, and now.

"That creep has more tricks than Carter has pills." Such was her fury that Ruth tossed out one of her mother's old metaphors, rather than concocting one of her own. "You must absolutely not go to the airport."

"I am going," Elisa retorted, suddenly deciding. Her privacy invaded, she was herself furious.

"He'll destroy your life. You'll become his slave." Ruth stalked and turned, sloshing gin. "Look what you've got here, Binks. You've got a future, you've got prospects. Commit yourself to him again and your happiness depends on his whims. He sees a pretty face and off he goes. And he will see a pretty face, Binks. Believe me, he will."

"It's my life," Elisa claimed, stalking now herself. "Not every life is your life. People make mistakes. They can learn from them." Her defense of Rafe astonished even herself.

"What he'll learn, sister, is that he can get away with it."

From there the conversation degenerated into shouts and tears and slammed doors. Ruth ended up on the couch getting drunk alone while one of Bob Hope's "Road" movies flickered unnoticed on the screen. Elisa stood cold on the balcony, wiping her eyes while calling out for her Romeo who had not been around for a week and who, in spite of her pleas, did not now appear. And from the cat's other owner, he of the morose apartment above the tobacco shop, no word had come since that bizarre evening when he suddenly turned to ice and drove away.

— 31 —

As Elisa was calling uselessly for her cat, Ramona Livingston collected her coat in the lobby of a hotel near Union Square and asked the desk clerk to call a cab. Her hands were shaking and as she turned from the desk she pushed them deep into the pockets of her jacket. The cold, wet wind blowing earlier had stopped now. Standing beneath the canopy, she watched soft rain fall through the lights touching the pavement with a sigh. She looked down the street and then at her watch. After one. Friday now.

The driver of a passing red Porsche turned on his wipers and slowed down looking at her. Moments later the Porsche came back around the corner, pulled to the curb and stopped. The driver leaned over and opened the passenger door window. He was about fifty, stocky with wavy, graying hair. He wore a blue denim shirt. Two or three of the fake-pearl snaps below his throat had been left open. Ramona looked at him without expression. He reminded her of a joke: the difference between a porcupine and a Porsche was that with a porcupine the pricks are on the outside. This one had a thick tuft of gray hair on his chest and three wavy creases on his forehead. He offered her a ride.

Ramona looked at him and then down the street to where her cab was approaching. She waited until the cab had pulled in behind the Porsche. The long-haired cab driver glanced at her, honked his horn and stared listlessly ahead.

"I only want to go home," she said to the cowboy.

He shrugged. "Whatever."

Inside, the Porsche smelled strongly of cigarettes and faintly of alcohol. From the tape deck came Kenny Rogers, his voice slurred by the swishing of the wiper blades and the whine of the engine as they pulled away. A brown felt Stetson with a puffy red and gold feather rising from the band had been on her seat and was now on her lap. It seemed to her a kind of statement, that hat.

"I was going to grab some breakfast before turning in," the man said. His voice was deep. resonant and slow. She glanced at the hands gripping the leather wheel-cover. Thick, pale fingers with black hairs bristling between the knuckles. "You got time for that?"

"I suppose," Ramona said, her eyes on the road.

His named was Kenny, "same as the singer," and he ran a club in Bakersfield. He ordered two eggs over easy, ham and hash browns, at a Doggie Diner, the two of them seated across from one another in a booth near a window. Ramona drank tea and nibbled at her toast. Kenny talked about dogs he had known, inspired perhaps by the name of the restaurant. Kenny liked dogs but he hated poodles. His second wife had brought a poodle to the marriage, "a nervous, loud, flit of a dog" that sank its teeth into Kenny's calf whenever it had a chance. One day, "when I was in a funk anyway," Kenny had kicked the dog ten feet across the room and over the couch.

"Three pointer," Kenny told her, "and end of marriage."

Ramona said she hated all dogs. That wasn't strictly accurate but she didn't bother explaining that it was more contempt than hatred she felt. The vicious ones she hated, but it was a dog's neediness that led to her contempt. The way they could be shaped by a bit of food, a pat on the head. And the smells, and their desire to lick your face. She could go on, but didn't.

Kenny said he hated cats worse than he hated poodles. His first wife had loved cats. "At least with the poodle I knew where I stood. Her Siamese attacked while I was asleep. Damn near bit my ear off." He leaned forward and showed Ramona the scar, a thin white curving line that began near the top rear of the lobe and ended at the bottom front.

To Ramona it looked more like a slice than a bite.

"That's because when I yanked him off his teeth were still sunk in. Took three stitches to close it up."

"End of first marriage?"

"Something like that," Kenny said. He wiped the plate with the last of the toast and chewed contented-ly, looking at her. He had a large, easy self-assurance about him. "You cold?" he asked after a moment.

She shook her head. It was true though she was trembling. She was trembling all over and couldn't stop. Little shivers from her feet up to her neck. The wavy creases in Kenny's forehead dropped, his eyes squinted. He reached across the table and with two fingers spread the collar of her coat.

"How'd that happen?"

"Some bastard," she said, looking away.

"One you care about?"

She shook her head again. "I bruise easy," she said.

Kenny wiped his lips with a paper napkin and then his fingers, slowly as if he were rubbing sand off very pretty stones.

"We all bruise easy," he said when he had finished.

He had a room on Lombard, one of those motels that seem pleasant enough until you try to move the bed lamp and discover it has been bolted to the nightstand. On the dresser was a bottle of Jack Daniels. A gray sock hung out of the suitcase, an empty glass rested on the table near the window. The bed had been lain on.

Ramona refused whiskey but she was glad Kenny had come along. "Thing to do when you been thrown, is climb back on. Right away, climb back on." Her dad used to say that. God, she hated that man and hoped he was dead, but he did have a couple of sayings she liked. That one and, "Even the Queen of England has to wipe her ass." That was another one she remembered.

Kenny poured some whiskey for himself and sat down on the edge of the bed. She knelt down and helped him pull off his boots. Hemorrhoids and cowboy boots, she thought—this guy brought to mind all her bad jokes—sooner or later every asshole gets them.

"Why do you wear these things?" she asked.

Kenny had lighted a cigarette. He blew out some smoke with a loud hiss and looked at the boots.

"Vanity," he admitted after a moment. "These are sea turtle. Had to be smuggled in. And those?"

Ramona looked at her heels. "I like to dress up," she said, slightly embarrassed. "At home I never had a chance. I guess it makes me feel more grown up, successful…pretty."

The cowboy shook his head. "You're not pretty, child. Don't you ever believe that. Pretty things are dime a dozen. You are beautiful. And that's rare, that's very rare."

Ramona blushed. Reaching forward she removed his socks. At mid-calf on his right leg she could feel a slight depression. Maybe there really have been a poodle.

Kenny had said he could relieve her trembling and he did, though not for the reasons he probably imagined. It was her skill that brought a sense of calm. Her attention to craft. That and her daring, her willingness to risk, to place herself again up close and alone with one those large and dangerous creatures who pass themselves off as harmless boys and men. Like the one earlier that evening, the shy, soft-voiced, married father of two from "the City of Love" who, as he put it, "doctored" CAT scanners and fetal heart monitors—and who had damned near murdered her. Like that one.

Kenny, it turned out, snored loudly and very disagreeably. The sound was not human at all, she decided. It seemed to be coming from a large, malfunctioning machine. No wonder the cat had attacked him.

Ramona climbed quietly from the bed. One of the things she had learned early on was to memorize where everything went as it came off. When she had dressed she stood for a moment in the darkened room and marveled again at the ferocity of his snoring. Then crouching down beside the chair, she felt for his jeans. This was not her line of work and it would be tricky. She remembered keys and loose change. The right front pocket, that was where he had stowed it back at the restaurant. Her hand felt the metal clip inset with a silver dollar holding a wad of bills. She pushed the money into the pocket of her coat and set the empty clip on the chair. It was a lot of money, though not more than what the firms and corporations paid, asking her to designate it "catering" or "escort service" or "consulting."

The wind had risen again and the rain came in gusts and splashed off the red Porsche as she hurried past. Somewhere near dawn, she thought, Kenny would rush bare-assed to the drapes fearing that she had made off with the car as well.

***

That Thursday evening, the evening before Good Friday, there had been a communion service at the church. The service commemorating the Last Supper was one of Lydia's favorites in the church year. But on this Thursday her mind was too rattled by the day's events to give it her full attention. Images of Janet and little Noah kept pressing in on her contemplation. She felt herself vacillating between gratitude and terror, between the impulse to jump up and shout out her thanks to God and dreading that on this night of high betrayal some part of her would reveal her most precious secret.

Harold, too, appeared distracted, and in a sense that was a relief. He had arrived home late and they had to rush to the service. He performed the rituals woodenly, popping mints into his mouth, his mind obviously dwelling on some problem at work. He had been thus all week and Lydia felt a deep sympathy for him. People in other professions could leave their work at the office, but there were times when a man in Harold's position simply could not do that. When emergencies came up his responsibilities were ongoing whether he was at home or in the office or, as on this evening, participating in a religious service.

They went to bed early, both of them seemingly eager to be unconscious for a while. But then shortly after three, Lydia woke. Her husband had moved. She lay very still and waited as he swung his feet over the side and sat a moment on the edge of the bed. She could feel him gathering himself up from the scatter of sleep, and she knew this was not just another trip to the toilet.

Harold went into the bathroom where Lydia could hear him shower and shave. As was her practice, so as to not further burden him, she kept her eyes closed when he returned, careful to maintain her slow, steady breathing as he dressed himself.

In preparation for emergencies he always kept an outfit hanging near the dresser, but on this occasion he did not touch it. The night before, after returning from the service, Harold had hung his best suit on the bathroom door, and then from its box in the closet he had taken down his gray homburg. He had not worn the homburg in months and when he set it beside his wallet on the chest of drawers she had teased him about it. "Is there a new secretary at the office?" she had asked. "It's the Easter season," he had said. "You should go out tomorrow and get yourself a new bonnet."

Lydia had scoffed at that, but now she thought maybe she would. Then on Sunday after the sunrise service they would have breakfast at a nice restaurant and then take a stroll around Jack London Square before they went to visit Noony. They would make a dashing couple, she thought.

When Harold was fully dressed he did an unusual thing. From the chest he removed some clothing that he stuffed into a duffle. The items were all dark, she could tell that much, and they included the black watch cap she could not remember him wearing since that Christmas when they visited her father's family back in Indiana.

Then, with his tie knotted and snug at his neck, his suit coat on and buttoned, homburg in hand, he quietly approached the bed, leaned over and kissed her on the cheek. It was all part of the ceremony. He knew she was awake and she knew he knew. But then he did something that surprised her. He touched a finger to her temple and brushed a few strands of hair back behind her ear. "Goodbye," he whispered, his voice husky and smelling of mint. Pleased, she broke her feigned sleep, and reaching a hand up behind his neck pulled him down and kissed him on the lips. "Supper?" she asked as he straightened up. "No, you go ahead," he said. "I'll be late."

Harold Manx noticed that his hand was quivering slightly as he directed the key toward the slot in the ignition. But he was all right. He backed out of the garage and allowed the engine to warm as he closed the garage door. He had not invested in a powered garage door. Professionally he was comfortable with technology, but in his personal life he preferred to ignore change unless it noticeably improved his situation. For the same reason he preferred walking up two or three flights of stairs to using an elevator.

A light shone from the living room of the house next door. That house had quickly changed hands a couple of times after the Bolcars sold it. But this latest family had been there a few years now and seemed to have settled in. Two teenage boys. It was to them that Harold attributed the odd light that now and then was left to burn through the night. The pavement glistened in the driveway but the wind and rain Ramona Livingston had walked through an hour earlier during her escape from the motel were ending now. The forecast called for skies to clear by midday, a prediction that greatly pleased him. Green digits on the dashboard announced two minutes after four.

His first stop was the nursing home in Alameda. Noony's room was second from the end on the north side of C wing. The outside door at the end of the wing could be reached from a walkway that climbed a gentle slope from a cluster of coastal oaks. The walkway was lighted but low near the ground so the lights wouldn't shine in the room windows. Through the window of the grated door he could see the length of the empty corridor down to the lobby where the nurses' station was located just around the corner. Drug supplies were kept secure, but for the most part the facility had been constructed to keep people in rather than out. The door would be locked but Harold had spent a lot of time at that end of the corridor and had come to know the door well. Well enough to trip the lock in a matter of seconds, well enough to know that his dismantling of the alarm system the previous weekend would not yet likely have been discovered.

He had thought to bring a towel which he placed outside the door and on which he now carefully wiped his shoes before stepping inside.

When Harold was seven his mother's favorite

horse, a mare named Curly, had broken the cannon bone in her right foreleg after stepping in a prairie dog hole. Seeing the horse stumbling about, her hoof flopping uselessly in the air, she had consented to have Harold's father to shoot it, urging him to hurry and be done with it. Harold had watched her drown kittens herself when the population grew too large in the barn, and had seen her decapitate many a chicken with a hatchet kept sunk in a stump, plunging the bird into scalding water and plucking the feathers, a fussy scolding sound coming from her lips, the feathers flying about, their hot, wet smell filling the air. None of this had been done for pleasure. She had mourned that horse, and generations of dogs as they reached the ends of their days. But she knew to do what had to be done, just as he did.

Mercifully she was asleep in the darkened room. For all his confidence he did not want to look into her eyes. There was no violence, no struggle. His approach was medicinal and certain. Autopsies were not performed on eighty-nine year old senile nursing home residents who died in their sleep. Back in the grove of oaks, water dripping from their heavy branches, the matted leaves and twigs slippery beneath his feet, Harold Manx vomited up the coffee and most of the scone he had eaten a short time before.

As Harold Manx was disgorging his breakfast and as the sun was first touching an isolated road in southwestern Colombia, a ranch hand on his way to work discovered the partially-decomposed body of a man whose hands and feet had been bound by electrical tape and whose face was hidden by a black bandana knotted at the back of his head. Authorities would identify the victim as a well-regarded local rancher, a husband and the father of two sons. His family had owned property in the region for several generations.

— 32 —

When Elisa woke that Friday morning and looked through the crack in the drapes, out through the sliding glass door to the balcony, she saw a moment's sun touch the leaves of the eucalyptus. The rain she had heard during the night, the wind that had battered the door, were gone now and the clouds were breaking up.

This had never been her room. Her mother called it that but it had not been hers, not really. By the time her parents moved to this condominium in the City she had already left to attend college in Portland. "You can have your old room back," her mother had said that wintery day when Elisa had telephoned from Oregon. But it had not been her room before and these last months, three of them now, had not made it so.

The storm had the eucalyptus smelling wonderful. The littering of leaf and bark on the balcony floor felt cold and slippery against her bare feet. A familiar feeling, this cool, damp morning by the Bay. In Oregonia she had never quite adapted to the summer heat. Rafe, who had learned about heat during his time in St. Louis, used to laugh at her complaints. "This is not hot," he would tease her. "Hot is when the temperature and the humidity are both in the nineties and your shirt and jeans cling to your skin."

Rafe's voice still providing commentary, a main character in the ongoing narrative streaming in her head. The first few days after she returned from Tahoe she had tried sitting zazen on her bed. Doing this in the early morning or before she went to sleep. But it hadn't worked. Her system had been too roiled. From her temples to her toes an uneasy energy bounded about, seemingly without purpose or design.

No sign of Romeo. And no word from Robin. Maybe she should call or stop by his place, to ask about the cat if nothing else. To grant her one-half interest, as it were, back to him. To tell him she would soon be leaving. And she was leaving. She would give her notice at work today. She would call Tom MacElhenney from the office. She obviously couldn't do it from here. She had chosen the plays she wanted to work on. She would bawl on the phone, she knew she would. She could never thank him enough for his patience, for the faith he had placed in her. And come evening she would meet with Rafe at the airport. They would talk. They would talk about possessions and how to divide them, about charting a civilized course that would allow them both to remain with the company. Or maybe not. Maybe it would all end differently. Moments of clarity, one conflicting with another, came and departed her mind quickly of late like characters entering and exiting a farce.

From the sanctity of the balcony she walked toward the perils of the kitchen. Her mother would not have given up. One of her strengths, if you could call it that, was that nothing convinced her. You could argue until your tongue lathered, but when you paused for breath she would repeat the same damn thing that had started the argument in the first place.

When the water was about to boil, when Elisa had the filter in place and the grinder had pulverized the beans, Ruth Bolcar stepped into the room wrapped in her purple robe. She looked even worse than she usually did at six-thirty in the morning. Perhaps she had resisted an eye-opener, Elisa thought. She struggles with it, has her small victories.

"About ready," Elisa said.

"I'll chew the beans."

"I've already ground them."

"Shit." A half-cough sort of a laugh. Ruth sat on a stool and took a drag from her cigarette. "You always were too formalistic, Binks. Me, I'm elemental." She waved the cigarette as if offering a visual aid. "It was your father who talked me into these filters. I prefer my smoke raw, my booze straight. I sounded best singing Wagner."

"Earth mother," Elisa said, pouring the water.

That cough-laugh again. "Earth mother on a dying planet facing a burnt-out sun."

The pleasure she took in that image was obvious, not simply the cleverness but the solace she found in its desolation. They were silent as the water percolated through the grounds. Elisa had turned on the radio. An accident on 101 just below the tunnel north of the Golden Gate Bridge. Inbound traffic was a mess.

"Call in sick" her mother suggested as Elisa poured the coffee. "We can play tourist. Go down to the wharf, have a banana split at Ghiradelli's. Shop for shoes. I love shopping for shoes. Lunch at…Clandestines! Have we been there since you came home?"

"I don't think so, Mom."

"Well, we must. Remember the summers, how we used to meet your father there for lunch once or twice a month?"

"Of course."

"We'd come in and he'd be standing there by the door slugging down gin with the boys and he'd look at our packages and wince. It was a routine that wince. One of his little performances. But that's one thing I'll say for Pug. All he ever did when we spent his money was wince. His money? See, I'm still saying it. His money! The wife of a lawyer for thirty-two years and he never bothered to tell me that I was entitled to half his earnings. *My* lawyer told me that. The 'community' Cleary said, had earned that money. Not Pug Bolcar, not the firm. The community."

Ruth took a sip of coffee followed by a deep drag on her cigarette. "You should check on it, Binks. It may be the same in Oregon. You can be sure Rafe has checked on it. That's why he's trying to crawl back into the picture."

The conversation had brought them to the edge of that painful subject and Ruth paused. Elisa concentrated on her coffee. It was hot and strong, just what she needed.

"All right. All right," Ruth finally said. "Mea culpa, mea culpa. I cover myself in ashes. I crawl up the stone steps pushing a marble with my nose. I prostrate myself before your adulthood."

"Come on, Mom."

"You want a hair shirt, I'll wear a hair shirt. Hey, I'm tough. When I was growing up there was no meat on Fridays. For Lent we gave up something real like jelly beans. I've been through it, kid. You want self-flagellation, you get self-flagellation. I'm a pro at that one. I know all the weak points."

Elisa was trembling. Part of her wanted to cry. To reach over and put her arms around her mother so they could cry together like two babies. Another part wanted to kick her in the teeth. How many times had she heard this totally self-serving, totally fraudulent crap. She placed her cup on the table to keep from spilling the precious coffee and looked away.

"Ah," said Ruth, watching her closely. "The stone idol does not respond. That's the way it's always been for me. No miracles. No tear falling from the painted plaster face of the Virgin. No weak smile from the Jesus on the plastic cross. You lights your candles, you spills your guts, but they are unmoved and so you walk away. Forgiveness is a rotting pie in the sky."

Elisa was crying now. She took a paper napkin from the counter and wiped her eyes.

"You were my last best hope and I drove you away. I was only trying to help, really I was—I know what these men are like—but I was wrong to try. You are an adult and you have to make your own way."

"Mom..."

"To see you sliding back now...the similarities are striking, Binks. Our lives are running in a strange parallel. It's just that it took me thirty-one years to get the guts to do what you did in four. To see him sneaking back into your life...I just couldn't stay out of it. I should have, but I couldn't."

"It's more than that, Mom. It's also the drinking. I don't want to drink. I don't want to see you drinking."

"I have that under control, Binks, I do. And we've had fun. It was like old times, you would come home from work. We had things to talk about."

"But we always had to drink. In Oregonia I would get home and do an hour's exercise. Here I drink. And the smoke."

"I see now. Yes, you're right, of course. I've ruined your health as well as your marriage. I've made you totally miserable, haven't I?" Ruth slid her empty cup across the counter. "A refill, dear? It's only coffee." As Elisa poured the coffee, Ruth added, "I'm driving you back to him. I can see that now."

"Mom."

"Not only did I chase you away from me, but I've chased you back to him. And that other young man? He seemed nice enough the time or two I met him. A little down at the mouth, a whipped puppy sort of look, don't you think, but pleasant in his way. Turned a bit doe-eyed when he looked at you. I noticed that. You should give him a call, Binks. Just because he hasn't called you, doesn't mean he's not interested. They lose their guts now and then, some men do. Maybe it's the good ones who do that. He may just need a sign, a little bucking up."

Elisa stood, cup in hand. "I have to shower, Mom. I'm going to be late as it is."

"He may just be busy, or out of town on business," Ruth continued. "So many men travel these days." She flicked the ash from her cigarette. "Would you at least save lunch for me, Binks? A fare-thee-well, if you like. Clandestines, like the old times. We can talk."

"Of course, Mom. And you know it's not a fare-thee-well."

Elisa watched her mother inhale deeply from the cigarette and realized that she had conceded nothing. At lunch the whole production would start all over again.

Elisa glanced at her watch. Three minutes before eight. She still had to cross Davis, walk half a block and then take the elevator to the third floor. She was going to be late. And she had to pee. The light at this intersection always caught her and the desire to urinate always became unbearable while she waited. If only she had enough self discipline to limit herself to a single cup before she left the house.

A foul smelling drunk stood at the curb beside her. She tried to step away but the crowd was thick and unyielding. A car wheeled around the opposite corner. Her attention was captured by its familiar color and shape—a white Audi. A blast from the horn, a quick wave. Her father. He must have a court date, she thought, to be hurrying to his office this early. She should call him, talk about what was happening with her and her mother.

Halfway across the street, running at the front of the crowd, Elisa realized she was not going to make it. At the far curb she angled quickly toward the first building. Through the revolving door, past the perfumes and the lingerie where a sharp right led her alongside women's shoes at a near run. Was someone following her? She could hear hurrying steps. Now, that was silly, she thought. Returns, credit department, another right—she knew the way by heart. The two-cup sprint. They could advertise it, charge an entrance fee, sell T-shirts. At the doorway she stopped and looked back. No one was behind her.

But then, back out on the street and hurrying again toward her office, Elisa saw a man standing at the red curb beside a large black car. He was immaculately dressed, a gray suit, white shirt, a conservative tie. But her attention had been captured by the oddity of a gray homburg on his head, that and something familiar about his face. In her rush she would have passed on except it was obvious now that he recognized her as well. An imposing figure, large, somber, seemingly from another time—or more precisely, seemingly out of time—he stood watching her without expression.

"Mr. Manx?" Elisa said, pausing.

"Binks, how good to see you."

Elisa smiled. She approached, reached out her hand. "Funny after all these years, that we should meet a second time."

Harold Manx took her hand and looked down into her eyes for a moment. "This meeting is no accident, Binks. I was waiting for you."

"Waiting? I don't understand."

"I need to speak with you. It is somewhat urgent." He released her hand and opened the passenger door of the car. "Get in, please."

"But…" She looked at her watch. "I'm already late."

"I've spoken with your employer. It's all been arranged." Elisa could feel his hand on her upper arm. He pressed her gently toward the open door. "We can talk better inside."

She took a step toward the car then planted her feet and leaned slightly against the pressure he was applying to her arm. "Mr. Manx, I…"

"I need your help, Binks. It's about Janet."

"Janet?"

He nodded.

"All right," she said, after a short hesitation. And accepting his guidance she slid into the passenger seat.

There was no hurry about the man. He closed her door and walked slowly around to the driver's side. Oblivious to the roar and rush of traffic, Harold

Manx removed the homburg and set it on the seat between them, his nearly hairless head pale and gleaming as he leaned in. Then he removed his coat revealing a brown shoulder holster and the weapon beneath his left arm. A large man, thick through the chest and shoulders. He folded the coat carefully and placed it in the back seat. Finally settled behind the wheel, he removed something from a pocket in his vest and placed it in his mouth. Elisa smelled wintergreen. Then he started the engine and pulled out into traffic.

"So what's this about Janet?" Elisa asked, a few blocks later, unable to restrain herself. "Is the news good?"

"Not now, Binks," Harold Manx said. "I'm becoming an old man and I can only do one thing at a time. Right now I'm driving. There are several tapes in the tray. Choose one if you wish. I believe the one in place is Horowitz, the pianist."

That 'Not now, Binks," the tone of it, sent her back to the third grade and a stout teacher with the name of Thorne, a Mrs. Thorne it had been, "shushing" her with a scowl. Her desk had been in the front row and she had always been eager to participate, a quality that had made her, as her mother would later be fond of reminding her, a "handful" at that age. Probably still was, she thought now.

Elisa started the tape and sat back in her seat. They were traveling westerly toward the Golden Gate. The incoming traffic was thick and harried as if each driver realized that more cars were entering the city than places were available to park them, a gigantic game of motorized musical chairs. On Lombard they passed a blue postal drop box where a few hours earlier Ramona Livingston, one fist in her coat pocket clutching Kenny's cash, had stood in the rain and gusting wind to hail a cab. Elisa felt now a moment's gratitude toward the man sitting beside her. That he had thought to make arrangements with her employer suggested a good intent, an underlying courtesy. Janet Manx, she thought, after all these years.

— 33 —

On that Friday morning Robin Durham was thinking about an early exit from work when he forced himself out of bed and into the office by six o'clock. He had the girls for the weekend, this being Easter. Traffic would be bad under the best of circumstances. He wanted to get an early start for Monterey.

But first there was work, specifically a report Fernald wanted to see before the weekend. Robin had not felt comfortable in the office of late. For one thing Gordon was down in the dumps. His wife had had an argument with her boss and was sending tapes to television stations from Tampa to Seattle. Gordon was distressed by this turn of events—being happy where he was—and he had chosen to discuss his options and lament his fate with Robin, usually while Robin was trying to get some work done.

Then there was the whole mess surrounding Chin and Manx, the Lackner and the Bolcar investigations.

The conflict with Elisa. He had promised Chin to not discuss their conversation about the Lackner assignment with anyone. However, about a week following that meeting, Robin had returned to Chin's office on his own accord. He wanted to be straightforward about this woman he had been dating whom it turned out was the daughter of Lawrence Bolcar, a man the department was investigating, an investigation that he, Durham, was directly involved with. He wanted to make clear how he had stepped away, broken it off. He also wanted to inform Chin of something Elisa had inadvertently told him before they separated: that there was bad blood between Harold Manx and Pug Bolcar. A personal thing, and it raised the question of whether the Chief should be heading up that investigation.

From Robin's point of view the meeting with Randall Chin had not gone well. Chin listened carefully but gave very little back. About the Bolcar case he would say nothing. That was the Chief's baby. If Manx had wanted Robin to know more, he would have told him. When Robin mentioned the long-lasting personal antagonism between the Chief and the man he was investigating, Chin grew very still.

Into the silence Robin said, "I've broken if off, for now anyway, but I would like to have nothing more to do with the investigation. My position is untenable, as you can see."

Chin wanted to know if he had he spoken to Harold Manx about this. He had not. And why not?

"I suspect he might want to use me to get information from her about her father."

"And you're not prepared to do that?"

"No," Robin said after a pause, "I'm not."

Chin pondered this. A hard man to read. He had just learned something about the department's newest agent but what he made of it was anybody's guess. Or maybe he was just like the rest of us, Robin thought. Too much on his mind already, resentful of hearing more bad news.

On Randall Chin's desk was a small wooden box-like container filled with small, round, brightly-polished stones. On each stone a face had been carved. Chin reached for the box, his gold watch flashing. For the next couple of minutes he poked through the stone faces as if in search of a particular one, a unique expression that would answer all of his problems. Finally, he looked up from the mob of faces scattered in front of him.

"Say nothing of what we have discussed here to anyone, Durham. And if the Chief asks you to do something more in the Bolcar investigation, I want to know immediately."

With that he had been dismissed. Everyone in the office seemed on edge. Gordon was a dreary wire service bringing him periodic dispatches detailing his wife's activities and the instabilities within the hierarchy of her station's management—for a few days it looked as though her boss would be leaving, though not for certain. Chin seemed nervous and irritable. Fernald—his easy-going charm once famous and now gone—had thrown Robin's draft report back in his face, claiming that he wanted more detail, more background. Harold Manx, meanwhile, appeared to be brooding in his private chambers.

And the Chief's chambers were indeed private in every way. Consistent with his fealty toward the public trust he had furnished it with his own funds. His strict adherence to rules and regulations was legendary. His expense account, it was said, was bone bare. If he stopped at his bank or made a personal purchase while on the job his mileage record would reflect the interruption and the mile or two of deviation subtracted from his request for reimbursement.

Robin's only view of Manx's office had occurred at the holiday party in mid-December. He had only been with the department a few weeks at the time but had been told the party offered a rare chance to peek inside. He found the door open and the Chief standing behind a makeshift bar serving a treacherous drink he called a boomerang. The usually taciturn boss wore a Santa Claus hat. His eyes gleamed with merriment and his eyebrows twitched as the blender roared away, giving the impression that his little performance was, in his eyes at least, amazingly clever and funny. Robin found the experience embarrassing but it did afford him a chance to look around. The Chief's taste in furniture ran to rich woods, tall bookcases, walnut file cabinets and desk. His chairs had leather seats. Western paintings on the walls, reproductions of Remington statuary standing about.

Those file cabinets, Gordon had later joked, while elegant with their wood exterior, were lined with lead. Had to be because of all the toxic information stored inside. Not only records of the investigations under Manx's control, but also files on individuals, both public and private, whose influence the Chief might one day need or who were in a position to threaten him. Included in this category were employees. Rise too high, too fast, the rumor went, and you might earn a private meeting with the Chief. Fernald, it was said, had been there, and had left the meeting a quieter, more docile man.

When Robin arrived at the office early that Friday morning the night officer and the clerk were just leaving. The phone lines were blinking on hold and the place empty. "The Chief is in his office," the clerk had told him as she entered the elevator that Robin was stepping out of. The staff shared an unacknowledged conspiracy to keep each other informed of the Chief's whereabouts.

The shredder had been removed from its customary position beside the copy machines and Robin could hear it grinding away behind the closed door to Manx's office. Robin was working at his desk a half hour later when the Chief stepped out.

"Ah, Durham. Good man, nose to the ground. On a fresh scent, are you?"

To Robin, the Chief appeared vigorous that morning, robust in a fine gray suit, jacket off, vest and holster in place, color on his scalp and face.

"Just a report," Robin admitted. "Fernald wants

it. Thought I could knock it out before the crowd shows up."

"Well, good to see you at it. Have you seen Charlie?"

Robin did not know a Charlie.

"Janitorial foreman. Big black guy, shaves his head. Probably on the fourth floor, or down in the cafeteria. Would you track him down, Durham? I need to get rid of some trash."

He found Charlie in the cafeteria chatting with a woman setting out pastries and bowls of chopped fruit. Charlie directed him to Ricardo on the fourth floor. Ricardo was not happy.

"What's the man want? I done that floor."

When they reached the office Manx was pushing the shredder back to its home base. Robin bent down to plug it in while the Chief instructed the scowling Ricardo to remove all the trash bags from his office. Then the two of them were alone for a moment.

"Anything new on the Lackner case?" Robin ventured, still on his haunches, a bit of hesitation in his voice.

"Good outcome," Manx reported matter-of-factly. "Webster has become a joint operation with the San Jose P.D."

"Good to hear," Robin said, regaining his feet. "And Bolcar? Anything ever come of that?"

The transformation on the Chief's face was remarkable. The color left and then abruptly returned, a deep red. Veins popped out on his temples. He was glaring at the younger man.

"Your role in that operation has been completed, Durham. Your job done. If I need you for anything further I'll let you know."

"Right, Chief."

Harold Manx rotated on the newly buffed floor and returned to his private space. Sometime after seven while Robin Durham was still struggling with the report, he saw the Chief, his coat on, hat in hand, walk through the office and out the door.

Pug Bolcar arrived at his office a few minutes after honking at Elisa. He had an eight-thirty settlement conference on the Ramona Livingston case and Ramona was not there. Nor had she called. Under the court's rules she had to be present at the conference, or at the very least available by phone. And the only number Pug had was that damned answering service.

"Try it again," he told Becky. "And keep trying it until something breaks loose."

Typical Friday for Becky. She handed him two telephone slips before he left her desk. Huddleston had called, the attorney handling the libel suit against the newspaper. Huddleston wanted to talk with him. It was important. The second call was from Vince Lackner. Lackner said he would be at Pug's office at eleven. According to the message it was urgent that he meet with him. The word "urgent" had been underlined. Not something Becky would have done without being told.

Pug did not have time to return the calls but

before he left for court Pete Miller demanded a minute of his time. The evening before, at Pug's direction, Miller had tracked down the man who had worked as foreman for the company that paved the parking lot where Ramona fell. Pug had recently learned that the man was no longer with the company. A falling out, perhaps? Would he testify about the absence of sand in the sealant? Pete had bad news. According to the ex-foreman, sand had been mixed with the sealant. Either this guy was lying or Pug's expert was wrong.

In the judge's chambers everyone was chugging coffee and shuffling through papers. Judge Eleanor Perrander had her clerk present and a court reporter. She insisted an agreement could be reached in this case and she was prepared to badger, and perhaps threaten to get it.

Her first question to Pug Bolcar: "So, where's the plaintiff, counsel?" She frowned at his excuses and recited the rules. Sanctions could be imposed. Under some circumstances Ramona's claim could be dismissed.

Pug explained that Ramona was committed to the case and had always been cooperative. He suggested they proceed without her. After some half-hearted posturing the other attorneys agreed, knowing that Ramona's absence placed them at an advantage.

There was talk from the defense about Ramona's shoes, a pair of worn-out sneakers that were said to be inappropriate for the wet conditions. They also argued that she had taken an indirect route from the bus stop across the parking lot to the store entrance, thereby causing her to unnecessarily use the sloping approach where she slipped and fell. The shoes, Pug responded, were standard, almost universal footwear these days, and the slope was part of the public approach designed by the builder, approved by the owner and paved by the paver. There followed a vigorous exchange over whether the approach was a ramp as defined by the building code. Pug contended it was, and the code required a non-slip surface on ramps. The building owner's attorney denied that the slope was a ramp. The paver's counsel claimed the approach, ramp or not, had been properly paved. Pug, holding his breath, relied heavily on his expert's report that the sealant had been improperly applied. To his relief the report was only weakly challenged. The paver's attorney, seeing himself as in the employ of the paver's insurer, had apparently not bothered to check out the sand question with the paver himself. But if there were no settlement, Pug thought, he almost certainly would check, before or during the trial.

After more than an hour of this, and still no Ramona, he reduced his demand from a hundred-thousand to eighty-five, knowing that their position was likely as strong now as it ever would be, especially if Ramona could not be tracked down by Monday morning, or if the report of his paving expert was seriously impugned.

The defendants came back with sixty-five

thousand. Judge Perrander wanted to know who was paying what. The attorney for the building owner's bankrupt insurance company said the state insurance authority agreed to shell out twenty-five. To go beyond that would require the approval of a governmental commission, and that could take weeks. A representative of the paver's insurer agreed to pay forty. The judge pressed and got him up to fifty. Now she was scowling at Pug Bolcar. Meet them in the middle, her look insisted, and we can all get this behind us.

Pug refused to come down. At eighty-five, he said, he was already shaving his fee to get his client what she deserved. And the judge had not met the plaintiff who would make an attractive and persuasive witness.

"And whose fault is that?" the judge growled. Then she turned her attention back to the defendants. She would not be trying this case, she said, but if she were, she would almost certainly rule that the sloping approach was legally a ramp. The message was clear. The defendants left the room again and returned in five minutes with the remaining ten grand. Where it came from they didn't say, and Pug didn't ask. Now he just had to find Ramona.

— 34 —

From a payphone in the courthouse Pug Bolcar called Ray Huddleston who said he had something he wanted Pug to hear. Just what he would not say. "You have to hear it in person." The man did not sound happy.

Huddleston's office was less than a block from the courthouse. Pug was there within five minutes, but Huddleston kept him waiting an additional fifteen, yet another sign of his attorney's displeasure. He used the delay to telephone Becky who said that Vince Lackner was already at the office. "He's very nervous," she said, her voice muffled, "I hope you get here soon." From the court he had learned that the conference was over so when Ramona had called a few minutes before Pug she got a number.

"Sorry," Ramona said when Pug reached her. "Did I blow it?" She sounded half asleep.

"You could have. As it turned out you only made it more complicated."

"I have a way of doing that. Are we going to trial?"

"That's up to you. Can we meet for lunch?"

"You aren't going to tell me, are you?"

"Not if I can get a lunch out of it."

"I see. Well…okay." She seemed to consider it a moment. Then she said, "I'm leaving town, Pug."

"You mean no time for lunch?"

"There's time for lunch. I mean, like leaving, going away, you know? If they offered us anything, I'll take it at this point."

"Are you all right, girl?"

"All right? Hey, I'm Lady Bounce." She sounded anything but.

Rayford Huddleston had a gold crown on a lower bicuspid that glinted when he talked. He never seemed to use more than five words in a sentence, never suggested indecision or lowered himself to the "ahs" or "you knows" that afflict most everyone else. When he wasn't in a trial, he ran triathlons or something similar. Moments after Pug got off the phone Huddleston came out. He ushered Pug into his office, and without further introduction walked to a tape player on his desk, pushed the play button, then stood looking out the window. Pug listened for a full five minutes before he reached over and turned it off.

"The quality," he said, "sounds professional."

"I'd say so." Huddleston turned. "The results of our discovery. I've listened to it all. There's obviously been some editing. But there's enough there to get the picture. It ends when you lose the hand. I've done some calculations, Pug." He motioned toward his desk. "The article was correct to the dollar. It may be embarrassing, but it's not libel."

"Where'd they get the damn thing?" Pug asked, feeling embarrassed indeed. "Who taped it?"

"I got the impression the paper needed someone's permission to release it. They refuse to say who or where." Huddleston was obviously struggling to control his anger. "They don't have to say. The question is, did they print the truth? The answer is on the tape. Unless you're prepared to testify that the tape is a fraud."

"No."

"Then I suggest we file a dismissal. You proceed in the face of this and you're risking a malicious prosecution suit. We both are."

"Goddamn it! Somebody was spying on me. It was Lackner's hotel room. That son of a bitch must have wired it."

Huddleston ejected the tape and handed it over. "That's your business. You told me you had been libeled."

Pug swallowed hard. "I apologize for that, Ray. I needed to find out who told them. You're right. Dismiss the damn thing."

"You know as well as I do. A lawyer's biggest headache…"

"…his client lying to him. Yeah, I know." Pug stood up. "You got me this, and I thank you for that. There's a son of a bitch in my office right now who needs to hear it."

There sat Vince Lackner, the narrow, brown eyes, looking like a caged wolf. Pug ignored him.

"Becky," he shouted going directly into his office, "get me that damn tape player out of the library." He grabbed the phone book, and finding the numbers he wanted, punched them into the phone. "Get me Patricia Pendar," he said when the party answered.

"Yes."

"This is Pug Bolcar. Who gave you that fucking tape?"

"Pug Bolcar," Ms. Pendar said in a bemused sort of way, as if recalling a humorous moment from the distant past. This followed by a slow husky chortle that he found infuriating.

"That's right. Who gave you the goddamned tape?"

The laugh again. "You're not being serious."

"You'll see if I'm being serious."

"What are you going to do, Lawrence 'Pug' Bolcar, ace lawyer," Patricia Pendar said sweetly, "sue me?"

Pug chose rather to slam down the receiver. "Becky!" he shouted just before she came through the door. He grabbed the tape player from her hands and put it on his desk. "Get Lackner in here, and close the door!"

In the outer office, Vince Lackner had been doing deep breathing exercises in an effort to stay calm as he waited for Pug to arrive. He entered now, his leather jacket unzipped. He stopped at the corner of Pug's desk.

"Pug, we have a problem. A serious problem."

"Listen to this," Pug said, removing the tape from his briefcase.

"It's an emergency."

"Sit down and listen, Vince."

Lackner sat down and Pug put on the tape. They both listened in silence for a few minutes.

"That's…that's the poker game?" Vince asked, stunned.

"That's right, Vince, every belch and dropped chip. I got it from the *Courier*."

"I don't understand."

Pug leaned forward, both hands on the desk, his large chest suspended over the tape player that continued to reproduce the idle shifting of bodies, the muttered words and the tumbling rattle of plastic chips that had taken place late that night three months earlier.

"Goddamn it, somebody taped our poker game and gave it to the newspaper! That's how they printed what I lost. Somebody gave them this."

"But…" Lackner stopped suddenly, thinking.

"But what, Vince?"

Vince paused. When he continued he spoke very carefully, "Then, it wasn't you?"

"Me!" Pug shouted, trembling with rage. "I told you it wasn't me!"

"It saved you fifty-five thousand."

"You think I taped myself and then turned the damned thing into the paper so I could cause myself all this grief?"

Vince Lackner's narrow eyes continued to stare at the moving tape.

"As if I knew in advance I was going to lose?"

Vince shrugged, and seeing the shrug, Pug found he needed to walk to the far corner of the room.

After a moment Vince said, "Pug, listen to me." He then explained that Carlos had returned to San Francisco the day before. He had insisted that Lackner fly him over the Rosyland property to see what was going on. They had circled the property several times. There was no sign of activity. No plants, no water lines, no greenhouses. No indication the road had even been used.

Pug had walked back to the desk, turned off

"Mom."

"Lo, a voice! Are we to anticipate a pronouncement?"

"Shut up, Mom! Can't you see you're only making it worse." Elisa blew her nose.

Ruth was smiling. "Should I get a stone tablet or are those provided? I can't ever remember. Did God give Moses the tablets or did he just dictate?"

"Mom, I'm going to see Rafe tonight."

"Let me make sure I get this down," Ruth said, reaching for a pencil and the shopping list. "'See Rafe tonight.' Yes? There's more, I suspect."

"Mom."

"Well, out with it. I know it's not granite but we can finalize it later." Ruth lit a new cigarette from the old, which she then snuffed in the ash tray. She looked at Elisa, her thin eyebrows plucked and drawn and raised inquisitively.

"I'm going back to the company. Back to Oregon."

"Ah." Ruth set down the pad and the part. She looked older suddenly, thin in the neck. The globlets at her jowls hanging like thick tears. This was the whipped look, a familiar stratagem to Elisa, but it touched her as it always did because the tragedy of her mother was that though she slid from role to role she believed them all.

"I don't think we're helping each other," Elisa added by way of explanation. "I think it's just the opposite."

"It's all my fault, I know it," Ruth admitted. Elisa sighed and started to protest but Ruth wasn't listening.

the tape and was punching the intercom, directing Becky to bring him a cup of coffee.

"So what? That's not my problem. You hired that guy. If he ran off with the money, that's your problem." Now he was poking in the drawer of his desk in search of a cigar. He needed something to do with his hands if he was going to keep them off Lackner.

"That's not the way Carlos sees it," Vince said. "He's making threats."

Pug's hands stopped and he looked up. Just then Becky came in with the coffee. The two men were silent. Did Mr. Lackner want tea? Mr. Lackner shook his head.

"What kind of threats?" Pug asked when Becky had closed the door.

"You'd better check on the whereabouts of your daughter."

"I know where my daughter is." Pug had found a cigar. He removed the wrapper and began to moisten the surface. "She's at work. I saw her this morning, a block from her office."

Vince persisted. "You'd better call her. Carlos wants to meet you on the Rosyland property. He told me he had a way of getting you there."

Pug put down the cigar and reached for his directory. He called the number and was told Elisa had not come in. There had been no word from her.

"But she has to be there," he insisted. "I saw her a couple of hours ago just outside your door."

"I'm sorry," the voice said. "She hasn't come in."

Pug broke the connection and punched in seven more numbers. "Ruth," he said, "is Binks there?"

"She's at work, Pug, you know that. You want the number?"

"I have the number. She's not there."

"She has to be. She left this morning. We're having lunch at Clandestines."

"What time?"

"Twelve-thirty."

"I'll meet you there."

"Pug, what's going on?"

"I don't know. I'll meet you at Clandestines."

Pug set down the receiver. He picked up the cigar and lit it. It tasted terrible and a moment later he smashed it out in the ashtray. The thing to do now was to not kill the man sitting across the desk from him.

— 35 —

About eight-thirty that Friday morning Elisa Gilbert and Harold Manx crossed the Golden Gate Bridge in comfortable traffic. On the tape deck Vladimir Horowitz was playing a Beethoven sonata to a live audience. The car's interior smelled of wintergreen. Clouds were breaking up and to the east a field of sun covered the inlet to San Francisco Bay, Alcatraz glinting in the light. His back straight, his eyes on the road, the steering wheel gripped with both hands, Elisa thought that Harold Manx would make an excellent model for a safe-driving campaign, one of those oh-so-earnest films high school students are subjected to, a voiceover going on about posture, mindfulness and sobriety. Except there was no voice. He had not said a word since he shushed her. Just his breath, a heavy, slightly raspy sound.

He had become considerably older, she realized. Heavier, graying, thicker in the jowls, a start of a ponch above the belt. Not older from that moment or two when she saw him at Lake Tahoe. Her state of mind that afternoon, being what it was, she had hardly noticed him at all beyond the ridiculous sweater. But from when they had lived in adjoining houses and Janet had been part of both their lives, fourteen years ago now.

"How's your mother?" he asked suddenly as they approached the tunnel north of the bridge. Two crinkled cars pushed off onto the median were all that remained of the accident Elisa and Ruth had heard described on the radio that morning.

"Mom's struggling," Elisa said. "She and dad got divorced last year."

Harold said he had heard something about that. He was not surprised. She had put up with a lot over the years.

"I knew her," he added when they had passed through the tunnel and emerged back into the light. "Before she was married."

Elisa was surprised.

"Not personally. I knew her singing. I saw her perform several times. There had been a community chorus in Oakland. And a choir at Mills. She sang with those. Solos at times. She had a fine voice, your mother. Her low notes were particularly rich and she could project them. That's uncommon with a soprano. After she married…after that she didn't sing much."

"Well, Michael was born soon after. Then, in a while I came along."

Harold Manx did not seem impressed by these excuses. "I don't think she was encouraged to keep it up," he said, adding after a moment, "It's the drinking, I suppose."

"Yes."

"I'm sorry to hear that. We weren't close as neighbors, not socially. But I remember an honesty about your mother, a fine intelligence. And a sense of vulnerability. All that came through in her singing."

Strange about the singing. Elisa's first reaction at the mention of it was embarrassment. Her mother drunk at a party, singing too loudly at the piano, going on too long while the audience drifted away, looking at each other in dismay. But she had other memories. A wedding or two, her mother practicing when she was very young. She would walk through the house, running the scales. The sound was alarming to a small child, frightful. Her mother seemed possessed of some great, uncaring power. And yet there was strength there as well, an independence, a sense of purpose. And she remembered the lullabies after the last story had been read and the book closed. Her voice gentle and comforting, and yes, Harold Manx was right, vulnerable.

"Is Noony well?" she asked, the subject being mothers. She had been about to call him Mr. Manx, which was what she had always called him. But it seemed too formal now and she wasn't ready just yet for Harold.

"Mother is dead."

"I'm sorry. Was it recently?"

"Early this morning."

"Oh!"

"It's a blessing that she finally died."

"Still it must be a shock," Elisa said. "I'm sorry for your loss."

"They fed her a kind of gruel that they forced down her throat with a gray plastic tube. A terrible thing to watch." He paused as though struggling to control his voice. "Sometimes she would suck on a bit of orange, but you couldn't count on that. They never bothered to put her teeth in. Lydia thought she was content, but Lydia was kidding herself. It's understandable," he added, glancing over. "Lydia always looks for the good. And she and Noony were very close."

"It's too bad you can't be with her today. I'm sure you could comfort each other."

"No, Lydia is very strong," he said firmly. "She can handle it."

There it was, that tone again. Janet, and she too, used to shudder when they heard it. At the sound of it all questions had been answered, the discussion ended, everything settled. Like Lydia, Janet was supposed to be very strong. And strong meant seeing the world the way Harold Manx saw it. Doing what he said needed to be done. Down the street the students at Berkeley were trampling everything decent. Huey Newton and his friends were running around Oakland calling policeman 'pigs' while over in San Francisco the streets were filled with drugged-out hippies. Everywhere the music was disgusting.

That had been Harold Manx's view of the period. And Janet Manx, though a mere child at the time, was being raised as the lawman's daughter. She was the example of how it should be done. It sometimes seemed as though Janet alone was destined to stand in the face of this anarchy, to turn back the tide. Poor, bespeckled Janet who loved books about horses set in far off places, books about people who died doing the right thing. "You said this was about Janet," Elisa offered, inviting him again to explain. They were moving north toward San Rafael. Condominiums and apartment complexes stacked on the hillsides like toys, the lovely green fed on winter's rains. She had been terrified of this man, she remembered now.

Harold Manx placed a new breath freshener in his mouth. He kept the roll in the pocket of his vest and he was adept at removing it with his right hand, peeling back the paper a notch with the nail of his thumb, separating a mint and slipping it into his mouth while his left hand remained all the while in control of the steering wheel. Elisa recognized suddenly that these mannerisms, so practiced and ritualized, were stalling devices, mechanisms to control the pace, employed to maintain his sense of control.

"I received a call yesterday," he said when at last he

spoke. "A male voice. No name given. He claimed to be a friend of Janet's."

"Really? So, she's in contact?"

"No," Harold Manx said, cutting her off with that tone again. "It could be a hoax, or even a trap. Over the years I have created many enemies. It's the nature of my work. That's why I said nothing to Lydia. After what she's been through another disappointment would break her heart. We had her back once before, you know. Would have, but your father...." The tape had ended some time before. He turned it over and pushed the play button. "Anyway, the voice on the phone said she wanted to meet with me. And here's where you come in. She would meet me, the voice said, but only if Lydia were present. I responded by saying that was impossible. I said that because I was still thinking the call probably had nothing to do with Janet. Someone was setting a trap for me. So, I suggested you in Lydia's place."

"I don't understand."

"My words to him were, 'What if I brought Binks?' I wanted to see how he reacted to that. If it was just some enemy of mine, he would have no idea who Binks was. How would he react? Anyway, there was a pause on the line, and then the voice said, 'That would be acceptable.'"

"I still don't understand."

"So, I'm hoping Janet really was with this guy and when she heard your name she agreed to the meeting."

"But why me? Why Lydia? Why anyone?"

"She's afraid I might try to detain her, obviously.

With you present that would be less likely."

"Will you...?"

"No, of course not. Janet's an adult now. Her life is her business. Anyway, that's all I know. We are supposed to be at a particular telephone booth at a certain time. I assume we will get further instructions at that point."

Elisa had turned and was sitting with her back against the door. "This is so exciting!" she exclaimed after a moment. "Aren't you excited?"

"Yes," he said, though he looked anything but.

"You know what this is, Harold? This is like field trips! Remember middle school, the endless routines day after day, the same boring classes, the same dead-dull teachers, and then one morning you walk into the homeroom and the teacher announces a field trip. You're all going to a fish hatchery, maybe, or the botanical gardens, or an almond orchard, a field trip. Something unexpected. A break from the madding routine of school. This is like that. A field trip, but this is even better because we don't know where we're going or what's going to happen. We could see Janet, or like you say, it could be a trap. Glad you brought that pistol along, Harold. We just might have to shoot our way out!"

Elisa felt giddy. Of course it was Janet, she was sure of it. And she was very happy that she would have some small part to play in it all. She reached down and took up Harold's gray homburg and plopped it on her head. It came to rest at her eyebrows, bending her ears out like they'd been curled. She pulled down the sun visor and examined herself in the mirror, tapping the top of the hat so it sank even lower on her head.

"You may just have lost a hat, Harold. This just may be the price you pay to have my services in this matter." That sentence sounded just like something her father might say, and hearing it made her laugh.

But Harold Manx was not laughing. To Elisa, at that moment he looked very sad. A large serious, sad man, both hands gripping the wheel, bushy eyebrows clinging like brambles to the side of a cliff. Seeing him thus she felt shamed and thoughtless. His daughter gone for years. And now on this very morning, his mother dead.

But the hat, she might just hold on to the hat.

As Robin Durham watched Harold Manx walk out of the office that morning, he felt very uneasy. The expression on the man's face when he had mentioned the Bolcar investigation had been bizarre. The only sense it made to Robin was that Randall Chin had violated his confidence and told the Chief about Elisa, about Robin's involvement with her. "Your job is done," Manx had said, meaning his work on the Bolcar investigation. Or had he meant more than that? Was the Chief making inquiries behind his back? Once all the information had come in, been collated and analyzed, was his *job* done, meaning his career with the department? That's the way the Chief was said to work, slowly, methodically, thoroughly. Then a quiet meeting in the inner sanctum followed by a shameful handing-over of keys, badge, files and weapon, a cleaning out of desk drawers, the photos of the girls swept off the desk and into a cardboard box conveniently provided for the purpose. A shoulder-slumping walk to the elevators.

Well, if his job was done, at least on the Bolcar investigation, the one thing he could do was telephone Elisa. He despised himself for not having contacted her earlier. He could have said something, had the decency at least to tell her he thought of her. But such was his respect for the omnipotence of Harold Manx that he put on his jacket and walked for two blocks before calling from a public phone. She wasn't at work. Yes, she had been scheduled to work. No one seemed to know where she was or when she might arrive. Who was calling? Robin declined to give his name. He would call back later.

Maybe his imagination was running away with him, he decided when he had returned to his desk. He should talk with Randall Chin. Robin had seen Chin come in earlier, but he had gone straight into a meeting with Fernald and three unfamiliar men and was still in there. Something was up.

Shortly after noon, the department received a phone call from Vince Lackner. Robin happened to be standing near the receptionist's desk at the time. His report finished, he was waiting around to talk to Chin. The receptionist, after trying unsuccessfully to sooth Lackner, looked at Robin with a pleading expression. With her hand over the mouthpiece she asked if he could please talk to this guy. He wants to speak with someone in authority but both Chin and Fernald were still in that damned, interminable meeting.

"How can I help you?" Robin asked, hoping Lackner would not recognize his voice.

"I need to talk to someone who has some authority around there."

"What's your problem?"

"My problem is your boss. He made a deal with me and I don't trust him. I've gone way out on a limb to help the department and all I get is grief. Manx is never satisfied. He tells me he's done with me and then he's back demanding more. I risk my life and my business for the department and now I find out that all this time he's been spying on me." Vince Lackner's voice was revving to a high whine. "And here's another thing. Your boss is involved in criminal activity himself. He's worse than the guys he's chasing. I know that for a fact. He kidnapped someone this morning and he's insisting on my help."

It was becoming clear from both the tone and the content that Vince Lackner was experiencing some kind of mental breakdown.

"Help him do what, Mr. Lackner?"

"Help him trick this guy."

"Trick this guy? The guy he kidnapped?" Robin rolled his eyes at the receptionist. She was laughing, hand over her mouth.

"No, he kidnapped a girl."

"I see. Mr. Manx kidnapped a girl." This for the benefit of the receptionist.

"The guy's daughter. The suspect's daughter. There has to be a file on this somewhere. It's a whole operation. I just want to make sure it's in that file that I am never bothered again."

"I'll need to know more, Mr. Lackner, if I going to locate this file you speak of. Do you have a name? I must have a name if I'm going to pull the file."

"It's all part of the operation. You obviously know nothing about this. Look in the file. Pug Bolcar, that's the guy he's after."

The receptionist was still laughing, wiping her eyes with a facial tissue, but Robin Durham had stopped smiling. "Are you saying Mr. Manx has kidnapped Mr. Bolcar's daughter?"

"Look in the file. There probably some legal way he can get around calling it kidnapping, but it's wrong, pure and simple. But I want assurances. If I'm going to go through with this, I need something in writing. I called my lawyer and of course he's unavailable and I call you and you're acting like it's a joke. This is no joke. Look in the file. I want something in writing that is ironclad, you hear me?"

There was a moment before Robin Durham could manage any words. Then he said, "I can assure you, Mr. Lackner, the department does not engage in criminal…"

"I got to go," Vince Lackner said, cutting him off. "Just remember what I said. I want it ironclad." Then he hung up.

"Oh my," said the receptionist. "What was that name he kept shouting?"

"Bolcar," Robin said pensively. "Pug Bolcar."

"I'll look, but I don't think we have an active investigation by that name. It doesn't sound at all familiar to me."

— 36 —

Vince Lackner hung up because Pug Bolcar and his ex wife were walking back to the bank of phones.

"She's not here," Pug said. It was not yet twelve-thirty but Pug had insisted they get to the restaurant early. His former wife had met them there. She seemed to Vince Lackner somewhat hysterical, looking about wildly. "And I just remembered," Pug continued, "that I'm supposed to have lunch with a client. She's waiting at Gilroy's. I've got to call Gilroy's, Ruth. A client is waiting for me there."

Lackner found himself alone with Pug's ex-wife, a woman he had met once a couple of years before and remembered as being much younger. She was fidgeting with her hands, an uneasy dance was going on from the hips down as if she had need of a toilet.

"We had a big fight, my daughter and I," the woman told him. "Just last night. Then this morning I was obnoxious. I drove her out, my own daughter. Why do we do things like that?"

Vince had no idea of what the woman was talking about. He wanted to be away from her. She was uncorked. She might suddenly start talking loudly or even begin to shout, yell out for her daughter, who knows? Nothing terrorized Vince Lackner so much as the possibility of a public scene. Besides, his own mind was preoccupied with Harold Manx. He needed time to think it through. Manx might have been following his every move for months. What did that mean for his life? Ruth Bolcar had stopped talking. She was staring at him, waiting for a response.

"Hmm," he said.

"She left her husband just after Christmas," the woman went on, glancing at Bolcar's thick back bent over the telephone. "Terrible story, the poor girl. She needed a refuge and came home to be with me. I loved every minute having her there, but I drove her away. I got drunk. I interfered with her life. I yelled at her. I treated her like shit." She took a tissue from her purse, dried her eyes and looked around. "What time is it?"

"Twenty-five till."

"Binks is always late anyway," Ruth Bolcar said.

They waited in silence, watching the door. When Pug joined them it was almost a quarter till one.

"Try Rafe again, Pug," Ruth Bolcar said. "She's gone back to Rafe."

"I just did. There's no answer."

"I made her hate me," the woman said. "Now she's gone."

"Don't blame yourself, Ruth," Pug said. "It's not your fault."

"She was prepared to say anything, just to get out of the house. She had no intention of meeting me for lunch. She's done with me. I'll probably never see her again."

There was a surprising tenderness in the way Pug Bolcar reached out and placed his arm around the shoulders of his former wife. Even Vince Lackner noticed it, lost in his own hard calculations.

"Do you want a drink, Ruth?" Pug asked.

"No, no thank you. I do, but I'm not going to."

"All right. Well, don't blame yourself. We don't know yet what happened, but I don't think it was your fault. Vince and I are going to go now. Do you want to stay awhile? I'll get you a table."

"I don't think so. She's not coming is, she?"

"I don't believe she is. I'll tell David to call you at home if she comes in."

"She's meeting Rafe somewhere," Ruth Bolcar said. "She was meeting him tonight anyway, but she probably thought I would try to interfere. Or maybe she's doing it for me, Pug. Do you think? Maybe she wants me to get help…"

"Maybe that's it, Ruth."

She was still talking as Pug Bolcar led her away. He spoke with the maitre d' and then walked her outside to find a cab. Lackner followed at a respectable distance. The sun was out but a cool breeze was whistling down the canyon between the buildings and Ruth Bolcar's neck seemed to sink into the collar of her jacket as she waited at the curb. Bolcar was talking to her, his eyes on hers. Lackner could not hear what they were saying and did not care to listen. Just get her a cab, he thought, so we can get on with this. It occurred to him, though, as they waited, that no paper or solemn promise could ever protect him from Harold Manx. That man held all the power. He was immensely clever and totally devious. What he had done to Pug Bolcar with the newspaper and then the idea that Bolcar had done it himself. The man had great skill and no qualms; his position gave him license to hound a person to his grave.

Finally, a cab came and Pug's ex-wife was driven away.

"I want the police in on this," Pug said when he came over. "If that Colombian bastard has kidnapped my daughter I'll see him hanged. This is my family we're talking about. What's with this guy anyway? Is he crazy or something?" They were walking rapidly toward Lackner's car. Pug was puffing. "He lays a hand on her, I'll kill the son of a bitch."

"The police will just be a problem, Pug. What are you going to tell them? That you had this deal to grow marijuana that went bad?"

"That the bastard kidnapped my daughter, that's what I'll tell them."

"Carlos just wants to talk. If you're willing to talk, nobody gets hurt. Call in the cops and you get SWAT teams and choppers. Not to mention newspapers and TV cameras. Push Carlos to the wall like that and bad things might happen. We'll make up a story about Jake. He had to go back to Hawaii, death in the family. We buy some time. Then we deal with him on our terms."

"Christ. All right, let's get up there." But then as they were driving out to the airport Pug had had another idea. "Maybe I should just pay the son of a bitch. Pay him and get it over with. Then call in the damn cops."

"Fine, tell him you'll pay him."

"Let's stop at your office. Give Tripper a call. He might be able to scare up the money in a couple of hours, assuming he's not out beating the bushes for some seven-foot jock. Then I got the money when we get there."

The man was in a panic, Lackner realized. But his own job was simple, at least up to a certain point. Get Bolcar up there, that was his job. Later it might get complicated.

"Not now, Pug. The longer he sits there…"

"You think he's going to turn her over on a promise? What's he, a fool?"

"He's not holding her for the money, damnit," Lackner said, irritated. "He just wants to talk."

Pug Bolcar took a deep breath and sat back in the seat. "All right. Let's talk."

By the time Ramona Livingston had reached her apartment that Friday morning it was almost three and she was speeding on some strange chemical-free euphoria. Emptying her purse and coat pocket, she totaled the take. More than six hundred dollars. She had a vision of herself. She was Lady Bounce. She operated behind appearances, her true self unseen. She would be a mover of assets, a creator of events. Men would seek her out. She would be like one of those exclusive restaurants, so confident its door was unmarked except perhaps by a lamp and a small plaque. The men would come filled with desire and in fear of her power. They would want sex, of course, but she would be untouchable except when she chose, and her choices would be free and spontaneous. Or maybe she would keep a man, a young, gentle man who was pursuing some craft or art. A poet maybe, or a composer of serious music. There had been such a young man in one of her classes at the university. Crew-necked sweaters, clever, he had charmed her, thought her innocent, taken her for coffee. But her life had been too complicated, her scramble too intense to fit him in. She would always move fast. She would have havens on different continents and in various climates. She would outfit a plane as others do travel homes. But never, never again would she have to submit herself to a man for money or power. That part of her life was over. And fear would be a thing of the past.

But the fear was not yet forgotten. As she lay down her spinning thoughts turned and began to claw at her. The men of the evening past grew ominous. Their qualities mixed and magnified. They were out there and they were angry. And anger made men huge. They loomed over you like large animals. They acted without warning and with no regret. Your fear enraged them, made them impersonal like some force of nature. Huddled in her bed, waiting for the sleeping pill to take hold, Ramona felt she had slapped God. And she waited now to see what He would do.

The pill did let her sleep—caused her to

oversleep as it turned out. But when she woke all the apprehensions had accrued like interest on a debt. She managed to call Pug's office and then later Pug called her. She was afraid to take a tranquilizer. If she was going to leave the apartment she had to be alert. Her fear, as terrible as it was, was the ally she needed if she was to go out there. And there were things to do. She started packing boxes. She called storage facilities. It all had to be done carefully. Several months' rent on the storage unit had to be paid in advance. No forwarding addresses. She didn't have one anyway, wasn't certain even where she would go. There were bank accounts, a start on some investments. She had to take all those records with her. She would need more cash. And she had to get to the airport.

At Gilroy's, Ramona asked for and received a corner table away from the windows that faced the street. She wore a dark turtleneck sweater to hide the bruises and dark glasses to cover her swollen eyes and she sat with her back against the wall. Pug was supposed to have been there at noon but he was late. Ramona drank bottled water and waited behind the menu, a large heavy construction backed with rice paper. Her glasses in combination with the dim lighting made the menu illegible. But that was all right. She wasn't hungry anyway.

When a waiter came and asked her name, she refused at first to give it. He had a dark beard; already by mid-day it cast a shadow over his face. There was a phone call, he explained, for a Ramona

Livingston. Who was it from, she wanted to know. The man did not know. She scowled at this, thinking him incompetent or perhaps devious, but she went to the phone.

Pug wanted to make it tomorrow. He had an emergency, a family matter, he called it. There would be no tomorrow, not in San Francisco, not for her, but she did not tell him that just then. He needed her approval on the settlement amount and she gave it. After his fee, the discovery costs he had fronted and the medical bills she had not yet paid, the amount coming to her would be less than half of the total. Some of that, he reminded her, would be taxable. And if she had the cosmetic surgery, that would take more of it.

Still, it was a leg up and it cheered her.

"Can I get the money today?"

That was impossible. Papers had to be drafted and signed. Checks needed to be written by insurance companies and mailed. It might take a month.

To Ramona Livingston a month seemed a long way from where she was. Even tomorrow was a distant port.

"What about tomorrow?" Pug wanted to know. "Could we have lunch?"

Not with her. Lady Bounce was going away. It was like the snow she remembered coming to the Palouse of eastern Washington, the way it blew and settled on everything. The way it cleaned a farmyard, erasing all the tracks, the traces of habits, the memories of where you had fallen and cut your knee, the routes to and from outbuildings. You could step out on that new snow of a morning and you, too, were new and light. You could set a new course and it would be fresh. It would reflect the exact you, the new you, the you you were at that moment. That, at least, was the way it seemed to Ramona Livingston standing in Gilroy's around twelve-thirty on that Friday, her eyes behind the sunglasses watching the door.

— 37 —

For Lydia Manx that Good Friday time passed slowly as she in her active imagination thought it must have passed for Jesus. Seven utterances in the hours he hung there. At the birth there had been angels, the stunning star, the shepherds amazed. But no divine presence witnessed his slow dying.

Good Friday to Lydia was a story of the absence of hope, the experience of God not being present. It was a day when physical matter lost its grace, she was thinking as she prepared her breakfast of cereal and fruit. Objects would be heavy, their edges harsh, their texture gritty. Dust clings, flies buzz and bite. There's a crick in the neck, a kink in the knee. One senses the violence of digestion, the resistance of hair, the weariness of the heart's beating. Sounds are isolated and distinct, falling away. The sky is high, distant. Prayers go off and touch nothing. Everyone is alone, isolated in his own itchy skin.

Hecklers pass the soldiers and the crowd gathered on the hill; slurs are thrown, anger is expressed. And pain, of course. The sheer agony of extracting oneself from a young and healthy body. But mostly, Lydia thought, it must have been an experience of time slowly passing, the sensation of waiting. For him, as well as for the others. The soldiers waiting for the three men to die so they could go home to their evening meals. The curious standing about, many leaving before it was over, bored, having business to attend to. His mother, others who followed him, waiting at a distance. At first they probably expected a miracle but hope faded as the hours stretched out and the sun moved toward the horizon. Finally it grew dark and they were still there, him hanging and they waiting, waiting without hope until the end.

The call had come in around six from the nursing home. It got Lydia out of bed. She telephoned Harold's office immediately but the lines were set on hold. She tried repeatedly for fifteen minutes and always got the same result. She waited awhile. When she tried again she was told her husband had left. The person taking the message did not know when he would return.

After breakfast Lydia prepared a cake and placed it in the oven. A funeral was scheduled for two that afternoon and she was on the funeral committee. The ladies of the committee prepared a meal for the mourners, set up tables in the church fellowship room. It was good to share food after a funeral, she believed. It healed and comforted. It drew one away from the grave's edge and back to the business of life. Who, she wondered, had prepared food that night for the mourners in Jerusalem?

Mid-afternoon, when the work of the funeral committee was finished, when the tables had been cleared and the dishes washed and dried and put away, Lydia again called Harold's office. He was not there, and according to his secretary he had not phoned in. She offered her condolences.

Lydia drove alone to the nursing home. Noony's room had been cleaned out, the bed made. Her possessions collected and stored in the office of the administrator's secretary. There were a couple of robes, a pair of slippers, a few toilet articles, the small ivy that had stood on the window sill that Lydia used to tend when she visited, a few cards left over from Christmas and Noony's February birthday, cards that Lydia had taped on the wall beside her bed.

None of it spoke of her mother-in-law, or had her touch, which had been brusque and firm. Lydia remembered suddenly that brusqueness, saw Noony again, whole and hardy. Death had a way of opening a life, spreading it out as if upon a scroll, and she was free now to consider Noony from any point without special concern for the old shell of a woman at the end.

One of the aides, Alison, an African-American woman who had known Noony when she was still somewhat active, walked with Lydia out to the car. This woman, who had washed Noony and changed her, who had combed her hair and turned her in bed and lifted her in and out of her wheelchair, was obviously saddened by Noony's death. Noony's fate was the same as every one of Alison's patients. They all came to await dying, but clearly Alison did not generalize in that way. Noony had been a personal presence for her, an individual with habits of eating and sleeping and defecating, a physical being with weight, with crannies that needed to be scrubbed, with a certain texture to her hair.

Lydia remembered then the Biblical story of a fellow named Joseph, not the Joseph who was Mary's husband, some other Joseph, who "went in boldly" to Pilate and asked for the body of Jesus which he then took down, wrapped in fine linen and laid in a sepulcher that he sealed with a large stone. In that dark hour when violence had once again had its way with life and death had come and hope had fled, a person for no gain had parted with some treasure and had risked his safety to do tenderly what had seemed to him the right and proper thing to do. And this woman, too, standing now beside the car, had done as much for Noony. The idea of it brought tears to Lydia's eyes. Alison probably thought the tears were for Noony, not realizing they were for her. But acts of grace had always struck Lydia with surprising force.

Back at the house Lydia received a phone call from her daughter. Janet reacted to Noony's death with a sharp intake of air. Hearing her soft sobs Lydia realized that Janet had harbored a shy fantasy that they would all eventually find a way to go back and start over. That her time away would be forgiven. No, not simply forgiven, erased.

"How did Dad take it?" Janet would ask before hanging up. It was the first time she had referred to

Harold as something other than "he".

"He doesn't know yet," Lydia said.

As she pondered her daughter's question she thought that Harold would experience an undercurrent of conflicting emotions. He would be capable and calm, but she would have to watch in the days following to see if she could be of help to him in some unspoken way. With these thoughts, and after another fruitless call to the office—he had said he would be late—Lydia changed her clothes and ventured out to the quiet of her garden.

"Where is this telephone booth?"

"It's a ways yet," Harold Manx said.

It had become country almost before she realized it. The sun was brilliant now and they were beginning to see the first signs of vineyards, nearly dormant at this time of year. The mature vines cut back, their thick short branches spread out like arms on the wires connecting the support poles. Visible in the new vineyards were white poles set at precise distances, each marking a newly planted vine. The poles, as they drove past, offered dancing patterns to the eye.

Inside the car there was no sense of dance. Harold could have been a robot driving along. When Elisa stopped talking, the interior filled with a thick silence smelling of wintergreen. She recognized now that something was amiss in that silence, some disconnect became evident to her. It wasn't just his silence. No, it was more than that. The possibility that he would be seeing his daughter again, seeing her this day for the first time in years, shouldn't that produce in him something, a sense of anticipation, an eagerness, a feeling of excitement? But she found none of that. Harold Manx struck her as solemn, distant, devoid of anything that might suggest enthusiasm. Perhaps he dared not hope, she thought, trying to justify his demeanor to herself. And of course he was in mourning for his mother. Even if he had thought it better for her to have finally died, still he would naturally experience a sense of loss. But these justifications did not resolve the incongruity troubling her. Like a style of dress once a la mode and now discarded, her sense of adventure, even celebration, had lost its allure. She had become uncomfortable, and so she talked, homburg on her head, eyes peering out from under the brim, staring at the road ahead.

"When I saw you in that hotel lobby in Tahoe three months ago I probably didn't tell you why I was there. That a few hours before I had found my husband having sex with another woman." She paused there for a moment, letting it sink in. "I say 'having sex,'" she continued. "They certainly weren't 'sleeping' together, far from that, and I can't bring myself to admit that they were making love. I mean, grappling in a darkened prop room, clothes thrown about, both of them married, though not to each other. That is not making love, in my estimation. There are other words, but the best I can muster is 'having sex.' If you have another suggestion, Harold, let me know."

Harold Manx did not suggest an alternative.

"You seemed to have been crying," he said.

"Not surprising, I probably had been. I could not believe he had done that. My Rafe? My husband? I kept asking myself: Who is this person? This can't be the man I have loved and married. Where has he gone? We'd been married over four years. Before the marriage we'd lived together for almost two years, nineteen months to be exact. I had never been unfaithful to him that whole time, never been seriously tempted, not after we moved in together. And I never had any suspicion he'd betrayed me. After, of course, I began rethinking the possibilities, all the women we have known, the opportunities he would have had.

"He denies there have been others, though he admits that with this woman it happened more than once. He tells me now they broke it off, that it's over. That's what he says, but who knows? That's the thing about betrayal, isn't it? Once someone has betrayed you, how can you know?"

Harold had nothing to add, though he did reach up to the visor, pull down a pair of sunglasses and put them on. To Elisa, Harold Manx looked awful in those sunglasses. He would probably look pretty silly, she decided, in any kind of sunglasses, but these in particular were definitely ridiculous.

"Harold," she asked, changing the subject rather abruptly, "did I tell you what I have become? My profession?"

"An office girl, I understand."

An *office girl?* Elisa almost choked. Now there

was a phrase. It sounded like somebody's pet. In the
same class with say "lap dog" or "house cat."

"No, no, not that! That's temporary. My career?"

"Career?"

"I'm a costume designer. That's who I am, Harold!"
And it struck her just then that, yes, that *is* who she
is. "I work for a theatre company. Up in Oregon. A
large, regional theatre company. It's a profession, and
the company is prestigious. And let me tell you, I'm
good at what I do. I dress the actors the way Janet and
I used to dress our dolls. Well, I don't dress them, of
course. I mean I design their costumes. That's what I
was doing when I found my husband…you know….
And I'm going back. That's what I have decided. I'm
going back to Oregon, back to the company, back to
my career."

"I see," Harold Manx said without enthusiasm.

The man was thoroughly irritating.

"Well, Harold," she said now. "I am sorry to
tell you this, but as a professional, I feel obligated.
Those sunglasses don't work. Those sunglasses are
in fact ugly."

She had hoped to shock him, get him off his
dime. But who could say what was going on behind
those absurd things? What he said was, "They serve
the purpose."

"Only a man," she responded, shaking her head.
"For one thing they are too big and heavy. The lens-
es are absurdly dark, the frames thick and black and
cheap. In a word, ugly. Besides, sunglasses say something, Harold. Movie stars wear sunglasses, mobsters,

playboys, yachtsmen. Sunglasses are a statement. Any designer would tell you that.

"We add them to a costume with great caution because they say so much. And different styles say different things. If the ones you choose clash with the character you want to create you have a problem. I had this actor once, okay, he must have been ten years older than me. New to the company, but experienced. Been around. Anyway, this guy decided to add a pair of sunglasses to his costume. Part of his 'business' he told me. He wanted to take them on and off. He wanted to push them up on his head, pull them down, do stuff with them. His 'business.' Well, here's what I told that guy, Harold. I said, 'Your twitches, your walk, your accent, the way you hold a cup of coffee, all that is your "business," but sunglasses are part of your costume and your costume is *my* business. So take off the sunglasses.' And guess what? The director backed me up. One hundred percent."

Harold just kept driving.

"And now I have before me this straight-arrow, aging man in an immaculate white shirt, suit trousers and a handsome vest sewn from quality fabric, gray-patterned with just a hint of blue, a nicely matching gray and muted-blue tie, and what's that, a pair of ridiculous sunglasses. Nothing personal here, just a bit of professional advice if you don't mind. But before you put those sunglasses on, Harold, had I costumed you, I would have been proud. Here we have a respectable, distinguished, successful gentleman of late middle-age. And now what do we have? We have a...well, pardon me, but we have a clown."

Harold touched his right thumb and index finger to the frame of the glasses but then left them there and returned his hand to the wheel.

"See, here's the thing, Harold. When you walk into a theatre …"

"Lydia and I didn't go to plays. Movies either."

Elisa felt her breath catch for a moment. Yes, she had heard him right. He had used the past tense. Not about Noony, about Lydia, about his life with Lydia.

"Well, I'm sorry to hear that, Harold. But I'm giving a hypothetical here. So, pretend, okay? When you walk into a theatre—not just you—anybody. When you walk in, the playwright and those of us on the stage and behind it, we make certain assumptions. You have come to see and hear a story and we are going to present that story to you, that's one assumption. Another is that we have all the information that makes up the story and you in the audience have none. So everything we say to you, and by that I mean everything—the way the stage is designed and colored; the furniture, if there is furniture; the paintings on the walls, if there are paintings or walls; the way the stage is lit; the way the actors enter and exit; the way they stand in relationship to each other; the way they move and sit and walk; their clothing or lack of clothing; not to mention the words they say or sing, or shout; all of that is delivering information to you, the audience.

And all of that has to be consistent with the overall purpose. It has to advance the audience's knowledge about the story being told. In a way it's like a dream, see. We are leading you into a dream and we want nothing to happen that wakes you from that dream. So if a character's suit, his voice, his age, the cut of his hair, all of that say one thing, but his sunglasses say something else, then the members of the audience don't know what to think. They wake up for a second, confused, caught in an incongruity."

Yes, *an incongruity*. Elisa paused and glanced over at Harold. They had just entered the cute little town of Hopland. He slowed down. He was meticulous about honoring speed limits, but whether he was paying any attention to the buildings or the locals walking the sidewalks, or for that matter, listening to anything she said, she could not determine, hidden as he was behind those absurd glasses.

"So now," she continued, "if I were costuming a character such as what I have described, and I wanted the impression to come gradually to the audience that this successful-looking man is really a comic figure, or say, a sly, sinister figure, that there is something inside him, in other words, that is contrary to his exterior persona, I might dress him like you are dressed today. Tasteful, even elegant, but then at some point early on, I would have him put on a pair of absurd sunglasses like the ones you have on just now. That might wake them for a moment, but it's consistent with the dream, you see. It will start to educate the audience, make them begin to realize that this character is not all he seems to be. That's all I'm saying, Harold. That and one more thing. As soon as we get a chance I'm going to buy you a pair of sunglasses that are appropriate for who you are."

"You don't need to buy me any sunglasses, Binks."

"I want to buy you some sunglasses, Harold. I really can't stand the ones you're wearing. Besides, I have to pee. Find a place where I can pee, and maybe they'll have sunglasses for sale."

"All right," he said. But as they drove through Hopland they passed a couple of service stations, and Harold Manx did not stop.

— 38 —

After Robin Durham got off the phone with Vince Lackner he started toward the conference room where Chin was still in his meeting. It was his intention to demand a few minutes of Chin's time. He was about ten feet from the door when David Gordon came out. What the hell was Gordon doing in there?

"Come on," Gordon said, grabbing his sleeve and leading him to the elevator and from there to the steps outside the building. Coming from the fluorescent interior, the sunshine caused them to stand squinting at each other.

"What's going on in there?" Robin asked, irritated. "It's been all morning. I got to talk to Chin."

"I got grilled, baby, up and down the pike. Remember that little job I did for Manx? That title search up in Humboldt?"

"Yeah."

"They wanted the whole story. What did Manx say about it? What did he give me? What did I find? Did I have a copy of the documents, the legal description of the property? Any maps? The works. Chin's trying to prove something to these guys. He's after the Chief, I can smell it."

"Jesus." Robin turned and started back inside. "I got to get in there."

"Where you going?"

"After this, job hunting probably."

Not an occasion for polite knocks. Robin opened the door of the conference room and stepped inside. And there they sat in the unhappy haze of Chin's cigarette smoke: five loosened ties and five half-empty coffee cups, Chin, Fernald and the three strangers. Not a smile in the lot. No one rising to greet him with a shake. The three strangers, he now realized, were straight from higher up. Not happy with the business at hand and clearly displeased by his interruption. Like fans at a tennis match, they all turned their heads in unison. Toward him, and then toward Chin, looking for pest control. Get him out of here, the looks were saying.

"Durham." Chin alone got to his feet. He had the look of a man who wished he was still in his office playing with the little stone faces. "Nobody called you in here."

"It's an emergency, sir. I need to talk to you."

"Seskin is operations officer. Talk to Seskin." Chun turned away.

"About Bolcar?" Robin asked. "About the Chief

and Vince Lackner?" That got their attention. "In private, sir."

Chin stared at him, slack-jawed, and then looked around the table. Nobody was trusting anybody at this point. Chin's expression to Durham: Aren't you the guy dating Bolcar's daughter? The others were probably wondering if Chin had staged his entrance for dramatic effect. Manx was a legend, Chin the ambitious Asian. Was he fomenting a distasteful coup attempt? Four suits staring at Chin, expressions cold. But Chin went with it.

"All right," he said. "Five minutes, gentlemen."

They went to Chin's office, Chin trailing smoke and embattled vibes. "What you got?" he said, when the door was closed.

Durham had made notes of the salient features. The shredder this morning, the bags of trash. The call from Lackner. The second call he had made to Elisa's office after Lackner's call had come in.

"So, was she there?"

"No, sir, though she was supposed to be. They don't know where she is."

"Maybe she's home sick."

"I have that number as well," Robin admitted. "No answer there."

"When was this?"

"Lackner, twelve-thirty, or thereabouts. My call to her office immediately after. Then following that, the call to the home."

Chin started for the door. "Follow me."

In the conference room, Robin had to repeat

his story. They wanted more detail. Just who was this Lackner and why should anyone believe him? How did Durham come to know Bolcar's daughter? Satisfied at last, the group of them marched single file to the inner office of Harold Manx. Durham had not been dismissed, so he went along, following the line of slapping, broad-soled shoes. The door was locked, causing everyone to stand around for a few seconds.

Then the young guy, the one with the slicked-back hair and the dark herringbone suit said: "Anybody got a key?"

"Not a chance," Chin said. "We'll have to take it off."

The young guy persisted. "You telling me? His secretary, janitorial, somebody must have a key."

Chin grimaced. "Durham, check it out."

Nancy, Harold Manx's secretary these past fifteen years, did not have a key to her boss's office. Charlie, the janitorial foreman, did not have a key, or a master that would fit it. "The Chief's office, you say? No way."

There followed another whispered conference in the hallway, the five of them clustered in a huddle. By this time all work had stopped and an audible hum was emanating through the department.

It took half an hour and a crowbar from the depths of the building to open the door to Harold Manx's office. Sandwiches were called for and delivered. Gordon was in cynics' heaven: a corridor of super sleuths standing around holding pastrami and swiss while they watched some old plumber-type mutter and curse as he wrenched on the recalcitrant door.

In the meantime Chin had Robin call Lackner's office. Lackner was not available. His secretary finally revealed that he had flown with one passenger to Eureka. A rental car awaited him there. Time of return? Unknown? The herringbone guy insisted he call Elisa's office again. Same result.

As an undergraduate, Robin had read about great archeological discoveries, about that moment when some archeologist had finally broken through to the inner room or the long-buried chamber of a cave. He recognized the sensation when at last the door was removed and everyone crowded forward and then paused at the opening. It was Randall Chin alone who entered. He went first to the walnut file cabinets. They were locked. He tilted them one at a time. "Empty," he said. "Empty."

By this time Robin and Gordon had followed Fernald and the out-of-towners through the door. On the desk was a stack of files. On each was a note summarizing the status of the investigation and the direction it needed to take. Beside it was a second stack. "Personnel," the note on them said, "For Chin's eyes only." On a table were several stacks of empty manila file folders, each with its metal binder removed. Beside them the box of used binders. The Chief had thought to not dispose of anything the department might have been able to make use of. Also on the desk was a sealed, number ten envelope with a name written on it.

"Who's Lydia?" Gordon asked, picking it up.

Randall Chin took the envelope and slipped it into his coat pocket. There followed another huddle, Chin with the outsiders. Then Chin came out.

"Durham," he said, "call the airport and reserve us a plane."

Lawrence "Pug" Bolcar sat in the Cessna twin, his legs apart. He had removed his tie, curled and rolled it into the pocket of his suit coat. His collar was open; the wind at the airport had tousled his hair. What looked like a permanent blush rode high on his cheekbones. His deep and heavy breathing seemed to resonate with the working engines.

When they reached cruising altitude Vince Lackner cut back slightly on the throttle and tried to settle in for the flight north. He, too, had dark thoughts to contend with.

They had just passed to the east of the Farallon Islands; Point Reyes National Seashore lay directly ahead. The line of surf running northward gave the illusion of a static white ribbon tracing the edge of the land; similarly deceptive was the scattering of whitecaps, which, from this altitude, gave the impression of having been permanently painted on the ocean's surface. The wind came at them from ten o'clock. It would slow their speed and push them landward but it felt steady to Lackner. High pressure re-establishing itself in the wake of the rain.

At the airport Pug had felt tightness in his chest as he paced up and down on the tarmac waiting for Lackner to complete his preparations. Now he felt caged. Lackner had brought a bag of food and drink on board. Pug refused the apple he was offered ("It's organic.") and now he watched as Vince took a large bite out of it.

As Vince chewed he provided details of his company, the equipment he used, what was leased and what he owned outright. Mostly he leased. "Saves on personnel and hangar space," he explained with military crispness. A tone of voice so different from the whine he had employed in the car from Clandestines down to the airport as he tried to explain his innocence about Jake the grower. ("It's just some mix up, Pug. I've known Jake for years. A bit eccentric but dependable. You think I haven't been put out by this? You think I don't have a business to run? I don't know why you're looking at me like that. If you hadn't been so sure Carlos had ratted on you…") And so forth. The same whine again to express his bafflement about who Carlos turned out to be. ("I knew nothing about him, Pug. Sure, I met him in Colombia. He seemed like a decent fellow. Invited me into his home. A nice ranch, a couple of sons. And he loved to play poker, that's all. I had no idea he'd turn into this. I figured he was an easy mark. I was doing you and Tripper a favor, that's the way I saw it. Why are you blaming me? I'm trying to help you out of a mess you created. If you had any idea of what this has cost me in time and money…") And so forth.

The more Pug thought about it, the more he realized that Vince Lackner's screw-ups were responsible for all of his troubles. First the damned Colombian, then the crook of a grower who probably grabbed the money and ran. Who was likely sitting on a beach in Hawaii, smoking dope about now rather than being here growing it. Meanwhile Lackner continued talking, "…and all over Southeast Asia, Bangkok, Jakarta, Singapore, Manila, we get to most of them regularly. Latin America too, of course."

"That I know about," Pug Bolcar said sourly.

North of Jenner they crossed back over the land though the Pacific was still visible on their left. Lackner had a jug of water beside him and was taking sips every few minutes.

After a lull in the conversation, Vince Lackner asked what seemed to Pug a very strange question, "You're around the courts all the time. Ever run into a cop named Manx? Harold Manx?"

"Christ, you know Manx?"

"Not really. I…"

"Well, I do. Not through the courts. We were neighbors once upon a time. That sorry bastard. How do you know him?"

Vince Lackner was fiddling with some switches. "I don't know him, not really. That's why I asked. He approached me the other day. He wants to set up a sting at the airport. Said he'd pay to use my office. I told him I had to think about it. So, you knew him, huh?"

Pug related the story about Janet and the court order. "I was audited three years running. I had false credit reports filed against me. For a while, at least, my phone was tapped, though I couldn't prove it, of course."

"How long ago was that?"

"Christ, I don't know. It's probably been six, seven years since that happened. Why?"

"Is he still hassling you?"

"I haven't had any problems the last three or four years. My daughter saw him in Tahoe over Christmas. He told Binks the daughter never came back. Can't blame her."

"While we were there?"

"What do you mean?"

"In Tahoe, she saw him. While we were there?"

"Yeah, sometime that week. I don't remember."

They were nearing the water again just north of Fort Bragg. The wind was more northerly here and Lackner made a slight correction.

"Sounds like I should back away," he said. "The money's not worth it."

"You got enough on your mind already, right Vince?" Pug made no effort to disguise his sarcasm.

Ahead the shoreline bulged westward. Soon they were flying over rugged, heavily forested coastal mountains.

"We're getting close," Lackner said. He had taken out some topographical maps and was studying them. He cut back on the throttle, dropped down and began a long, clockwise sweep of the terrain. "Kind of a dangerous game," he muttered. "Some dope grower might think we're the law and take a potshot at us."

"Not *your* dope grower, obviously."

"Ours," Lackner said, correcting him.

The exchange brought a taste of vomit to Pug Bolcar's throat. "You chose the bastard, Vince. First the goddamned Colombian with his fucking manicured fingernails and now this asshole. I could wring your neck. I really could. And if anything happens to Binks I will. I swear it."

Lackner ignored this. He was following a road now, flying just north of it in an easterly direction.

"Recognize your place?"

"Are you kidding?" Pug was looking out the side window. "I was only there once or twice, years ago. By car. It's all just timber to me."

"Well, it's coming up here." Lackner swept across the road and then banked back to the north. "There, it's right below you. That dirt road. And there's a cabin in the clearing ahead."

"Okay," Pug said. "Is that it? I don't know."

"That's it."

"Wait, there's a goddamn car down there. Big black thing. A Lincoln or something. Is that Carlos?"

"Must be," Vince Lackner said after a pause.

They were past it now and Pug was craning over his shoulder. "Make another loop. I want to see if Binks is there."

But Lackner had straightened out and was pulling back on the throttle.

"I just wanted him to know we're coming," he said. "We've got to pick up our car. It's an hour's drive or more to get back to this place."

— 39 —

The long-awaited phone booth where he had said they would receive instructions stood at a corner of a gas station near the air compressor where, for a quarter, you could add a few pounds of pressure to your tires had you the need, which they did not. A small town, set in a narrow valley surrounded by trees. A young couple stood at the road's edge a few yards away, hoisting their thumbs at each passing car, he in jeans, she in a full-length skirt. Elisa noticed the skirt immediately. It was lovely, fitted at the hips and then flaring out, a soft gray, edging toward silver and with colors of darker gray, maybe a touch of black, an abstract horizontal pattern suggesting cityscapes. A thrift store find probably. Wildly inappropriate for hitchhiking through northern California, but attractive for all that.

In Elisa's mind everything had changed, though Harold Manx had said nothing, and she was not prepared yet to confront him directly.

A half-hour south he had finally stopped at a fast food franchise so she could relieve herself. He had followed her inside like a guard dog and was waiting at the restroom door when she came out.

"Hungry?" she asked, scowling at the menu board from beneath the brim of the homburg.

"We don't have time for that," he had said, still wearing the absurd sunglasses. Taking her arm, he tried to guide her out the door. She resisted the pressure, planting her feet beside a booth where an Hispanic woman sat with two small children.

The woman looking up at them, maybe somewhat alarmed.

"You don't have to do that, Harold," Elisa said. "I don't know what's going on, but I'm not going to run away."

"No." He released his grip.

"I'm going to see this through."

"Yes," he said.

"Maybe the boxed salad is edible. I can bring it along, eat in the car."

"If that's what you want."

"A bite for you? A sandwich or something?"

"No, no thank you."

He offered to pay but she pulled cash from her purse and paid herself. Now at the gas station Harold extracted himself from the car, taking the keys with him. He had put his coat on to enter the food franchise and had not taken it off. The weapon under his arm seemed an embarrassment to him, like a body part that should not be exposed.

"Wait in the car," he said, and walking to the phone booth, made a pretense of glancing at his watch.

Elisa did not wait in the car. It was midday now and quite warm. She tossed the mass of plastic containers, napkins and utensils left from the salad into a trash barrel by the pumps. The female hitchhiker approached her, wanting to know if they were traveling north.

"I have no idea where we're going or why," Elisa admitted.

The woman did not seem to find this surprising. "I like your hat," she said.

"Thanks. You can talk to that man over there watching us. But I don't think he's in the habit of picking up hitchhikers."

"Yeah, car like that. But I thought maybe you."

"It's his car," Elisa said. "I'm just…" What was she really? "I have to pick up something in the store."

Among the snacks and sodas and six-packs of beer Elisa found a rack of sunglasses. She was trying on a pair when Harold came through the door.

"Try these," she said. "Aviators. Not great, but better than what you have on."

"We have to go."

"Harold, really." The man behind the counter looked capable of tossing a grizzly out the door. Elisa looked at the man and then at Harold Manx. "Try them on."

Harold Manx took off his sunglasses and tried on the new pair.

"Better," she said. "Definitely better."

"Binks."

"Buy them, Harold."

Harold purchased the sunglasses, a couple of chocolate bars and the bottle of water Elisa handed him. On the way back to the car Elisa tossed the old glasses into the trash barrel.

They did drive north but Harold left the hitchhikers standing in the sun. "Sorry," Elisa shouted out the window. "Your skirt is beautiful."

The highway alternated now between two and

four lanes. And the country felt more remote to her. Dense conifer forest pushing against the shoulders, a creek appearing and disappearing alongside the road. Solitary structures now and then, dirt roads leading off into the trees, cut banks raw and steep and unstable looking. A country only marginally peopled.

"Oh, my God!" she exclaimed into this emptiness. "Mom! I was supposed to have lunch with my mother. I have to call her. I do, Harold. I have to. I'm sure she's worried sick. We had a fight this morning. She probably thinks I stood her up, or something."

Harold did not see it as a problem. "When you were late, she would have called your employer, Binks. That would have been the obvious thing to do. Your office would have explained what I told them. That you are assisting the department on a matter of some importance."

"And what exactly is that?"

"I told you." Harold Manx said flatly. He looked about as silly in these glasses as he had in the original pair but at least now she could see his profile better, see what his eyes were doing. And what they did was glance at her, just a glance. "And if she still had concerns she would have called my office. They would have filled her in."

That glance had not been comforting.

"I want to call her," Elisa repeated. "The next phone booth we see, the next store, station, whatever. I want to call her."

Harold picked one of the chocolate bars off the

seat and handed it to her.

"Open this, please. I need a little something. And help yourself."

Nothing said for the next ten or fifteen minutes. The tape deck silent, the aroma of mint replaced faintly with chocolate. A store came into view on their left, a couple of abandoned fuel pumps, a large tank needing a coat of paint, a faded American flag rustling listlessly on a tall pole, a phone booth in plain sight beside the pole. They passed without stopping. Elisa decided to resume talking.

"A few hours after I saw you in the hotel lobby that afternoon, I was unfaithful to my husband."

She was leaning against the door again, watching him. He was quite fastidious with the chocolate bar that she had opened and set on the seat beside him, breaking off small squares with his right hand and lifting them one at a time to his mouth. Taking his time, letting each square melt on his tongue. He did not comment.

"You are the only person in the world I have ever told this to," she continued. "I'm making my confession, Harold. It seems in order, given the circumstances."

Harold Manx kept his eyes on the road, both hands on the wheel, a slight movement around the mouth to reposition the melting chocolate. He had developed small creases that curled down from the corners of his lips, as if his mouth were full of tadpoles and the tails of two of them had escaped. She did not remember those creases. Surely she would have noticed them, made some comment to Janet about the tadpoles sneaking out of her father's mouth.

"And the man I was unfaithful with is a man you know."

This caused him to glance over.

"A man you work with. One of your subordinates. I didn't know that at the time, of course. He made up some story. What would you call it? A cover maybe? One of the many euphemisms we have for a lie. A 'cover story,' or 'working undercover.' That's what it means, doesn't it? Under the cover of a lie. Your subordinate told me he was studying snow in the Sierras, something like that. That he was a scientist rather than a cop. It didn't matter to me. He could have said he was most anything and it would not have mattered. It wasn't him I was interested in. Not that night. I was into tit-for-tat. Revenge. Revenge against my husband." She paused and positioned herself so she was staring straight at him. "You know about revenge, don't you, Harold? How it eats at you. The hunger for it."

"Durham," Harold Manx said, reaching down for another square of chocolate.

"Bingo."

"You made the connection later?"

"He told me, later. We saw each other a few times in the City, and then suddenly he broke it off."

"Did he say why? Why he broke it off?" Harold Manx holding the square of chocolate between thumb and index finger, gripping the wheel with his remaining fingers. The voiceover in the movie saying, "If you must eat something while driving, remember to keep your eyes on the road and both hands on the wheel whenever possible."

"Not really. Something about work. Another cover story. Which is to say, another lie."

"It may have been well intended. A justification, if not a full explanation."

"A cover story," Elisa said again. "Which is to say, a lie."

Harold Manx placed the chocolate square in his mouth and put both hands back on the wheel. A short time later he turned off the highway. They passed through a grove of huge, old redwoods and then a mile or two later he turned onto a steep dirt road.

"This doesn't have anything to do with Janet, does it Harold?"

"This has everything to do with Janet," he said.

About the time Harold's Cadillac began bouncing up the road, throwing dust, Rafe Gilbert was enjoying a standing ovation in the smaller of the company's two indoor theatres. They had just finished another performance of Sam Shepard's "Buried Child," Rafe having played Vince, and he and the rest of the cast were being wildly rewarded.

Who can explain an audience? he thought, bowing toward the glaring footlights. A Friday afternoon, a performance that had not gone particularly well, a play that is determinedly degenerate and depressing, and the audience was going bonkers. Must be a crowd of English majors. A different group seeing the same performance would have marched out like zombies and groped their way down the street toward a stiff drink.

And a stiff drink was just what Ferguson (Tilden) and Rand (Bradley) were expecting to have with Rafe. It had become a ritual whenever they had a weekend matinee, and Fridays counted for weekends. Another cast would be performing Shaw's "Man and Superman" in the large theatre that evening and a third, a Fugard in the stage they were now exiting. While others worked, said Ferguson to Rand in the presence of Rafe, the three of them would be eating food with too much grease and listening to jazz at the Cypress Cup.

"Can't make it," said Rafe to his friends. "I'm flying to San Francisco."

"I smell wife," said Ferguson to Rand.

"Agreed," said Rand to Ferguson. "That and an obvious fit of backsliding."

"Momentary lapse," suggested Ferguson. "The last quiver of a dying conscience."

"Thing to do is drown it," said Ollie Rand to Rafe. "Nothing kills a conscience quicker than alcohol. Two or three drinks and there'll be no perils of air travel, no terrifying encounters with she, the woman scorned."

"This is true, my lad," added Ferguson. "That's been proven. Alcohol is what doctors use, after all, to kill germs. And what is a conscience, but an insidious germ by another name?"

Rafe, who had been only half-following this banter, looked up from the mirror. "A conscience is a germ?"

"Or," suggested Rand to Ferguson, ignoring Rafe, "our boy here may simply be horny. Sweetie run off. Lady Macbeth back in her castle."

"Having washed her hands of the whole sordid mess," observed Ferguson.

"The original washer of hands, Lady Macbeth," said Rand. "None does it better."

"Either way," said Ferguson with considerable cheer, "alcohol is the answer."

"Gentlemen, what alcohol brings is what our master has taught us: 'face painting, sleep and urine.' And when I have finished removing this paint from my face, I'm off to San Francisco."

"His true love for to see," announced Ollie Rand.

"To see, or not to see," Rafe said grimly. "That is precisely the question."

From the time their plane pulled up and away from the cabin in the woods, Pug Bolcar fell into deep thought. He did not speak again until they had landed and were in the terminal, walking toward the car rental booth. The bits of information tumbling around in his head did not add up the way they were supposed to. He felt a chill come over him and decided he needed to try a new approach.

"Let me get this, Vince," he said in a voice that

he hoped sounded almost cordial. "The fact that you own the plane doesn't mean it didn't cost you to fly up here."

Vince looked surprised but muttered his thanks.

"The reservation is in the name of Pacific Transport," said the clerk, looking at the card.

"No need to change your paperwork. Just put the charge on my card and list me as the principal driver."

"I can drive, Pug."

"You'll be navigating, Vince. I see you brought the maps."

On the drive south, Pug felt like he did the first morning of a new trial.

"Vince," he said after they had gone some distance, "we've had our difficulties over this. That's the truth of the matter. But at this point, it looks like we're in it together, so let's go over what we know."

"All right." Vince Lackner sipped water and watched the road, his voice wary.

"You're a bright guy. You play a decent game of poker. You're a skilled pilot, a professional. You own and manage a complex business."

"Thank you. I do my best. It's not easy."

"I'm sure it's not. To operate a fleet of aircraft that has to be maintained and paid for. Your buy-in must have been huge, complex financing arrangements, heavy debt service."

"Debt service is eating me up, Pug. Interest rates being what they are. And this thing. I would have been on my way to Tokyo today but for this. Nice job, easy money. Four executives on their way to a convention. My pilots were all committed. I had to hand the work over to a competitor."

"That's tough," Pug agreed. "And all the countries you fly into and out of, all of them, I suppose, have their own sets of laws and regulations."

"Absolutely. Each one is unique."

"I'm impressed," Pug admitted. "You get in, you get out. You have assets to protect, on the ground and in the air.'

"That's right."

"You take possession of shipments in one country and deliver them to another. You have to secure insurance that protects you in all those jurisdictions. You rent storage facilities. You get shipments through customs, pay tariffs. Different rules, different languages to deal with."

"That's it. That's what I face on a regular basis. That's my job. Endless details, hassles that need to be resolved."

"And I assume you have to contend with a certain level of corruption."

Vince smiled, glancing over. "Let's say there are rituals, Pug, formalities. You have to know the local customs, who's in charge, the lay of the land, as they say."

"I see. Well, like I said, that's very impressive."

"I do my best."

"Yes, I'm sure you do. So, Vince, let's talk about Jake."

"Jake?"

"The grower. That Jake."

Vince Lackner had his hand in the food bag. He withdrew a granola bar and opened the wrapper with his teeth. "Would you like one?"

"Not at the moment," Pug said.

"Jake."

"Yes, Jake. This guy from Hawaii you know so well. Who, like you, is skilled at what he does. Who, you assured me, has experience in this line of work. The one we could trust to do the job. That Jake."

"Pug...?" Vince chewing rapidly.

"Who now is nowhere to be found. Who promised to do work that has not been done or even started. Who seems to have absconded with my ten grand."

"I'm sure he has an explanation."

"Whose actions have resulted in the kidnapping of my daughter." The thought caused Pug to slap the wheel.

"Pug..."

They were on a freeway headed south. Miles back they had passed herds of cattle beside the road. But now they were in forested hills, following a river. Pug slowed down. He was trying to keep it under the limit. The last thing he needed was a siren and lights flashing up his tailpipe.

"It doesn't add up, Vince. A man with your skill and experience mixed up with this level of incompetence. And you seemingly so clueless. No idea what happened, no way to contact the man. It doesn't compute."

"Like I said, Pug..."

"But leave that aside for a moment, Vince. Let's talk about your hotel room in Lake Tahoe. The one with that magnificent view out the floor-to-ceiling windows. The view you were so proud of. Apparently, that room was bugged, Vince. Either you, or Carlos, or Tripper wore a wire, or the room itself had been fitted with one or more microphones. And from the quality of the tape we listened to, it sounds like the latter. Can we agree on that? That from the quality of the tape the room itself was bugged?"

"Yes," Vince Lackner agreed quietly. "It must have been."

"And you're telling me that once again you have no idea? That a man with your skill and experience, knowing that you did not bug the room, assuring me that Carlos did not, knowing that neither I nor Tripper could possibly have entered your room and installed a microphone, that you have no clue who did?"

To that question, Vince Lackner did not respond. He was looking at the map spread across his lap.

"Our exit is coming up," he said. "A couple of miles."

"There are a couple of other things I've been thinking about, Vince," Pug continued. "That night at your office, the night I met this Jake fellow and gave you the money. The place was lit up like Broadway, Vince. You care to comment on that?"

"Not now, Pug. I want to make sure we get the right exit. It's coming up."

"And finally, Vince, there was the strange question

you asked me as we were flying up here."

"Here, this one. Turn here. Now, at the end of the ramp, take the road that goes right."

The road, once they reached it, was vaguely familiar to Pug. Not the road so much as the grove of giant redwoods it passed beneath before heading up into the hills. Yes, he had been here, the shade, the cool, damp feeling beneath the trees. Nice to come off a freeway and into this. He had had a vague plan at one time to develop the property a bit. Build a nicer cabin. Use it as a getaway.

They were traveling westerly now toward the ocean. As they hair-pinned up the hillside, Vince Lackner instructed him to turn left onto a dirt road that was narrow and deeply rutted. Atop a small post set in the ground a red plastic strip fluttered in the breeze. How convenient, Pug thought. They had been invited to a party and the host had marked the path with brightly colored flags.

More climbing and then at the top, an even narrower dirt road with a second red plastic strip. Pug made the turn. He stopped the car and rolled down the window.

It was very still. The forest surrounding them had been logged over a few years before, leaving a scattering of young trees, old snags, a tangle of bushes and brambles.

"Back to the question you asked on the flight up," Pug said. "The one about…"

"Harold Manx?" Vince suggested.

Pug Bolcar sighed. "Yes, the one about Harold

Manx."

— 40 —

"I'm cold and these ropes are hurting my wrists."

Elisa Gilbert sat on a wooden box in the doorway of an abandoned and filthy cabin, the homburg on her head, her hands and feet bound with orange nylon cord. The last direct light had left the clearing and the temperature was beginning to fall. She knew the whole story now. She had become bait, set on a box like a slab of cheese placed on a trap.

Harold Manx went to the trunk of the car and returned with a plaid blanket that he draped over her shoulders. Green and red, not her favorite colors, certainly not with the outfit she was wearing. Harold had changed clothes a short time before. Gone, folded and placed in the back seat, were the white shirt, the suit and tie. Dark slacks now, that ridiculous sweater with the leather football sewn across the front, the same one (there couldn't possibly be two of them!) he had worn in Tahoe. A black watch cap on his head. A modest man, he had stepped behind the opened car door to make the change.

"She's alive, Harold," Elisa said as he spread the blanket over her shoulders.

"She's dead."

"She's alive. You can't kid yourself like that. If she had died you would have heard. She's alive and one day she'll come home."

"She's gone."

"Somewhere out there she's growing as a human

being. She's facing her challenges. Part of her is missing you and Lydia. One day she will have the courage to come home. She will come to ask for your forgiveness."

"You're being clever, Binks, but it won't work. Janet is gone and she's gone because of him."

"Lydia knows better. I'm sure of that. Lydia is a woman and she's waiting."

"My business is with your father," he said, turning away. He had set the pistol on the car hood when he went for the blanket. Now he picked it up again and held it in his right hand. A dark thing, it seemed to Elisa. An ominous, dark object hanging absently from his fingers as if it were some forgotten extension of his arm. He stood looking beyond the car, watching up the road through the trees.

"You're going to kill me, aren't you? You'll have to in the end."

"You are not going to die!" he said, suddenly angry.

"You're sure of that?"

"That's right."

"How can you know? You can't know that anymore than you know Janet is dead. You're afraid of the possibilities, Harold. You shut them out, walling yourself in with false certainties. Tell me something. Are you going to die?"

"Yes."

"Today?"

"That's right."

"And my father?"

"Not necessarily."

"Do you want him to die?"

"I want him to pay." Harold Manx was pacing now, back and forth in front of the parked car. "He has never paid. He always comes out on top. Your father is slime. I want to hear him beg for your life. That's what I want. I want to hear him beg for your life the way I begged for Janet's life. And whether he lives or dies depends on how he does that. How honestly, how sincerely he begs."

He turned and stood directly in front of her, looking down. "Do you think your father is capable of honestly begging for his daughter's life? That's what I did. I begged him to give me more time. 'Give me twelve hours. At least four, give me that.' But no, not Pug Bolcar. Well, do you?"

When Elisa hesitated, Harold Manx snorted.

"That's what I thought," he said.

"And if he doesn't?"

"Then I kill him. And after him, and after I have released you, then myself."

It was very still now. The juncos that had been rustling in the duff near the cabin wall had flown to a leafy branch to spend the night. To the west the sky was lucent, a milky blue growing darker by the minute. Harold Manx resumed pacing. In his dark clothing he had become little more than a shadow moving back and forth in front of her.

"He will," she said finally. "If he has to."

"I see you have your doubts. You think he won't bring himself to beg. Not even for you. He'll want to argue, won't he? He'll deny he did anything wrong. He'll say it's all my fault. He'll probably threaten to sue me. That's a laugh."

He said it was a laugh but he did not laugh and neither did she. Of course he would argue, she realized, that's who he was.

As she watched Harold Manx pace, entering her view and then momentarily stepping out of it, coming and going, back and forth, she felt complicit in a strange way, as if she had somehow participated in bringing this moment into being; this shell of a cabin; this small clearing; this desolate, empty place; this failing light; this tortured man with his dark gun. It wasn't that she should have refused to get into the car with him, or have run away when he got out to play that charade about getting instructions on the phone. No, it was more fundamental than that. It had to do with what they shared, with what she and Harold Manx had in common.

"I am truly sorry for what happened to you, Harold. I'm sorry for you and for Lydia and for Janet." How she wished at moment that she could speak to Rafe: "I forgive you," she would say to him. "I'm not carrying this weight any longer. I may not come back to you, but I'm letting the rage go. I'm letting it go."

Harold just kept pacing.

"You want to die," she said quietly as he passed in front of her. "That's the difference between us: you want to die and I don't." That truly was the difference, she realized. He had carried it on his back so long he wanted it to reach around and kill him.

"I want justice."

"You mean revenge."

"It's the same thing. Justice, revenge, the same thing. I've been society's avenger for a long time, Binks. You can talk about deterrence or rehabilitation, about getting people off the streets for the protection of society. But it all comes down to revenge. And yes, that's what I want. I want revenge."

"Well, what I want is to go home. You're making a terrible mistake, Harold, and you know it. Let's go home so I can call my husband, so you can bury your mother. So you can comfort your wife. So the two of you can welcome Janet when she finally turns your way. You think you want to die but you're just afraid to let it go. We're all afraid. So what? Let's go home."

Suddenly, Harold Manx turned and began to run in her direction. For a moment she thought he intended to physically attack her. But he stepped past, bumping her shoulder. Then she saw them too, car lights topping the rise and wavering in the distance.

The car topped the rise and the lights illuminated the doorway of the small cabin and Rafe Gilbert got up from his seat near an empty gate at San Francisco International, where he had been sprawled out with a copy of *Sports Illustrated*. For the fifth time he called the courtesy phone system to ask that Elisa Gilbert be paged. "She is on the list, sir," he was told. "She has been paged and we will continue to page her." The voice was not friendly.

Rafe replied that he knew she was on the list but he had not heard her name called for a while. His voice wasn't friendly either. Then he called Ruth Bolcar's number and got the machine again. The law office was closed. He did not have a home number for Elisa's father and none was listed in the fat, tattered directory dangling below the payphone. As he started back toward his seat a voice in his mind spoke to him, "She has answered the page, you fool. She's answered it by not coming." That voice ridiculed the other voices. The ones saying he should call the police, the hospital emergency rooms.

When they paged Elisa again a few minutes later, Ramona Livingston heard the announcement. She was flying standby and she had heard the name several times while she waited. She did not remember Elisa's last name, having heard it only that one time back in South Lake Tahoe, but the repeated announcement resonated with her. It made her think of Pug and his daughter. She imagined that the Elisa being summoned, was Pug's daughter and that someone was trying desperately to reach her.

As she walked down the boarding ramp, feeling safe for the first time in twenty-four hours, Ramona's mind began to play with the possibilities. The man trying to reach Elisa—it was a man, she decided— had worked with her at a bank. No, at the betting windows of a race track. That's right, adjoining windows. Together over the past few months they had embezzled a quarter-million dollars in bills of various denominations. Management had become suspicious and they had agreed to meet at the airport, where, disguised as newlyweds, they would transport the cash to the safety of a Geneva bank. The man now frantically trying to contact her had the plane tickets. Elisa had the cash, and obviously, Elisa had skipped. The fantasy greatly pleased Ramona as she stowed her carry-on luggage and settled into her seat.

But then as she fastened her seatbelt she realized that the shadows she had hoped to leave at the gate had entered effortlessly and were now taking seats all around her. It wasn't fair. There should be a machine, Ramona thought, like those metal detectors you walk through. When you come out the other side, all the bad thoughts would have been crisped. They would have fallen away, light as ash. A flight attendant came by with a selection of magazines. Lady Bounce glanced at *Vogue* but the one she chose was *Business Week*.

Tripper McLain also heard Elisa's name announced. He was leaving for a scouting trip in the Midwest. He and Scotts Berger, his chief scout, had tickets for the NCAA Final Four. Berger was very high on a point guard at one of the Big Ten schools. Tripper did not see Ramona, whom he might have recognized, nor Rafe, whom he probably would not have. But hearing Elisa's name brought Ruth Bolcar to mind. They should have her over for dinner, he thought. He would mention it to Helen. McLain liked Ruth. She made a delightful dinner guest, assuming she kept her drinking under control, and she might have some interesting scuttlebutt on Conden's senate race.

On the flight Tripper met a pleasant fellow named Chip Woodward, who it turned out was the general manager of news at Channel 3. Woodward was a basketball fan. Loved the game, he said. But he also hinted that there were problems at the station, a power struggle of some kind going on. He didn't mention names but he let drop that he was on his way to Cleveland for a job interview. "Maybe I'll become a Cavaliers' fan," he said ruefully.

Ruth Bolcar that evening was not thinking of dinner parties or her brother's race for public office. She was stone sober—the only way to do this—and she had taken a taxi to the hospital. The cabbie dropped her at the door of the emergency room, which was not where she was going, but a pale man waiting there pointed her in the right direction. At first she had thought she would go away somewhere. One of those places they advertise with quiet and greenery and natural food. But she was a city girl and the scoop on the talk shows was that this program in a wing of the hospital was among the best. For Ruth, the whole thing was tied up with her daughter. Binks not meeting her at Clandestines for lunch made a statement, a statement confirmed by her absence through the afternoon.

Her signature on the admission form, when at long last it came to that, shivered and then tumbled off at the end as if falling into a chasm. The intake worker, as she looked through the form, thought the signature revealed the strength of Ruth's demon. But Ruth saw it as a lure cast out on deep waters, tempting her daughter home.

Lydia Manx that evening had a job cleaning her hands and her produce. She had thinned and weeded the young carrots. She no longer had to plant dill. The seeds she did not harvest in the fall fell to the ground and brought forth new sprouts in the spring. Scattered through the garden, the tender shoots of dill were nearly identical with the young carrots, differing only minutely in color and pattern of leaf. The task was to remove the dill from the rows of carrots without dispatching too many of the planted crop. The soil had been in nearly perfect condition for this project: not saturated but still moist from the rain, it readily surrendered the departing roots and molded beneath the pressure of her fingers to embrace those that remained. It was a hands-and-knees project, a contemplation not to be hurried. Like that man Joseph, she thought, she had begun the resurrection.

She returned to the house when the failing light made detection difficult and her fingers were becoming cold. In a colander she carried the largest of the removed carrots, some leaves of red-leaf lettuce, a couple of tender spring radishes and a palm full of dill shoots, her salad in the rough. When Harold returned late from a day in the field, he usually called first from the office to say he was starting home.

Many of Lydia's evenings had been like this, working in the kitchen while a corner of her mind awaited that call. Tonight she already knew he would be late so she set about preparing dinner, a tuna casserole with snow peas that she could easily reheat when Harold arrived.

In tribute to the season, her favorite station was playing Mozart's *Requiem Mass*. A part of her mind was on the music, a part on the preparation of the food. But once the casserole was in the oven and the salad drained and chopped and as she moved absently about the kitchen tidying up, she heard herself at prayer. She prayed first for Noony, and then for Janet and Noah, for Harold and for herself, and then for others known and unknown. Lydia Manx, grounded in her myth, in her myth praying, praying for us all.

The car stopped a hundred or so yards from the cabin but the headlights remained on, the high beams shining in her face. The familiar smell of wintergreen came to her, the sound of Harold Manx's breath above and behind her. A minute passed and then a figure appeared in the lights and began to walk toward the cabin.

My father is coming to his death, she thought, and she had a flash of that night in Tahoe. He in his turtleneck and jacket, leaning out over the curb, the cars churning slush. "Anybody can cross a street at the corner, Binks."

"Dad, stop! Stay…!"

Harold Manx slapped his hand across her mouth

and nose, choking her voice and cutting off her breath. The force of it pressed her head back against the base of his chest, the homburg falling to the cabin floor.

He held her that way for no more than a second or two. "I'm sorry," he blurted out, releasing his grip. "Binks, I'm sorry." He bent down, picked up the hat and placed it clumsily back on her head, his breath rasping, the barrel of the pistol bumping cold against her cheek. Then he stood behind her, his left hand on her shoulder, and the two of them watched as the figure slowly approached, the headlights bright in their eyes.

It was not her father. She did not recognize at first who it was—a male, tall, not her father, but beyond that…

"Hi," the man said when he stopped about ten feet away.

"Hi."

"Are you all right?"

"I've been better."

"Durham, what the hell are you doing here? And where's Bolcar?"

"Harold wants to kill my father."

"He's back with the others, Chief."

"He does, Robin. That's what this is all about. He intends to kill my father."

"What others, Durham? Back where?"

"Well, Lackner's there, Chin, those guys in suits. Tessler. I think that's the name of one of them. "

"Harold…?"

"Short guy, greasy hair? Talks like he's from New York, Boston maybe?"

"Yeah, could be. East Coast somewhere."

"Gordon Tessler," Harold Manx said. "From the prosecutor's office. Ambitious. Very political. What's he doing here?"

"So, my dad…?

"I understand some newspaper called the office, Chief. About releasing a tape or something. Chin took the call and then started looking into it. Ended up calling Tessler."

"My dad, Robin…?"

"Yes, he's okay."

"Tessler and Chin," Harold Manx said.

"Harold, I'm cold and I'm hungry. My wrists are raw from this damn rope. And those lights are hurting my eyes. Take me home. I'll ride with you."

"The pair of them."

"We'll go see Lydia. We'll bury Noony. I'd like to pay my respects."

Elisa felt Harold Manx's hand squeeze her shoulder. The sudden pressure almost caused her to faint with fright, though later she would realize it had been a caress.

"All right, Binks," he said. "Untie her, Durham. The two of you wait with the others. I'll meet you there."

"Don't leave him alone," Elisa whispered as Robin bent to untie her. "He's…!"

The windows were open and the night still. He and

Lackner sat in the back seat of their rental car, ordered to stay there while outside the others paced around. The shot, when he heard it, sounded strangely innocent as if some kid a mile or so away had taken a potshot at a tin can. Then, when the Chinese guy brought the car to a sliding stop at the cabin door and Pug leaped out, he found his daughter sobbing in the arms of a man who until a few minutes earlier he had known only as Jake the marijuana grower.

EPILOGUE

Back in San Francisco, damage control was handled by Randall Chin, acting director. His dexterity with language and facts had long endeared him to prosecutors who found that his incident reports, crafted while details were still warm and flexible, tended to withstand cross examination months later. The envelope in his pocket never got to Lydia and the press release was long on the Chief's many accomplishments and short on the details of his death. At Elisa's insistence, Pug Bolcar agreed to not sue the department. Elisa wanted nothing done that could harm Lydia or Janet, whom she met in a tear-filled reunion the following day.

So Harold Manx was buried beside his mother and in praise for his many accomplishments. His coffin was flag-draped, its path from church to hearse a corridor lined with uniformed officers from counties, cities and the federal government. Kind words appeared in Patricia Pendar's column and sentimental ones flowed from the perky mouth of Roseanne Harden, everyone's sweetheart at Channel 3 News.

From her hospital room Ruth watched the news

reports and read the column. Pug Bolcar did not read the column or attend the funeral; he had a doctor's appointment and was at that hour walking a treadmill toward a bypass. Vince Lackner did not attend the service either. Randall Chin had given him what amounted to a Get Out of Jail Free card and he was in his favorite place in all the world: the cockpit of an airplane somewhere over the Pacific. But Elisa was there. She sat with the family, with Lydia, double-struck, her grief amplified by doubt, with Janet, who struggled not to blame herself, and with young Noah, grandson of the honored man, who as the preacher droned on, passed from lap to lap among the three of them, his eyes bright and alive.

Later, when the rites had been said at the gravesite and the crowd was dispersing back toward their cars, Elisa and Robin walked together among the stones. It was mid-afternoon, a beautiful spring day. Her car was already packed and it would be well after dark when she finally reached Oregonia. She would be driving the interstate alone, avoiding semis and roaming the dial for strong signals. Tom and Marilyn MacElhenney had offered to put her up until other arrangements could be made. She would, they said, be welcome at any hour. But it was afternoon now, the grounds were dappled with sun and the shadows cast by large oaks, and she and Robin walked alone together, talking among the stones.

Doug Ingold is married and the father of two. He divides his time between the Redwood Coast of northern California, and the Sunshine Coast of southern British Columbia.